Fake Out Hearts

Nikki Lawson

For More Information:
nikkilawsonauthor.com

For updates on new releases, giveaways, and other fun stuff, sign up for my newsletter!

Note: although this book is overall a sweet and fluffy romance with a green flag hero, it does deal with a few potentially sensitive subjects, including references to infertility and an eating disorder.

*To all the readers who want to be called "my wife"
by a tatted up hockey player with a filthy mouth.*

*Bonus points if you want him to be so possessive
that he'll make you come in front of your ex
just to prove you're his.*

Theo Camden is waiting for you...

Chapter 1

Theo

Steaming hot water from the team shower pounds against my scalp and runs down the length of me. It's almost enough to distract me from my disaster of a failed pass tonight. Almost.

The rest of the Aces are shouting and bantering in the showers around me, but their voices meld into a jumble of background noise as scenes from the game we just played flash in my mind like I'm playing it all over again.

"We're down to the wire, but Camden has the puck and what could be the start of a real turnaround here, folks!" The announcer's booming voice echoes in my head, urging me on. The game is tied and there's less than a minute left on the clock, but that's all the time I need.

A wet towel claps against bare skin and a shout rings out in sync with the crowd howling in my memory.

The Prowler's nervous goalie steels himself as I hurtle toward him, picking up speed like a freight train. There's nothing in my way, and the poor fucker knows I'm about to hit him with everything I've got.

"Wake up, Camden!" Noah, our team captain, barks, and I can't tell if I'm hearing him in my memory, in reality, or both.

1

I keep hammering down the ice as my vision turns black at the edges and every muscle in my legs screams along with the crowd. They know as well as I do that I've got this. They've seen me sink easier shots than this before.

"Camden!" Noah's voice shouts from two worlds at once.

One of the Prowlers appears out of nowhere, trucking at me from my right like his life depends on it, and I panic. Fuck, he's moving too fast. I'm not gonna make it.

"Goddamn it, Camden!" Noah's voice hounds me again.

This time I look. Noah is farther up the ice and alone to the left of the goalie. If I act fast, I can pass to him before the asshole Prowler chasing me figures out what's happening. If Noah takes the shot from there, the goalie will never see it coming and the game is guaranteed to be ours. But I've got a wide-open shot from here!

"Did you get hit so hard you lost your hearing or something?" Noah asks and shoves me gently.

I almost fall on my face as someone checks me from behind. The rink blurs around me while I fumble, and when I stabilize, my face blazes as I see my least favorite person rocketing down the ice in the other direction with the puck.

"That Kaplan guy has gotta be the biggest prick around," Reese, our left winger and co-captain, says from the other side of the showers like he's reading my mind, and I snap out of my daydream. The other Aces must have finished cleaning up a while ago, judging by how dry and clothed they all are. But Noah is standing there and looking at me like I grew a second head.

Fuck. How long have I been zoned out?

"Right? And we were on our A-game tonight too," Sawyer, our defenseman says, and my eyes dart away from Noah's piercing blue pair. We both know damn well Sawyer isn't including me in that after my shitty play cost us the game against our biggest rivals tonight.

"Home ice advantage, I guess," Reese offers with a shrug, but our goalie, Grant, scoffs and shakes his head.

"No such thing. We fumbled it."

"Alright, alright, enough with the pity party. I'm ready to forget about tonight." Maxim Federov, one of our forwards, holds his hands up. "Who's down to get this press crap out of the way so we can go drink away the sting?"

"Don't have to ask me twice," Reese says and heads for the door. Everyone follows him, even Grant, which is a shock. Well, everyone except for Noah. He watches the rest of the team file out of the showers into the locker room and leans against the wall beside me with his arms crossed.

"You alright?"

I look up at him with the same cocky grin that's won over the media and the fans for years.

"Yeah, I'm fine."

"You sure about that? That's twice today you've locked up on me," he says, and I flinch.

"Just enjoying the hot water. Don't worry about it."

It's bullshit, and I can tell from the look he shoots me that he's not buying it. Why would he? Everyone's seen that my game has been off all season, but even I don't know why. It's like I've lost my spark, that drive that kept me hungry and hustling. I keep trying to get out of this rut, but nothing is working and it's really starting to piss me off.

If I'd just taken the fucking shot... hell, even if I'd passed to Noah, it would've changed everything, I'm sure of it. But I froze and Kaplan won the goddamn game because of it.

Noah's not gonna let my crappy playing off the hook forever, but I definitely don't want to talk about it right now, so I towel off, get dressed, and square up to look him in the eye because he's still staring at me expectantly.

"I'm *fine*," I insist, and he throws his hands up.

"Alright, but it's not me you need to convince. The press is waiting, so fix your face before you go out there. You don't have to talk to me, but there's no getting out of talking to them."

"This face? Nothing to fix," I say and flash him another grin before we stride out to face the swarm of reporters who have already gathered in the press room.

"Theo! Theo! What happened out there? How are you feeling after that last-minute steal by Kaplan?" a young guy from the local news asks.

My stomach twists and my fists clench at the mention of Kaplan, but I grin at the reporter and shrug.

"Not much to say. We played our best, but we got outplayed. Might be hard to believe, but even the Aces can't win every game," I say to laughter.

Noah catches my eye and nods approvingly, but all I see is the way he looked at me right before Kaplan checked me in the back.

"Anything you would've done differently?" another reporter asks from the rear of the crowd, clearly not getting the hint that I don't want to talk about this.

"Having eyes in the back of my head might've helped," I say to more laughter. "But in all seriousness, no. I'm proud of the way the Aces played tonight."

Even as the words leave my mouth, they feel hollow. But what the hell am I supposed to say? I'm not about to give Kaplan the satisfaction of knowing he got to me, and I don't want Noah sweating me any more than he already is, so I decide to cut things short.

"I don't want the bus to leave me in Prowler territory, so I'd better get going. See you at the next one," I say and push my way through the reporters and don't stop moving until I'm out of the stadium and safely on the team bus with the rest of the Aces.

Noah follows not long after and I pretend like I'm listening as we do our usual post-game debrief on the way to our hotel, but I'm barely picking up any of it. None of it matters anyway because I know exactly where things went wrong and who's to blame.

Thankfully, the guys leave me alone while they argue in the hotel lobby over which bar to go to. I don't really care where as long as there's plenty of stiff drinks and hopefully, a hot woman or two to take my mind off all of this crap.

Eventually, the concierge suggests a local sports bar called Pitcher Perfect that's only a few blocks away, so we drop our stuff off in our rooms and pile back into the bus to head over. The whole drive passes in a blur without me noticing much of it until I'm standing at the door with the rest of the team.

From the outside, the place looks like every other sports bar I've ever been to, all low lighting, high top tables, and flat screen TVs. And I can see through the windows that it's fucking packed with people wearing Prowlers jerseys, which is just great.

"Ladies first," Reese jokes as he holds the door open for me, so I sock him on the arm on my way past. "Ouch! Someone's feeling feisty tonight."

"Gotta keep my shot arm strong somehow," I say and stroll past him like I'm the most unbothered dude in the room even though I'd much rather be back at the hotel with a bottle of something from room service.

The roar of conversation washes over me as I stop in the waiting area and take it all in. Peanut shells crunch under my feet, and the place reeks of stale IPA, which makes me hate it even more, but I'm too far in to back out now. I glance around the room, scoping out the available talent, and freeze when I spot a head full of familiar, wavy dark hair across the bar.

The woman it's attached to is thin and gorgeous, with a small but muscular body and toned calves shooting from her denim jeans that scream she's a dancer. She's got her back to me, and I cringe when I realize she's wearing a Prowlers jersey too, but I can't help staring at her anyway. Where do I know her from? I can't place it.

Laughter erupts at the crowded table she's sitting at, and I spot someone carrying a boom mic as they loop around the edge of the table to hold it over the head of a smug face I'd very much like to punch. Two goons with cameras on their shoulders follow, and my blood curdles.

Because Shawn Kaplan is here.

With his stupid fucking reality TV show crew.

And that means the woman I can't take my eyes off must be Becca, his girlfriend.

We've met a few times before, most recently after a home game when I found them arguing outside a bar. Kaplan was a total dick to her, only worried about how she was making him look by wearing his jersey—like that's anything to be upset about. I still think she'd look much better wearing mine, and I'm debating walking over to tell her that again when a hand clamps around my bicep.

"Relax, Camden," Noah whispers in my ear, but I barely hear him. "Remember what I told you about Kaplan: he's got it out for you. Don't take the bait, especially not here."

"Easy for you to say. He didn't make a fucking fool out of you today," I mutter back, but Noah squeezes my arm so hard that I wince.

"Exactly. So don't let him do it again."

"Fine," I hiss through gritted teeth. "I'll play nice. For now."

"Good. Come on," Noah says and practically drags me to an open table on the opposite side of the bar, far enough away that I can't start shit, but not far enough that I can't see every irritating moment happening at Kaplan's table.

The waitress comes a few seconds later, a young brunette with striking hazel eyes and a teasing smile.

"Good evening, gents. I'd say welcome to Pitcher Perfect, but this isn't exactly Aces territory," she says with a grin and gestures at the Prowlers jersey she's wearing too. Of course. "Oh, come on, lighten up. I'm kidding. You played great tonight too, but you all look like you could use a drink, so what can I get you?"

I'm first to bark an order for a triple whiskey on the rocks. The waitress raises her eyebrows at me but doesn't say anything, which is the right move. The rest of the team orders a round of drinks and we all sit watching the sideshow that is Kaplan's table of sycophants while we wait for the booze to show.

A few minutes later, the waitress returns with a tray balancing our drinks on her shoulder. I snatch the whiskey glass off the tray before she can lower it to the table and down most of it in one go.

"Okaaay, so it's one of those kind of nights, huh?" she teases as she hands out the other drinks. "Round two?"

"Stat."

"Can you believe this prick really has cameras follow him everywhere?" Reese asks, tilting his head in Kaplan's direction as the waitress vanishes into the crowd. "Who the fuck does he think he is? An honorary Kardashian?"

"He's got a big enough ego to be one," Sawyer answers and everyone laughs but me. I finish the last of my whiskey instead and watch as Becca shifts in her seat toward Kaplan. She tries to put her hand on the small of his back, but he shrugs her off. She tries again a few moments later and this time he swats her hand away and scowls at her.

"Easy, Camden," Noah warns in my ear again. He must have been watching me the entire time, which pisses me off even more. I don't need a babysitter. "Not your circus, not your monkeys."

I open my mouth to tell him to piss off, but a fresh round of shouts erupts from Kaplan's table, cutting me off. Becca jumps from her chair, knocking it to the floor with a crash, and the assholes with the cameras point them right in her face as

7

the whole bar goes silent and stares. What the hell is happening?

"Are you serious right now?" Becca mumbles at Kaplan through the hand clapped over her mouth. It's so quiet in the bar that I hear every word. Kaplan shrugs and flashes her the smuggest look I've ever seen.

"As serious as your insecurity," Kaplan fires back, and I'm on my feet before I realize it because I know exactly what's going on.

Kaplan is about to break up with her.

In public.

On camera.

Chapter 2

Becca

The room feels like it's spinning around me, like I'm the imploding star that this scene revolves around. It's so obvious what's happening, but I don't want to believe it. The bar has fallen so quiet that I can hear my heart hammering in my ears, and my throat is so tight that I can barely breathe—which is exactly what I need to be doing right now.

I can't see them, but I feel every pair of eyes in the bar pricking against my skin like knives, and the bright lights from the cameras aimed at my face cause spots to appear in my vision. Then Shawn swims into view wearing a mocking smile, and although it only intensifies my anxiety, at least I have something to anchor to.

He throws his arms wide, welcoming the watching crowd in. "Oh, come on, babe. It's just not a good fit, but you already know that. Look at you, you're falling apart. You're too shy for the cameras.

Yeah, because you're making an ass out of me in public. Again. The thought scorches through my brain, and I start to say something back, but Shawn talks over me.

"You don't have the same ambition that I do," he says, his

voice louder. He moves so close to me that I can smell the alcohol on his breath, then leans forward until his face is only a few inches from mine. "And it's so obvious to me what's really going on here. You're jealous because I spend so much time with women infinitely hotter than you."

My stomach roils and my cheeks flame. I feel like I might throw up, but that's the last thing I want to happen right now. I refuse to give Shawn the satisfaction of breaking me down in front of his audience, both here in the bar and watching at home.

"Are you seriously going to do this now? In front of all these people?" I ask, my voice coming out much firmer than I feel.

Shawn just shrugs, like I'm the most insignificant person in his world right now. And honestly? That's exactly how I feel—small and worthless and easily discardable.

"It's been a long time coming," he says, giving me an almost pitying look that makes my stomach sour.

He reaches out for me, but I step back. Even the idea of him touching me makes my skin crawl. I'd sooner jump into a bed of bugs than let him put his hands on me ever again. Shawn has embarrassed me in public more times than I can count, but this one takes the cake.

"Look, it's not you." He holds out his hands, chuckling almost smugly. "It's me. I just... I need someone more on my level, you know? Maybe it's because you're Canadian or something, I don't know, but you're just too *bland.*"

A wild urge to laugh bubbles up in my gut because this is all fucking insane. It can't be happening, right? This is just the latest cruel stunt his producers have cooked up for the show. It must be, because there's no way in hell it's real. After all the shit I've put up with from him, *he's* dumping *me?* It's absurd.

I stiffen and reach for my drink. "How's this for bland, you asshole?"

Before I can stop myself, I throw the contents of the glass right in his face.

Ice bounces from his cheeks to the floor, and the remnants of my gin and tonic drip off his chin, spotting his shirt. The bewildered look he flashes me should make me feel like a superstar, but shame, embarrassment, and hurt course through me instead.

The bar erupts in shouts and the cameras catch it all, but I whip on my heel and bolt for the nearest door before I have to listen to one more word from Shawn or any of his lackeys. Part of me regrets throwing the drink at him because I know I just gave him exactly what he wanted—a sob story for his scripted little life—but another part of me is past the point of caring.

I burst through an unmarked door into an alley on the side of the bar and gulp down the night air. My trembling hands wrap around me like I'm trying to literally hold myself together, to keep my twisting insides from spilling out all over the ground.

"Come on, Becca, breathe," I mutter to myself. "It's okay. Don't let him get to you. He's an asshole. A total asshole."

"That's putting it lightly," a deep voice says, and I jump. I spin around expecting to confront someone from Shawn's team, but find a towering, dark-haired guy with striking but warm green eyes that rake over me instead. His jaw shifts as he grits his teeth, and I recognize him right away.

"You," I whisper, barely able to believe who it is. Theo Camden. He's the right winger for the Aces. I've seen him around and talked to him once after a game a while back. What are the odds he'd run into me after two separate fights with Shawn? Given the dysfunctional track record Shawn and I had, pretty high, I guess.

Honestly, I could use the company, but I don't really want anyone to see me like this, much less someone I really shouldn't be talking to. What if the cameras find us out here? It's pretty much a guarantee that one of Shawn's sick producers demanded the crew follow me. My only question is which corner they're lurking behind because the last thing I want is to give Shawn even more footage that he can play on loop to make me look like the villain.

"That looked rough." Theo steps closer. "You okay?"

"I'm fine," I tell him with a shrug.

He laughs and shakes his head. "I don't believe that for a second."

He keeps moving closer, and I think he's going to try to pull me in for a hug, but instead, he leans his back against the wall next to me. We're close enough now that I pick up the smell of his soap, something with hints of amber and spice. He must have come here fresh out of the locker room showers. It's a struggle, but I push the thought out of my mind.

"I know, I'm a mess," I choke in a combination of a laugh and cry before my hands fly up to cover my face. "God, that was so embarrassing."

That doesn't even begin to describe the shame percolating in my gut.

I peek a glance at Theo through my fingers and find him staring down at me from almost a foot above, a concerned look on his face.

"Okay, it still is," I breathe, my cheeks heating.

"Don't be embarrassed. For what it's worth, I've wanted to punch Shawn more times than I can remember in my career, but never as much as I wanted to tonight. Making a woman cry, especially in front of a room of people, is the lowest of the low. He's lucky my guys were there to stop me."

It warms my heart a little to know at least someone in the room cared—because judging from the total silence, I didn't think a soul did. I drop my hands to steal another look at Theo and find him wearing the same playful grin I've seen so many times on TV. I don't know what possessed him to follow me out here, but I'm glad he did because talking to him is distracting me enough to avoid falling to pieces.

"It's Theo, right?"

His smile widens and he nods. "Good memory."

"But terrible judgment?"

Theo chuckles. "No comment. But yeah, we've really gotta stop meeting like this."

I burst out laughing, unable to stop myself. At this point, I don't know what else to do. Shawn turned me into a laughing-stock for the whole world to see, and I feel like such an idiot for letting it happen. Again.

Standing out in the alley talking to a member of the Aces, Shawn's biggest rival team, isn't making the night any less bizarre, but somehow it feels right. Especially knowing that if Shawn ever gets wind of it, he'll be furious. Good. The prick deserves it after what he just put me through.

"I swear, I'm never letting myself fall in love again," I blurt and regret it almost instantly, but Theo tips his head in agreement.

"Can't say I blame you. I decided pretty much the same thing after my divorce."

My eyes snap to his. "I didn't know you were ever married. Or divorced. I'm sorry. We don't have to talk about that, I was just venting."

"Nothing to be sorry about," Theo assures me with another shrug. "I was young and stupid. She and I barely knew each other, and we moved way too fast. But it's a long story that's not worth getting into."

I chew on my lip, torn between wanting to ask more and leaving it alone. It's not really any of my business, but talking to him is helping calm me down. I'm still working up the courage to press for more when he lifts a full bottle of top shelf whiskey I didn't even realize he was holding until now. He shakes it at me, and the amber contents glug and swirl inside.

"I don't really want to be here any more than you do right now. Want to bounce?" he asks, and I lift my eyebrows at him.

"Where'd you get that?"

"Bought it from the bartender on my way out. So, what do you say?"

Each of the chorus of voices in my head screams at me to say no. I don't give a damn what Shawn would think, but I know that if even one of the Prowlers or, god forbid, Shawn's camera crew, spots me leaving with Theo and a bottle of booze, they'll spin it into a salacious story that will dog me—and Theo—for the rest of our lives. It would be exactly the kind of red meat they wouldn't be able to resist.

But then again, why should I care? Shawn just dumped me on camera, which means our breakup will be broadcast on national television. And I'm sick to death of playing a part in his soap opera anyway, so it's not like I owe him a shred of respect. Or anything, really.

Besides, what better way is there to prove I'm not the bland girl he thinks I am than by doing something bold like this? And maybe even a little bit reckless?

My heart hammers in my chest, and my lower lip locks between my teeth. Part of me wants to torch this bridge and never look back, but there's another, meeker part of me that's still worried what Shawn will say or do.

It's that realization that pushes me over the edge. I'm done caring about Shawn. Forever.

"You know what? I'd love to," I finally answer.

Theo beams, smiling broadly as a dimple appears in his cheek. He offers me his free hand, and before I have the chance to second guess myself, I follow him out of the alley into the cool LA night.

Chapter 3

Theo

It's kind of surreal to be walking side-by-side with Becca on LA's salty-breeze streets. I could've imagined any number of ways this night would play out, but this wasn't one of them. Not that I'm complaining. I don't know where we're going, and Becca doesn't seem to either, but it doesn't matter as long as we get away from the bar and the media circus.

I glance over at Becca, who's staring down at her shoes while she walks. She takes deceptively big strides from those short but toned legs, and I can't help but think how beautiful she is from head to toe. Or noticing the way her smooth, ivory skin sparkles in the moonlight. Like she can feel me looking, her gold-flecked brown eyes drift up to mine, and my heart clenches when I spot tears drying on her cheeks.

Has she been crying this whole time? Was it something I said? Fuck.

"You know, I really wasn't lying earlier when I told you I wanted to beat the hell out of Kaplan," I say, testing the waters and trying to keep things light. I don't want to rush her or scare her off. Hell, I don't even know what I was thinking when I chased after her, I just knew I had to do something because seeing her dash out of the bar was like a knife in my side.

Becca laughs and pushes a strand of her dark, wavy hair behind one ear. "Oh, I believe you. What stopped you?"

I thumb the stopper out of the bottle of Macallan with a pop. "I saw you crying, and I couldn't stand it. I bought this because I was gonna break it over Kaplan's head, but I figured you needed it more, so I came after you instead," I say, and her smile widens.

"I don't know much about whiskey, but I definitely think that would've been a waste."

I hold the bottle out to her. "Anything spent on Kaplan is a waste. Here, you first."

Becca smiles and reaches for it. Our fingers brush as she takes the bottle, and I swear I feel something spark between us, a powerful—and dangerous—undercurrent. Her skin is even softer than it looks, but there's a quiet strength to her grip. It must be her dancing background. Thinking about it makes me wonder what other surprises are hidden under her soft exterior, but I push the thought out of my mind.

With a sheepish, adorable look, Becca tips the bottle gingerly up to her lips and takes a little sip. I love how she's delicate about it but unafraid to get down and dirty by drinking right from the bottle. She really is full of surprises.

"Kaplan never deserved you," I mutter, unable to stop myself. But fuck it, it's true, and she needs to hear it. There's probably no one else in her orbit who could or would be honest with her about him like this. "And I wasn't lying back when I told you that you deserve a guy who thinks you look beautiful no matter what you wear. A guy who treats you like a princess."

Her cheeks are flushed, but I can't tell if it's from what I said, what she just went through, or if the whiskey is already kicking in. She's tiny, barely five foot seven, so it wouldn't surprise me if she's a lightweight.

"Thanks," she says and passes the bottle back. I suck down a healthy swig because after what just came out of my mouth, I have a feeling I'm gonna need the liquid courage myself if this keeps going. The whiskey tingles all the way down and warms my stomach, putting me at ease. At least for now.

"Can I ask you something?"

Becca shrugs, her eyes flitting from mine to the pavement and back. "What?"

"Why'd you stay with an asshole like that for so long?"

She sighs, shrinking in on herself, and I worry I might have hurt her feelings. "Good question."

"Sorry if that's too forward. You can tell me to fuck off if you don't want to talk about it, by the way."

Becca laughs and throws her hands in the air. "No, it's okay. I don't know why, honestly," she says and falls silent for a few moments. I don't know where she's gone, but I see the thoughts playing out on her face like a movie.

"Okay, that's not true," she finally says. "I do know why. My mom moved around a ton when I was younger, always falling for some guy or another and bailing when things got hard. You live what you learn, right?" she finishes with a half-hearted shrug.

"Something like that, yeah. That must've been tough though. I'm sorry."

"Thanks. And yeah, it was. She dragged me all over Canada. I never really made friends or felt like I had a place to call home, so I guess at some level it was nice to finally find somewhere to land with Shawn. I always told myself I'd never do the same things she did when I got older, but I guess because I was so determined not to be like her, I overcommitted and stayed way too long with someone I knew wasn't right for me."

"I get that," I say before taking another swig and handing her the bottle. "My ex was a lot like your mom, actually. She

17

could never stay in one place for too long at a time. I swear, it was like she had to keep moving or she'd die."

Becca takes another drink from the bottle, more assertively this time, and nods with a wince as she swallows her mouthful of whiskey. She drags the back of her free hand across her mouth and sighs. "Yeah, sounds just like my mom."

"I'm sorry if this out of line since I barely know you and all, but I know exactly what it's like trying to escape your past," I start and watch her face for a reaction. She doesn't recoil and doesn't try to stop me, she just keeps staring at me with those wide, full brown eyes of hers. "But maybe... I don't know, sometimes I think maybe running too hard from it means you're still letting it define who you are."

Becca stops abruptly and lets out a sad little laugh that melds with the lapping waves of the ocean not far behind her.

Shit. I went too far and put my foot in my mouth again, didn't I?

My heart skips what feels like several beats while I listen to the waves crash in and out along with my thoughts. I'm tempted to fill the silence, to change the subject again, but I hold my tongue and wait what feels like forever for her to say something.

"It's not really my past I'm worried about," Becca says, toeing at a rock on the sidewalk.

"What do you mean?"

"Well, what you said just now made me realize I'm not going to get to do all the things I came to the US to do. God, I was so naive. I came here with all these big dreams and aspirations for my dance career, but Shawn sucked me into his world like a black hole and it's all ruined now."

"You can still do all that stuff you said, you know. Your dreams don't have to die just because you kicked a self-absorbed asshat to the curb."

Becca frowns. "No, I can't. I'm Canadian, and the only reason I'm allowed to be here is because I got a visa to work on

Shawn's stupid TV show. He's *definitely* going to kick me off it now."

"Shit. No job, no visa," I say as understanding dawns, and Becca nods.

"Exactly. And most of my 'friends' here are Shawn's, so it's not like I'll have anyone in LA who will miss me. But I don't have anyone to go back to in Canada, either."

I gaze down at her, torn between keeping quiet and saying what I really want to say. Maybe it's the whiskey talking, but there are words burning at the tip of my tongue, so I decide to let them out.

"You have at least one person here who'll miss you."

Becca's soft brown eyes lock onto mine, jolting me. I don't know what it is about this woman, but I can't deny there's something there. Something meteoric and gravitational.

"Oh, really? Who's that?"

"Me."

Her eyelashes flutter as she blinks, surprise reflecting in her eyes. Then she laughs, shaking her head as she hands the bottle back to me. "You don't even know me."

"I know you well enough."

"Okay, then what's my favorite color?"

I freeze, knowing it's a trap, and search her outfit for clues. But she's wearing Kaplan's Prowlers jersey, which is way too big on her, and cut-off denim shorts, so there aren't any dead giveaways.

"Blue," I say, and she scrunches up her nose.

"That's everyone's favorite color, so I'll chalk that one up to a lucky guess. What else have you got?"

"I know you're a dancer."

"Because I literally just told you that," she says after a beat, and we laugh together.

"Nah, I knew before you said it tonight. You told me the last time I saw you, but you also said you were 'sort of' a dancer. I still don't know what that means."

Becca stares at me for a second before the hint of a smile creeps across her face. "You remembered that?"

"What can I say? You're unforgettable. And apparently, you really like Macallan whiskey," I say as I hold up the bottle and swish it to demonstrate how much she's already had. We're already halfway through the bottle, and at this rate, it'll be finished in the next few minutes.

"Actually, it's the first time I've ever had it."

"Really? I would've guessed Kaplan had expensive taste, so sounds like I chose wisely," I say before hitting the bottle again myself. A buzz is already humming at the back of my head, but I can't tell if that's the whiskey or my nerves talking. And I don't really care because I'm enjoying this so much. I could stand out here on the shore listening to the water and talking to Becca until the sun came up and never get tired of it.

"Are you ever gonna tell me what exactly it means to 'sort of' be a dancer?"

Becca shrugs. "It means I let a shitty man derail all my dreams. Just like my mom."

Rage bubbles in my stomach, warring with the whiskey. If I didn't already fucking hate Kaplan, I sure as hell would now. Becca is right, I don't really know her that well at all. But I can already tell she's sweet and genuine, a true princess, and Kaplan never deserved a second of her time.

If I ever get in a room alone with that asshole again...

Kaplan has no idea how badly he fucked up by driving her away like he did, but I resolve to make him see it by treating Becca the way she deserves—often and publicly. No amount of punches to his smug fucking face could ever substitute for the joy that would bring me. And I could really use more joy in my life right about now.

"You know what?" Becca says, her expression brightening a

little. "I don't want to think about anything sad right now. I want to do something fun."

She starts toeing off her shoes as she speaks, and I cock my head at her

"What are you doing?"

"Come on," she says and takes me by the hand, pulling me off the sidewalk and onto the sand beside it before I can object. Between the shifting sand and the swirling in my head, it's hard to keep my balance, so she gets ahead of me. But eventually, I stumble up to her where she's standing with her feet in the water as it laps back and forth up the beach.

Becca lifts a teasing eyebrow at me, her oversized jersey fluttering in the breeze that's coming off the water. "Aren't you going to join me? Or is the big bad hockey player scared of the ocean?"

"Oh, please. I've lived through Colorado winters. The Pacific doesn't scare me in the slightest."

"Then prove it. I dare you."

"I'll take that dare, princess."

I kick off my own shoes on the sand behind us so they won't get wet. The sand sifts between my toes, and the water comes rushing up the beach, soaking me and sending a chill tearing up my spine.

"Holy shit, that's colder than I thought it would be!" I hiss, and Becca tosses her head back in laughter.

"Those Colorado winters must not be that cold," she teases and starts moving farther into the water.

It's up to her knees when she lets out a yelp and almost falls over, but my hand darts out like I'm interrupting a pass to catch her, pulling her against me. Her heaving chest presses into my side, and she glances up at me, her golden-brown eyes gleaming in the moonlight and searching my face.

We stare at each other, frozen, for what feels like forever. I keep her suspended like the world paused around us in the middle of a dance, and I feel her heartbeat pounding against my ribs. Mine is hammering just as hard. Maybe I never should've followed Becca, much less left with her.

And maybe this is all a terrible idea, but then why does it feel so right? And why does she fit perfectly in my arms?

Becca swallows hard and licks her lips. The way they sparkle in the moonlight stirs something in me, something urgent and dangerous, and I feel myself teetering on the edge of control. I want to kiss her, feel those luscious lips against mine. But I know we shouldn't be doing this. She knows we shouldn't be doing this. Yet neither of us moves.

Tension crackles between us, and I can see on her moonlit porcelain face that a flurry of thoughts are racing through her head too.

I lean forward, ignoring the voice in my head that's warning me not to get myself tangled up in more of Kaplan's drama. I know that's exactly what I'm inviting, but with Becca in my arms, staring up at me with desire burning in her gorgeous brown eyes... I don't care.

"Theo," she whispers, just loud enough I can hear it over the water lapping against the shore.

"Fuck it," I mutter, then drop my head to press my lips to hers.

Chapter 4

Becca

Theo kisses me with a hunger and passion I can't ever remember feeling, and my body responds on its own, arching up into him. I'm a little dazed by it all and feeling like I'm living a dream sequence, but there's no denying my attraction to him is real. And this is one dream I don't want to wake up from. I want to savor it.

He pulls me to my feet and cradles my head in his hands to kiss me deeper. I have to stand on my tiptoes to reach his mouth, so I jump into his arms and he catches me, his powerful arms holding me in place by the underside of my thighs like I'm as light as air. His hands wind up my back, plunging under the Prowlers jersey dangling off me, and his fingertips dig into the skin beneath.

"Come back to my hotel with me," he mutters when we finally break.

"Okay," I answer immediately, and he sets me back down on my feet.

We hurry out of the water, hand-in-hand, and rush to get our shoes back on. I'm definitely feeling the whiskey now, which makes standing on one foot at a time difficult. We both almost fall over more than once and can't stop laughing at each other. The sand sticks between my toes, but it's the furthest thing from my mind. All I can think about is what this dark-haired, tanned mountain of a man is going to look like without his clothes on.

Theo already has his phone out by the time we get back to the road. "I just ordered an Uber. Should be here any second. Gotta love LA."

"Wait, where's the whiskey?"

Theo shrugs. "No clue. Dropped it on the beach or in the water, I guess. But I don't think we're going to be needing it the rest of the night," he says with a laugh and flashes me that devilish grin of his again. He trails a fingertip down my arm, and goosebumps echo after it, warming my core and wetting my panties.

Part of me can't believe I'm doing this, but I don't have the time to second guess it because a black sedan that can only be our ride is rolling to a stop at the curb in front of us. Theo hurries over and opens the door for me.

"After you, princess," he says, holding a hand out to help me into the car, which is probably a good thing because between the whiskey and my attraction to him, I'm feeling a little unsteady but not at all unsure.

I climb into the back seat, and he slides in next to me but not without hitting his head on the door. My snort turns into giggles when he shoots me a look, but he can't keep his laughter in either, especially when the driver, a thin guy not much older than us, glares at us in the rearview. He has to know we've been drinking, but what does he expect? It's the night of a Prowlers' game in LA.

When we're both seated and belted in, the driver taps a few times on his phone to get the directions to Theo's hotel up and running, then hits play on some generic house music. Traffic isn't as bad as it normally is after a game, but it's still dense enough that he has to bob and weave between lanes and other cars.

Theo can't keep his hands off me. One finds its way to my thigh, making me jump, but he doesn't stop. He wedges it between my knees and pushes my legs apart to snake his fingers farther up toward the leg of my shorts. They slip under the hem easily, and when his fingertips brush against the edge of my panties, my breath catches in my throat.

This isn't like me at all, but then again, maybe it is. I've been trapped in Shawn's reality TV nightmare for so long that I'm not really sure what's true about me and what isn't anymore. Over the years, I twisted myself in knots to make him happy until I was unrecognizable. But the hungry look Theo shoots me as he toys with the band of my panties thaws a part of me that was so deeply frozen I'd forgotten it existed until now.

So much for being bland, huh?

"Can you be quiet?" Theo whispers in my ear, the heady, sexy scent of whiskey on his breath filling my nose. I nod through a fresh round of goosebumps, so he pushes his hand past the band of my panties. "Do you want me to stop?"

I shake my head hard, and I see him grinning in the reflection of the rearview. Light from the streetlamps plays across his face in flashes as we weave in and out of traffic, and I breathe in sharply to keep from gasping when he presses a fingertip inside me. He pulls out just as unexpectedly and wiggles up to my clit, teasing it with soft, gentle flicks against the calloused pad of his fingertip. It takes everything I have to hold in the moan building in my stomach. Not to grind against his hand and get myself off faster.

His finger traces agonizing circles against my clit, and my hands grip the seat cushion to keep myself from screaming when he suddenly changes direction. The sensation is too much, and I can feel an orgasm already welling up inside me. No one has ever gotten me off like this. Maybe it's the thrill of getting caught combined with the person I'm doing it with, but I'm not going to be able to hold it back much longer.

I melt into the seat and the car around me falls away while I lose myself to the incredible pleasure Theo's giving me. I feel adrift in a sea of sensation that's both too much and not enough at the same time. My body rocks in rhythm to Theo's soft strokes against my clit, and I have to grit my teeth to fight the tingling that's quickly becoming a burning in my core.

Just as my eyes flutter shut and my breathing stops, the car jerks to a halt. If I wasn't so dazed, I'd be annoyed that it stopped just as I was about to crash over the finish line. Theo yanks his hand from my shorts, smirks, and licks his fingers, sending heat racing through me. The boldness of it startles and arouses me, but I'm so breathless I can't form the words to comment on it.

"We're here," the driver snaps as Theo throws the door open and the cabin lights flare. He's glaring at us in the rearview again. He's not stupid, he must know we're up to something, but Theo ignores him and hurries out of the car.

He offers me a hand up again, which is good because my legs are wobbling and every nerve is still on fire. He kicks the door closed, and the driver peels off as I stand on the curb with the world spinning around me.

Theo's hand squeezes mine, grounding me somewhat, before he leads me toward the hotel's entrance. I'm still so close to coming that with every jelly-legged step I take toward the lobby, I feel the subtle friction of my panties against my clit make little shockwaves that edge me closer and closer.

Theo stops outside the elevator and presses his lips against my ear. "Don't come yet. Not like this. I want my face buried between your legs when you do," he says, and it's a good thing he's still holding my hand because his words make my vision swim.

"Okay," I whimper back. It's the best I can do. Every nerve

in my body feels like it's screaming, and it's so loud in my head that I can barely think straight. He could tell me to strip down and lie on one of the sofas here in the lobby, and I wouldn't have the resolve to fight him.

Theo repeatedly smashes the button to call for the lift, but someone must have just gotten out because it dings and the door swishes open almost immediately. He pulls me inside by the hand and hammers the button to close the door before anyone can join us.

Clearly, he wants me all to himself for this ride, and my heart races at the thought of what he's going to do as soon as the doors close.

They seal shut, and Theo uses his body weight to push and press me against the cold metal of the wall. Goosebumps ripple up my back, and Theo hoists me up to crash his lips into mine.

He's grinding against me, pushing the rock-hard bulge of his cock into the crotch of my shorts and giving my clit a new shock of pleasure with each thrust. Heat courses through my body like I jumped into a steaming bath and I'm so turned on I can barely breathe, much less think.

"You're so fucking beautiful, princess," Theo groans when he pulls away. He rests his forehead against mine while he catches his breath, and all I can do is cling to his shoulders helplessly. "I bet you taste twice as good as you look. I can't wait to find out."

"Mmm," I whimper, unable to form coherent words, but it doesn't matter because his lips are on mine again. He forces them apart with his tongue and swipes it over mine, and the raw passion in the way he does it melts me. He's not asking for permission. He's taking what he wants. And I'm so fucking wet that I wouldn't dream of stopping him.

The elevator dings when we arrive at his floor, and he lowers me to my feet carefully before pulling me out of the elevator and down the hall toward his room. We're moving so fast we're almost running, but Theo doesn't seem to care in the slightest who sees us or worry we might run into someone he knows. The only thing he's focused on is fishing his keycard out of his pocket.

"Fucking hell," he curses when he tries to cram the card into the slot and misses because his hands are shaking. He turns around to plant a quick kiss on my lips, then tries again. He must've put it in too fast though, because the little light above the slot flashes red. "Dammit."

It's stupid, but the way he's so desperate to get me into his room only makes me want him more. He makes *me* feel wanted, something I've never really felt with Shawn. With him, sex always felt like an obligation, something he ordered up when and however he wanted. And it wasn't like I could say no or had any say whatsoever in how it went.

If I'd left it up to him, he probably would've brought the cameras in the bedroom with us.

The thought makes me angry, so I push it away. I'm a world away from Shawn right now, and that's exactly how I want it.

"Here, let me try," I whisper and take the keycard from him.

I put the card in slowly but firmly, and the light flashes green as the lock disengages.

"Thank fuck," Theo growls and pushes it open with his foot to pull me inside by the hand.

As soon as we're inside, he shoves the door closed, then presses me up against it. His lips meet mine in a hungry kiss, his hands going to the hem of the jersey I'm wearing. He pulls away just long enough to tug it over my head in one fluid motion and toss it to the floor. I've got a tank top and bra on underneath, and even though he hasn't even gotten me naked yet, Theo's eyes heat as he drinks me in.

The way he's looking at me makes something warm pool low in my belly, and I finish what he started, pulling off my tank top before unhooking my bra and sliding it down my arms.

"Jesus fucking Christ," Theo murmurs as his hands trail up my ribcage toward my breasts. "You're even more beautiful than I imagined, princess."

Cupping each breast, he traces circles around my nipples with the pads of his thumbs and I can't hold back the groan that leaks out of me because they're so sensitive.

"I've been dying to taste you since we got in the Uber. And now you're all mine," he says and attacks my neck with his mouth, kissing and sucking all the way up it until he reaches my lips.

"*Fuck,*" I breathe into his mouth. "Take me."

Theo drops to his knees and rips my shorts and panties down together like there's nothing holding them in place. Before my brain can catch up, his tongue flicks against my swollen clit and I cry out in shock and ecstasy. His hotel is probably packed with people, including his teammates, but I'm way too turned on to care. And something tells me Theo isn't going to hold back for their sake either.

"You like that?" he breathes into my pussy, his hot breath like fire against my clit.

"Oh my god, yes!" I gasp. "I'm so close already."

"Good. Because I want you to soak my fucking face, princess," he says and sucks my clit into his mouth, lapping at it with his tongue. My fingers shoot to his short, dark hair and wind themselves up in it as the orgasm I've been fighting for the last thirty minutes or more comes roaring to the surface.

He drags his mouth away from my clit and buries the tip of his tongue in my pussy. As soon as it pierces my folds, I let out a sound somewhere between a groan and scream because there's no way I can keep the dam from breaking.

"That's it, let it out," Theo encourages me before he buries his face between my legs again. The warmth of his breath and the vibration of his hungry groan sends me into the stratosphere.

My fingertips dig into his scalp as the orgasm crashes over

me, but Theo doesn't let up. He keeps sucking and licking every part of me he can get his mouth on, and the pleasure is so intense that my knees start to buckle. For a second, I'm afraid I'm going to pass out.

But Theo hoists me up by my thighs, just like he did in the water earlier, and holds me in place against the door as the last of my orgasm trickles out of me and he continues eating me. My body twitches and convulses against his face, and I jolt every time his tongue or mouth grazes my electrified clit. Finally, it passes, and I dissolve against the door behind me, breathless and wordless.

"That was fucking amazing." Theo smirks as he looks up at me, his emerald eyes flashing with desire and admiration. "Do it again."

"What? Are you serious?" I gasp. Shawn almost never got me off, let alone more than once in a session. As soon as he finished, we were done, so to have an incredibly hot wall of muscle like Theo still between my legs begging for more leaves me at a loss for words but makes me wonder how much else I've been missing out on these last few years.

"Dead serious," he says. The adorable dimple in his left cheek appears, melting any chance I had of resistance. He nuzzles my still-throbbing clit with the tip of his nose, pushing a little whimper out of me.

"I—I don't know if I can."

"Oh, I beg to differ," he says and flicks my clit with his tongue. A shock courses through me and I gasp. "You'll never know until you try."

"Theo, I can barely stand," I beg, and I'm not kidding. My legs have turned to Jell-O, and if it weren't for his hulking arms literally holding me up, I'd be a quaking puddle on the floor.

"Let me help you then," he says and lifts one of my legs over his shoulder, pulling me closer to him. With my body pinned like this, it isn't like I can say no, so when he slips his tongue between my folds again, my head drops back on its own, thudding against the door as another moan claws its way up my throat. No one has ever made me feel like this before.

"That's it. Good girl," he praises me between licks, but his words barely register. I feel like I'm leaving my body and the only thing keeping me rooted is the feeling of my fingers twisted in his hair. And incredibly enough, I already feel another orgasm rumbling to life in the depths of my core. That's another first.

"Oh my god, Theo," I groan as the rumbling swells into a burning of nerve endings on fire. My second orgasm sneaks up and pummels me, crashing through me like the waves on the LA shore. I grind myself down against his face, gasping at the electric feeling of his stubble rasping against my sensitive skin. Wave after wave of pleasure fills me, forcing my eyes shut and the breath out of my lungs. My toes curl so tightly that it's sweetly painful.

When it passes, I slump back against the wall, but Theo still isn't finished with me.

He grabs my other leg and throws it over his shoulder as well. I yelp when I lose contact with the floor, but his broad shoulders keep me suspended easily as my back rests against the wall. He's not a lot taller than Shawn, who was just as muscular and built from playing hockey too, but Theo feels bigger and stronger somehow. It's amazing how our bodies just seem to fit together, to read each other.

Theo never pulls away or stops eating me for a second. If I weren't so overridden with pleasure, I'd be amazed at his ability to hold me up and devour me at the same time. I'm starting to feel a little dizzy from the whiskey, the multiple orgasms, and being held up like this, but I'm not at all sure I'm ready for it to be over yet. My entire nervous system is screaming in overload, but I don't want him to stop.

"The more you come, the sweeter you taste, princess," Theo mutters against me, making me shiver.

He slows down, licking torturously slow circles around the very edges of my white-hot clit. My thighs squeeze his head, and my fingers claw into his scalp, but that only seems to egg him on.

"I want one more," he growls.

"Oh god," I gasp, my pulse racing. "Are you serious? You already blew my mind twice. I don't think I can come again. I—"

Whatever I was about to say gets swallowed up by a gasp as he laps at my clit again. Then he draws back to fix those devastating green eyes of his on me, but this time he's not smiling. Something burns in his eyes, hot enough to send sparks racing through my veins.

"You can. And you *will*," he demands, then drops his head again.

He kisses, licks, and nips at every inch of my pussy, and I fall apart. Noises even I can't describe are flowing out of my mouth like a woman possessed. Maybe it's because I've already come twice and everything is extra sensitive, but it takes even less time for a third orgasm to bubble over.

Jesus, this man is going to break me. Maybe he already has.

The thought races through my head on repeat, clashing with the sound of his wet and hungry lapping at my equally wet pussy and thighs until my body starts tensing. As yet another orgasm shockwaves through me, my back arches against the door, and he groans his approval as I fall apart on his face for a third time.

Finally, he pulls himself away from me and scoops me up into his arms. I couldn't walk even if I wanted to right now, so I focus on catching my breath while he carries me to the bed. He lowers me down onto the edge on my back, its pillowy top hugging me. But I can tell from the animalistic look in his eyes we aren't done.

"I told you that you deserved someone who'd treat you like a princess," he says, smirking.

"Forget being a princess, I feel like a fucking god*dess* right now," I whisper and watch as he pulls his wallet from his back pocket. He flips it open and pulls a condom out, then tears it open with his teeth.

"Because you are. And don't you ever forget it." He rips his shirt up over his head with his free hand, revealing a toned body I couldn't even have dreamed of.

Tattoos litter his chest and arms, more than I can count or keep track of. They're barely visible in the moonlight streaming in through the open window beside us, but a crouched, snarling tiger on his left pec catches my eye as he unbuttons his jeans. It reminds me so much of him—threatening on the outside, and wild inside.

And it's hot as hell.

I stare up at this untamed animal of a man towering over me with my heart racing and my clit throbbing. And as he peels his boxers down his marbled muscle thighs, I can't stop myself from gasping.

Because *every* part of him is huge.

Chapter 5

Theo

My cock twitches under Becca's gaze, and desire thrums through me all over again. Watching her drink in my tattoos like she was trying to memorize every one of them was one of the hottest things I've ever seen, but the intense mix of awe, heat, and intimidation playing out on her face makes precum dribble from my cock head.

I take my cock in my hand and stroke it a few times. "If you keep looking at me like that, I'm gonna come before I ever get inside you."

Blush races across her cheeks and her eyes dart up to mine. "Oh, uh, sorry. I wasn't trying to stare, it's just... you're beautiful. And I had no idea you had so much ink."

"I bet there's a lot you don't know about me," I say as I crawl onto the bed over her, forcing her onto her back. I kiss my way up her body, starting at the tender insides of her thighs, and love the way she jolts every time my lips touch her. If she was mine, I'd treat her like this every fucking night, just so she never forgot how important she is to me.

"Then tell me," she whispers back, and it drives me crazy.

Not that I'm bragging, but I've hooked up with more than

my fair share of puck bunnies over the years. The thing is, most of them don't give a shit about anything other than getting the bragging rights of bagging an Aces player for a night. And maybe it's because I have so many, but I've never had a single woman ask me about the story behind my tattoos—not that I would've told them anyway.

But the fact that Becca's insisting on it does something to me.

"I have a tattoo for every major event in my life," I say as my mouth hovers over her still-wet pussy. My tongue flicks against her swollen clit and she moans, tossing her head side to side on the bed.

"I want to know the story behind them all," she says as she lifts her hips up, desperate to get my mouth back on her. But I move farther up instead, placing tender kisses on her ribs and breasts until my mouth eventually finds hers. Our tongues tangle, and Becca wraps her legs around my waist, pressing my cock head against her slippery folds.

It feels fucking incredible, so I reach down to grip myself and drag the head up and down her slick creases while we keep kissing. Becca moans into my mouth when my cock grazes her clit, and although I'd never go bare on a hookup like this, I'm more tempted than I've ever been. With as many times as she's already gotten off, her pussy is probably on fire, so I know she'd feel amazing without a condom in the way, but I wouldn't dare. I told Becca she deserves to be treated like a princess, and I'm going to live up to it.

But when my cock accidentally notches up against her entrance, forcing a gasp out of both of us, I stop immediately. "Fuck, where'd that condom go?"

I fumble around for it in the dark because I know I dropped it somewhere on the bed after I opened it, and finally my fingers find the foil of the wrapper.

I don't ever want to let her go, but I reluctantly pull back so I can roll the condom on, and Becca watches every second of it with her lower lip snagged between her teeth. I've thought she was gorgeous from the second I laid eyes on her but seeing her bared out in front of me like this with raw desire written all over her face adds a whole new layer to her beauty.

I have a past, and so does she. We all do. But I'm starting to see that there is so much more to this woman than she's ever let anyone see, and I'm determined to show her she can trust me with it. That I'm not just another selfish prick like Kaplan or the deadbeats her mom got with who will use her for what he wants and throw her away.

She's special. She might not see it yet, but I do, and I'm going to do everything I can to make it clear. Even if it's only for one night.

When I finish rolling the condom all the way on, Becca swallows.

"You okay?"

"Yeah, it's just... can you go slow? I've never been with a guy as, well, big as you are."

It's so sweet and innocent that desire floods my veins all over again, so I lean over her and gently kiss her forehead. "I promise I'll go slow, princess," I say, brushing her hair out of her face. "I'll make it good for you. But I want you to take every inch of my cock. Do you think you can do that?"

"Yes. I want that," she whimpers softly, and I can't hold back anymore.

I find her entrance again and start pushing in, watching her face for even the slightest hint of pain. As she opens up for me, her eyes widen, and a faint gasp leaks out of her.

"You're so tight," I groan as I reach down to thumb her clit, hoping it'll ease the stretch for her. "Fucking hell."

She writhes beneath me as I press deeper inside, biting her lower lip as she hooks her legs around the backs of mine, pulling me even closer.

"That's it," I grit out. "You're doing amazing."

"Is it all the way in?" she whimpers.

Something hungry and possessive rises up inside me, making me feel almost feral. "Not quite. You've only taken about half. You want more? You think you can handle it?"

Her gorgeous eyes flare wide, but then she nods firmly, rolling her hips beneath me and making me slip a little deeper inside her. "Yes. I want all of it. All of you. I can take it."

I grin, my cock throbbing. "Of course you can. You can do anything you set your mind to, princess."

She laughs softly at that, but the sound turns into a breathy moan as I pull out and then slide another inch into her tight pussy.

"So. Big," she gasps.

"You're killing me, princess," I groan, resting my forehead against hers as our breaths dance together in the space between us. "I'm gonna fall apart before I give you everything. You feel too damn good."

"So do you. It's... it's so *much*, Theo."

"Not too much for you," I promise.

I keep toying with her clit, and she slowly starts to relax as she gets turned on all over again. Inch by inch, I disappear inside her until our hips meet. I have to stop and take a breath because the sensation of her squeezing all around me is almost too much to take, and judging from the look on her face, she feels the same.

"Good girl," I say and stroke her cheek with the backs of my fingers. "I knew you could do it."

"Oh my god," she moans, grinding against me as she squirms on the bed, her pussy clenching around my entire length. "Please move. I need more. Please."

The way she begs, digging her nails into my back, sets me on fire. I draw almost all the way out and thrust back in force-fully, and Becca cries out, her nails digging into my skin. She arches beneath me, so hungry and responsive. It's fucking incredible.

"You're driving me crazy," I groan as I push her legs farther apart and pull out until only my head is still inside her.

After working her over as much as I have, and seeing the way she's responding to my cock inside her, I'm so turned on that I could come at any second. But I'm determined not to go until she does again. Her needs and pleasure will always come first for me.

Becca whimpers in response, a sound that turns into a scream as I drive in again and start to thrust in a steady rhythm. Her hand drops to her clit, and she works circles across it with her fingertips. I want—no, *need*—to get closer, so I lock my hands under her knees and push them to her chest, making it even easier to bury myself inside her. She's so wet that I can feel it coating my cock as I pick up the pace, pistoning my hips.

"Yes," Becca breathes, begging and urging me on at the same time.

We settle into a fast but steady rhythm, in and out, and her moaning fills the room. The whole floor can probably hear us, but I don't give a fuck. The only thing that matters to me is the beautiful woman in front of me and the way I'm making her feel.

It takes less than a minute of this for her fingers to start moving faster against her clit. And when her legs start trembling in my hands, I know she's getting close again, but she's not the only one. It's taking every ounce of concentration and grit I've honed after years on the ice not to erupt, especially when her eyes flutter open and lock on mine. She chews her lip and nods eagerly at me. That's good because I feel myself racing toward orgasm too and I don't think I can hold it back anymore.

This is the best sex I've ever had.

It's not the first time I've thought it, but it's not just about the physicality. Of course her soft skin feels amazing, and of course I'm losing it to the wet, slippery grip of her pussy, but it's the connection between us that's really pushing things to a new level.

She's been so vulnerable tonight, both by choice and by circumstance. After what she went through with Kaplan, she would've had every right to tell me to fuck off when I followed her outside, but she didn't. Maybe it's jumping the gun, but that makes me feel like Becca trusts me in a way that no other woman has before. Why else would she be here with me right now if she didn't? This isn't just a rebound thing, I know it isn't. I've had more than enough of those to know the difference.

But even with my ex, who I really thought I loved, I've never felt this bonded during sex. That has to mean something. It just has to.

Becca's latest whimper slams me back into my body, where the pleasure building is becoming unbearable. I match my thrusting to the speed of her hand and after a few more deep pumps, Becca's breath catches in her throat, and she goes rigid under me until a scream builds in her stomach and erupts out of her with her orgasm. She bucks up against and grips me, sending me right over the edge with her. My eyes squeeze shut, and I lose all sense of time and place as I come so hard with her that I stop breathing.

When it's over, I slump over her with my forehead against hers, heaving. I don't want to crush her, so I hold myself up by my hands, and it takes all my strength. Becca looks up at me, flushed and breathless and beautiful.

"Wow," she whispers, barely able to get the words out. "That was incredible."

"You're damn right it was, princess," I say and plant a soft kiss on her forehead. I'm in no hurry for this to be over, so I hold myself in place above her, staring into her beautiful eyes and trying to memorize the moment. I hope not, but I know there's a chance I might never see her again after tonight, so I don't want to forget this.

She smiles up at me as her hand reaches up to the tiger tattoo on my pec. She drags a nail around its outline, summoning goosebumps to the surface of my skin.

"You said earlier that each tattoo you have commemorates a moment in your life," she whispers.

"Yeah?"

"What was this one for?" she asks, and I have to laugh. "What? What's funny?"

"Nothing, it's just... the story behind that one is kind of stupid."

"I love it. Tell me," she insists, tracing the tattoo again. The story really is stupid, but after what we just shared, how can I say no to anything this woman wants? She doesn't even know how much she's gotten to me.

"It commemorates me being a teenage idiot," I say as I lie down facing her without pulling out and hug her into me. She rests her head on my shoulder and keeps tracing the tattoo. "But in all seriousness, it was the first tattoo I ever got. One of my buddies in high school dared me to do it. He thought I was too chicken shit to go through with it, so of course I had to prove him wrong."

Becca lifts her head and smirks at me. "Typical teenage boy behavior."

"Exactly."

"What about this one?" she asks, moving her finger over to a tattoo of a flame-tipped arrow wrapped in a parchment banner on my other pec. "Is that Latin?"

"Yeah. 'Audaces fortuna iuvat.' It means 'fortune favors the bold.'"

"What's the story behind that?"

"A hockey coach of mine in high school inspired that one. I

think he was probably the only person who ever believed in me when I was a kid. He really pushed me because he saw my potential. Playing on his team, the Archers, made me realize I could really make something of myself if I wanted to. He passed away about a year after I graduated, so I got that tattoo to remember him by. And to remind myself to keep shooting for my goals."

Becca beams at me. "That's really sweet. But I'm sorry to hear he passed."

"I was too. Crushed, actually."

Her fingers drift up to the base of my collarbone where she stops on yet another tattoo that runs along it, a string of numbers in a loopy, script font. "What about this one? Is it a date?" she asks, thankfully changing the subject.

"It is. That was when I signed my first ever NHL contract," I say, and I can't help smiling about it. It was a long time ago now, but I still remember how on top of the world I felt that day. It took years of blood, sweat, and tears to make it to the NHL, but I did it.

"Wow. I didn't realize you'd been playing professionally this long," she says. "No offense," she adds in a hurry.

I laugh and kiss her forehead again. "None taken. Most people don't know much about my career before the Aces. Even hardcore hockey fans like you."

"I hope to learn," she says, her eyes locked on mine, and it does something to me. This woman is full of surprises, and I'm not really sure what I did to make her so interested in me, but I can tell she means it. She's not just saying the things she thinks a star hockey player would want to hear like some of the other girls I've been with over the years.

"I'll tell you anything you want to know," I say, surprising myself. There is something about Becca that makes her so easy to talk to, so disarming. I can't put my finger on what it is, but she defuses me, makes me feel like I can let my walls down.

Even just a little bit. And it feels great to let go of some of that tension.

"Anything?" she whispers, her eyes drifting to my left arm, and I already know where she's going.

"Anything," I insist, but when her fingers sweep to the two golden rings joined together on my bicep, it still summons a little stab of bittersweetness.

"Was this one for when you got married?" she asks.

"When we got engaged, actually." I don't know what else to say that I haven't already told Becca about. I made my peace with that part of my life, but I don't talk about it often for a reason.

"So, then this one...?" She trails off, her fingers running over the pair of dates beneath the rings.

"One for the day we married, another for the day we got divorced. Yeah."

Becca presses her forehead against me, staring deeply into my eyes with a mixture of admiration and tenderness. "Thank you."

"For what?"

"Being so open. I mean, we technically just met and all," she says, and we laugh together. "But seriously, I appreciate it. Maybe it's weird to say, but it's inspiring," she says, and I feel myself getting hard again inside her.

"What do you mean?"

"Well, if you can get through that and still be one of the best hockey players in the NHL, it makes me think I'll be okay too," she says without any idea just how *off* I've been lately. If anyone's in need of inspiration, it's me. And it's probably way too soon to even be thinking this way, but I can't help wondering if she could be the thing to finally pull me out of the funk I've been in—if she could give me a reason to want to play again.

"You're going to be more than okay," I tell her, and nudge my nose against hers.

"How do you know that?"

"Because you're way too fucking amazing for the world not to see it," I say, and she chuckles but it's forced, so I look her right in the eyes. "I mean it, princess. Don't ever let anyone or anything take your light away."

"Theo," she whispers as a tear streaks down her cheek, and then her lips are on mine again. My cock swells inside her in response, and Becca moans into my mouth as I stretch her.

When there's a pause in the kiss, I pull back. "If it takes doing this with you all night to get you to believe me, I will. I don't want you to just know how amazing I think you are. I want you to *feel* it."

"I want that too," she says, sending a rush of blood to my cock.

"Then I think I'd better find another condom," I say and don't hesitate. I pull gently out of her and hurry to the bathroom to get rid of the used condom and dig another out of my overnight bag. I roll it on and head back to the bed where I find Becca lying on her back with her knees spread, welcoming me in.

"I can't get enough of you," I groan. "I want you all night."

"Then what are you waiting for?" she teases, so I climb over her and hover there, notching my swollen cock head against her entrance.

Her legs instinctively wrap around my waist as she pulls me into her. We moan together as I slide inside, and she's already loosened up enough that I can take a few easy strokes to warm up. Becca chews her lip and nods at me, encouraging me. But as hot as it is, I want more.

I pull out and lift her off the bed to spin her onto her hands and knees. Becca seems surprised at first but doesn't fight it. She actually looks over her shoulder at me, still with her lip locked between her teeth, and I lose it. My hands clap onto her beautiful ass to grope it, and she moans in response.

"Do you have any idea how beautiful you are?" I ask and give her cheek a clap. She whimpers but doesn't say anything, just arches her back, practically begging me back into her. "Good girl," I say as I line up and slide inside, forcing a long, low moan out of her.

She buries her face in the pillow to drown out the noise, but I don't give a damn who hears—I want the whole hotel to know how amazing I'm making this woman feel. And more importantly, I want her to feel how amazing she is, just like I told her.

So I keep pounding away at her, my hips clapping against her cheeks, until the whole room echoes with her moans. Not even the pillow is enough to muffle them.

"I can't get enough of you," I mumble and lift her up by the stomach, pulling her back against my chest. She wraps one arm around my neck to hold herself in place, so I reach farther down and rub her swollen clit between two fingers. She shudders against me and gasps each time I thrust into her.

Each little noise she makes nudges me closer to orgasm, and I lose myself to the sound. The room falls away until all I can see and feel is Becca against and around me. My mouth finds her neck, kissing and nibbling at the soft, sensitive skin there while my fingers continue stroking her clit.

"That's it, that's my princess," I encourage her. "Do you feel how amazing you are now? Do you?"

"Yes!" Becca gasps. Her eyes are squeezed shut, her mouth hanging open, and I can feel from the way she's gripping me that she's getting close again too. But it's still not good enough for me. I still want more.

No, I *need* more. So I pull out abruptly, making her gasp and shudder again, then fall on my back on the bed beside her.

"What are you do—" she starts, but yelps when I lift her up and spin her around to straddle me. Her legs fall on either side of my chest, and I try to lower her back down on my cock to ride me, but she puts her hands on my thighs and hesitates.

"I want to see you ride me. Is that okay?" I ask.

"Yeah, it's fine. I've just, uh, never done it like this before. Shawn wasn't into me being on top."

"Can't say I'm surprised. But you're fucking gorgeous, so that's his loss," I say in awe as I reach up to cup her breasts, and she beams down at me. She spreads her legs a little farther and sinks down onto me. I watch my cock disappear inside her, inch after inch, and the little gasp she lets out when my hips meet her thighs sends a thrum through my whole shaft.

"You're in control now," I tell her. "Take your pleasure." She chews her lip again nervously and blush appears on her cheeks. "You deserve it, princess. So go on, take it."

With a tiny nod, she lifts upward, gripping and pulling me along with her. The sensation is incredible as she glides up my shaft. It's so intense I can't help my eyes fluttering, but I want to drink it all in so I fight to keep them open. Becca sinks all the way back down slowly and watches my face the entire time with an intensity and heat in her gaze that I haven't seen from her before.

It's fucking maddening in all the best ways.

"That's it. It feels good for you, doesn't it?"

"Yeah," she breathes, nodding eagerly. My hands fall from her breasts to her fingers, which I lock between mine and squeeze.

"Then don't stop. Go as fast or slow as you want. But don't you dare stop."

"Okay," she says confidently and rises back up before crashing down on me again.

"Oh my god," I groan because I really am under her control. With her hands in mine to keep her steady, she lifts up onto her feet from her knees, squatting and pulling me even deeper into her. She tosses her head back in ecstasy as she loses herself in the feeling of me filling her, and the sight alone is enough to send me over the edge.

"That's it. Come for me, just like this. I want to see it," I tell her, but all she can do is moan in reply. She's riding even faster now, bouncing on me with a hungry desperation, and I know she's getting close. My cock is so stiff it hurts, and I feel my balls tightening. If she keeps going like this, I'm not going to last much longer either.

"Fuck yeah, princess. Take it!"

She falls back onto her knees, but I can't fight it anymore, so I grip her by the hips to pull her down at the same time I crash into my orgasm. I drive a few more forceful pumps into her like this before a moan erupts out of her. Her legs start to tremble, and then she's coming too, gasping and clawing at the sheets as her orgasm wracks her body in waves.

She slumps over me when it passes, her petite frame withering against mine. Her hands rest on my chest, holding herself up while she tries to catch her breath.

"That. Was. Incredible," she says through gulps of air. But she must be spent, because she falls forward onto me, her head resting next to mine. Her warm breath teases my ear.

"You're incredible," I say, trailing my fingers up and down her spine. She laughs, sending tingles through my cock. "Fucking hell. That was amazing."

"Easily the best I've ever had," she says, her voice somewhat muffled by the sheets.

"Well, with Kaplan, I'm sure that's not a very high bar to clear, but I'll take it as a compliment regardless."

She laughs again and rests her forearms on my chest so she can hover over me. Her beautiful, wavy dark hair dangles in my face and across my shoulders.

"It was definitely a compliment. And trust me, there's zero competition."

"Good answer," I say and steal a kiss.

She nuzzles her face into my neck as we fall silent, her soft breathing filling my ear while I stroke her back. A few moments later, I smile when I hear a little snore sneak out of her. I can't say I blame her for being exhausted after tonight. I wish I could keep her right here, just like this, all night, but we'd both wake up sore and regretful.

"Becca?" I whisper, and she stirs.

"Mm?"

"I'm just gonna lay you down, princess," I say and gently roll her off me onto the bed.

She curls up on her side, pulling her legs toward herself, and I sneak away to the bathroom to get rid of the condom. When I crawl back into bed beside her, she mumbles something I can't make out, but doesn't resist when I wrap one arm around her and pull her back against my chest. I bury my face in her hair and kiss the back of her neck.

I can't get close enough to her, and I'm not ready to let her go. For the rest of the night, at least, I don't have to. The thought brings a smile to my face, and I fall asleep to the gentle rise and fall of her exhausted breathing.

Chapter 6

Becca

My eyes flutter open and land on Theo's arm wrapped around me. Neither of us remembered to close the blinds before we fell asleep, so the bright morning sun is streaming through the window. I blink against the brightness and smile as flashes of the night drift back into my mind.

My body hurts from head to toe, but in a way I've never experienced before. I've had plenty of sore days from dancing, but those don't compare to the sweet sex ache I feel in every joint and muscle. Theo truly worked me over last night, and even after we fell asleep, he wasn't finished. At some point, I woke up with him hard against me, and we started all over again.

I don't know if he did it just to make me feel better about my breakup with Shawn, but regardless, it worked. I've known for way longer than I'd like to admit that it was time to move on, and that I never should have gotten with him in the first place, so in a way it's a relief that it's over.

It doesn't change the fact that it fucking sucks to be broken up with on national TV, but even with that Shawn did me a favor. Because now there isn't a sliver of doubt in my mind that this is the right thing for me. I used to get emotional even thinking about leaving him, but now it just feels like a relief.

It's over, and I'm starting to see our "relationship" for what it really was: totally toxic. It's hard to feel anything but good about letting go of something like that.

I glance over my shoulder at Theo. He's still out cold and breathing evenly, but the memory of what he did to me pretty much all night long makes my clit throb. I know it was just rebound sex, but holy shit, was it incredible. I wasn't lying when I told him it was the best I'd ever had. And it will probably remain the best for a long time.

Part of me wants to thank him, but how would I even do that? Somehow, waking him up to say, "Thanks for screwing my brains out last night" doesn't feel quite right—even though he'd probably appreciate it. But I also have the pieces of my life to put back together after Shawn's dumping, so I decide that maybe it's better I just get on with things.

I carefully crawl out from under Theo's arm, and thankfully, he doesn't wake up. He's probably just as exhausted as I am, if not more. I mean, he did most of the work. I have to scour the room to find my clothes since they landed everywhere but in one place, and I'm just pulling my shorts up to button them when Theo stirs.

"Going somewhere?" he asks, his voice rough from sleep. He holds a hand up to his face to block out the light and fixes me with his sexy grin and even sexier set of dimples.

"Well, my life kind of fell apart last night and I'm on borrowed time, so yeah, I need to get going," I say as I finish buttoning my shorts. He flashes me a sad smile, so I walk back to the bed and sit down beside him, pressing a soft kiss to his lips. "But thank you for last night. It was exactly what I needed."

"My pleasure," he says, his grin widening.

God, that fucking dimple.

He looks so gorgeous like this, sleepy and mussed with that

half smile on his face. It's so damn tempting to strip all my clothes back off and climb into bed with him, just stay here having amazing sex all day and forget about everything else, but I can't. Eventually, reality will catch up with me. It always does.

"What are you gonna do?" Theo asks as he pushes himself up on the bed. I let out a sigh and try not to let myself get overwhelmed by the daunting truth of what's coming.

"That's a great question. I honestly don't really know."

"So, what then? You just wander around until the answer comes?"

"No. More like I go and pack my things and try not to have a nervous breakdown about the fact that I'm probably getting deported any second now."

Theo chuckles at that, but then his expression turns serious. "There has to be something you can do, right? You're too amazing for this country to lose you."

I know he's just saying that to make me feel better, but it makes something warm spread through my chest. Unfortunately, I don't think he's right.

"I don't know," I say with a shrug. "Without work in the US, the only other thing I can think of that would get me a green card in a hurry is marriage. And that's obviously not going to happen now."

Theo's green eyes snap back to mine at that. He stares at me for a long moment, and I can see something brewing behind his eyes.

"You really want to stay in this country?" he asks.

"Yes, more than anything," I blurt, and embarrassment floods my face at how quickly the words came out.

But I mean it. I came here to pursue a career in dance, and there's still so much I haven't done that I promised myself I would do. So much that got shoved to the backburner because of Shawn.

"Okay." Theo nods. "Then I have an idea. It's kind of crazy, but hear me out before you say anything, alright?"

I nod, my brows furrowed. I have no clue where he's going with this. "Alright."

He hesitates for a second, then shakes his head. "Actually, maybe this is a bad idea. I shouldn't even say it."

"Oh, come on, you can't leave me hanging like that. I'm too curious now!" I laugh, leaning toward him a little. "Whatever it is, just tell me."

Theo stares me in the eyes with an unreadable expression for what feels like forever before he finally speaks. "Well... what if we got married?"

My jaw drops.

It's a good thing I'm already sitting on the bed, otherwise I'd probably fall over.

That idea is more than a little crazy. It's completely insane. For all intents and purposes, he and I just met, and now after a whirlwind night of sex, he wants me to marry him? I don't think I've ever heard anything as crazy—and that includes all the shit that came out of Shawn's mouth.

"What?" I murmur, still not sure I heard him right.

"I told you it was kind of crazy, but it could work! If we got married, you'd get a green card, right? You could stay in the country."

I blink at him, barely processing his words. I'm still stuck on the 'let's get married' part.

"Theo, that's really sweet of you, but—"

"I mean, you said it yourself, right?" He keeps going, his tone gaining even more conviction. "You don't really have any roots or anyone to go back to in Canada. So why not just stay in the US? You could come to Denver with me. We'll stay married for a couple of years, and then you'll have permanent residency and can keep pursuing all your dreams here. We can go our separate ways when it's all settled."

It's madness. Total lunacy. The delusions of a guy still basking in the post-sex glow or something, I don't know. He really is sweet to even think of it, but there's no way in hell that would work. I wouldn't be the first woman to try it, and surely the US government is on to people doing that kind of thing by now. That's the sort of stuff that only works in the movies.

But what if it *did* work?

I want to kick myself for even entertaining it, but I can't ignore the fact that Theo just threw me a golden lifeline to stay in the US—even if it is totally fucking bonkers. He's right though, I'd rather take up under a bridge than go back to Canada at this point, especially with so much unfinished business here. And I mean, I was willing to be with a piece of shit like Shawn to stay in the US, so would fake marrying Theo really be any different?

It's so wild and reckless though. I can't really do this. Can I?

Theo takes both of my hands in his and squeezes them. "Come on, Becca. Don't let Shawn ruin your future, your dreams. Don't let him write the last word in your story here."

His words are so earnest, so heartfelt, that they spark something in me. Theo doesn't really know me from Eve, but he's apparently willing to marry me just to give me a shot at my dreams. That has to mean something, right? Plenty of women around the world have spent years daydreaming about and would probably kill for an opportunity like this, so I have to wonder if I'd be crazy *not* to say yes.

You're just too bland. Shawn's stinging words echo in my ears, coming from nowhere, and my heart hardens. Not that I owe him a damn thing, but Theo's right. I can't let him be the thing that undoes my future—I owe myself enough respect not to let that happen after all I've put up with from him.

"Are you sure about this?" I ask, barely able to get the words out through my vise-like throat. "*Really* sure? No strings attached or anything? We just get married, play house for a couple of years, and that's that?"

"It's whatever you want or need it to be. And I mean that. I'm doing this for you, princess."

His use of the word sends goosebumps scattering over my skin, and I know that I can't possibly turn him down. This is the lifeline I need, and I'd never forgive myself if I walked away from it.

"What do you say?" Theo asks, pulling me back into the moment with another squeeze of my hands and a soft grin. "Will you marry me?"

I pull back all the words that are swirling in my head to make way for the only one that matters.

"Yes."

Chapter 7

Theo

I'm smiling so hard my entire face hurts. This is completely fucking nuts, and we both know it is, but I don't care. From the second the idea popped into my head, I've steadily grown more and more sure of it, and it seems like Becca has too because she can't stop smiling either.

I really do want to help her because it's the right thing to do, and that's enough of a reason on its own. But more than that, I refuse to let her asshole ex screw her over by dumping her and getting her booted from the country.

Navigating this isn't going to be easy, and I'm not cavalier about that. Generally, I try to avoid interacting with the government as much as possible, but marrying a foreigner isn't exactly the most uncommon thing in the world, so it's not like we're blazing a whole new trail here. And as long as we color in the lines, we won't have anything to worry about.

Sure, the government will grill us about our relationship history and want us to prove that we're really a unit with shared finances and living arrangements and all that other crap, but we don't have to worry about that right now. We still have plenty of time to sort all that out, and thanks to being a member of the Aces and the money that brings, we'll have access to some of the best lawyers in the country.

"What do we do now? Run down to the county courthouse and make it official?" Becca asks.

"No way. If we're gonna do this, we're doing it right." I chuckle, then reach for my phone on the bedside table next to me. I fell asleep and forgot to charge it, so the battery is low, but there's still plenty of charge to make a few phone calls. And that's all I need.

"What does that mean?" she asks, leaning forward to steal a glance at my screen as my fingers fly across it. But I've already started a call, so I hold it up to my ear so she can't see who I'm calling.

"No peeking." I grin at her. "If we're gonna have a shotgun wedding, we might as well do it in the most classic place."

"What about the team? Don't you have to travel back to Denver today? Or play a game somewhere or something?"

"Nope. The Aces are staying an extra night here in LA before we head back to Denver, so I've got time. Now hold that thought," I say as the line clicks over to an automated voice recording. I smash the zero button on my keypad until I get a live agent.

"Good morning, Mr. Camden, and thank you for calling North Star Travel. My name is Holly, and I'll be your dedicated personal concierge today. How can I help you?"

"Good morning, Holly," I say, smiling at Becca because I know she can hear every word. "I need help booking a flight for two from LAX to Las Vegas today. As soon as you can find, and preferably in first class, but I'll take whatever is available."

"Of course, Mr. Camden. Do you have a preference on airline?"

"Doesn't matter."

"Okay. Do you mind if I put you on a brief hold while I search?"

"That's fine."

"Great. I'll be back with you in a few minutes." Holly switches me over to a hold, and generic pop music fills my ear.

"I can't believe you're doing this. That *we're* doing this," Becca says, staring at me in disbelief, but she laughs after a second. "You know this is totally insane, right?"

I shrug. "I like to move fast when things feel right. Doesn't make me crazy. Makes me decisive."

"Right, 'decisive.' That's the word," Becca says, although she seems to be getting just as caught up in this as I am.

"So, your favorite color really is blue, right?" I ask, and she lifts her eyebrows at me.

"Uh, yeah. But we already went over that."

"I know. But if we're gonna sell this marriage as the real deal, we'd better make sure our stories match and we've got all the details right."

"Oh god," Becca groans, slumping over on the bed. "You're right. I didn't even think of that. I don't know anything about you!"

I reach for her hand and give it a squeeze. "Hey, don't worry. We've still got plenty of time to go over all that."

"What are we going to say about how we met? And why we decided to get married so fast? I mean, the breakup and every-thing that happened last night was on camera. It'll wind up on Shawn's show for sure."

I frown at the mention of her ex. "Not *all* of it was on camera. Shawn the asshole dumping you was, sure, but the cameras were nowhere around the two of us after that. We can just say there was a connection between us that neither one of us could deny."

She flushes a little, biting her lower lip as she looks at me.

What I just said isn't far from the truth, and I know it. There *was* a connection between us that felt pretty fucking undeniable in the moment. But that's why I feel certain this will work. Even though I only proposed marriage because I know how badly she wants to stay in the country, the kernel of truth will be there when we talk about how we met and how we just clicked.

"But isn't it going to look suspicious that you and I decided to get married the day after Shawn dumped me though?" Becca asks, the flicker of heat fading from her eyes as worry replaces it.

As much as I wish I did, I don't have a good answer for that question. She's right, there's a chance some people will think that the two of us had something going on *before* her breakup with Shawn, and the last thing either of us wants is to give that douche a chance to spin the story in his favor. And I'm sure that once he hears about this, he's going to lose it and do everything he can to interfere just out of principal.

But I'm not going to let any of that stop us.

"People fall in love and get married overnight all the time. Britney Spears did it, so why can't we?"

She laughs and shakes her head. "I don't know if that's the best example, but sure."

"Fortune favors the bold, remember?" I ask, and she flashes me a warm smile as her eyes drift to the matching tattoo.

"Okay. Yeah, you're right. We'll figure it out."

The pop music in my ear halts as Holly comes back on the line. "Mr. Camden, are you still with me?"

"Yes, ma'am. I hope you have good news?"

"I do. I've held two first class tickets on a flight this afternoon, departing at 1:15 P.M. Will that work for you?"

I hold the phone from my ear to check the time. It's just after nine, so that should give us plenty of time to get something to eat, pack, and get to the airport.

"That sounds perfect."

"Excellent. I'll go ahead and make the reservation for you then. Would you like me to charge the card we have on file?"

"That's fine," I say, and Holly goes silent briefly. I hear her clicking around on her computer for a few seconds.

"There we go. You should receive an email confirmation shortly with your flight details and confirmation number. Will you also need transportation to the airport?"

"I can handle that, but thanks."

"My pleasure, Mr. Camden. Have a safe flight and enjoy the rest of your day."

"Oh, I will," I say and flash a grin at Becca before hanging up. When the call disconnects, I see an email notification with the flight details, just like Holly said. I hold the screen up to Becca. "We're going to Vegas, princess."

"Oh my god. We're doing this, aren't we? We're really doing this! But wait, I don't have any clothes, or even a toothbrush."

"Don't worry about any of that," I say, giving her hand another squeeze. I still haven't let it go, and I don't want to. "We can buy whatever you need on the way or when we get there. But we need to get some food in our stomachs first, so let's find something to eat before we head to the airport, okay?"

"Yeah, right, of course." Becca nods. "But I don't know if I have the appetite for anything, to be honest."

"After all the calories we burned last night? Yeah, you're gonna need to eat," I say, and she blushes. I jump out of bed and throw my clothes on from the night before. I didn't really have time to unpack any of the rest of my stuff, so it doesn't take long for me to round it all up.

"Are you okay?" I ask as I zip my suitcase. Becca's staring out the window and digging at one of her cuticles with her thumb. "You're being awfully quiet."

"Yeah, I'm fine. I just have a lot on my mind."

"I get that. This is a lot to take in. Penny for your thoughts?"

She twists on the bed to face me, her dark hair falling over one shoulder. The look of girlish innocence on her face knifes me in the heart all over again—she really is one of the sweetest women I think I've ever met. I know this is the right thing to do, and that it'll change her life for the better in a thousand different ways, but if she's having any second thoughts about it, I'd rather know now than *after* we tie the knot.

"I don't have the words to tell you how much this means to me, Theo," she says. "It's both the craziest and nicest thing anyone has ever done for me. But I still can't believe you're doing it. Or understand why."

I zip my suitcase the rest of the way closed and sit down next to her on the bed. I push a lock of her hair behind one of her ears, and she smiles at me. "Well, believe it, because I am. And I'm doing it because you deserve it after everything you've put up with from Shawn, after all the time and dreams he's stolen from you. Now it's your time to shine."

"Thank you," she whispers through the tears forming in her eyes. She brushes them away in a hurry with the back of her hand. "I don't know what else to say."

"You don't have to say anything," I tell her and peck a kiss on her forehead before standing up and offering her a hand. "Now come on. We don't want to be late to our own wedding, do we?"

Becca laughs and rests her hand in mine. I pull her up and she runs to the door to hold it open so I can wheel my stuff out. In the elevator, I call for another Uber on the ride down, and by the time we're done checking out at the front desk, a driver's already waiting for us at the curb. Thankfully, it's not the same uptight asshole from the night before.

An older guy steps out of the car and smiles as he helps us load my stuff in the trunk.

"Heading to the airport, I assume?" he asks with a knowing

smile. I'm pretty sure he recognizes me, but he's doing a good job of keeping his excitement hidden.

"Yeah, but do you mind if we stop to get a bite to eat first?"

"Not at all. What did you have in mind?"

I turn to Becca, who's already climbing into the back seat. "What's your favorite cuisine?"

"Shouldn't you already know that?" she asks, her brows lifted.

"Why do you think I'm asking?"

She laughs and shakes her head. "Indian."

"Really? Me too. Never would've guessed that about you, but Indian it is. Take us to the best place you know of, please," I tell the driver and get into the car next to Becca.

"I'm not sure if any of the Indian restaurants will be open this early, but I'll see what I can find," he says and spends a few seconds tapping around on his phone after he gets in the driver's seat. "Doesn't look like any are. Anything else sound good?" he asks, staring at me in the rearview.

"I wasn't sure about that for breakfast anyway. You okay with just grabbing something at the airport instead?" I ask Becca, and she nods. "Okay, then let's just head to LAX."

"You got it," the driver says and throws the car in drive.

We merge into the traffic that's already getting heavy, and I realize it's probably a good thing we're leaving early. I told Becca not to worry, but honestly, I don't have a clue how much time we really have to do this thing. I'm also not entirely sure she's going to be able to get on a plane, but like I told her, it's not like someone in the government is just sitting and waiting to switch off her visa.

Her hand rests on the seat between us, and I wrestle with whether I should hold it. We're about to get married, sure, but that doesn't mean we're an item. It strikes me that I don't really know where the line is anymore, or how we're going to navigate what's real versus what we're putting on for the feds and the cameras.

It takes more than an hour to get to the airport, but we make it in one piece and on time. Becca helps me unload my suitcases, and we head inside to a nearby kiosk to get our boarding passes. My heart hammers in my chest as I clumsily punch in her information, but when the machine asks for her passport to scan it, it goes through without a hitch.

"See? You aren't a fugitive just yet," I say, although I'm not sure who I'm comforting. Becca laughs and tucks her passport back into her pocket.

"The word 'yet' is doing a lot of heavy lifting there. I still can't believe we're doing this," she says and wipes her palms on her shorts.

"Getting cold feet already? You aren't gonna leave me at the altar, are you?"

"No, not at all. Don't be ridiculous," she says, and the smile that cracks her face sparks a warmth that spreads through me. It's going to be fine. This is all going to work out. It has to, for her sake. I'd never let myself live it down if I failed her on this.

"I just really hate airport security. It's always stressed me out," Becca adds.

"That's universal," I say and offer her my hand. "But don't worry, I'll be there with you through the whole terrible ordeal. Ready to get strip searched?"

"Oh god, don't joke about that," she says, the color draining from her face.

"Sorry, sorry." I make a face. "Bad timing. Come on, it'll be fine. The sooner we get this over with, the sooner we can get some food and get married. In that order."

Becca laughs, and I see her shoulders drop a bit. Good. I don't want her to worry about a damn thing right now. She's got more than enough on her plate. Just like I told her, we check my suitcases, but I keep a duffel bag with me and we breeze through security without an incident, then emerge into the cramped quarters of LAX's terminal three.

Unfortunately, there isn't much to choose from when it comes to food, so we end up stopping at—where else—a sports bar type of place that serves chicken and beer. It's ridiculous, but somehow it feels right given how Becca and I met and how all of this started.

"Think this will be enough to hold you over?" I tease as we sit down with our greasy food a few minutes later.

She laughs. "The flight is barely an hour long, so I think I'll survive."

"Wonder if that means they'll even have food service in first class?"

Becca's brows shoot up and she pauses with a chicken tender halfway to her mouth. "First class?"

"Yeah, didn't you know? It's on your boarding pass."

She drops her chicken back in the basket. "You didn't have to do that."

"True. I didn't have to marry you either, but here we are," I say, and again she smiles, but it falls quickly as something else seems to dawn on her. "What's wrong?"

"I just realized I don't have anything to wear. How am I supposed get married without a dress?" She gestures to her clothes—just cutoff shorts and a tank top, since she deliberately stuffed Kaplan's jersey in the hotel room trash before we left.

"Don't worry about that either. I've got you covered," I say and lift the duffel bag I brought with me off the empty seat next to us.

"Please don't tell me you have a wedding dress you bring with you to every game," she says, and it's my turn to laugh.

"It's not a wedding dress, but I think you'll appreciate it anyway."

"What, you aren't going to show me?"

"Not yet. I want it to be a surprise. Besides, my fingers are all greasy, so I don't want to ruin it."

"Don't you think I've had enough surprises lately?" she asks as she retrieves her chicken and takes a bite of it.

"You definitely have. But this is a good one. Trust me."

"That's the name of the game right now, isn't it? Trust."

I reach across the table and give one of her hands a squeeze. "It is. It's all going to be fine. Perfect, even. I promise."

"Okay. I believe you," she says, letting out a slow breath as someone makes an announcement that our flight to Vegas is now boarding at gate twenty-four.

"That's us. You ready to go?"

"Ready as I'll ever be," she says, although she steals another bite of chicken as I grab the duffel bag and rummage in my pocket for my boarding pass. We probably don't need to be in such a hurry, especially since we're flying first class, but I figure the sooner we're on that plane, the better.

We rush across the terminal and join the priority boarding lane, and to my surprise, Becca takes my hand. I give her another reassuring squeeze and flash her a grin, which seems to work. She hands the agent her boarding pass first, and the agent doesn't even glance at it before she scans it on the machine she's standing behind and hands it back.

"Enjoy your flight, and welcome aboard," she says in monotone while reaching for my boarding pass. Becca and I jog down the ramp and take our seats in the second row. Normally, I always claim the window seat, but I let her have it. Something tells me she's going to need the distraction, and even I have to admit that the view as we come into the desert of Vegas is beautiful.

As soon as we're seated, a flight attendant our age approaches. "Good afternoon, and welcome aboard. Can I get you something to drink? Maybe a mimosa or a glass of champagne?" she asks, smiling at us.

"Two glasses of champagne, please," I order for us, and the attendant nods before returning to the galley. Becca stares at me.

"Champagne? This early?"

"We have a wedding to celebrate, don't we?"

Becca laughs and nods. "Yeah. I guess we do." She rests her hand on the little drink tray between us, so I place mine on hers, and she links her fingers between mine. I know our upcoming wedding isn't real, and that this feeling won't last, but goddamn if it doesn't feel like it could.

The flight attendant returns a few moments later carrying a tray with two small, bubbling glasses of champagne. She hands one to each of us, and I clink my glass against Becca's.

"To new beginnings?"

"To new beginnings," Becca agrees and takes a healthy sip.

~

We touch down in Vegas just under an hour later, and as soon as we're on the ground, I switch my dying phone off airplane mode —because we still need to find a chapel to get this thing done in. I probably should've done it before we left, but I figure there can't be too many people trying to get married on a whim in the middle of the afternoon, even in Vegas. We're bound to find something.

"There! That one," Becca says, pointing at a place called The Little Church of the West in the search results. I tap on it to look at some of the pictures and see that it's tiny, old, dark as hell inside, and made almost entirely out of stained wood. It's not exactly what I would've chosen, but if that's what Becca wants, that's what I'll give her.

"You're sure?"

"Positive. It's so quaint and cute. It reminds me of an old log cabin or something." Her cheeks are still rosy from the champagne, and it's such a good look on her.

"Looks like it's only about ten minutes away from the airport too, so that's convenient."

"Isn't that the point of this whole thing?"

"Exactly," I say, and flash Becca a grin before switching over to the Uber app to order another ride. Hopefully, I can charge my phone at the chapel, otherwise I'm not sure how we're going to find a place to stay tonight or get back to Denver tomorrow.

We're one of the first off the plane, which means we're also one of the first to have to stand and wait for our bags to show up. But that gives me time to call the chapel and book something. Just like I thought, they're pretty much wide open for the whole day, so I snag the first appointment they have.

After my bags finally show up, we rush outside to the ride share area and load into another Uber. The driver smirks at us in the rearview when he sees where we're heading.

"It's been a while since I've had one of these. Congratulations," he says, and Becca smiles nervously.

The closer we get to the chapel, the realer it gets that we're doing this. Thankfully, the ride isn't long, so neither of us have time to psyche ourselves out about it. What's funny is that, of the two of us, Becca seems to be way calmer about the whole thing now. It's like we flipped roles or something.

The driver parks on the curb outside a chapel that's somehow even smaller than it looked in the photos online. If I hadn't already looked it up, I probably never would've noticed it tucked into a grove of trees next to an empty parking lot—the most Vegas thing in the world. The little brown building has one steeple that doesn't even reach past the trees beside it, and the place looks like it can't hold more than maybe fifty people.

"It's adorable," Becca says as we climb out of the car, and if she's happy, that's all that matters to me. I lug all my bags out of the trunk and hike them up on the curb, then follow her to the door. I keep expecting some cheesy Elvis impersonator to pop out to greet us, but no one does, so I check my phone and see we're about thirty minutes early.

"I guess we should probably get changed," I say, and Becca spins on her heel to face me.

"Does that mean it's surprise time?" she asks, glancing at my duffel bag. I grin and nod.

"It does. This isn't exactly traditional wedding garb, but we aren't exactly doing a traditional wedding either, so I think it fits," I say and hoist the bag up to unzip it.

I pull out one of my jerseys and shake it to unfold it, and Becca stares at it for a second before she walks over to run her hands across the silky material.

"I know Kaplan didn't like you wearing his jersey because it was too baggy and 'unflattering' on you, but I also know that Kaplan is a fucking dick, so I thought you'd look much better in mine," I say.

Becca bites back a smile, a gorgeous blush climbing up her cheeks. "It's perfect."

She takes the jersey from me and pulls it over her head. It's obviously not the first time I've seen her wearing a hockey jersey, but when she turns around to pull her wavy dark hair up through the jersey's neck hole, I see "CAMDEN" etched across her back for a second before her hair drapes over it. The sight of my name on her back stirs something inside me. Something possessive and protective that I can't remember feeling for a long time.

Becca faces me again, still beaming, and with the bright desert sun streaming through the trees down on her beautiful face, she looks even more flawless than usual. She has a glow to her, a radiance, that makes it hard to focus on anything else in my view.

Holy shit. I'm really about to marry this woman.

Even though we're only a matter of minutes away from

sealing the deal, it still doesn't feel real. But when the door to the chapel opens and, of course, out steps a badly-dressed Elvis impersonator, it gets real fast. I shake my head to clear it and take a deep breath before offering Becca my hand and one last grin.

"You ready to be my wife?" I ask, and she drags in a deep breath and lets it out in a long, slow exhale before reaching for my hand.

"Let's do it."

Chapter 8

Becca

As soon as Theo's hand touches mine, an electric shock of awareness courses up my arm. It's such a simple gesture, but it's intimate at the same time, and my heart starts pounding in response.

Oh my god. We're doing this. We're really getting married.

Even as we're walking toward the chapel entrance with an Elvis impersonator escorting us, it's still hard to believe. Barely more than twenty-four hours ago, Shawn and I were still a couple, and I didn't have the faintest clue he was going to break up with me. Or that my whole life was going to turn upside down overnight.

The fake Elvis, complete with a sequined jacket and over-sprayed pompadour, is giving us a very fast, very "fine print at the end of a TV ad" explanation of how the whole ceremony is going to work, but I can't process any of it. All I can focus on is the feeling of my hand in Theo's because it's the only thing keeping me from floating away like a kid's balloon animal.

And then we're stepping inside, and I feel like I'm watching it all play out from outside myself, like I'm seated in the tiny wooden pews. Everything is in place, perfectly set up and picturesque. There's an old chandelier hanging from the A-frame ceiling, flanked by two large candelabras on the floor. A woman sits with her back to us at an ancient looking organ, and the Elvis impersonator has already taken his place beside her on the altar.

Wait, is he officiating?

I have to bite back a laugh because it strikes me just how ridiculous all of this is. I mean, I'm wearing a hockey jersey to my wedding and Theo's still in street clothes. I never imagined my first trip to Vegas would be to marry a stranger. But what's more ridiculous, tying the knot with someone I just met for a green card or staying with an abusive asshole for the same reason? As crazy as it is, I still somehow believe I'm doing the right thing because this is going to unlock a whole new world for me.

But then the organ strikes the opening chords to "Here Comes the Bride," and I snap back into my body. Theo flashes me a grin, and all I can do is smile back. I told him I wouldn't leave him at the altar, and I meant it, but my heart slams against my chest with every step I take closer to Elvis.

We reach the altar long before the song is over, and there isn't another soul in the chapel, but Elvis still throws his hands wide like he's performing for a sold-out audience anyway as the song comes to an end. He flashes me a toothy grin and a cliché wink.

"Ladies and gentlemen, we gather here today to join in holy matrimony..." he starts, then pauses to glance at a small slip of paper in his hand. "Theo Camden and Becca Summers."

Theo snorts, and I can't help joining him because it's such a stark reminder of how slapdash this whole thing is. We booked this appointment not even an hour ago, and it was so sudden that the officiant didn't even have time to memorize our names. But he's clearly done this thousands of times because he recites the rest of his spiel from memory.

"Mr. Camden, would you like to share a few words?" he asks Theo when he's finished, and Theo nods. I turn to face him, and he takes both of my hands in his.

"Becca," he starts, and I hold my breath. It didn't even occur to me to come up with vows, but now that I'm staring into Theo's piercing green eyes and he's clearing his throat to say his, I feel stupid for overlooking it.

"From the first moment I laid eyes on you, I knew you were special. And that one day, whenever I got the chance, I'd make you see and believe it too," he says, and my throat squeezes shut —because he already has. For fuck's sake, he's marrying me so I can stay in the country, and if that doesn't make a girl feel special, then I don't know what will.

"I may not know you very well, but anyone with eyes can see how brave and kind and smart you are. That's why it killed me when I saw the sad look on your face the night I met you. I saw that beautiful light in you going out, and I promised myself I'd never let you feel that way ever again, so long as you were in my life. And now you'll always be in my life, no matter what happens, so I hope you'll always be smiling. That's my mission from now on— to make you feel like the princess you are. To be a haven you need for as long as you need it."

By the time he finishes, I'm melting a little inside. I had no idea he had felt any of that, or that he paid much attention to me at all that night when we ran into each other outside The Hideout.

Theo and Elvis are both staring at me expectantly, waiting for me to say something in response. But how the hell am I supposed to follow *that?*

I clear my throat and wipe my eyes with the back of my hand. I lock eyes with Theo, my heart pounding while I search for something to say. And then the words come all at once, pouring out of me in a wave.

"I've never known anyone like you," I whisper. "Someone

who would bend over backward, move heaven and earth, just to help a stranger. Someone who could turn the absolute worst night of my life into the best. I don't know if I'll ever be able to express how grateful I am, but even though this is crazy, I'm glad I'm doing it with you."

I finish speaking, and Theo beams at me and squeezes my hands.

Elvis the officiant holds a heart-shaped pillow down to us. Two golden bands sparkle in the chandelier's light, and my breath catches in my throat. This is it, the moment of truth. Theo reaches for one of the bands, and I offer him my left hand. He lines up the ring with my finger but doesn't put it on yet.

"Becca Summers, do you take this man, Theo Camden, to be your lawfully wedded husband, to have and to hold, in sickness and in health, until death do you part?" Elvis asks, and I feel like my heart is trying to claw its way out of my throat.

"I—I do," I stammer, and Theo slides the ring onto my finger. I'm not sure how the chapel got the ring size right since I didn't give them any measurements, but it fits perfectly. And now it's my turn, so I take the other ring and repeat Theo's movements. Elvis turns to him.

"Theo Camden, do you take this woman, Becca Summers, to be your lawfully wedded wife, to have and to hold, in sickness and in health, until death do you part?"

"Abso-fucking-lutely I do," Theo says, and I laugh as I put the band on his finger.

"Then by the power vested in me by the state of Nevada, I now pronounce you husband and wife. You may kiss the bride," Elvis announces.

Theo and I lean into each other. Our lips meet, and our arms wrap around each other, holding us in place. Our mouths don't open, probably since neither of us are sure where we stand with that kind of thing right now, but the kiss goes on much longer than I meant for it to.

Theo finally pulls away, and I stumble a bit when my body leans forward on its own like it's chasing his lips. My nervous system is thrumming, and my cheeks flush with embarrassment at the realization. We just got married, but we aren't together. Not really. This is all for show.

Theo flashes me his easy, charming grin.

"You're not a stranger anymore, princess. You're my wife," he says. I beam at him while the organ strikes up its haunting chords again, and despite the roiling, churning feeling in my stomach, I hold on to his hand for dear life and let him lead me out of the chapel.

Because I don't have any idea what comes next.

The next two hours pass in a blur that I can barely keep track of. One moment, I'm signing what feels like an endless flow of legal forms while the Elvis impersonator beams at me, and the next, I'm standing in line waiting to board a plane back to LA. I feel like I teleported from the chapel to the airport because I have no recollection of what happened in between, but staring down at the new ring on my finger never fails to anchor me back in reality.

Because this is real now. Very real. I just married Theo Camden in a shotgun wedding barely more than twenty-four hours after getting dumped on camera. And the basic but sufficient gold band the chapel provided me is irrefutable proof of what we just did. I couldn't take this back even if I wanted to, and as crazy as this spur-of-the-moment wedding was, what's crazier is that I'm not sure I want to.

Still, all at once, a wave of nerves crashes over me, sucking me into their undertow, and I struggle to breathe.

Have I completely lost it? At some level, I feel like if I'm already asking myself the question, I already know the answer. But my body seems to know what to do without my input, so I watch my hand pass a boarding pass to the gate agent on its own, then follow Theo down the jet bridge and into our first class return seats, this time in the first row.

I take the window seat again, more because I need something to distract myself with than anything else, and immediately my gaze drifts out to the tarmac. The workers zip around beneath the plane on foot and in carts, transporting the baggage and fuel and supplies for the plane. It strikes me how ordinary their days must be, especially compared to mine. And I can't help wondering how many other shotgun brides have found themselves feeling the exact way I do now on this very same plane.

Theo's hand finds mine, jolting me out of my thoughts as he murmurs, "You're freaking out, aren't you?"

I let out a little laugh, unable to help it. "How did you know?"

"You haven't said a word in at least an hour, and you haven't looked me in the eye in about as long, so call it an educated guess," he says, then flashes his signature grin at me.

"Am I really that easy to read?"

He shrugs. "I'm your husband. I'm supposed to be able to pick up on these things, right?"

I know his words are meant to comfort me, but the word 'husband' makes my stomach flutter all over again. He must see the nerves playing out on my face, because he squeezes my hand and twists in his chair to face me.

"Becca, listen to me," he says, dropping his head a little to hold my gaze. "This is all going to work out great, okay? After we're married for a couple of years, you'll get your permanent residency without having to work on Shawn's shitty reality TV show. And you can pursue your dreams. All of them. Everything you came here to do."

I nod but still can't seem to find any words. This all still feels so surreal, like it's happening to someone else and I'm just an observer along for the ride.

Theo strokes my thumb with his, his expression patient and gentle. "Would it help if we talked about some of the little details?"

"Yes!" I say in a rush, because I'm realizing how badly I need it. How badly I need to feel the ground under my feet again, even if it isn't concretely in place yet.

"Okay. Well, for starters, I think sleeping together again should be firmly off the table. What do you think?"

I nod. "Agreed. That won't do anything other than complicate the whole situation even more."

"Exactly. How do you feel about PDA though? If we're going to sell this thing as real, we'll probably need some of that, especially in public."

"Oh god," I groan, and Theo's eyes shoot wide.

"What? What's wrong?"

"It just hit me how public all of this is actually going to be. I mean, you're a hockey player—a well-known one. And I just left another one of those with a TV show for you. The media is going to have a field day with this."

"Only as much as we let them," Theo insists, and all I can do is stare at him as half a dozen examples of people violated and ruined—or worse—by the paparazzi flash through my mind. Princess Diana. Britney Spears. Lindsey Lohan. The list is endless. What makes him think we'll be any different?

"Theo, you can't promise that. You can't control them. You know that as well as I do."

"You're right, I can't control them. But I can control their access. Plenty of power couples manage to dodge the press and keep their personal lives away from the tabloids."

"And how the hell are we gonna do that?"

Theo bites his lower lip and shoots me a serious look. "You'll have to move in with me in Denver," he says, and I feel like the entire plane is spinning around me, like we've already taken off and are crashing back down.

It makes perfect sense. Of course I'll have to live with him—he's my husband now, after all—but it hadn't occurred to me yet.

"I know it's a huge step, but we have to do it to sell the story of our marriage, and there's no better way to keep the world out than to build a fortress," Theo says, keeping his voice low—which is probably a good idea, because for all we know, there could be someone in the seats around us listening to or recording our every word. Like it or not, Theo is an almost instantly recognizable guy, so it's almost guaranteed someone on this plane has placed who he is.

"Right. Okay, yeah," I murmur, slowly coming around to the idea. "But we can't stay inside the house forever. How are we going to handle being out in public?"

"We'll cross that bridge when we get there. Luckily, we still have some time before that will be an issue."

"We do?"

"Yeah. I'm flying back to Denver with the team later today, and we don't have another game for a few days. That should give us enough time to work out all the logistics, get you settled in Denver with me, and let me break the news to the rest of the Aces. I'm sure the PR team will have some ideas too."

"About what?"

"How to handle the media, how to keep things as private as we can, that sort of stuff," Theo answers, and I breathe a sigh of relief because for a second, I worried I was already getting signed up for some social media campaign. And I'm not anywhere near ready for that.

"Okay," I say and take another deep breath. It's all going to be fine, just like Theo said. And I might barely know him, but I believe he knows what he's doing with the press. He's had years of experience dealing with this sort of thing, much more than I do, so I'm going to have to trust him.

Because if we're really going to sell this marriage as authentic, I'm going to have to start acting like it. If the media sees me falling to pieces in public, that will sink our ship before it even sets sail, so I'm going to have to learn to put on a brave face and do the dance.

And if there's anything I know how to do, it's dance. I'll just have to keep putting one foot in the front of the other, one move at a time. The first move is getting back to LA to pack up my things and tie up the loose ends I have back there. Thankfully, there aren't many, and the realization makes me grateful I wasn't more integrated in Shawn's life. This could be so much messier than it is.

"Buckle up, princess," Theo says gently, snapping me out of my thoughts. "We'll be taking off soon."

Without me noticing, the plane has already pushed back from the gate and began taxiing toward the runway, so I belt myself in, take another deep breath, and sit back in my seat. Theo squeezes my hand again, and when I glance over at him, he gives me a small, private smile.

"Thank you," I tell him. "I needed that."

"Anything for my wife," he says as the roar of the plane's engines floods the cabin.

We're soaring above the red-orange meteorite that is the Vegas desert just a few minutes later, and as the city's casinos and sprawling highways grow smaller and smaller in the window, I decide to leave all my worries there too.

Yes, what Theo and I just did is crazy, but it's going to work.

It has to, because my dreams depend on it, and because I'm finally coming around to believing that after all the shit I've been through in my life, I deserve it.

The flight attendant brings us a second round of champagne, and Theo asks her if he can borrow a phone charger before we clink our glasses together again. The bubbling liquid strangely calms my stomach, and I watch with a smile as Theo plugs his phone into the jack built into his seat and starts tapping away on the screen, making notes of all the things he needs to do and people he needs to call when he has signal again. I don't have to say a single thing because he has it all covered. Movers. My flight to Denver. Grocery delivery for whatever I want or need. Everything's there.

We touch down back at LAX about an hour later, and as soon as the wheels touch the tarmac, Theo flips his phone out of airplane mode and starts placing calls. After all the time I've spent being Shawn's glorified personal assistant, managing his calendar and filming schedule for him, being taken care of like this really does make me feel like a princess.

After grabbing Theo's bags, we spill out in the warm LA afternoon and into an Uber that's already waiting to take us back to my place. Theo stays on the phone for most of the journey, but I don't mind. For once, I'm happy to let someone else take the wheel.

But as soon as we pull up to the curb outside my place, Theo pockets his phone and returns his attention to me. "Are you okay? Sorry I've been so distracted."

"I'm fine, and I understand. Thank you for taking care of all that stuff. I don't think I could've handled it."

He smiles at me. "Yes, you could've. But I wanted to do it for you. Do you mind waiting here for me for a second so I can walk her inside?" he asks the driver, and when they agree, Theo climbs out of the car with me. He walks me to my door, and we stand in front of it uncomfortably, neither of us sure what to say or do.

"I guess I should give this back to you now. You'll probably be needing it before I will," I say after a beat, then reach up to lift his jersey over my head.

But before I can complete the motion, he reaches out to stop me.

"No. Keep it." He leans forward a bit like he's going to kiss me, then freezes for a second before planting an innocent peck on my cheek. "I'll see you soon, wife," he says in a low voice, then reaches for my ring hand to give it a squeeze.

"Yeah, see you soon," I breathe. He steps back, and I stand in the doorway watching him walk back to the car. "Wait, Theo!" I call after him, and he spins around like he's back on the ice. "Shouldn't we, uh, trade phone numbers or something?"

He grins and pulls out his phone. "Oh, damn. Can't believe I almost forgot about that. What's your number?"

I recite it to him, and his thumbs fly across the screen as he types it in.

"Got it." He nods. "Oh, hold still for a second."

"Why?"

"I need a picture to go with it."

"Oh. Okay." I laugh, then lean against the door frame with a smile.

His phone makes a clicking sound as he snaps the photo, and he checks the screen, a slow smile spreading across his face.

"Perfect." He looks up at me, a momentary flash of heat passing through his expression. "And I still think you look better wearing my jersey, princess."

My stomach swoops a little, and I run my hands over the fabric of the jersey, hoping he doesn't notice the goosebumps scattering over my arms. "Thanks. We'll talk soon?"

"Can't wait."

He raps his knuckles against the door frame, then turns and strides back to the Uber, and I don't tear my gaze away from the car until it rounds the corner and disappears. Even after he's gone, I stay where I am, frozen in my doorframe and blinking absently as I try to process everything that's happened in the past twenty-four hours.

I can't believe I just got married.

Or that Theo Camden, the bad boy of the NHL, is now my husband.

Chapter 9

Theo

I can't stop smiling. In the Uber all the way back to the airport and onto the private plane with the rest of the Aces, a smile never leaves my face. The guys are all talking, cracking jokes, being their usual rowdy selves, but all I can think about is what I just did. What *we* just did.

Becca and I got married.

Every time I think those five words, my smile widens and my stomach flips over. I'm still wearing the rinky dink gold band the chapel provided, and I keep catching myself glancing down at it just to make sure it's still there. That we really did get married, and it wasn't all some game loss-induced fever dream.

But it's there, gold and solid, and it's not going anywhere. After I throw my bag in the overhead bin and take the window seat next to Noah in the front row, I stare outside and trace the band with my thumb absently while the plane rolls into position for takeoff. My mind is racing with all the big changes that have already happened and will continue to happen, but the funny thing is, I'm not really stressed about them.

It's just like I told Becca—everything is going to be fine. She might not believe it yet, but I do, and I'm hoping that my optimism will be enough for both of us for now. It's definitely going to take some time to adjust to all of this, and I don't blame her for being worried about the media—especially with Kaplan's vulture TV crew still circling—but we can handle all that.

"Hey, Camden. You listening?"

Noah's deep voice cuts through the thoughts galloping through my mind, and I glance over at him.

"Sorry, what?"

"I just asked you why you've been so quiet today," his says, his keen blue eyes fixed on me. "You've been off in left field for a couple of days now. Everything okay?"

"Oh, yeah, everything's fine. Just have a lot going on."

"Cagey much?"

Noah arches a brow at me, then jolts in his seat when the plane lurches forward. He grips Margo's hand like his life depends on it until he realizes we aren't in the air yet, just making a turn on the runway. When he notices me smirking at him, he rolls his eyes.

"Don't look at me like that. You know I fucking hate flying," he grumbles, and I can't help laughing. "But seriously, what's going on with you?"

I can't keep it a secret forever, but I'm not sure I'm ready for the whole team to hear yet, so I twist around in my seat to see who's sitting where. My stomach drops as I realize that Margo is leaning forward a little in her seat beside Noah, looking at me curiously. Well, whatever. She'd find out from Noah almost immediately anyway since they're together now, and she probably needs to know since she's the team's social media manager.

I turn to face them both as I declare, "I got married today."

Margo almost chokes, and Noah's blue eyes widen.

"I'm sorry, what did you just say?"

"Come on, dude, you heard me. I got married."

"*Married?*" Margo keeps her voice to a low hiss, but it still catches Reese's attention where he's sitting in the aisle seat right in front of me. He turns around in his seat, his eyebrows shooting up. Luckily, no one else around us seems to have heard her. I'm not really ready for the whole team to know about this yet.

"Are you serious? And why am I just now hearing about it?" Noah asks, shaking his head like he's trying to force his brain to process this new information.

"I was trying to keep things quiet for a while."

"Why?" He narrows his eyes. "Who did you marry?"

He probably isn't going to like my answer no matter how I frame it, so I decide I might as well rip the band-aid off in one go.

"Becca Summers."

Just as I expected, Noah's eyebrows skyrocket up his face. "You mean the same Becca who was dating Shawn Kaplan? The one we saw get dumped at the bar last night? *That* Becca Summers?"

I nod. "Yeah, that's the one."

"Holy shit," Reese mutters from in front of me, sounding just as shocked as Noah.

I guess I can't blame them. I'd be shocked too if one of them had done what I just did. But they don't know what's really going on, so who are they to judge?

"Fucking hell, Camden. Are you crazy?" Noah mutters.

I can't help but chuckle at that. "Well, that's always been up for debate, hasn't it? But I promise I was of sound mind when I said my vows."

"How did this all happen?" Margo asks, still holding Noah's hand as she leans toward me a little. "Were you two seeing each other before last night, or...?"

I hesitate, unsure of how to answer that question. I mean, the true answer is no, but I also don't want them to know that my relationship with Becca technically started as a hookup. And since we've already promised each other that won't happen again, it's not relevant to the larger story anyway. "No, but we knew each other. We talked once or twice before last night."

"And now you're married?" Noah asks incredulously.

"Yeah. I don't expect you to understand, but I had my reasons." I lower my voice so that no one else will be able to hear us. "In case you forgot, Kaplan dumped Becca last night, on camera. And she was an employee of his dumb show. I offered to marry her to get her a green card so she could stay in the country and chase her dreams."

"Oh." Margo blinks. "That's surprisingly sweet of you."

I arch a brow. "Surprisingly?"

She makes a face. "I didn't mean it like that. It's just... that's a huge thing to do for someone, Theo."

My stomach does that weird flipping over thing again. "I know."

Noah blows out a breath, running a hand through his dark brown hair. "Did you think this all the way through before you tied the knot with someone you barely know? And someone who used to date your arch-nemesis, no less?"

"Of course I did," I lie. "I know what I'm doing."

"I sure hope so." He shakes his head, looking concerned.

"Listen, Theo, I don't mean to be insensitive or anything, but have you thought about how this might impact your ability to meet someone for yourself?" Margo asks gently.

"What do you mean?"

"Well, if you're married to Becca for a couple of years while you wait for her to get permanent residency status in the US, that's a long time where you won't be able to date anyone else. You know, have a real relationship."

I shrug. "That doesn't matter to me. I'm not looking for love anyway. I'm way more focused on my career right now, and I've already tried the whole 'real' marriage thing once. It blew up spectacularly, so if this fake marriage does nothing other than helping Becca, I've got no qualms about it."

Margo gives me a penetrating look, studying my face. Then she nods slowly. "Alright. If you're sure."

She leans back in her seat as we finally take off. But even Noah's fear of flying isn't enough to distract him from asking more questions. Once we're in the air, he leans over so that no one else can hear what he has to say.

"*Please* tell me you aren't just doing this to fuck with Kaplan."

I shake my head firmly. "No. It has nothing to do with that fucker and everything to do with Becca."

He looks me in the eyes for several long seconds, probably searching for any hint that I'm lying to him, but he can look all he wants. He won't find one. I'm telling the truth.

Finally, he nods just like Margo did. "Okay. But I'm serious, man. Don't let this feud with Kaplan get any worse. You hear me?"

"Loud and clear," I say, giving a little salute.

The truth is, I still want to rip Kaplan's fucking head off for what he did to Becca, but I know better than to say that out loud to anyone—least of all to my team captain.

Thankfully, he leaves it at that. Reese doesn't say anything else either, and the plane grows quiet as everyone settles in for the flight.

Good. I've got things to do.

I pull my phone from my pocket and tap into Becca's contact info. I had to copy her number down in a hurry, so I didn't even have time to give her contact entry a name. I tap to edit it and instead of putting her name, I write, "My Wife" with a ring emoji. Then I set the picture I took of her at her place earlier as her contact photo and my phone's wallpaper.

It's hard not to smile at her beautiful smile staring back at me, so I linger for a moment to drink in the details. Snapping her picture was such an impromptu thing that she couldn't have prepared for it, and that's what makes me think her smile is genuine.

As insane as all of this is, it's worth it if it put that expression on her face.

Grinning to myself, I pocket my phone again and nestle up against the window, hoping to get a little sleep before we land in Denver.

Because I have a lot to do when we get back.

~

I'm just pulling into the garage of my loft in Denver a few hours later when my phone rings. Thinking it might be Becca, I fumble for the phone where I dropped it into my car's cupholder, but when I bring it up to my face, I'm surprised to see that it's my mom calling instead. I swipe to answer automatically.

"Hey, Mom."

"Hey, sweetie. How are you doing?"

"Pretty good, thanks. I actually just pulled in at home after an away game," I say as I finish parking and climb out of my car to unload my bags. "How have you been?"

"Oh, don't worry about me. I'm fine. I just wanted to make sure *you* were okay. Is everything alright in your world?"

"Yeah, everything's great. Why?" I ask, a flicker of worry lighting in my chest.

"Well, I read an article about you this morning..."

Her voice trails off, and I groan.

"Oh, come on, Mom! I've told you a million times to stay away from that tabloid crap. You know it's all made up."

"I know, I know, but this one wasn't a tabloid piece! It was in a sports magazine I saw at the doctor's office, and it was talking about how you've been having a rough season," she says, and my stomach sinks.

Shit. Are the vultures already circling? Have I really been playing that badly?

"But the worst part was at the very end when the article said there's speculation you might be dropped after your contract is up with the Aces if you can't turn things around. And you know, I *am* your mother, so I worry. It's what I do. Are you sure you're okay?"

It's her genuine concern that twists the knife even deeper in my chest. Because the truth is I *have* been playing like shit this season, and it doesn't take a paid analyst to see it, either. The part that pisses me off the most about it though, is that I don't even know what's wrong or how to fix it. Or if I even can.

Are the Aces really thinking about dropping me?

I shake my head to clear the thought before it can even fully form. I can't let that shit take root because it's a self-fulfilling prophecy. And it's only going to make me play worse than I already am.

"I'm totally fine, Mom. I promise," I insist. "And I don't care where you find those articles, they're all trash. If I've told you once, I've told you a million times: the only person who knows a thing about my life is me. Everything else is sensationalized with some angle or another."

"Okay. But you know if you need anything—anything at all —your father and I are here for you."

"I know. And I appreciate it," I say, even though there's a bit of a knot in my stomach.

I've always been close with my parents, so it kills me not to be totally honest with my mom, especially when it's clear she's genuinely concerned about me, but now isn't the right time to have the 'I just got married' conversation with her.

"I'm okay though," I reassure her. "Honestly. I'm just having a bit of a rough patch on the ice. You know, even Gretzky had a few sketchy seasons."

"Good point." She laughs, sounding less worried, which gives me enough breathing room to start hauling my bags inside.

"What's going on with you and dad?" I ask, changing the subject. "What was the doctor's appointment for this morning?"

"Oh, nothing to worry about, just my usual checkup. Apparently, my doctor is leaving to start his own practice soon, so I'll probably be moving along with him, but that was probably the most exciting thing about the visit."

"Then I'd say it was a pretty good visit," I comment, drawing another laugh from her.

"What about you? Have you seen a doctor lately?"

"Of course I have, Mom," I assure her as I lug my bags through the parking garage toward the elevator. There aren't many other units in my building, which is nice because it means the elevator is almost always free, and that's true today too. "I'm a professional hockey player, remember? I see doctors more than I see you at this point."

"And isn't that a shame?"

"It is. I miss you and Dad. Maybe we can get together sometime soon," I say, and I almost tell her about the fact that I got married today but catch myself at the last second. I need to tell her, but I need to do it in the right way, and this isn't it. It wouldn't be fair to her or to Becca, especially without talking to my wife about it first.

"I'd love that. You're always welcome, sweetie, anytime you have the time." She clicks her tongue against her teeth. "Well, I should probably let you go so you can get settled in. I'm sure you have a lot to take care of now that you're back home."

"Yeah, I do. But it was great to hear from you. I love you."

"Love you too. Take care."

"You too. Bye, Mom."

I hang up just as the elevator arrives, but her words follow me out and into the hallway. I know it's stupid and a waste of time, but I can't stop thinking about what she said about commentators harping on about my performance this season.

But there isn't anything I can do about it at the moment. Those pinheads are going to talk regardless—it's what they get paid to do—so I use my phone to unlock my unit's door and drop my bags just inside the door that opens into the kitchen. With both hands free, I tap over to the camera and snap a quick picture of my living room with its incredible view of the Rocky Mountains thanks to the wrap-around floor-to-ceiling windows and vaulted roof, then attach it to a message I send to Becca.

ME: The mountains are waiting for you. *smile emoji*

Chapter 10

Becca

I'm still wearing Theo's jersey as I quickly pack my somewhat meager belongings into boxes, and when I stop to take a break, I realize that the jersey still smells like him.

Part of me wants to breathe it and him in, inhaling the scent of amber and spice, but I don't have time. I might not have a lot of stuff to pack, since I like to keep my possessions light—another behavior I probably picked up from growing up with my mother. But there's enough that I have to be conscious of my time.

It helps that Shawn never gave me much space in his condo, even after two years together. Then again, there wasn't a lot of room left with his ego taking up so much mass. But at least that means I won't have to face him to get back anything I care about, and that's a mercy because I don't know how I'd behave around him right now. Especially now that I have nothing left to lose.

But I'd be a liar if I said it didn't hurt. I still can't believe he'd so casually throw me away like I meant nothing to him at all. It makes me wonder if I ever mattered to him, or if I was always just a prop in his staged life, something to make him look and feel better until the season was over and he recast me with a younger model.

My phone rings from the other side of the room, thankfully saving me from a spiral I have no business going down right now. I step over and around half-full boxes and scattered possessions to get to my phone where it sits on the kitchen counter, and freeze when I see the name on the screen.

It's Peyton, one of the crew members on Shawn's reality show. I'm tempted to decline the call, but Peyton was one of the few friends I managed to make in LA. The city's reputation as a fake and shallow place was definitely true in my experience, so I had a hard time making friends that weren't also part of Shawn's orbit.

But I don't want to disappear from the city without at least getting a chance to say goodbye and thanks to Peyton, so I pick up the phone.

"Hey, girl," I answer.

"Becca! I'm so glad you picked up. I was worried you might not after what happened."

Great, so she already knows. Not that I'm surprised given her job and proximity to Shawn, but I'm still not fully prepared to have this conversation—and I'm not entirely sure I can trust her with the truth of what's happened since.

"Yeah, it's been a wild couple of days," I say, which is the understatement of my lifetime.

"I've heard. That's why I called. I saw the footage of the breakup the crew captured earlier, and I just wanted to make sure you were okay," Peyton says, and my heart thaws almost instantly. She and I were real friends, so maybe it shouldn't be a shock that she cares, but it still catches me off-guard.

"I'm weirdly at peace with it," I admit, surprising myself.

She scoffs. "Really? Then you're a better woman than I am."

"I don't know about that. It's just that sometimes you know

when it's time to move on, and my time came. Maybe not in the way I would've liked, but it came anyway."

"Holy shit, Becca. I'm so sorry. This whole thing is awful."

"It's not your fault. It's not like you scripted it or anything."

"I know, but still. No woman should have to go through something like this."

"Plenty of women before me have gone through worse than this."

Peyton laughs. "Okay, you got me there. What are you going to do now? I mean, I know about your residency situation and all."

There it is, the million-dollar question. I want to be honest with Peyton, but I'm scared. The green card arrangement is complicated, and I don't want to do anything that might jeopardize what Theo and I have done.

"It's okay, you don't have to answer that if you don't want to," Peyton says when I don't reply. "You know what? Are you free to meet for coffee or something?"

"Uh, I'm in the middle of packing right now, but—"

"Packing?" Peyton frowns. "Are you going back to Canada already? Damn."

"No, not to Canada. It's a long story," I say through a sigh. I really should finish packing, but taking a break to spend some time with one of the only friends I have in LA is too appealing to turn down. "I'll tell you all about it over a cup. Where do you want to meet?"

"Are you sure? I don't want to ruin your schedule."

"Of course, I'm sure. Besides, I could really use a caffeine jolt right now."

"Perfect. Then let's meet at Keen Bean in, like, twenty minutes? Does that work?"

"See you there," I say and hang up, feeling better already. The rest of my stuff can wait, so I leave it where it is and grab my purse and keys before locking up and leaving. I make it to

Keen Bean, a small local coffee place not far from my apartment, right on time.

Peyton's already standing outside the shop waiting for me when I pull up, and I can't help smiling at what she's wearing. She's always been on the more alternative end of the spectrum, so her dark eye makeup, multiple piercings, and plaid skirt with fishnet leggings fits her perfectly.

"I'm glad you agreed to come out," she greets me as I climb out of the car, pulling me in for a hug.

"Thanks for the invite. I needed it more than you know," I say, and follow her into the shop. It has a rustic look with exposed venting and stained, coffee-brown concrete floors, and every piece of furniture in the place is a handmade piece of matching wood. Between the quiet ambiance and the smell of fresh grounds in the air, I feel my shoulders drop almost as soon as we step through the front door.

"Order whatever you want, it's on me," Peyton says.

"Are you sure?"

"Positive. It's the least I can do for you after all of this."

"Thanks, Peyton," I say and try not to tear up as I approach the barista. I don't need anything super fancy, so I order a quad Americano and an apple scone to go with it. Peyton, however, orders up something I couldn't repeat even if I tried, but she's much more into coffee than I'll ever be.

We pick a high-top table toward the back of the shop where there aren't many other people and settle in. Peyton smiles at me sadly while she drums her black-painted fingernails on the knotted, polished wood of the table.

"Seriously, are you okay? Screw everything else, I just want to check in on you."

I shrug. "Like I said, I'm weirdly relieved by it all. It's like a weight finally lifted and I can breathe again."

"I get that. Getting cut from an asshole's world will have that effect on a girl," she says bluntly, and my eyebrows rise.

I've always known Peyton wasn't Shawn's biggest fan, but I've never heard her talk about him like this so openly—or at least not around me. She smirks at my reaction. "What? I figure I can let it all out with you now, right?"

"Yeah, go nuts."

"Good. Because he *is* an asshole, and not just to you."

"I'm not surprised in the slightest to hear that."

"And I'm relieved you aren't. You know, pretty much the entire crew hates his guts, but he's our meal ticket, like it or not, so we're stuck with him."

"I know the feeling," I say, and Peyton chuckles.

"I bet you do. But I still can't believe he pulled that shit with you in public with the cameras rolling. That's a new low, even for him," she says, shaking her head.

"How bad would it sound if I told you I'm used to that kind of thing by now?"

"Pretty bad, not gonna lie," Peyton says, and we laugh together. It's dark, but in a weird way, it's helping me feel better. Her validation—and reality check—are things I needed more than I realized. At least the rose-colored glasses aren't slipping on.

The barista calls Peyton's name to let her know our drinks are ready. "Hold that thought," she says and gets up to grab our coffees. She returns a few seconds later and sets my americano in front of me, so I pop the lid off and start blowing on its surface. The boiling water they make them with always makes it too hot for me to drink at first.

Peyton sits stirring her complicated coffee concoction with a stirring stick she grabbed on her way back. She stares at me through the steam pouring out of it, and I can tell there's something she wants to talk about but can't find the words.

"What's on your mind?" I ask before braving a sip. It's still hot, but it's at least not scalding my mouth.

Peyton sighs and lets go of her stirrer. It spins around the cardboard cup along with the liquid before it stops. "I have to be honest. I didn't just invite you out to check in on you."

"I kind of figured that. Whatever it is, just say it. I can handle it. I'm a big girl."

Peyton smiles at me, but there's a hint of sadness in the corners of her mouth. "I don't know for sure that anything is in the works, but I wanted to warn you that there's still tons of b-roll footage of you—and I do mean tons—that we shot, and Shawn can still use any or all of it thanks to the waiver in the contract you signed."

My stomach twists in a mixture of anger and resentment. I don't have the words to describe how much I hate that fact. But it's a fact, no matter how I feel about it, so Peyton's right to remind me. And I appreciate her doing it, although I'd much rather push the thought from my mind.

Part of me thinks even Shawn wouldn't do something shitty with that footage, but after what's happened in the last few days, I'm not naïve enough to believe it anymore. He dumped me in front of a bunch cameras in a crowded bar, for fuck's sake, so there's probably no low he won't sink to—especially if he thinks it'll benefit his image somehow.

I spent so much of my relationship with Shawn trying to justify his behavior, clinging to the image of who I thought he was when we first started dating. But that image has been shattered into a million, jagged pieces now, and there's no going back. The only thing I see him as now is the asshole he really is and always was.

"Are you okay?" Peyton asks, concern etched all over her face.

"Yeah, I'm fine. Just boiling a little."

"Can't blame you there. Like I said, as far as I know, there isn't anything being worked on right now, but you probably know better than I do that there's a good chance it'll happen eventually."

"Throwing a drink in a narcissistic asshole's face on camera will do that for a girl," I say, and Peyton bursts out laughing.

"I'm still proud of you for that one. I'll never forget the look on his face. I had to watch it so many times while reviewing the footage, and it never got old. It never will."

"He deserved worse."

"Oh, *so* much worse," Peyton agrees. "But you know what they say. What goes around comes around and all that."

"I hope so."

"You and me both," Peyton says. "But I'm glad you're not letting this get in your head."

"Are you kidding? I've already given him years of my life I can't get back. Those days are over."

"Good for you. But I guess that brings us back to the elephant in the room. You said you were packing when I called, so what's that all about? What are you going to do now?"

"Don't worry, I'm not going back to Canada. Not yet anyway."

"Okay... then where are you going?"

"I'm moving to Denver."

"Oh!" Peyton eyebrows shoot up toward her hairline. "What's taking you there?"

"I'm going to pursue all the dreams I unceremoniously threw on the backburner when I got together with Shawn," I answer, intentionally keeping my answer vague.

It's not that I don't trust Peyton with the truth, I just think it's probably best to keep the wedding to myself for a while longer. Or at least until I'm out of town. God only knows what Shawn will do when he gets wind of that.

"Hell yeah." Peyton nods in approval, beaming at me. "It's good to see your spark coming back, I have to say. It's been a while since I've seen that in you."

"It's amazing how much better you feel when you kick a piece of shit to the curb," I say, and although Peyton nods, she has no idea just how true it is. Seemingly overnight, my entire world has changed, and almost all for the better. Maybe I'm crazy, maybe I'm still more naïve than I'd like to admit, but I have a feeling that somehow, it's all going to work out. That Theo's right.

"Big mood," Peyton says, still smiling. "But hold up, I need to grab some more creamer for this," she says and heads back to the condiment table without another word. I pick my phone up off the table where it's been lying face down while we talked, and my heart skips a beat when I see a text from Theo that he just sent a couple of minutes before.

THEO: The mountains are waiting for you. *smile emoji*

There's a picture of what must be his living room attached, and it looks gorgeous. I don't know what kind of place I expected him to live in, but it wasn't this. The décor has an outdoorsy vibe, rustic and masculine, but with softened edges of tasteful color here and there. Did he decorate it himself? He did an amazing job if so.

And then there's the view outside the windows. Holy shit. There's a wrap-around balcony that looks out on a beautiful, sweeping mountain range dotted with snow. It reminds me of home in a way, familiar but just different enough to be new and exciting.

I can't help the grin that splits my face as I start typing a reply.

ME: When is that flight again?

Chapter 11

Theo

I don't know what feels worse: my aching body after another rough practice, or the way I beat up on myself for it when I step into the showers after. Usually, the hot water helps clear my head after a few grueling hours on the ice, but today it just seems to keep bringing up more thoughts along with the rising steam.

I feel like I'm caught in a fucked-up loop. I know I haven't been playing my best lately—and so does everyone else, according to my mom—and even though I know better, I can't help carrying that bullshit with me every time I lace up my skates. Which only makes me play worse. Rinse, repeat.

It's infuriating. But the worst part about it is that I don't know how to make it stop. Or if I even can. And now that I know there's speculation about the Aces not renewing my contract...

Knock it the fuck off, Camden. There's no time for a pity party.

I shake my head under the water to try and clear it. I can't give in to that irritating little voice nagging at me in the back of my head because it's a slippery slope that never leads to anything good. Besides, Becca's arriving today, so I need to get my shit together for her sake. She has enough to worry about, I don't need her worrying about me too.

I wash up quickly, towel off, and get dressed. I'm hoping not to have a run-in with Noah or any of the other guys before I slip out of here to head to the airport, but no luck. As soon as I step out of the locker room, I find Noah waiting for me, leaning up against the thick plexiglass barrier between the ice and the stands. His arms are crossed over his chest, and he's got that disapproving dad look on his face that he does so well.

"What's the rush?" he asks.

"I've got somewhere to be," I answer cryptically, and Noah chuckles.

"Come on, Camden, cut the crap. You're going to pick up Becca, aren't you?"

"So what if I am?" I'm not really in the mood to explain myself after the beating I just took on the ice, mentally and physically. So maybe I'm being a little too forceful with Noah, but whatever. To my surprise, he sighs and drops his arms.

"What you do in your personal life is your business. I'm hardly one to talk shit about mixing work and pleasure," he says, referring to his relationship with Margo. Well, at least he's not totally oblivious. "I'm just worried about you, man. You've been having a rough time lately, and I'm concerned this Becca situation could, well, you know," he continues and shrugs.

"No, I don't," I say flatly, even though I know exactly where he's going with this.

"I don't know, *distract* you more," he says, and although it stings, I don't take the bait. "I don't say that because I don't want you to be happy, Camden. You know me better than that by now. I just want to see you get your groove back. I don't like seeing you struggle like this."

"Thanks," I say, surprised. Maybe I didn't know where he was going with this conversation.

"Of course. I'm your captain, I'll always have your back. Just be careful with this whole Becca thing, okay? I don't want to see you get hurt or get into any trouble over it."

"It won't be a problem, I promise," I insist, and Noah nods.

"Alright. I trust you. Now you'd better get going before you're late to pick up your new wife," he says with a grin, and I punch him on the shoulder on my way out of the arena. It's a short drive from there to the airport, so I'm a few minutes early. We're not supposed to linger in the pickup area, but I don't give a damn, so I park right outside the door to baggage claim and decide to text Becca.

ME: I'm here and right outside the door when you're ready. Hopefully, the cops don't run me off before then.

She doesn't answer, but she's probably in a rush to get her bags and get outside. I'm sure she'll check her phone when she has a second, so I relax in my seat and wait. But I don't have to wait long before the gorgeous, dark-haired woman who is now my wife steps out of the sliding doors and flashes me a beaming smile when she spots me through the tinted windows of my car.

Fuck, she's even more beautiful than I remembered.

I jump out of the car and hurry over to take the two giant rolling bags she brought with her. She shipped the rest of her belongings out, and they all arrived last night, so this is probably the most important stuff she needed to carry with her.

I'm not sure what's appropriate as a greeting, so I lean in to kiss her on the cheek, but she does the same thing, and we end up knocking our foreheads together.

"Ow." She laughs softly, putting a hand to her head.

"Shit, sorry." I take her hand, checking to make sure she doesn't have a bump on her forehead or anything. "I guess we're going to need to practice that one a bit more."

"Right. Sorry, I'm just not used to this. But... it's good to see you again," she adds, her cheeks flushing an adorable pink color.

"Yeah, you too, princess," I say.

We're still standing very close together, and I realize I haven't dropped her hand yet. She smells amazing, a combination of vanilla and lavender that I remember well from our night together, and as our gazes meet, I realize that as crazy as it sounds, I missed her.

I clear my throat, forcing myself to let go of her delicate hand and step back. "How was your flight?"

"It was great," she answers as she passes me her bags. "Thank you so much for getting the ticket. You really didn't have to buy me a seat in first class."

"I wanted you to be comfortable," I tell her with a shrug as I wheel her bags to my car and open the trunk to load them. "I'm sure you've been busy with getting ready for the move, so I figured you could use a break. By the way, the rest of your stuff arrived last night, so you'll just have to figure out where you want to put everything."

"Oh, perfect. Did it all get there in one piece?"

"As far as I can tell, yeah, but I didn't look too closely. Didn't want to be nosy." I wink at her as I finish storing her bags, then lead her to the passenger side to open the door.

"Wow." She grins as she climbs in. "I don't think Shawn opened a door for me once the entire time we were together."

I bite back a scowl, a fresh burst of anger at Kaplan rising inside me. I hate the way he lowered her expectations of what she deserves from the world and the people in her life.

Resting my hand on the frame of the car, I drop my head a little as I hold the door open, catching her gaze. "He wasn't good enough for you."

Something soft and vulnerable flashes across her face, and she nods. She glances around at the leather seats of my car, then back up at me.

"Well, thank you for picking me up. I don't think he ever did anything like this either. I would've driven my car out here, but..." She grimaces. "Well, it's a bit of a beater, and I wasn't sure it would make the drive. I left it with Peyton for now, but I'll see about getting it shipped out to Denver soon."

"That won't be necessary," I say, making a snap decision.

She frowns. "It seems like it is. I know there's public transportation here, but I'm guessing I'll need a car. You can't drive me around all the time."

I chuckle. "No, I guess I can't. But if you're worried about your car breaking down, I'd rather have you in something safer. I'll buy you a new one."

Becca stares at me, her eyes widening. Her mouth opens and closes several times before any words come out. "You'll what?"

"I'll buy you a new car."

"Theo." She swallows, shaking her head. "I can't accept that. Marrying me for citizenship is one thing, but buying me a brand new car? I really, really appreciate it, and it's amazingly nice of you to offer, but—"

"No buts." I shake my head firmly, crouching down by the open door of the car so that she won't have to crane her neck to hold my gaze. "You're my wife now, and my wife deserves the best. And you don't have to thank me for anything."

"Are you sure?" She tugs her bottom lip between her teeth, a tiny line appearing between her eyebrows. "You've already helped me so much. I don't want to take advantage of your generosity."

"You're not." I rest a hand on her knee, giving a little squeeze. "I'm doing all of this because I *want* to. I want to help you." I lower my voice a little, letting her hear the truth in my words. "This whole marriage thing might be fake, but that doesn't mean I'm not going to take care of you while you're my wife. That part is real. Okay?"

Becca nods, her eyes glistening as she blinks rapidly. "Okay," she whispers. "Thank you, Theo."

I grin, then check to make sure all her limbs are in the car before I close the door and walk around to the driver's side. I climb in and start the car before glancing over at her.

"Oh, we need to make a stop on the way back to my place. Is that alright?"

"Sure. What are we stopping for?"

I glance at the plain golden band on her ring finger. "We've got to get you a proper ring, princess."

Her gaze follows mine, and her jaw falls open a little. "Oh! Theo, that's really not necessary."

"I know it isn't, but remember what I told you? I'm doing this because I want to. If you're going to be my wife, I want you to *like* the ring I put on your finger. Don't forget, you'll be wearing it for a couple of years, so it might as well be one that you choose and that makes you feel amazing to wear."

Becca laughs incredulously and leans back against her seat. "I keep thinking I'm in a dream I'm about to wake up from."

"Nope. This is real life," I assure her, pulling away from the curb. "We already have an appointment at a jeweler, so let's get going before we're late."

I navigate us away from the pickup area to head into downtown Denver, where Rockset Jewelry waits. The airport is about forty minutes away from downtown with traffic, so it takes a good while to get where we're going, and Becca doesn't say much during the drive.

"Everything okay?" I ask as I parallel park on the street.

"Yeah, just taking in all the sights. I've never been to Denver before. It's beautiful."

"It really is. Oh, and I probably should've warned you about the elevation."

"What about it?" Becca asks as she takes off her seatbelt.

"The oxygen is thinner up here, so basic activities like walking take more out of you than they would somewhere else. And you've gotta be careful with the alcohol too. It'll sneak up on you. Not that I'd know anything about that," I say with a grin.

"Good to know."

"Ready to shop?"

"As ready as I'll ever be," she says and climbs out of the car. She waits for me on the curb while I get out, and I offer her my hand when I join her. She stares at it and hesitates for a second but smiles and links her fingers between mine.

Rockset is a somewhat new jeweler in town. They just opened a couple years ago, but I did my research, and they've got the best of the best in terms of stones and craftsmanship, which is exactly what I want for Becca. They cut most of their stones themselves, and all their bands are handmade. They're expensive because of that, but I don't care how much her ring costs. I just want Becca to be happy.

As soon as we step inside, I can tell the place has money. Like a lot of businesses around here, their aesthetic is a mix of modern clean lines and rustic accents. The place even *smells* expensive, and I can see in the look on Becca's face that she's picking up on it too. She flashes me a worried look, but I squeeze her hand to reassure her. I wouldn't have brought her here if I couldn't afford to buy any ring in the place, and I definitely can. I'm not one of those professional sports guys who likes to blow their money on stupid shit like sports cars and mansions, so I've got plenty to spare.

"Good afternoon," says a thin, hipster-looking guy sporting a full, clean-cut red beard and leather apron says as he steps out from behind a door beyond the counter. His matching red hair is slicked back and juts out from the base of his head in a wave. "You must be Mr. and Mrs. Camden. I'm Oliver, the owner," he continues and offers each of us a hand to shake. "Pleased to meet you both."

"The pleasure's all ours," I say with a grin.

"I understand you're looking for a replacement wedding

ring?" Oliver asks, reaching for Becca's ring hand. She offers it to him for inspection, and he smiles at her kindly. "Nothing wrong with a classic gold band—if it ain't broke, don't fix it—but something tells me you're looking for a ring that's a little more personal."

"That's *exactly* what we're looking for," I answer, and he nods.

"Well, you're welcome to look at the rings we already have cut, of course, but if you don't see anything that works, we offer custom cuts as well," he explains, gesturing at the huge display case dividing us. He glances at Becca. "Do you have an idea of what kind of stone you'd like?"

She chews her lip and gives him an uncertain look. "Uh, no, not really. To be honest, I wasn't expecting to be here today, so I haven't given it a lot of thought."

"The classic wedding ring surprise," Oliver says, flashing me a playful smile. "No worries. Let's start with your favorite color, then."

"Blue," she answers confidently.

"Excellent choice. Mine too, although that's probably obvious," Oliver says as he waves a hand over one of the nearby jewelry cases that is filled with different shades of blue gemstones. "Do any of these catch your eye?"

"Oh, I like that one." Becca leans over to point at a delicate looking silver band with an ivy-like design that wraps and folds around itself. Oliver opens the case from behind and reaches for it, and when Becca spots the price tag underneath, she whips around to me with her eyes wide open. Admittedly, it's expensive, but I can afford it.

"Don't worry about it," I whisper to her so Oliver can't hear.

"Go ahead, try it on. I'm not sure what size you are, but it looks like it might fit," he says as he slides the little velvet display across the glass to Becca.

"Here, let me help." I step forward and tug the ring off the display before taking Becca's hand in mine. I gently remove the gold band and set it on the glass, then slip the new ring on. It fits like it was custom made for her.

"It's perfect," Becca whispers, so quietly that even I barely hear her.

"Then I guess we don't really need to keep looking, do we?"

"But Theo, it's so expensive," she says, glancing over her shoulder back at the price tag in the display case. "With everything else you're already doing for me, this is too much."

I cradle her face to kiss her forehead. "Nothing is too much for you. Remember that." I turn to Oliver and nod to him. "We'll take it."

"Then I'll get things settled. Feel free to keep it on, I'll just put your old band in its box," he tells Becca, and all she can do is stare at him as he packs everything up and starts closing out the transaction. I toss my credit card on the counter and smile at Becca, but she can't take her eyes off the ring. She turns her hand back and forth in the light, admiring the way the baby blue gem sparkles in the light.

"Do you like it?"

"Are you kidding? I love it."

"Good. Because you get to keep it for the rest of your life." She beams at me, and I stand there taking in the ring's beauty with her while Oliver takes care of the finances. It doesn't take long for him to finalize everything, and when he's finished, he passes me a few sheets of paper and a fancy blue velvet box with Becca's gold band inside.

"Congratulations," Oliver says and shakes my hand before I lead Becca out of the shop and back to my car. She climbs inside quietly, and as we pull away, I catch her still staring down at the ring.

"Are you sure you like it?"

"Of course I do!"

"Okay, okay. Then is something else on your mind? You're being pretty quiet."

Becca shrugs and finally takes her eyes off the ring to meet mine. "I don't know, I guess this is all just getting very real very fast. I mean, I just got off a flight here and the next thing I know, I'm getting a surprise of a lifetime in the form of a beautiful and *very* expensive wedding ring."

"Yeah, I get that. It's a lot to take in. Are you having second thoughts?"

"No, not at all. I'm just feeling a little overwhelmed by how, well, good things are turning out for me. After Shawn dumped me, I thought I was going to have to run home with my tail between my legs, but I feel like I'm living in a fairy tale instead. It's surreal. And still hard to believe."

I reach over to rest my hand on hers. "Believe it. You can stop waiting for the other shoe to drop because it's not going to happen. You're right, this *is* real. We're doing this. And everything is going to be perfect."

"I believe you. I do. But it's just going to take some time for me to adjust."

"Totally understandable. You can take all the time you need," I say, and leave it at that. Thankfully, the view on the drive back to my place is stunning. You can't really look anywhere without seeing the mountains, and there's still a light dusting of snow on the peaks.

"It's so beautiful here," Becca mumbles as she stares out the window. "It reminds me a lot of home. I missed the mountains and snow while I was living in Los Angeles. I never got a chance to get out of LA and up into the mountains in California."

It's such a small detail, but it makes me smile because I love the snow and mountains too. Big cities are great and tons of fun, but in my opinion, nothing can beat the rugged natural beauty of the Rocky Mountains. Some people get tired of the views after a while, but I don't understand how they could. They change throughout the year, and every season brings some incredible new sight.

It reminds me of Becca and all the ways she continues to surprise me.

We pull into the garage of my building a few minutes later and I climb right out, but Becca hesitates in the passenger seat. She's staring down at her ring again and adjusting it on her finger.

"Everything okay?" I ask, leaning into the car, and she glances over at me with her bottom lip trapped between her teeth.

"Yeah, I was just thinking."

"About what?"

"I... I want fidelity." Her voice isn't steady, but the intense look she gives me is. "I know this marriage isn't real, and I'm not trying to pretend it is, but I still don't want you seeing anyone else on the side."

Without a word, I walk around the car to her side, open the door, and kneel beside her.

"Becca, listen to me. I meant what I said. For as long as I'm your husband, I'll take care of you. And that includes not being with anyone else." Reaching out, I grip her chin between my thumb and forefinger, holding her gaze. "I can't offer you my heart, but I can offer you that."

Something flashes in her eyes, powerful but hard to read, and she nods.

"Thank you," she breathes.

I trace my thumb lightly along the curve of her jaw, just a tiny movement. "And I want the same from you too. As long as we're married, I want to know that there's no other man in your life."

She blinks, looking almost taken aback, as if she wasn't expecting me to want that claim on her. Then she nods again, licking her lips.

"Of course. I don't want to be with anyone else."

"Good."

I rise smoothly to my feet and offer her a hand to help her out of the car, and as she rests her delicate palm on mine and I close my fingers around hers, I can't quite explain the feeling of satisfaction that floods my chest.

Chapter 12

Becca

My jaw drops when I step into Theo's condo. I've already seen it in the picture he sent me, but the picture didn't do it justice. The furniture is so high-end that it looks like something out of a magazine—I can only guess at what it must have cost. And the high ceilings and windows let light pour in from every angle, which gives the entire condo a warm glow and feel.

He has a corner unit that looks right out at the mountains and it's a killer view. I almost start crying again when I realize that this is my home now, and that I'll get to spend every morning on that wraparound balcony admiring the mountains while I sip my coffee.

"Welcome home," Theo says, and when I turn to face him, he's blushing and rubbing the back of his neck. Is he embarrassed? "From the looks of the place, it'll probably surprise you to hear, but I grew up poor. Buying this place felt more than a little bonkers back when I did."

"I don't blame you for falling in love with it. It's amazing," I say and take a slow spin around to drink in more of the details.

"I'm glad you like it. And don't be shy, make it your home. When I first moved in, I was afraid to touch anything in here."

He chuckles, and I laugh with him because it's not hard to believe. Everything in the condo screams money, but there are hints that it's lived in too. There are dishes in the sink, and I'm pretty sure I spot a stray sock by the stairs to the loft.

"It definitely feels expensive, but it weirdly feels like a home too, if that makes sense?" I say.

"It makes perfect sense! That's exactly how I felt. It wasn't exactly the place I imagined buying beforehand, but it felt right."

"It sure feels a lot better than the staged film set that was Shawn's place," I murmur, and Theo scoffs.

"Imagine that. Fake ass. But seriously, feel free to make this place your own and make yourself comfortable however you want."

"Thank you, but honestly, I'm not sure I even know how to do that," I tell him.

Theo shoots me a skeptical look, his brows stitched together. "Oh, come on, I saw your apartment. You've got some decorating chops."

"I can't take credit for that. Shawn's crew designed most of it."

"Wow. He really did script every last detail, didn't he?"

"You have no idea. But I'm not kidding. I don't know the first thing about making a place a home. I've never really had one to try it with before."

"Well, you do now." Theo walks over to take both of my hands in his. "Come on, I'll give you the grand tour. I mean, it's not very big, but still."

He doesn't wait for an answer before tugging me over to the metal, exposed staircase that leads up to the loft and the master bedroom. He spots the sock at the foot of the stairs and gives me a nervous glance.

"Uh, sorry about that. I must have dropped it when I was doing laundry before practice. I swear I'm not a slob."

"I'm hardly in a position to judge."

He chuckles, his eyes warming as he leads me into another room. "This is the master bedroom."

Similar to the living room, this room features a very high ceiling, but it slants down to a point near the bed in the far corner, giving the room an angular, almost mountainous feel itself. I love the way the design naturally pulls my eye.

But when I glance around and see no other beds or doors, my heart skips a beat. Is this the only bedroom in the condo? I know we're married and all, but does Theo expect us to share a bed already?

I'm trying to figure out whether that excites or scares me, but I get my answer when he brings me back downstairs and into a hall off the kitchen where another bedroom waits.

"This will be your room," he says and opens it, revealing a large but mostly empty space, aside from a bed, dresser, and all my boxes stacked against the far wall. "As you can see, it's pretty much a blank slate. I rarely have company over other than my parents, so I haven't done anything with it, but I figure that'll give you the chance to try some things out. Is it okay?"

"It's great, yeah." I nod, already thinking of where I'll put some of my things. Not that there's much to place, but still.

"Awesome. Then I'll leave you be for a while so you can get settled. Help yourself to anything in the house. The fridge is fully stocked, but I'm not a cook myself, so we'll have to figure that out. Not that I expect you to cook for me or anything like that," he adds in a hurry, and I smile at him.

"I like cooking, actually, but I appreciate the consideration. And, well, everything else you've done for me. Seriously, Theo. I don't have the words."

"Good, because you don't need them. Go ahead, make yourself at home. I'll go get your bags out of the car."

He grins at me, then disappears back down the hall. I stand there staring at the room for a few seconds, feeling like a total fish out of water. It's just like Theo said, I'm almost afraid to touch anything. Because as much as he insists that this is my home now too, I still feel like an intruder.

I close the door to the bedroom, more to put myself at ease than for privacy, and walk over to the bed to sit on the edge of it. The movers Theo hired did a great job with all my stuff. As far as I can tell, there aren't even any dented corners, so it's highly unlikely any of my things got damaged in the move.

I labeled everything, but with the way they're stacked, I can't read them, so I reach for the nearest one at the top of the stack and peel away the tape. It turns out it's the last box I packed with all the odds and ends that wouldn't fit in anywhere else. I sift through it since I can't remember everything that's inside, and my heart clenches when I spot a bright red maple leaf at the bottom of the box. It's a little wall decoration that my mom bought for me when I was a kid, and somehow, I've managed to keep it across all the many moves we've made.

"Maybe this will help make it feel more like home," I mutter and pull the leaf out of the box. There's a little hole built into the top of the middle leaf for a nail, so I scan the walls to see if one is already around. There isn't, but I do find a little tab on the back of the bedroom door that's probably supposed to hold a robe or something like that.

I get up and walk the leaf over, and it fits perfectly on the tab. "There," I say with a smile, running my fingers over the cool metal. I'm farther away from home than I thought I'd ever be, literally and figuratively, but it isn't the first time. I kept this same decoration hanging above my bed in my apartment back in LA because I got so homesick at first.

Shawn was really the only person I knew in town, other than his network of teammates and TV crew. It strikes me that, for as long as he and I were together, and for as long as I lived in LA, it never really did feel like home. And it's crazy because I literally just got here, but as I take another look around the room in Theo's condo, I already feel better about it than I ever did about LA.

A knock on the bedroom door startles me, and I step back just in time as Theo opens it and pokes his head in. "Sorry to bother you, but I've got your bags."

"Oh, it's okay, I was just hanging something. Come on in," I say and step aside to let him wheel my bags through. He puts them on the other side of the room with my boxes, then stands to admire the maple leaf.

"Nice. I like it. Very homey."

"My mom bought it for me forever ago. I think I've had it since I was like ten."

"If maple leaves could talk, huh?"

"It's probably best that this one can't," I say, and Theo laughs.

"You're probably right. Are you getting hungry? I was thinking about ordering something. How do you feel about Indian since we didn't get it the other day?"

I'm not particularly hungry, but I don't want to be rude and turn him down—especially when he's trying to make up for missing out the last time. "That sounds amazing."

"Awesome. I know the perfect place."

"I take it you order out a lot?"

Theo blushes. "Yeah, but not always. I cook occasionally. I'm sure you saw the dishes in the sink."

"Occasionally?"

"Yeah, you know, when the mood strikes."

"So almost never?"

"Okay, you caught me." He chuckles as he pulls out his phone. "Do you know what you want?"

"Chicken korma," I answer without a moment's hesitation.

Theo looks up from his phone to give me that playful grin of his. "Damn, that was fast."

I shrug. "It's my favorite dish. Hard to go wrong with it no matter where you order it from."

"Noted. Want any naan bread to go with it?"

"Garlic, please."

"That's my girl." He taps around on the screen a few more times, then tucks his phone back into his pocket. "Alright, order's placed. Should be here in about fifteen minutes. Do you want any help with any of this stuff?"

He gestures toward my bags and boxes, but I shake my head.

"I'm okay. There's nothing heavy or anything in there. Honestly, I'm not really in the mood to go through it all right now anyway. I have the basics in my travel bag, so I'll probably just dive into this tomorrow."

"Okay, sounds good. I'll let you know when the food gets here." Theo raps his knuckles on the door frame and goes to leave my room, and instead of lingering where I am, I follow him. I can't hide out in here forever. At some point we're going to have to get used to sharing a house and being in the same area at the same time, so we might as well rip this awkward bandage off now.

Theo settles his tall frame on the L-shaped couch that angles around the living room and frames the big-screen TV at the center of it. "Make yourself comfortable."

I sit down on the opposite side of the couch, and he glances over at me, a wry smile curving his lips. "Is it just me, or is this weird?"

"You think?"

We laugh together and Theo shakes his head. "Well, I guess it only has to be as weird as we make it, right?"

"I don't know how to *not* make this weird."

"Sharing a meal is as good a place to start as any. Isn't that what they did in 'ye olden days'?"

"Then I hope it gets here soon so I at least have something to do with my hands," I say, and Theo chuckles. He checks his phone for an update.

"Looks like it's already on its way. Should be here any minute."

"Great."

"So, uh, how do you like your room? Will it work for you?"

"I'm in no position to complain."

Theo shoots me a look. "You know that's not what I meant."

Thankfully, a bell sounds from somewhere in the condo, saving me from my own awkwardness, and Theo jumps up off the couch. "There's the food. Be right back," he says and strides toward the door. I hear him talking with the delivery guy but can't make out or focus on what they're saying because I still can't quite believe I'm here.

As I sit in this amazing living room, with this incredible view, I feel like I'm watching a movie of someone else's life. Which is hilarious when I think about it because I've spent most of the last few years of my life literally being a side character in someone else's story. But I'm still not comfortable being the one in the spotlight.

My fingers splay out across the textured leather of the couch just to root me, to convince me it's not all going to disappear if I blink. I can't think of a time I ever sat on a couch this nice, much less called one mine. Shawn could've afforded things like this if he wanted them, but that was the key: he had to want it. I try to remember a single time he did something nice for me and come up empty.

Meanwhile, Theo has married me, moved me into his house, and welcomed me into his life all while barely knowing me. He and Shawn might both be famous hockey players, but that's about it in terms of their similarities. I don't really understand what Theo sees in me or why he's doing all of this for me, because it really is crazy, but it doesn't change the fact that he is. That I'm here.

I turn on the couch to find him standing at the kitchen island watching me. "You okay?"

"Better than I've been in a long time," I say with a smile.

Maybe I'm just as crazy as he is, but I'm starting to trust him and that this is all going to work out. I've lived my whole life waiting for the other shoe to drop, so I don't really know how to turn that off, but being here and sharing something as simple as takeout Indian with him makes me want to try.

"That's what I like to hear." Theo grins as he walks back into the living room with two plastic containers and utensils.

He hands me my chicken korma and sits right next to me to set his meal on the glass-topped coffee table in front of us. We settle into a comfortable silence as we start to eat, and I take a few bites of the food.

It really is amazing, easily up there with the best Indian food I've ever had. And when combined with the bread, it's perfection. But all the nerves of the past few days have affected my appetite, and I'm already feeling full, so I leave the tray on the table after a bit and lean back on the couch to admire the view of the mountains.

"I don't think I'll ever get tired of looking at this," I admit in a quiet voice.

"That makes two of us."

"It's always been a dream of mine to live close to the mountains like this, but I didn't think it would ever actually happen."

Theo sets his tray down next to mine and leans back on the couch too. We stare at the mountains for a few moments until he turns his head to face me and smiles. "What other dreams do you have?"

I purse my lips. "Hm. I don't even know where to start, aside from the fact that I've dreamed of getting a dog ever since I was a little girl. But the time never seemed right for it."

"That's a good start." He nods approvingly. "What else?"

"I've always wanted to travel to Italy."

His face lights up. "Oh, that's a good one. Italy is amazing. What else? Making a career out of dancing? That must be a big one for you."

I tilt my head. "Yes and no. I used to dream of being part of a professional dance company, but even though I still love to perform, my dreams are different these days. What I really want to do is partner with a dance company and teach classes. Inspire the next generation of dancers."

"That's awesome. I've thought about teaching hockey someday too when I'm too old and busted to keep getting banged up on the ice. Not that I'm implying you're old or busted. Far from it." He shakes his head emphatically, making me chuckle. "But seriously, you should pursue it. No dream is too big or too small, and it's never too late."

"It's a big part of why I wanted to stay in the US," I admit. "So once things settle down a bit, I'll definitely look into it."

"You'll be an amazing teacher, I can already tell."

I cock my head. "Really? Why is that?"

"You're patient, you're one of the sweetest people I've ever met, and you know your shit. What else would anyone need in a teacher?"

He ticks the reasons off on his finger as he lists them, and I chuckle. "I should get you to write my resume for me."

"Happy to do it." His green eyes dance with amusement. "Besides being a fake husband, I make an excellent hype man."

I can't help but laugh, nudging him with my shoulder. "I'll keep that in mind."

He bumps my shoulder back, then glances down at the containers on the coffee table. "Are you finished?"

"I think for now, yeah. I wasn't very hungry, but I'll eat the rest later."

"Okay. I'll put it away for you."

He rises to his feet as he gathers up our food. I can't tell if this is something he'd do for any guest in his house, or if he's going out of his way to welcome me, but I decide it doesn't matter. It's sweet, regardless.

"I never would've guessed you're such a gentleman," I tell him, tilting my head as I look up at him.

He looks even taller than usual as he stands over me, flashing that irresistible grin again. Something I can't quite read passes across his expression as he shakes his head.

"That's probably because I'm not always a gentleman," he says, his voice dropping a little.

What does that mean?

I can't tell if he's flirting with me or referring to his bad boy reputation, but my face flushes, and heat rushes through my entire body as memories of our first night together race through my mind.

You shouldn't be thinking about that right now, I scold myself.

But Theo is still staring at me, making my heart pound even harder, and a little voice in the back of my head screams at me to break our gaze. I know I should, but I still can't bring myself to do it.

Then Theo abruptly steps around the couch and heads to the kitchen, giving me a chance to catch my breath.

"I'm, uh, going to go wash up," I say and push myself off the couch where I'm currently melting.

"There's a second bathroom in the same hall by your room," he calls after me as I pass him, so I hurry down the hall, hoping he can't see the redness I know is all over my face. I make it to the bathroom and close and lock the door behind me before throwing on the faucet like it'll cover the sound of my hammering heart.

Remember the rules.

Chapter 13

Theo

I pad downstairs the next morning in my boxers without thinking. I'm so used to living alone that it doesn't even occur to me that it's bad idea—until I get to the bottom of the stairs and find Becca in the living room doing yoga.

She's standing on a rubber mat with her back to me, deep into a lunging leg stretch with her arms raised over her head, and I know I shouldn't watch, but I'm frozen. I'm lucky she didn't hear or see me coming down the stairs, but I don't want to risk making any noise on my way back up to alert her that I was ever there.

And I can't bring myself to peel my eyes away.

She's wearing a skin-tight workout uniform that's powder blue, just like the ring I bought her, and the definition of her dancer's frame beneath the thin fabric does something to me. I've already seen and experienced her entire body, so it's not like it should be a surprise, but seeing her muscles flex through the cutout hole in the back of her top makes my breath catch in my throat.

My cock twitches, a flash of heat rushing through me. But

we already agreed we weren't going to do that anymore, so I need to nip this in the bud.

I clear my throat loudly enough that she'll hear, and she jumps a little. Her head spins around to find me, and although she's blushing a bit, she smiles. "Sorry. I hope I'm not in the way."

"Of course not. This is your space too, remember?" I say as I leave the stairs and head into the kitchen. Her eyes follow me, and I remember that I'm not wearing anything other than my boxers, which probably isn't helping her stay focused either.

"Uh, sorry." I gesture to myself. "I guess I'm not used to having a roommate yet myself. I won't make this a habit."

Becca laughs and shrugs. "It's your house, you can wear whatever you want or don't want." I shoot her a look, and the gorgeous blush on her cheeks deepens. "Okay, okay, within reason, obviously."

My cock twitches as her gaze drops again before she drags it away. I clear my throat, willing my body not to respond to her attention or the filthy memories flooding my mind.

"You're welcome to do yoga wherever you want," I tell her. "But I forgot to mention during the tour yesterday, I actually have a home gym that you're welcome to use. It's upstairs."

"Oh. Thanks." Becca gives me a funny look, then chuckles.

"What?" I ask.

"Nothing." She crosses her arms over her chest. "It's just funny. The whole time I dated Shawn, he never once made me feel at home in his space. And I've only been fake married to you for like a week, and living with you for a day, but I already feel more welcome with you than I ever did with him."

I'm sure she doesn't mean for it to, but anger flares up in me anyway. I walk closer to her, and she watches me intently.

"I understand why you'd make those kind of comparisons," I tell her in a low voice. "But you're not with Shawn anymore. And if I have one goal in this marriage, it's to make sure that you realize a fuckhead like that was never worthy of you. Because you're worth so much more."

Becca chews her lip, her body swaying forward a little. For a second, I swear she's about to lean in to kiss me. We're so close that I can feel the warmth of her body radiating into mine. She smells intoxicating, a sweet mixture of vanilla and lavender that makes me want to bury my face in her hair and inhale deeply.

My breathing picks up along with my pulse, and I can tell from the blood pumping in my ears that my boxers are leaving nothing to the imagination. I know I'm getting hard, but there's no way I could hide it now even if I tried.

Becca's throat moves as she swallows, then she steps back and leans down to start rolling up her mat. "Um, I'll check out the gym tomorrow. I was just finishing up for today anyway."

"Okay." I nod, trying to ignore the sudden hoarseness of my voice. "Well, I was gonna make myself some breakfast, and I'd bet you could use some carbs after that workout. Can I make you something?"

She glances up at me, a tiny smile tugging at her lips. She doesn't even have to say it, but I'm positive Shawn never fucking cooked for her.

"Sure," she says. "If you'll have enough of whatever you're making, I'll have some."

"Great." I chuckle. "Just as a warning, I'm not the world's best cook. But basic breakfast stuff, I can handle."

"Thanks. I'm going to go get cleaned up then," she says and leaves with her mat tucked under her arm.

I wait until I hear the shower running in her bathroom, then run back upstairs to put some clothes on. If I were by myself, I wouldn't bother, but especially after the charged moment we just had, I figure it's for the best.

Back in the kitchen, I crack several eggs into a bowl and whisk them up with some salt, pepper, and my secret ingredient: tajin seasoning. When they're ready, I heat a pan on the induction stove and pour the mix in. The surface gets hot almost immediately, so I get to scrambling them and drop the heat as low as it'll go so I can toast some bread in the countertop oven by the stove.

I'm just pulling the toast out—and burning myself in the process—when Becca comes back into the kitchen. Her hair's still wet, and she's changed into a plain, loose-fitting set of pink sweats, but she still looks great. Unfortunately, I realize when I check the butter dish on the counter that I'm completely out of it. I glance at her over my shoulder to where she sits at the kitchen island on one of the high-top, cushioned stools.

"Looks like I'm out of butter, but I think I have some avocado if you'd rather have that on your toast."

"Sounds good," she says, smiling, so I snag one out of a little dish I keep on the island and pull a cutting board from a custom-made slot built into the island's side. The knives hang magnetically from a strip next to the stove, so I grab one of those and get to work slicing up the avocado.

"So have you, uh, told anyone yet? About us, I mean?" Becca asks while she watches me.

"I told Noah, but he'd already figured it out anyway," I admit, and although she doesn't look thrilled about it, she nods.

"That was probably inevitable. I bet you spend more time with him and the other Aces than anyone else."

"Exactly. They were gonna find out one way or another, so I figured it was probably best to rip the bandage off quick."

Becca reaches over the counter to steal a slice of the avocado and takes a little bite. It's adorable. "Mm, right. What about your parents?"

"Not yet. I'll have to tell them at some point, obviously, but I'm still trying to figure out the right time." I grab a bowl out of one of the cabinets and drop the slices of avocado into it, then smush them together with the back of the wooden spoon I've been using to scramble the eggs.

"Yeah, it's big news. You don't want to give anyone a heart attack. Especially since they wouldn't even know I existed until after we were already married."

"Ugh, yeah, I'm not looking forward to it. But it'll be fine. I'm close with my parents, so I'm sure they'll understand, even if they're concerned at first. What about you? Have you told anyone yet?"

Becca shakes her head. "Not a soul."

"Really? Not even your mom?"

"No. We don't talk very often, so it hasn't really come up. She'll probably still be the first I tell though. I mean, it's not like I have a lot of other people to share the news with, you know?"

"Yeah, I get that." I pull a couple plates out of the cabinet and load one up with eggs, a couple pieces of toast, and a fork, then pass it to her. "It's not much, but bon appetit."

"This is really sweet of you, Theo," she says, although she doesn't dig in. She pokes at the eggs with her fork for a few seconds but ends up setting it down on her plate. "You said you're close with your parents. Tell me more about them."

I make my plate before sitting down at the stool next to hers. "Where to start? They've always been my biggest supporters, especially my mom. That can make them a little overbearing sometimes, but I know they mean well, so it doesn't bother me too much anymore."

"They sound lovely. How long have they been together?"

I laugh because I honestly don't know. "Uh, good question. Long enough that I don't think the number matters anymore."

"Is that code for you admitting you don't know?"

"Sure is," I say, and Becca chuckles. She spreads some of the avocado on her toast and takes a little nibble off one corner. She doesn't seem to be eating much, but maybe she's just a slow eater? We definitely don't have that in common, but that's okay.

"You know, they've had their struggles over the years, just like any married couple, but I think they love each other more now than they ever have. It kind of makes me jealous sometimes, especially since it seems to come so easily for them," I say, although I don't know where it's coming from. I've never told anyone that before, even though it's true.

"Why jealous?"

I shrug. "With my lifestyle and always being on the road, it makes it hard to find someone to be with and really keep the connection going. Someone who gets it. So I don't know, sometimes I worry I won't ever find what they have."

"I know the feeling," Becca says, and her gaze drifts off to the side.

"What do you mean?"

"I love my mom, and I know she loves me, but there's a weird sort of distance between us. There always has been, mostly because of the way she can't stop bouncing around. She's always made room for the men in her life, but she hasn't ever done the same for me."

"I'm sorry." I can't imagine how or why anyone wouldn't want to be close to her, but hearing this about her relationship with her mom just makes me feel even more protective of her.

Becca shrugs. "I appreciate it, but it's not your fault. Nothing for you to be sorry about."

"I guess you've lived the roadie lifestyle too, but in a very different way."

"Right. And not by choice. I've watched my mom chase after so many men that never really wanted her and who just ended up breaking her heart. And then I went and did the same damn thing, so at this point, I'm sort of convinced that's all love is. Chasing and heartbreak."

I have to fight the urge to hug her, to tell her all the ways I want to make sure she feels taken care of now, especially since she clearly missed out on that with her mom—and that dickhead Kaplan. My parents never had much money growing up, so we had more than our fair share of struggles, but they always made

123

me feel loved and appreciated, no matter how hard we were struggling.

I can tell from how quiet she's gotten that Becca probably doesn't want to keep talking about this, so I let the silence settle while we eat. She leaves half of her eggs on her plate and only eats one piece of the toast before pushing her plate away. I hope the conversation didn't get so heavy it ruined her appetite.

"So I guess it turns out I'm an even worse cook than I realized, huh?" I joke.

Her eyes widen, and she shakes her head vigorously. "No, no! I'm sorry. It's not that at all. I just... don't have much of an appetite when I've got a lot on my mind, if that makes sense."

"It makes perfect sense." I cock my head at her and grin. "So then why don't we do something to take your mind off all that?"

Becca lifts an eyebrow at me. "Like what? I've had a lot of big surprises lately."

"Nothing bad," I reassure her. "I have a home game tonight, and I was wondering if maybe you'd like to come?"

Her face lights up, excitement blooming across her beautiful features. "Are you kidding? I'd love to!"

Something warm fills my chest. I fucking love how much she loves hockey. "Great. I'll get you a rinkside ticket."

"But what about the rest of the team? Aren't they going to have a million questions?"

"Oh, I'm sure they will, but we can handle that. I mean, assuming it's not too much for you this soon?"

"No. I need a distraction, and a hockey game is just about the best thing I could think of. Plus, it'll be nice to get out and start meeting some new people."

"Awesome. I need to start getting ready for warmup practice before the game, but I'll send you the details on how to get in later. Are you good if I order an Uber to take you to the arena? Your new car won't be delivered until tomorrow."

"Oh." She looks a little flustered at the reminder that I

bought her a car, and she flashes me a shy smile as she says, "That sounds great. It'll give me a chance to learn my way around the city a bit before I start before I start driving myself around."

"Okay, great. Then I'll see you at the arena later tonight?"

"I wouldn't miss it."

~

I'm just about to stuff my phone into my locker room cubby later that day when I get a text from Becca saying she's at the arena.

ME: Awesome, glad you made it. You can come to the family lounge to say hi, if you want.

BECCA: Sure. Where is it again?

I give her the directions, then throw my things into my locker and hurry over to the lounge. We still have a bit of time before the game starts, and I'm glad she got here early. I want to see her before I get out on the ice.

I find Becca hovering near the entrance to the family and friends lounge, looking gorgeous as always. She doesn't see me at first, and I can't help stopping in my tracks and grinning at the sight of her. We're technically married now, but it's still somewhat surreal to see her standing there waiting for me.

But before I can walk over to greet my wife, Maxim Federov strides up to her. He grins, chatting her up like he's at some sort of speed dating event. Becca gives him a polite smile, nodding along with whatever he's saying.

I frown.

She's such a sweet, open-hearted person that she may not even be aware he's hitting on her—but I sure as fuck am. I've seen him flash that same smile at plenty of puck bunnies in bars over the years.

My hands curl into fists, my jaw going tight. It's irrational to be pissed off, seeing as how most of my teammates still don't know Becca and I are an item, much less married. But rational thought can't override the sudden feeling of possessiveness that rises up in me.

I stride over to where the two of them are standing, brushing past Maxim and wrapping an arm around Becca's waist, pulling her tight against me. She shoots me a startled look, but her body melts against mine as if it's an instinctual reaction.

"I see you've met my wife," I say coolly.

Maxim does a double-take, his blond eyebrows shooting up his forehead.

"*Wife?*" He glances between me and Becca. "Shit, I'm so sorry. I had no idea. Uh, congrats?"

"Thanks. Good to see you, princess." I use two fingers to tilt Becca's chin up, then lean down to press a soft kiss to her lips.

Her breath catches a little, her arm wrapping around my back like she's trying to steady herself. The kiss goes on for a heartbeat longer than I meant it to, but I can't seem to pull away. When we finally break apart, her tongue darts out to trace her lower lip like she's tasting me there.

"Thank you for coming to see me play," I tell her, keeping my gaze on her even though I'm well aware of Maxim watching us both curiously.

"Of course," she whispers, her voice a little breathy. "Like I said, I wouldn't miss it."

"Uh, it was nice to meet you, Mrs. Camden," Maxim says, clearing his throat as he backs away. He shoots me an apologetic, slightly confused look, then turns and strides off toward the locker room.

"What was that all about?" Becca asks when we're alone. My arm is still wrapped around her, and as if she realizes that we no longer have an audience to perform for, she slowly steps away from me. I drop my arm, already missing the warmth of her body against mine.

"Most of the rest of the team doesn't know about us yet," I

tell her. "Maxim included. Or at least, he didn't know until now."

"So you were, what? Claiming me?"

She laughs softly, but the grin slips from her face as I nod, my expression serious.

"Oh." She swallows. "You don't have to do that. It's just fake. Just for show."

I close the distance between us, unable to help myself. My fingers come up to toy with a lock of her soft dark hair as I drop my head to meet her gaze. "It may be fake, but there's no way in hell I'm letting any of my teammates hit on you while we're married. If this were real, I would've been out of my mind with jealousy, seeing you smile at another man. Because I'd want every single one of your smiles, princess. Every one of your laughs. All of them."

Her breath hitches, and I realize in a rush that I probably spoke too honestly. But then a small smile tugs at her lips, and she whispers, "As long as we're married, you can have them."

Something warm explodes in my chest at that. I glance around, half hoping that someone else will have entered the lounge to give me an excuse to kiss Becca again as part of our 'married couple' act. But unfortunately, the place is empty.

It's probably just as well. She tastes just as fucking amazing as she did the first time I kissed her, and I need to be doing my best to forget about that fact, rather than giving myself constant reminders.

"I should get back out there," Becca says, breaking the moment of silence between us. She gestures in the direction of the stands. "I want to get a snack before the game."

"Good plan." I nod, releasing her hair and stepping back. "See you out there."

"Okay." She hesitates, then surprises me by throwing her arms around me. "Thank you. Good luck tonight," she whispers into my ear.

"I don't need it. I've already got all the luck I need right here," I say, grinning.

She laughs, the musical sound pouring into my ear. I don't want to let her go, but I've got a game to get ready for, so I press a quick kiss to her cheek before leaving heading back to the locker room to finish getting geared up. Maxim is in there when I enter, and he glances over at me as he laces up his skates.

"So, you tied the knot, huh?"

I nod, aware of several of my teammates glancing our way. I have no doubt that he told all of them the news as soon as he got to the locker room. "Sure did."

"Recently?"

"Yeah, it's new. Very new."

"Damn, I had no idea. Sorry, man. I never would've approached her if I'd known. Are we good?"

I stare him right in the eye to make sure he gets the message. "Yeah. As long as you never hit on my wife again, we'll be totally fine."

Maxim grimaces, clearing his throat uncomfortably as he holds his hands up in a gesture of peace. "Yeah, you got it. I'm not trying to get my ass kicked over something like that. I promise."

My possessiveness surprises even me, because it's not an act. Becca's not really mine, but I still feel responsible for her. And I sure as hell don't want any other men—not even my teammates—hitting on her. Kaplan may not have appreciated what he had, but I know I'm not the only one who sees what a catch she is.

"Forget it," I say, forcing my shoulders to relax. "We're good. Let's just focus on winning this game."

"Now that I can do." Maxim nods and turns his focus back to getting ready.

I try to clear my head while I'm finishing gearing up. There's a lot riding on this game tonight, not least of all my reputation. Noah and the rest of the guys are going to be watching me like a hawk, looking for even the slightest indication that my relationship with Becca really is the distraction they're already convinced it is.

No doubt the team management will be watching me closer now too. Not that I needed the extra scrutiny from them, if the rumors about my contract hold any weight. But I can't focus on any of that right now. All I can do is put one skate in front of the other and make sure that I play like the badass I know I am.

With Becca here, that should be easier than ever. So as my skates meet the ice for our warmup, I immediately scan the stands for her and find her sitting rinkside, right where she belongs. She beams and waves at me, then stands up to take off her coat and show off my jersey she's wearing underneath.

It's all I need.

Chapter 14

Becca

Even with the distance between us and his face shield, I can see Theo beaming back at me. He raises his stick in his gloved hand at me, and my heart gives a little flutter in my chest. I sit back down and watch him take a few warmup laps around his team's side of the ice, getting faster and looser with each lap. It amazes me how naturally he floats across the ice. There's so little friction that it's almost like he's not wearing skates at all.

"You must be Becca!"

A curvy redheaded woman beams at me as she marches toward me with a woman I recognize as Margo, the Aces' social media lead and Noah's fiancée. Margo and I haven't met before, but I remember seeing and hearing about her when the news of her relationship with Noah broke.

"I'm Callie, and this is Margo," the redhead says and throws her arms out at me for a hug.

"Nice to meet you both," I say and hug Callie, then Margo.

I don't know what I expected from the other girlfriends and wives of the team, but I'm sort of surprised they're being so warm and welcoming, especially with how quickly all of this happened for me and Theo.

"I'd say we've heard a lot about you, but that wouldn't be very true," Margo says with a smile when we break. "Anyway, sorry for the ambush, but Theo told us you were coming so we thought we'd find you to properly welcome you to the family."

"Thanks," I say, although it's not enough to describe how grateful I feel. Given my history with Shawn and the abrupt way that Theo and I got married, I kind of assumed the other women would be rude or at the very least distrustful of me for snatching their friend and inserting myself into their space, so it's reassuring to see that isn't the case.

"Is this your first Aces game?" Callie asks as she sits down next to me in the stands.

"Not the first, no. But I used to cheer for the other side when I was at an Aces game," I say, and Margo laughs.

"Yeah, your jersey kind of gives away that you've changed teams. We thought you were trying to keep it more on the downlow."

I shrug. "I mean, we can't keep it a secret from the rest of the team forever, right? Might as well get out in front of it."

I sound much more confident than I feel, but Margo must be buying it because she smiles and nods.

"Spoken like someone who's familiar with how all of this PR stuff works."

"I was with a reality TV star for a couple of years, so I know a thing or two. What about you, Callie? What's your connection to the team?"

"I'm with Reese," she answers, beaming as she finds him out on the ice.

The guys are all taking turns making practice shots at the goalie now, so it's not hard to see who's who. After Reese takes his shot, he swoops around the back side of the goal and blows a kiss to Callie. She catches it and rests it against her heart. It's kind of corny, but it makes me smile, regardless.

Noah's next in line, and Margo watches him with the kind

of look only a woman in love would wear. Surprising no one, Noah sinks the shot, then points his stick right at Margo in the stands and winks at her.

He mouths, "That one's for you," and she calls back, "I love you!"

It's Theo's turn, and he comes barreling down the ice toward Grant, the Aces' goalie, like he's got a thirst for blood. His hands whip back and forward, sending the puck rocketing at Grant like a heat-seeking missile, and although Grant dives to the left to stop it, the puck shoots through his outstretched hands and sinks into the net anyway.

Theo comes to a hard stop by twisting to one side and digging his skates into the ice, showering the Plexiglass barrier with spray. He finds me in the stands and locks eyes with me, making my heart start to race, then skates slowly over to the glass. He kisses his glove, then presses it against the glass.

"Becca, look!" Margo nudges me, pointing up at the gigantic screens that hang above the ice.

The crowd camera is active, and it's zoomed in on my face. I watch myself blush, and I don't know what comes over me, but I kiss my fingertips and press my hand to the glass against his. The cameras catch the whole thing, making it loud and clear to everyone who's watching that he and I are together, but I can barely focus on anything other than the hammering of my pulse in my ears.

Because Theo is claiming me, very publicly, and I don't know how to describe the way that makes me feel.

We stand staring at each other for a few moments, our hands touching through the glass, until Theo finally winks at me and skates away. With my heart still pounding, I return to the stands and find Callie wearing a teasing smile.

"So much for keeping things on the downlow, huh?"

"Yeah, I guess so," I say, and although my neck is hot and flushed, I don't really mind. But I don't have time to linger on it, because a buzzer sounds, announcing the end of warmup, and within minutes, the arena doors open like flood gates and the stands start to overflow with eager fans of both teams racing to their seats.

The Aces leave the ice and I feel adrenaline coursing through me. I can't remember the last time I was genuinely excited to watch a hockey game. With Shawn, I always dreaded them, because no matter if the Prowlers won or lost, he'd find something to complain or agonize about after. And he'd always find some way to blame me for it.

I used to be an Aces fan, years ago. But with their rivalry with the Prowlers, rooting for them in Shawn's presence was basically blasphemy, so I had to give that up quickly. Thinking about it makes me realize just how much I had to give up for Shawn, so many things that were such a big part of who I was.

Knowing I'll never have to do any of that again is the most liberating feeling I've had in years. My future with Theo and in the USA is about as uncertain as it could be, but I'd still much rather be in this situation than spend another second shackled to Shawn.

I realize I don't even know who the Aces are playing against until the other team drifts out onto the ice a few minutes later. I don't recognize their black-and-gold jerseys, but the scoreboard above the ice updates to show an illustrated logo, announcing them as the Vegas Cobras.

The teams line up on the ice and skate past each other, bumping fists in a show of respect for each other and the game, before taking their sides at center ice. There are still fans finding their seats, but for the most part, everyone's settled and eagerly watching the ice, including me. Excitement crackles in my veins at the tension as the guys form up around the referee, waiting for him to drop the puck so they can lunge.

I'm on the edge of my seat watching, and the game hasn't even started yet. We're on the Aces' side of the ice, so I find

Theo exactly where he's supposed to be on the right wing, flanking Noah. Each of the guys looks like they could leap at any second, so when the buzzer sounds and the ref drops the puck, everything becomes a blur that's hard to follow.

I don't see how it happens, but the Aces win the puck, and Noah's already soaring down the ice with it in his possession. Margo lets out a loud whoop beside me and jumps out of her seat to cheer him on. Theo's trailing him, doing his best to stay in the way of the other team and keep the path clear for Noah, and it works.

When he's just a few yards away from the net, Noah swings his stick back in one graceful arc and sends the puck flying, catching the Cobras' goalie off guard. And just like that, the Aces are up one to nothing in a matter of seconds. I leap out of my seat with all the other Aces fans, shouting and losing my mind along with them. The Aces have always been a force to be reckoned with, easily one of the best teams in the league, and they're showing it right off the bat tonight.

I don't know anything about the Cobras, but they'd better wake up quick before they get steamrolled. The teams return to center ice, and this time the Cobras' center takes the puck, but Theo's on him immediately, hounding him all the way down the ice. He's just about to shoulder the guy when he changes direction abruptly and sends Theo soaring past him to crash into the boards.

Theo bounces off them and quickly recovers, and I can tell from the way he's hustling back toward the guy that he's pissed about getting feinted. But the Cobras player must know that Theo is out for blood, because again, just as Theo is about to catch up to him, he sinks a pass to a teammate, soaring the puck just out of Theo's reach. Theo slams the ice with his stick and course corrects.

"He's psyching himself out," I grumble.

"Yeah, he's been having a rough season, the poor guy," Callie shouts over all the noise in the arena.

"What do you mean?"

"I don't know, he's just been sort of..."

"Off his game," Margo finishes for her. "Noah's been worried about him. Not even he's sure what's going on with Theo, but he's concerned."

I don't like the sound of that at all. From what I knew of Theo, he's an incredible player with the reputation to match. So to hear he's been struggling, especially without a clear reason, makes me worry. He's seemed so upbeat and positive since I started spending more time with him, so I don't think there's anything major going on. But then again, I don't exactly know him very well, so he could just as easily be hiding something from me too.

I really hope it doesn't have anything to do with us. I dismiss the thought almost as soon as I hear it in my head, because I know it's stupid. Callie just said that Theo has been having problems all season, so that predates him marrying me. Is that what he meant when he called me his good luck earlier?

Shouting from the fans on the other side of the arena jars me out of my thoughts, and I groan as I see that the Cobras have just scored a goal of their own.

"Maybe they're not as sleepy as I thought," I groan to Margo, and she nods.

"Yeah, it took them a bit to warm up, but they're a good team. They won't make a win easy for our guys, but god, do we need it."

I completely forgot in the whirlwind that has been the last week, but Margo's words remind me that the Aces lost their last game against the Prowlers. Losing to anyone sucks, but losing to your biggest rival is probably one of the most morale-sinking things that could happen to a professional team.

The Cobras and Aces take turns scoring on each other until

the game stands tied three to three in the third period. Both teams aren't skating as fast or as strong as they started, but that's probably because they're getting exhausted. But there's only a about a minute left on the clock, and overtime would be a disaster at this point, so the Aces really need to sink one last goal to end this.

Like he's reading my mind, Theo lunges at the next puck drop and takes it, then blurs down the ice. It reminds me of the way he played against the Prowlers before, the shot he could've made if he'd passed to Noah before Shawn back-checked him.

I'm on my feet without realizing, screaming his name and watching with rising anxiety as he barrels toward the Cobras' goalie. I'm starting to worry he's going to blow right past the net when, at the very last second, he pivots and passes to Maxim, who fires as soon as the puck touches his stick.

He sinks it, and the crowd leaps to their feet, roaring their approval.

The Aces are up four to three with less than thirty seconds on the clock.

Theo might not have scored the goal himself, but there's no denying he probably just won the game for the Aces, so if that doesn't make him feel better, I don't know what will. The fans on our side of the arena are losing their minds, jumping up and down and singing, and I can't help joining them.

This is why I got into hockey in the first place. It's been so long since I felt this way at a game that I completely forgot how much I love it—and how much I've missed it.

Theo immediately finds me in the stands and holds his stick up at me in triumph. He's smiling so widely that his mouthguard is falling out. The crowd camera locks on me again, and even though there are many more eyes on me this time, I care even less. Let them talk.

The remainder of the game passes in a blur, but it doesn't matter. It was over as soon as the Aces scored their last goal, but when the buzzer sounds announcing the end of the game, our side of the arena erupts anyway. Callie, Margo, and I take turns hugging each other, and it strikes me that I can't remember sharing genuine joy after winning a game like this.

"Come on, let's get back to the family and friends lounge," Margo shouts over the noise.

I follow her and Callie outside and through the maze of halls that they seem to know like the backs of their hands to the lounge. There are a few other women who I assume are the wives or girlfriends of the rest of the Aces already there, but they're talking to each other, so we leave them be.

"What a game!" Margo says now that I can actually hear her again. "I really hope they got that winning goal on camera. We're going to loop that shot all over our social media."

"Oh, I'm sure the official feed got it, but even if they didn't, you can take it to the bank that one of the fans in the stands got a clip we can use," Callie says, and Margo nods.

"And what an amazing first game for you to be here, Becca," she adds, smiling at me. "What did you think?"

"I'm speechless, honestly. That was electric. I've always loved hockey, but there's nothing better than a tight game like that to get your blood pumping."

"Right? Our guys played so well tonight. I wonder if this is the start of Theo's turn around? I really hope so."

"Me too," I say, thinking about the rough season they said he's had. If anything would help him course correct, it's a night like this. Who wouldn't feel on top of their game after scoring a winning pass and shot like that?

"Do you want a snack or a drink or anything? It's probably going to be a while before the guys get here, so you're welcome to anything in here," Margo says, pointing at the wall of catered food and drinks beyond us.

"I'm okay for now," I say, keeping my eye on the door.

I can't wait to see Theo, to hear all about that pass he made

—and what he thinks of how things went for our grand debut tonight. But I don't have to wait much longer, because Theo appears just a few minutes later, still wearing his jersey.

I rush over to him to give him a hug. He's still wet after a shower, but I don't care.

"Congratulations!" I say and squeeze him tight. "That pass was so amazing."

Theo chuckles, drawing back a little to look me in the eyes. "See? I told you I had all the luck I needed."

The urge to kiss him swells in me, but I hesitate. The cameras aren't around anymore, and I don't want to overdo it, so I just rub his arms and beam at him instead.

"Guess this means our relationship isn't a secret anymore, huh?"

He laughs and shakes his head. "No, but I'm not mad about it. We wouldn't be able to keep it a secret forever, so we might as well let the whole world know at once, right?"

"That's almost exactly what I said to Callie and Margo. Thanks for roping them into my welcoming committee."

"Oh, they volunteered. They're all dying to get to know you."

"That makes perfect sense. I did kind of come out of nowhere."

"You sure did. Anyway, you ready to get out of here?" he asks, taking my hand in his.

"Are you all done with the press and everything?"

Theo shrugs. "As done as I can be. I'm sure they'll be waiting to ambush us when we leave, especially after tonight, but it's nothing I can't handle. That *we* can't handle."

"Alright. Let's do this."

He raises his eyebrows at me. "You sound so confident."

"It's like you said, everything's going to be fine. And I'm going to have to get used to this at some point, so no time like the present, right?"

"You're full of surprises," he says and uses his free hand to pull my head toward him so he can press a kiss to my forehead. It's a chaste, perfectly innocent gesture, but the feel of his lips on my skin makes my breath hitch a little anyway. "Let's go."

I don't know where we're heading, but I let Theo lead me through a series of doors until we eventually emerge into the cold Denver night. We must have come out of a back door because hardly anyone is there—other than a few smart reporters who must have staked the place out. They're smoking and talking to each other until they spot us. Theo picks up the pace a bit, so I try to match it, but he's hard to keep up with, and the reporters are too quick for us anyway.

"Theo, Theo! Congratulations on the great game tonight. How do you feel?" one of them asks while another aims a camera at us and blinds us with a flood light.

"Outstanding. But I'd feel even better if you just let me get home," Theo answers, grinning at the guy.

"Sure, but one more question for you before we get out of your hair," the reporter says, then looks over his shoulder at the others like he's looking for approval. The camera guy nods, so the reporter faces us again. "Is this your new girlfriend?"

Theo turns his grin on me, making my heart flutter. He raises an eyebrow at me like he's asking for permission, and even though my throat is as dry as the Denver night, I nod.

His grin widens just a little as he announces, "Nope. She's more than just my girlfriend. She's my wife."

"Wife? Whoa, that's a big development. Did you elope?"

"Sorry, but you've already asked your last question," Theo says without looking at the reporter. He keeps his eyes locked on mine, then tilts my chin up using just a finger. His hand drifts up to my face, where he rests it on my cheek, and my head swirls. Theo leans in closer to whisper to me. "If you don't want me to kiss you, stop me right now."

I say nothing, standing there frozen, until his lips find mine.

And then all at once, it's like I come surging back to life. I grip his waist to keep my hands from exploring every other part of his body. He's so brightly illuminated by the camera light that I can barely make out the details of his face, but I can feel them, so intensely that it's dizzying.

All his kisses affect me, but this one, this one's different. When our lips finally part, I'm still soaring, trying my best to catch my breath. But the reporters must be satisfied with the footage they got, because the camera light clicks off, plunging us back into relative darkness, and Theo takes the opportunity to give them the slip.

He leads me to his car, and we're quiet on the whole journey. But as soon as he opens the passenger door for me and I drop inside, I let out the breath I didn't even realize I'd been holding. Theo climbs into the driver's seat and starts the car, and although he's grinning at me, there's a tightness in his eyes. I want to ask what's going on, but he puts the car in reverse and speeds out of the parking lot, probably hoping to put as much distance between us and the reporters as possible.

We drive in silence for a few minutes until finally Theo breaks it.

"Okay, okay. Now that we're alone, you can be honest. You don't have to pretend for the cameras anymore. I know I played like shit tonight. Hell, I've played like shit this whole season. Everyone else knows it too."

I wince because that's not what I was thinking at all. "No, you're amazing! I mean, are you kidding? You helped score the winning goal tonight."

"Yeah, keyword: helped. I didn't score it."

"So what? Your team still won! Doesn't that count for something?"

He sighs and melts into his seat. "No. Not really."

I'm not sure if it's my place to ask, since I'm not actually his wife, but I don't have a clue where all of this is coming from, especially after the amazing kiss we just shared. Theo seemed on top of the world after winning the game, so I can't help wondering if something else is going on.

I decide to risk it. If we're going to be living together, we're going to have to learn to talk to each other about all kinds of things—especially the uncomfortable parts.

"What's been going on with you this season?"

Theo taps the steering wheel with his hand. "Fuck, I wish I knew. Nothing has happened. It's not like I got injured or someone died or anything like that that would make sense. I'm just... off. I'm trying harder, I mean I'm really pushing the hell out of myself, but it's like there's still a wall there or something. It's frustrating as fuck."

Without thinking about it, my hand finds his leg. "I've had struggles like that with dance sometimes."

Theo's eyes dart to mine. "Really?"

"Yeah, definitely. There were times where nothing was wrong, literally nothing. From the outside, it probably seemed to everyone around me like I had it all. A superstar boyfriend, a superstar life in the States, and a role on a TV show. Who wouldn't be jealous of all that?"

He scoffs. "Anyone who knows what an asshole Kaplan is."

I laugh and pat his leg. "Okay, fair. But the point stands. There were still times where I just didn't want to dance at all. The spark wasn't there, and that scared the hell out of me, because if I didn't have dance, then what did I have?"

"That's exactly how I feel! Hockey is my fucking life. So if I can't even do that anymore, then what good am I?"

I knew there had to be more to this than just playing poorly. "Don't say that. There's plenty more that's good about you than just your skills on the ice. This whole situation between us is living proof."

Theo glances over at me, his eyes flashing in the headlights that pass us, but I can see the tension in his shoulders melting with every passing second. Finally, he sighs. "You're right. Thanks for the reality check. I'm sure you don't want to sit and listen to me bitch and complain anyway. I'm sorry."

"No need to be sorry. It's normal to get down on yourself, especially when things aren't going right. I know the feeling. That's all I was trying to say."

He changes hands on the steering wheel to rest one on mine. He strokes the back of my hand with his thumb. "Thank you. I needed that."

"I'm your wife, remember? That's what I'm supposed to do," I say, and Theo beams at me. We fall quiet for the rest of the drive, and his hand never leaves mine. But I'm not complaining, even if I'm starting to get more and more confused about where the line between real and fake in this relationship lies—and if it even matters where the line is.

When we get home, I go to my room to change into something more comfortable. An oversized t-shirt and shorts are the first thing I find in the bags I still haven't fully unpacked, so I slip them on and pad back out into the kitchen to see what Theo's up to and grab a snack since I haven't eaten dinner yet.

Theo is standing at the kitchen island looking through the mail that I brought in for him earlier. He looks up at me, then freezes, his gaze locked on me. The smile that had started to spread across his face drops away as his jaw clenches, and I bite my lip.

Did he get some bad news in the mail?

"Is everything okay?" I ask tentatively after he stares at me in silence for a long moment. "What's wrong?"

"That's a man's shirt. Is it Kaplan's?" he finally asks.

My heart drops into my stomach—because it is. And all at once, I'm crystal clear on what the problem is.

"Oh." I flush, looking down at myself. "Um, yes. I just threw a bunch of stuff in my bag when I was packing up my apartment. I totally forgot he gave this to me, it was a long time ago. I've been wearing it as a sleep shirt for months."

Something flashes through Theo's eyes, and he steps around the kitchen island, striding toward me with an intense look on his face. He doesn't stop until he's standing so close to me that I can see the shadow of stubble on his jawline. My heart hammers in my chest like it's going to burst, and when he takes my hand, I jump slightly.

"I don't like anything that belonged to that prick touching your skin," he says in a low voice.

Heat floods my veins, and I'm viscerally aware of the warmth of his palm against mine.

"What do you want me to do about it?" I ask, and it comes out as a whisper.

"Take it off."

My breath catches. "W-what?"

"Take. It. Off."

I freeze for a heartbeat, my gaze locked with his. I feel like I'm drowning in the depths of his dark green eyes, like the world is tilting wildly beneath us. The command in his voice is undeniable, and I move on instinct, gripping the bottom of the shirt and pulling it up over my head, right here in the kitchen. As soon as it's off, he snatches it out of my hands—and in one powerful movement, he tears it at the side seam, ripping it nearly in two.

Holy shit.

My jaw drops open, an unaccountable rush of heat flooding my veins. Why did that turn me on so much?

We stand in loaded silence, staring at each other from mere inches apart, our breaths mingling between us. Theo's gaze drops from my face, trailing downward for a brief moment, and I can feel his focus like a physical touch. My stomach is a molten pool as my skin prickles with awareness, and I drag in a shallow breath.

One of us needs to break this tension before something happens that we can't take back. Before we cross a line we've already agreed we can't afford to cross ever again.

But I can't move.

I lick my lips, and Theo's gaze darts back up as if drawn by the movement. His nostrils flare, his eyes darkening... and then he takes a slow step backward, holding out the torn shirt to me.

"You'd better go back to your room, princess," he says in a low voice.

"Why?" I whisper.

He swallows, his Adam's apple bobbing. "Like I told you before, I'm not always a gentleman. And right now, I'm not feeling very gentlemanly at all."

My heart feels like it stops as his words wash over me. It takes everything I have not to give in to the maddening desire to pull him toward me, to say to hell with all the rules and crush my lips against his for real this time. But the voice in the back of my head grows steadily louder as reason takes over.

Forcing my reluctant body into motion, I take the shirt from his outstretched hand and slip down the hall back to my room. I drop the tattered fabric on the bed and step into the bathroom, turning the faucet to the coldest temperature possible and holding my hands under the flow of water. I splash it on my face, gasping slightly at the chill, but it's still not enough to put out the fire burning through my veins.

I'm going to need a shower—a freezing one—before bed. Because there's no way in hell I'm going to be able to sleep like this.

I never thought being fake married would be this difficult, I think as I stare at my flushed face in the mirror.

And if tonight is any indication, I don't have a clue how I'm going to make it through two years of this without exploding.

Chapter 15

Theo

I'm staring at Noah through his face shield while we're crouched, our sticks clutched tight, and the fierce look he's giving me in these five-on-five drills would normally get my blood racing, but practice is the furthest thing from my mind right now.

When Coach Dunaway blows his whistle, I'm so distracted that I don't even register the drill has started for a few seconds. Dunaway blows the whistle again to get my attention.

"What the hell are you doing, Camden? Wake up!" he bellows, and although I skate after Noah and the others, my heart isn't in it.

Everywhere I look, the only thing I can see is Becca.

Her cheering me on in the rinkside seats. Her hand on my leg while she talked sense into me. The look of confusion and raw desire she gave me when she tore off her shirt, just like I ordered her to. She didn't even hesitate.

I'm halfway down the ice when I realize that I'm losing focus again, all my blood rushing south at the memory of how she looked in that moment.

"What fucking planet are you on right now, bro?" Noah asks

a few moments later when he comes to a hard stop in front of me, sending shaved ice showering into the air. He waves a hand in front of my face like I've gone blind or something. "It's like you aren't even here."

"Not gonna lie, I kind of wish I wasn't."

Noah's eyes narrow at me, and he scoffs. "No one's forcing you. At this point, practice might go a little smoother if you weren't. So make up your mind. Are you in or out?"

He always knows exactly what to say to motivate me, and this isn't any different. "Don't worry, I'll get it together, Dad."

"Atta boy." Noah snorts, then glides back to center ice for a repeat of the drill.

I don't even know what the point of practicing these starts is anymore. We've all done it thousands of times by now, but Dunaway is convinced that it was the weakest part of our game against the Cobras last week, so it's apparently his new crusade.

When I square up in front of Noah again, both he and Dunaway are watching me. I don't want either of them on my case right now, and I don't want to give them any more reasons to think I'm losing my edge, so I keep my eyes locked on the puck. As soon as the drill starts, I'm on it, slapping the other guys' sticks away and barreling down the ice.

Probably because of how checked out I've been today, none of them saw me coming, so I get a huge head start. And I can tell from the grimace on Grant's face as he tenses up to block my shot that he knows I'm about to give it all I've got.

He's right.

I pull back and swing so hard it hurts, but Grant doesn't even bother trying to block the shot. It would probably take his arm off if he did. Instead, the puck rockets into the net, which barely holds it, so I spin around and hold my stick high.

"That better?" I shout to Noah and Dunaway. They exchange looks, and Noah rips off his helmet, then spits out his mouth guard.

146

"It's a start," he says, and I roll my eyes. Now he's just trying to piss me off, and it's working.

"Alright, I think that's enough for today," Dunaway declares as I'm skating toward Noah. "Let's not overdo it. We've got plenty of time to drill before our next game. Glad to see you've still got some fight left in you, Camden," he says and claps me on the back when I stop near him.

I follow the rest of the guys off the ice and into the locker room. I didn't play the worst I could've today, and Dunaway's comment should probably make me feel better, but the shot I just made feels more like a bandage on a broken arm. One little scrap of praise in practice damn sure doesn't feel like a permanent step in the right direction.

Still, I'll take my wins when and where I can get them.

Everyone showers up, and while I'm getting dressed, Noah strolls over to me. "Good work today," he says, and I have to do a double take because I'm not sure I heard him right.

"What?"

Noah laughs. "You heard me. I mean, it wasn't all great, but that steal and shot you made at the end there made me think maybe you really haven't lost your touch."

"So much for a compliment."

"Hey, it *is* a compliment. But maybe that's the key to getting your groove back. We'll just have to piss you off before every game. Or maybe we can convince the arena crew to broadcast a picture of Kaplan on all the screens. That should do it."

"Very funny." But honestly, as much as I don't want to admit it, it would probably work. Nothing pisses me off more than the sight of that fucker, especially these days.

"I get it. You've got a lot on your plate right now. Which reminds me: how are things with Becca going since she moved in?"

I'm not surprised he's asking, but I am kind of surprised that he seems genuinely curious. "Things are going really well, honestly."

"Yeah?"

"Yeah. She's really sweet, and we get along great. It's actually way easier to be married to her than I thought it would be. Not that I thought it would be a problem, but..." I trail off, and Noah picks right up on it like a bloodhound.

"But what?"

I don't really want to have this conversation right now, but I know my friend means well, and he's one of the few people I could ever share this with anyway. He's still staring at me, waiting for an answer, so I sigh.

"It's just hard to have her in my house, in my living space, with her stuff and her scent everywhere. I swear I'll never get the scent of lavender and vanilla out of my nostrils, and it's addictive as hell. I'm so fucking attracted to her. I guess... I guess I didn't expect it to be this hard."

Noah flashes me a sympathetic smile. "Don't take this the wrong way, but I warned you about that. This whole thing is complicated as hell. You can't really date someone else or anything, and Becca is firmly off limits, so you're in for a long two years of this kind of frustration."

My stomach tightens at the thought of even dating someone else, and that catches me off-guard. Sure, I'm pretty much always turned on with Becca in the house these days, but that doesn't mean I want to just fuck some other woman to take the edge off.

I only want *one* woman.

But I can't have her.

And I know that, and that this is what I signed up for. But that doesn't make it any easier.

Noah claps me on the shoulder. "Sorry, man. I don't envy the blue balls you're gonna have, but you've got this. I have faith in you. What you did for Becca was a really decent thing to do, even if I gave you a bit of shit for it in the beginning."

That wasn't what I expected from him, but I'll take it. "Yeah, you're right. It'll be fine. It has to be."

"You're damn right it does. 'Till death do us part' and all that," he says, leaning against the locker behind him.

My stomach twists again—mostly because I don't actually have any idea how long Becca and I are going to have to fake this. It should be as short as a couple of years, but it could take longer if we want to be extra safe and make sure she'll maintain her residency after the divorce.

"How are your parents taking the news?" Noah asks, cocking his head.

I groan. "Fine, but goddamn do I wish I'd told them before announcing it to the whole world in the press like I did."

"Uh, yeah, that might've been a good idea."

"Yeah, you should've heard my mom when she called the other day. I mean, she was happy for me on the one hand, but she was upset she had to find out that way."

"Can't say I blame her. It probably brought up all kinds of questions."

"You have no idea. She wants me to be happy, so I don't blame her for being skeptical about how fast this happened, but I couldn't bring myself to tell her about the green card thing. I'm not sure she'd understand."

"Well, to be fair, it's a lot for anyone to wrap their head around. But I know you're close with your parents, so I'm sure they'll come around eventually. Assuming you tell them someday."

"I'll have to eventually. I'm just taking my time."

"I bet they'd understand more than you think they would. Anyway, I've gotta get going. Keep this energy up, yeah?"

"I'll try," I say and grin at him. Noah smiles back and leaves me alone in the locker room to finish cleaning myself up. I'm not really sure why, but talking to him makes me feel better, so I leave the arena with a smile on my face and a confidence I haven't felt in a while.

Maybe I need to take my own advice and start believing everything is going to be fine. As easy as it is to buy into the fear that everyone's out to get me right now, I can't. Playing hockey is like riding a bike—once you learn it, you never really forget. So yeah, I might be in a slump right now, but dwelling on it all the time isn't doing anything other than making a self-fulfilling prophecy out of it. The more I let myself get weighed down by all of this, the more likely I'll make it that something bad will happen.

Becca is right. I helped score the winning goal in our last game, and I just left the other guys in my dust on the ice. The only thing in my way is me. And I've got to knock that shit off.

I climb into my car and drive home with the windows cracked just to feel the cold night air on my face. Something about the crisp chill always helps clear my mind. I don't know what Becca is up to, but I don't want to bring home any negativity to her. She has enough of her own to worry about, so she doesn't need my crap piled on top.

And I don't want a repeat of what happened between us the other night, either, so hopefully the cold air will help tamp that down too. This fake marriage thing is already hard enough, and the tension that has been building between us lately isn't helping. I need to get it and myself under control, because the last thing I want is to ruin this. For Becca's sake.

When I walk into the condo, I don't see any sign of her, so I wonder if she's gone out until I remember that I saw her car parked in the garage. So, unless she went for a walk or something, she's here somewhere.

"Becca? I'm home," I call down the hall toward her room, but I get no response.

When I peek around the corner, I see her bedroom door is

wide open, but she's not inside. Then I hear the faint thud of music coming from somewhere in the house.

I follow it back into the kitchen and realize it's coming from the gym, so Becca must be upstairs. I head that way, and the music grows louder. She's blasting some sort of upbeat pop anthem, and hearing it makes me realize that, until now, I didn't have a clue what kind of music she likes. But somehow, this fits her perfectly.

When I reach the doorway of the gym, I stop. Becca is on the far side of the room, where there are several mirrors mounted on the wall. She kicks and spins, her body moving as fluidly and gracefully as water, and I realize she's practicing her dancing.

I shouldn't be watching her like this, but I can't take my eyes off her.

Her movements perfectly match the tempo of the song, and I can't tell if this a routine she's memorized or if she's improvising, but it looks flawless either way.

But then she spots me in the reflection and freezes. Her face flushes immediately, and she drops her arms as she hurries over to her phone, which is sitting on one of the weightlifting benches to stop the music. She must have paired her phone to the speaker system.

"Oh, Theo! Sorry, I didn't know when you'd be home," she says a little breathlessly.

"No need to be sorry. I'm the one walking in on you. I tried to get your attention, but..."

"No, it's fine. There's no way I was going to hear you over that," she says, waving away my apology.

"Well, sorry for interrupting you, but... wow. You're good. Like, *incredibly* good."

Her blush deepens and she waves me away. "I'm not the most amazing dancer technically."

"I'm no expert, but I know a few things about moving your body, and that looked pretty fucking perfect to me."

She blushes at my compliment. "I don't know what happens, but when I'm dancing, everything else just kind of falls away. I get into this flow state. It's like this perfect harmony between my mind and body, like there's no lag at all between my thoughts and my movements. I love feeling that way. Everything else just melts away."

The passion in her voice makes me smile because I know exactly what she means.

"I have the same thing happen when I'm out on the ice sometimes," I admit. "It's like my stick and skates become a part of me, another few limbs or something."

"Exactly!" She beams. "I don't know about you, but I get a kind of tunnel vision when it happens. Like nothing else exists but the next step."

"Yeah, I get that. But for me, it's usually when I'm barreling down the ice toward a goalie like a heat-seeking missile," I say.

She laughs again, her brown eyes bright. "That makes sense." She sits down on the bench and sighs, still catching her breath. "You know, I think dancing and hockey have a lot more in common than most people think."

"Really?" I ask as I step over to the little mini fridge set against one wall and grab her a bottle of water. I always keep it stocked with that and electrolyte drinks for after my workouts.

I hand the bottle to her, and our fingers graze as she takes it. An electric shock seems to shoot up my arm, and I try to shake it off. Every fucking time we touch, I swear I can feel some kind of static charge build between us, but I've been trying to ignore it.

It's hard as hell though.

Becca takes a sip of water, her delicate throat moving as she swallows. I tear my gaze away, suddenly finding the weight rack incredibly interesting.

"You know…"

Her voice draws my attention back to her, and I shoot a glance her way.

"What?" I ask.

She chews her lower lip, recapping the bottle. "I've been thinking about something. You told me the other night that you were in a kind of slump, right? And you didn't really know why."

I blow out a breath, my shoulders slumping a little. I hate that she knows that about me, but at this point, who doesn't?

"Yeah. It's been an issue pretty much all season."

"Well, what if what's missing is that flow state we were just talking about? Like maybe that's the missing piece. You're too distracted to slip into that headspace," she says.

It takes everything I have not to wince at her use of the word 'distracted,' because that's exactly what Noah accused me of being with Becca. But this slump I've been in started long before I married her, so there's no way she's the cause of it.

I shrug. "Could be. That would make a lot of sense."

She hesitates, and I can tell from the look on her face that she wants to says something else but isn't sure if she should.

"What is it?" I ask, keeping my voice gentle. I don't want her to worry about anything she might say.

Her lips pull to one side. "I hate to even ask this, but I feel like I have to. You aren't having problems with hockey because of... because of me, are you?"

My hand darts out to rest on her shoulder, and I give a little squeeze. "No way, princess. Not at all. It was a problem for me way before we started all of this. I really don't know what's behind it, but it's definitely not you, so please don't let that get in your head, okay?"

Becca nods and smiles. "Okay. I believe you." She stands up from the bench, her worried expression morphing into a playful look. "But I have an idea."

"Why don't I like the sound of that?" I cock my head warily, and she laughs.

"Nothing painful, I promise. I just know that when I'm in a rut, sometimes it helps me to try something totally different. We get stuck in routines, you know? And then we get bored, and nothing kills passion like boredom. So why don't you try something new?"

I raise an eyebrow. "That depends on what you have in mind."

She holds out a hand, her brown eyes dancing. "Dance with me."

"Oh, no." I shake my head, making a face. "I give new meaning to the phrase two left feet. You'll lose all respect for me if I even try this."

"I've seen the way you skate. You couldn't suck at this if you tried. Come on, just give it a shot. For me?"

She gazes up at me with a pleading expression on her delicate features, and my heart thuds against my ribs.

Fuck. I don't think she knows this, but I doubt there's a single thing I could deny her when she looks at me like that.

"Okay." I sigh, chuckling under my breath. "I'll try. But whatever happens in this room stays in this room. You promise?"

She motions like she's zipping her lips closed. "Your secrets are safe with me," she vows, then wiggles her outstretched hand at me, so I take it. "Have you ever danced before?"

"I mean, sure, when I'm out at a bar and feeling the music, but I wouldn't exactly call it professional dancing. Not like what you do."

Her musical laugh fills the air. "No way, dancing in bars still counts. *All* kinds of dance are still dance. For today though, we'll start off slow with a step tap."

"A what step?"

"Here, I'll show you."

She drops my hand and stands in front of the mirror with

her feet close together but not touching. She counts down, then moves her left foot to the side, following it with her right, which she taps on the floor gently. She repeats the motion in the opposite direction. It's a simple movement, but somehow, she makes even that look elegant as hell.

"See?" she asks, looking at me expectantly. "Simple. Now you try."

"Fine, but I can't watch myself do this," I say and turn slightly so I won't have to see my reflection in the mirror. Becca laughs while I put my heels together and picture her movements in my mind.

Come on, Camden. You're a professional hockey player, for fuck's sake. You can do this.

I take a deep breath and step to the left, then try to bring my right foot over fluidly, but even without the mirror I can tell I'm moving as stiffly as a piece of wood. Becca steps around behind me and puts her hands on my hips, catching me off guard.

"It's all in the hips. You've gotta loosen them up. Bounce with it a little bit, you know? Otherwise, you look like a tree."

"Ouch."

"Too harsh?"

"I'm a big boy, I can handle it," I say, and glance over my shoulder to find her smiling at me.

"Good. Give it another try, but remember, keep it loose."

I try again, and I can tell from the ease of the motion that I'm doing better this time, but I still feel like an idiot. I can only imagine how awkward I must look. So when Becca snorts after a few seconds, I give up and spin around with my hands thrown up in the air, admitting defeat.

"See, I told you I'm bad at this."

"Yeah, no offense, but I can see why you're a hockey player," she teases, and I burst out laughing.

"Does that mean I'm off the hook?"

Becca pauses to think for a few moments, then shakes her

head. "So maybe the dancing itself isn't your thing, but I have another idea."

I groan. "What now?"

"Be my dance partner. The routine I was working on I usually do with a guy. It's a duo thing, but I obviously can't practice those parts by myself."

"After what you just saw, are you sure that's a good idea?"

Becca laughs. "Don't worry, you don't really need to dance for this part. I just need your strength."

"For what?"

"There's a part where I'll come running to you and jump. You catch me in your arms, then lift me up and spin me around, like this," she says, demonstrating with her hands in the air while she spins. "Think you can handle that?"

I shrug. "One way to find out, I guess."

"Just don't drop me, okay?"

"Never," I say, then get in position farther away from her. She strikes a dramatic pose with her arms flung out to either side.

"Ready?"

"Ready as I'll ever be," I answer, so she counts down, and the next thing I know, she's kicking and spinning toward me, closing the distance until there's only a few feet left between us. Then she jumps, flinging herself at me, and I manage to catch her and lift her, but as we spin together, my feet get tangled up in each other, and we almost go down. But I right us at the last second, and plant her safely back on the ground.

Her chest is pressed against mine, heaving, and I can feel her heartbeat pounding along with mine. She's staring into my eyes, practically smoldering, and I feel a current rippling between us. Her arms drape over my shoulders, and she chews her lip. Being this close, touching her like this, is driving me crazy, and my body is responding.

Becca pulls away abruptly and smooths out her clothes.

"Yup, definitely a hockey player," she says, and we laugh together, breaking the tension. "Thanks for trying anyway."

"Yeah, sure, no problem," I tell her hoarsely. I don't know what else to say, and I can't really think straight through the buzzing in my brain. I'm just glad we didn't get carried away again.

"I'm gonna go catch a shower," Becca says as she gathers her things from the weight bench.

"Okay," I say, and step aside to let her head for the stairs. She's almost at the top when I call back out to her. "Hey, uh, can I ask you a favor?"

She pauses and turns to look down at me with a curious expression. "To quote you, that depends on what it is."

I laugh. "Good one. It's nothing too serious, but I have a gala coming up in a few weeks that I have to go to. And I was wondering if you'd want to come along? You know, to see just how bad of a dancer I really am?"

Becca beams. "I wouldn't miss that for the world," she says, and leaves me standing there with a stupid smile on my face and a pounding heart.

Chapter 16

Becca

The Denver air is crisp, but I love the feeling of it along with the beaming sun on my face. It's been a couple weeks since I moved, and I'm still getting used to things, but the city is starting to feel like home.

It helps that Theo insisted on buying me a bunch of winter clothes since I didn't have many after my time living in LA. If it weren't for that, I wouldn't be taking the daily walks around town that have helped me learn the layout and settle into living here.

Maybe it's some sort of PTSD or something, but feeling the brisk, cutting air makes me realize how much I missed it while living in California. The constantly perfect temperatures in LA were amazing, so I get why the place is so expensive, but that was also part of the reason it never felt like home to me.

My phone buzzes in my coat pocket, so I pull it out, expecting it to be Theo. But it's my mom, speaking of home. I stare at the screen for a few seconds, debating whether to take the call. It's been a while since the last time we talked, and I still haven't told her about the wedding or what's going on with me, so I decide to swipe and answer. No time like the present.

"Hey, Mom."

"How's my American girl?" she asks, and I sigh softly. She's made the same dumb joke every time we've talked since I moved to the States

"Can't complain. I'm out on a walk right now."

"Oh, I bet the weather is just perfect out in LA. I'm jealous. It's freezing up here."

"I don't know, I think it's pretty similar here in Denver," I say and wait for her reaction. The line goes quiet for a few seconds before it clicks in her mind.

"Wait, Denver? I thought you were living in Los Angeles. Are you on vacation or something?"

"You could call it that. But it's more of a permanent vacation."

"That sounds nice," she says, totally unfazed. I guess I shouldn't be surprised—she's never shown much interest in my life—but it still catches me off guard. If this were my daughter in a foreign country telling me something like this, I'd be freaking out.

"What brought you to Denver?"

She obviously hasn't been keeping up with Shawn's reality show. To be fair, I've made a point to avoid it myself, so I'm not sure if he ever aired our breakup, but I'd be shocked if he didn't. Still, even though I know she won't really care, my heart is pounding in my chest as I wrestle with telling her the truth.

"I got married."

"About time! Welcome to the club," she says, and I have to bite back an incredulous laugh.

That's probably easy to say for a woman who falls in and out of love like she's trying on different dinner dresses, but for the rest of us, we usually only try to do it once. Then again, my mom has never really been like most women I know.

"You'll have to tell Shawn congratulations for me," my mom trills.

159

"Um, he's actually not the one I married. We broke up. I'm married to a man named Theo Camden, another hockey player."

"Oh." That seems to take her aback a little, but she bounces back quickly, her voice regaining its usual airiness as she asks, "Did he get you a nice ring?"

I stare down at the ice-blue stone on my left hand and smile, despite knowing she's probably more interested in the cost of the ring than how perfectly it seems to fit me. "Yeah, he really outdid himself."

"Well, I'm glad to hear that. And if he's a hockey player, I'm sure he can take good care of you. So you're on your honeymoon, then?"

While this time with Theo could be called a honeymoon phase, it's not really like that, so I'm not sure how to answer.

"Sort of," I say with a shrug.

There's no real point in going into detail because I'm sure she won't care or remember most of what I'd say. And I'm getting close to the building where I'm scheduled for an interview with a dance company, Curtain Call, so I need to get off the phone.

"Did you need something?" I ask. "Or were you just calling to catch up?"

"No, no, everything's fine here. Just thought I'd say hi and see how the Americans were treating you."

Much better than you ever did, I think, but thankfully manage to keep it to myself.

"Say hi to your new husband for me," she continues. "Tell him I'm looking forward to meeting him sometime."

"Yeah, will do. Talk to you later, Mom," I say, shaking my head slightly. She's been promising to come visit me for years and hasn't made it happen yet.

We say our goodbyes, and I drop my phone back into my pocket, then stand outside the building for a few moments to gather myself. I was in a great, upbeat mood before she called, but she's knocked me off-kilter, as usual. I sigh and shake my head, trying to clear it.

As much as it bothers me that my mom is so checked out and self-absorbed, part of me realizes it's probably easier this way. I couldn't imagine having to handle the reaction of super hands-on parents like Theo's when they found out he's married some random girl they've never met. For me, it was never a worry how my mom would react, so I guess that's the upside and downside of having an absentee parent.

After taking a few more deep breaths, I let it go and walk into the building. The head of the company personally invited me to interview with him after I applied for a position teaching kids how to dance, so I'm assuming that's a good sign, but I'm nervous either way.

There's a directory posted on the wall of the lobby with all the different businesses listed, so I find Curtain Call on the third floor and skip the elevator in favor of the stairs. Hopefully, the little burst of physical activity will help me burn off some of my nerves. I emerge onto the third floor and find a pair of glass doors with the Curtain Call logo etched on them waiting for me.

"Good morning," a blonde woman my age greets me when I step inside. "Are you Becca Summers?"

"Good morning. And yes, I am," I say and offer her my hand to shake. She takes it and gives it a gentle squeeze.

"Great. I'm Caroline, the studio head," she says, and my nerves ratchet back up. I wasn't expecting to meet her right off the bat. "Thanks for coming in. I'm so excited to talk with you."

"Me too. Thank you for the opportunity."

"Come on, I'll give you a tour of the studio while we chat," she says and steps out from behind the front desk to open another set of doors that lead into the actual dance space. It's huge and the warm, polished wooden floors instantly put me at ease. This is the kind of space I'm intimately familiar with, the kind of place I could see myself spending hours in.

"This is the main studio space we have, but there's an overflow studio over this way," Caroline says, pointing to our right. The adjacent studio is a bit smaller than this one, but it's comparable. "Our classes are pretty full, but business has been picking up, so I'm glad we have the space to accommodate all the new students. And hopefully someone with your background to teach them," she adds with a smile.

As much as I hate it, I feel blush blooming on my cheeks. "I would love that."

"Well, you seem like you could be a great fit. What got you into dance?"

"I kind of stumbled into it when I was young, honestly. My family moved around a lot, so most traditional after school stuff wasn't an option for me, but dance was something I could take with me no matter where we were living. And it gave me something to ground myself in when everything else was in motion."

"Sounds a bit similar to my background. Have you taught before?"

"Not formally, no, but I've done a lot of coaching and drills with other students and colleagues in my time."

"That tracks. You've been at this for a long time. But I noticed there was quite a gap in your resume where you weren't dancing for a while," Caroline says, and my heart skips a beat. I figured she'd ask about that at some point, but I've still been dreading the question. "Did that have something to do with your move to the States?" she asks, and I breathe a sigh of relief because that wasn't at all where I was expecting her to go with it.

"Yeah, exactly. I took a bit of a detour where I worked on a TV show for a while, but that didn't pan out, so I'm back to my first true love."

"Ah, the classic Hollywood dream, huh?" Caroline asks with a warm smile, and we laugh.

"It's a hard trap to resist."

"Hey, I get it. We've all got big dreams. But honestly, dancer to dancer, I'm glad to hear you're back in this world. I can already tell that's where your heart really is."

"It's been a while since I've heard anyone say that, so thanks."

"My pleasure. So like I said, we're expanding pretty quickly here. We already have some educational programming going on, but honestly, I don't really know what I'm doing with it. I'm hoping that's where you might come in."

"What are the age ranges you're teaching now?"

"Mostly younger, ages ten and under."

"I was hoping you'd say that. I love working with kids. Something about their excitement and enthusiasm makes me fall in love with dancing all over again."

"I love that. You'd probably be teaching several classes a week, is that something you have the bandwidth for?"

"Definitely. My calendar is wide open right now, so that shouldn't be a problem."

Caroline smiles and nods. "Awesome. Honestly, that's all the questions I had for you. Do you have anything you want to ask me?"

"Well, I do have one thing," I start, watching her face. She raises her eyebrows slightly, showing she's open. "Assuming it goes that far, my residency status won't be a problem, will it?"

"We'll figure it out. You were working in the States before, so it shouldn't be a problem. Maybe just some extra paperwork, but nothing to worry about."

"Great. Well, thank you so much for your time, Caroline," I say and shake her hand again.

"Of course. We'll definitely be in touch," she says and walks me back out to the lobby. "Have a good day."

"Same to you," I say and leave the building with a smile and hope that nothing can take away. Teaching dance is something I've always wanted to do, but I put it off for so long. And all because Shawn never supported me in it. He didn't like me doing anything at all that took my focus off him, and he never understood why I wanted to teach dance rather than be a dancer.

As far as Shawn was concerned, if I wasn't doing the dancing myself, performing and getting all the awards and accolades—and making him look good by extension—then it was pointless. But I've realized what was actually pointless was trying to make him happy.

My phone buzzes in my pocket again, so I pull it out and find a text from Shawn. I laugh because it's like my thoughts summoned him or something. I haven't heard a peep from him since the night we broke up, which is fine by me, but I knew that would have to end eventually.

SHAWN: Is it true? Did you really marry Theo fucking Camden?

I hesitate with my thumbs hovering over the keyboard. They're shaking, and I hate how much power he still has over me, even when he's hundreds of miles away and can't do anything to me anymore. I'm tired of this, of him, and I don't have to put up with any of it.

ME: Yes. But that's none of your business. Because I'm none of your business anymore.

I'm tempted to block him, but something in me tells me not to, so I mute his notifications instead and shove my phone back in my pocket. So much for the smile and hope I thought nothing could take away from me. No one can ruin my mood better than Shawn Kaplan, even when he's removed from my life.

Frustrated, I head back to Theo's condo in a hurry. Maybe a good workout will help me get my head back on straight. I just had a great interview, and I'm ninety percent sure I'm going to get hired. I have to stay focused on everything that's going right for me, not the little things that are going wrong.

But my phone buzzes again. I'm all but convinced it's Shawn using one of his crew's phones to harass me, so I ignore it, knowing that there will probably be a flood of texts and I don't want to read any of them. But they don't come. So by the time I've covered a few more blocks, I pull out my phone while holding my breath, but it isn't Shawn at all. It's Theo.

THEO: How'd the interview go?

I tap to reply right away.

ME: It was amazing! The studio head was really impressed with my background.

THEO: Congrats! I'm sure you'll get it. They'd be crazy not to hire someone like you with your skills and training.

ME: Aww, thanks. I hope you're right!

I hesitate again, thinking about whether I should tell him about the text I got from Shawn. But he seems to have backed off and I don't want to put Theo in a bad mood, so I decide against it. My phone vibrates again, and a picture appears in my thread with Theo. It's a photo of a large, adorable golden retriever with its tongue lolling out and a goofy, happy look on its face.

ME: OMG, he's so cute!

THEO: I'm glad you think so, because I'm adopting him.

ME: WHAT? Seriously?

THEO: Seriously. Didn't you say you always wanted a dog?

I can't believe he remembered that. It was an offhand comment I made that first night after I moved into his loft, so I'm shocked it even registered, let alone that it stuck in his brain enough to do something like this.

ME: I did. But Theo, you don't have to do this. You're spoiling me!

THEO: I keep telling you, princess. I like spoiling you. We'll see you when you get home.

He sends another picture, this time of him kneeling so the dog can jump all over him and lick his face. It's blurry from the action but I can still make it out, and it makes me laugh.

I'm still several blocks away from the condo, so I'm sure he'll beat me back, but I hurry anyway. I still can't believe he got me a dog. Especially after he's already bought me an incredibly expensive ring and a brand new car. As much as Theo calls me a princess, I'm really starting to feel like one.

Half an hour or so later when I let myself into the condo with my key, as soon as the door opens, a golden blur comes charging at me. The dog jumps up, resting its paws on my stomach, and whimpers excitedly.

"Welcome home," Theo calls from the living room where he's standing with a red rubber chew toy in one hand. "I think it's safe to say he likes you."

I scratch the dog's head and laugh at the way his tongue flops everywhere. But true to a dog's chaotic nature, he loses interest and bolts back to Theo, where he jumps up and tries to snatch the chew toy from his hand.

"No, no," Theo warns. "Watch this. Sit!" Instantly, the dog parks on his haunches, staring up at Theo expectantly with his tail and tongue wagging. "Good boy." He drops the toy, and the dog snatches it out of thin air so quickly that I almost miss it. Then he trots over to me to drop the toy at my feet.

"Think he wants to play?"

"Oh, he *definitely* wants to play. Toss it here," Theo says, holding his hands out.

I scoop up the toy and throw it toward him. The dog bounds in his direction and skids to a stop at Theo's feet, then sits and stares up at him again.

"He's learning!" Theo laughs, a warm, happy sound. "I know he seems kind of dopey, but he really is a smart dog."

"If he's already responding to commands like this, that's a great sign. He's definitely not a puppy, but he seems pretty young."

"The vet wasn't sure exactly how old he was since he was a stray, but their best guess is that he's about three years old."

"Poor guy. I wonder if he got lost or separated from his family?"

Theo shrugs and tosses the toy to the other side of the condo, making the dog bolt after it. "No idea. The vet said he just wandered into someone's yard one night, so they brought him in. But he wasn't wearing a collar or microchipped or anything, so they had no way of tracking down his owners. They put up flyers around town and online, but no one claimed him, so they put him up for adoption."

"He definitely seems like he grew up with people though," I say, and Theo nods.

"For sure. I mean, golden retrievers are usually good with people, but you can tell he's used to being around humans. What do you want to name him?" he asks after the dog brings the toy back to him to play tug of war.

I bite my lip, smiling at the fact that Theo wants me to name the dog. It makes it feel more real, like this sweet animal is really mine. Really *ours*.

"What about Milo?"

"I like it." Theo glances down at the retriever, who's currently swinging the toy around in his teeth like a shark. "What do you think, Milo?"

The dog barks loudly, filling the whole condo, and Theo laughs.

"Alright, Milo it is." He pats Milo's head a few times, and I come over to join them.

Milo rolls over onto his side, showing his stomach, so I give him a few tummy rubs. He's so cute it's almost unbearable, and it's impossible to leave him alone. But thankfully, neither of us have anything else going on, so we spend the whole rest of the day playing with him and taking him for a walk around the block.

Between that and the long walk I had earlier back and forth to the dance studio, I'm exhausted by the time we get home. So I tell Theo I'm going to turn in early, pet Milo goodnight, and head to my room. I get into my pajamas before going to wash my face and brush my teeth, then climb into bed and plug my phone in to charge while I spend a few minutes scrolling before I call it a night.

But a red badge on my messages app grabs my attention first. Did I miss a text while I was busy with Milo? Without thinking, I tap into it and my heart crashes into my stomach when I realize it's another message from Shawn. I try to close out of the thread quickly enough that I can't read anything, but not quickly enough.

SHAWN: I always knew you were a gold digger.

The words loop in my head like an annoying pop song I can't shake. I throw my phone down on the bed beside me, roll onto my back, and pull the covers over my head. I was having such a good day, and I don't want to let my shitty ex ruin that.

He's gone, Becca. Don't let him keep living in your head rent free.

I take a series of deep breaths to try and calm myself down, but my heart won't stop hammering, so I roll over to grab my phone and put on one of the sleep playlists I use sometimes when I'm having trouble drifting off. The soothing sound of rain falling in a forest somewhere almost immediately soothes me, so I close my eyes and let it wash over me. I lie there for what feels like hours, tossing and turning to the sound of the rain, and sleep never comes.

But then fear swells in my chest, and I'm running, as fast as my feet will carry me. I don't know who or what I'm running from, but I know that I don't want to be anywhere near them. Even stealing a glance over my shoulder doesn't reveal anything about who or what's chasing me. They're just a terrifying black mass, gaining ground, and for every step I take, they seem to take six.

I just keep running until I'm winded and exhausted and feeling like I'm ready to throw up. And then the ground disappears from beneath me, and as my body lurches over the edge, I jolt awake, sitting bolt upright in bed on the verge of screaming.

"It was a nightmare, Becca. Breathe," I whisper to myself through the tears that are streaming down my face. I've had this nightmare many times before, ever since I was a kid, but it's been years since the last time I had it. And I can't remember the last time it was this vivid.

I don't want to be alone right now. I *can't* be alone right now.

My body is drenched in cold sweat, and the blankets are all tangled up around me. I claw my way out of them because they feel suffocating and constricting, then fumble with my phone to turn off the rain sounds that are still going. It's then that I see it's after two in the morning, so I must have been asleep for a lot longer than I realized.

As soon as I'm free, I pad to the kitchen and onward to the staircase leading to the second floor, but as soon as my foot touches the first step, I freeze. Milo lifts his head from where he's sleeping in the living room, huffing softly as he cocks his head at me.

I shouldn't do this. It's a bad idea for so many reasons, but I'm still scared, and I know I'm not going to be able to feel safe enough to go back to sleep if I can't feel someone breathing near me.

Before I can waffle any further, I charge up the rest of the stairs and push Theo's cracked bedroom door open. As soon as I

169

step inside, he stirs, rolling over to face me. He reaches for a bedside lamp and flips it on, and when he sees my face, he hurries to sit up.

"Jesus, what's wrong? Are you okay?"

"I had a nightmare, and I know this is crazy, but I really need to not be alone right now," I blurt as tears bubble in the back of my throat again. Theo lifts the covers, beckoning me in, and I don't think twice before crawling into bed and entangling myself around him like an intrusive vine. His arms wrap around me, holding me close, and he strokes my back.

"It's okay. The nightmare's over. You're safe here, Becca. You're safe here," he whispers, over and over again. He traces soft circles on my back, and I try to focus on his relaxed, easy breathing to bring my heart rate down. The last of my tears leak out as the fear gradually begins to fade.

I'm a little embarrassed to even be in this situation in the first place, but I'm also grateful I had someone to turn to. This isn't something Shawn ever would've done for me, and I'd forgotten how good it feels to just be held through something intense.

"Are you okay?" Theo whispers, and I nod against his chest, although my heart is still beating a bit faster than I'd like.

"Yeah. Thank you."

"Of course. You're always safe with me."

I'm starting to believe that, so I take a series of deep breaths, and somehow my eyelids start to feel heavy again. And the soothing feel of Theo's fingers running across my back along with the soft pumping of his heart in my ear lulls me back to sleep.

Chapter 17

Theo

I wake up to the feeling of Becca's curly hair tickling my face, filling my nostrils with her sweet smell. My arms are still wrapped around her, and even though my left arm has fallen asleep a little in this position, it's a pleasant tingling. It's not the most comfortable position, but I could stay like this forever.

Feeling her body against mine like this again is stirring other parts of me awake too. Parts of me that have no business waking up. But I don't want to break the moment any sooner than I have to, so I squeeze my eyes shut and will away the images that flash through my mind of the first night we shared together.

But she stirs, thankfully shaking my mind back into the present. I can't see her face, but I sense the exact moment she places where she is. Her entire body tenses, but I rub her back.

"It's okay. Nothing happened," I whisper.

Still, she wiggles out of my grip enough to lift her face up so she can turn toward me a little. Her eyes search mine, and then she lets out a breath, shaking her head before letting it fall against my chest.

"So, uh, what *did* happen last night?" I ask.

"I had a nightmare. A bad one," she mumbles.

"Yeah, I noticed. What was it about? I mean, if you want to talk about it."

Becca sighs but doesn't reply for a few seconds. Finally, she tilts her face back up to mine. "It's a recurring nightmare I've had since I was a little girl. There's this big, black *thing* chasing me, and I run as hard and fast as I can from it, but I never put any distance between us. And it never catches me, either, so I just keep running, totally terrified."

I stroke her arm. "God, that sounds terrible. I'm sorry."

"It is terrible. I feel like I'm having a heart attack every time I wake up from that, but it's been years since I've had that dream."

"Do you think something brought it on then?"

Becca hesitates, then pushes a bunch of her hair out of her face. "Yeah, I guess. But I don't know what."

"What do you think it means? I'm no Carl Jung, but it sure sounds like it's trying to tell you something."

She laughs. "I don't know. But I always had that dream around the times my mom was about to uproot us again for some man she thought she was in love with, so that probably has something to do with it."

Her words are a knife's point pressed right into my heart. I wince because I hate hearing her say that, hate hearing the pain and sadness in her voice. I don't ever want her to feel that way with me, whether our marriage is real or fake. Making sure to keep my touch soothing and gentle, I tuck a lock of hair behind one of her ears.

"You don't deserve to feel that way, Becca. Ever," I say, and tears form in the corners of her eyes. She leans into my touch, and I'm suddenly intensely aware of how close together we're lying. Of all the places where her soft body is pressed against mine. Our eyes stay locked together, and I can't seem to stop stroking her arm as she tugs her lower lip between her teeth. I can't hear her thoughts, but they're practically screaming on her face. She's wrestling with this as much as I am.

Letting her sleep with me was a bad idea, and I knew it as soon as I offered last night. Because the temptation was always going to be there. Like I told her, I'm not always a gentleman, and with her in particular, it's getting harder and harder to control myself. I don't know what it is about her.

She's so close to me that I feel her heart slamming against her ribcage. One of her hands is resting on my chest, just on top of the tiger tattoo she told me she loves so much. The edges of my vision start to darken until she's all I can see, and my body is howling at me to make a move while my brain screams just as loudly to end this before it gets even more problematic than it already is.

But an invisible thread pulls us together, and before either of us knows what's happening, our lips crash. She tastes so incredible that a groan escapes me while my arms tighten around her, pulling her as close as I can possibly get. It's like I want to mold her body to mine, to fuse us together or something.

Her hands are roaming all over my body now, gripping at any inch of skin she can grasp. And when my tongue pushes her lips apart to find hers, my cock pulses with arousal. She doesn't fight me at all, almost like she wants this to happen as badly as I do.

But as quickly as the moment came on, we break. Reality snaps back into place, and we're staring at each other, breathing hard and in disbelief. We both know we shouldn't be doing this, that it's a clear violation of the rules we established at the start. Tension still crackles between us, charging the air and pulling me back in, but somehow, I resist. Somehow.

"I—I should go back to my room," she mutters.

I nod, despite my cock practically screaming at me. "Right."

Becca slips out of my bed quickly, as if she's afraid she'll change her mind if she doesn't move fast enough.

I watch her leave with her lithe, toned body and sleep-mussed hair. She disappears around the corner, and when I hear her footsteps plodding down the stairs, I fall back into bed and press my fists into my eyes.

"Fuck," I groan.

I can't believe I let this happen *again*, especially after the talk I just had with Noah about all of this. Pissed at myself, I shove one hand under the blankets to grip my cock and give it a squeeze, hoping that cutting off the blood flow will speed up the deflation. But it just makes me harder, and I know from experience that there's only one way to take care of a problem like this.

I fling the blankets off and peel away what's left of my clothes on my way to the shower. I don't bother closing the ensuite bathroom door, too focused on the mess of thoughts, emotions, and arousal churning inside me. Despite the winter cold, the water gets hot almost immediately, so I step inside and groan at the feel of the cascading jets hitting my tense body.

But even that isn't enough to distract me from thoughts of Becca, from the way she felt and tasted just now to the things we did together that first night. The images flash through my head like a disconnected film reel, jumping from one scene to another and back again, but all I can see is her and her beautiful body.

And all I can think about are the things I still want to do to her.

My hand finds my aching, swollen cock again and gives it a stroke. I'm so turned on that even one little jerk is electric. I rest my free hand against the tile to steady myself and jerk myself harder and faster, really working myself into it. It doesn't take long for my eyes to squeeze shut and for a familiar tingle to take root in my core.

"Becca," I groan, and a sharp intake of breath makes me jump. I whirl in the shower, nearly slipping on the soaking tile, and find her standing in the doorway to the bathroom. She's rooted in place, her mouth hanging open.

Holy shit. Was she watching me this whole time?

"Sorry, I... I can't find my phone and I thought maybe I left it in here," Becca stammers.

I nod, still gripping myself with my gaze locked on hers. She's not showing any signs of wanting to leave. And she isn't hiding the fact that she's drinking in the sight of me right now, either.

I don't know what comes over me, but I give myself another long, slow stroke and can't fight the groan it draws out of me. Her breath catches in her throat, and it only makes me bolder.

"Do you ever touch yourself while thinking of your husband?" I ask, and Becca's face floods with red. Her teeth capture her lower lip, but she doesn't look away.

Instead, she nods.

"Yes."

Heat courses through me. As much as I wanted to hear her say that, I wasn't sure she would. And now all caution is out the window because there's no turning back. "Do it now. Let me see."

Becca hesitates, looking around the room like someone else might be with us to see. But when she's satisfied no one else is around, she slips a hand inside her loose-fitting sleep shorts and begins moving it in slow circles against herself. So I join her, and she matches her stroking to my rhythm.

We aren't touching each other, and this isn't technically sex, so is it too far? Fuck it. I don't know or care anymore because I couldn't take my eyes off her even if I wanted to—and I definitely don't want to. Judging from the way Becca shoves her shorts and panties down to her ankles, I'm guessing she doesn't either.

She slips two fingers inside herself and lets out a little moan that makes my cock jerk, which she doesn't miss. She licks her lips at the sight, and all I can think about is how much I'd love to feel them wrapped around me. To see her beautiful face looking up at me.

The glass in the shower stall is fogging up, blocking our view, so I shove it open. Steam rolls out into the bathroom toward her, and when it clears, giving her a full look at me, her mouth falls open a little.

I lift my free hand and beckon her closer with my fingers. Again, she hesitates, as if internally warring over whether she should dare get any closer, but eventually she steps out of the tangle of her shorts and panties and moves toward me.

She stops just on the other side of the shower, and she's so close now I can hear her heavy breathing even over the hiss of the water. I stroke myself a few times, nodding at her, and she resumes. Her thumb traces circles around her clit, making her squint.

"That's it, that's my wife. Show me how good this makes you feel," I say, and watch as goosebumps erupt across her soft skin. She reaches out like she's going to rest her hand on my chest and my entire body tenses with anticipation, but she stops just before she reaches me and puts her palm on the foggy glass of the shower. Her head drops to my cock like she's asking me for more, so I pick up my stroking.

"Do you like that?"

"Yes," she hisses.

"Is this how you imagine me when you touch yourself?"

She lets out a long exhale and nods, seeming unable to speak. She drags her palm slowly across her clit, making herself shudder, and hunger swells in me. I'm beyond tempted to pick her up and carry her back to my bed to do all the things and more I've been thinking about.

But I can't. I don't know what will happen if we cross that line again—but that doesn't mean we can't get right up to it.

"How turned on are you?"

Her eyes snap to mine. "*Very*," she whispers, a slight rasp in her voice.

"Fuck. Me too. But I'm not going to come until you do. Can you do that for your husband?"

Becca shivers, her hand writhing against the shower wall. "I can't stop it."

"Then do it. Show me," I say, picking up the speed of my strokes. I want to come with her, at the exact moment she teeters over the edge. We might not be able to share an orgasm like we did that first night, but this is close enough. And after all the tension between us lately, coupled with this incredible moment, my cock is so hard and swollen it hurts. I need the release as badly as I know she does.

Becca puts her fingers in a V-shape around her clit and rubs it between them. Her face is flushed, and her breathing turns erratic and labored while she speeds toward climax. It takes everything I have not to reach out, to slip my fingers inside her to truly push her over the edge. But somehow, I manage to keep my hands to myself—literally and figuratively.

Watching her breathe and please herself makes my cock swell, and I feel my body tense as release builds inside me. Becca gasps and her eyes flutter shut as she pushes a finger into herself. A ragged moan stutters in the back of her throat, and her hips roll against her hand while her legs tremble. She comes with a long, low groan, but she keeps herself standing using the shower wall.

I realize I've stopped breathing, so I gulp down air and turn in the shower as my own orgasm sweeps through me. I spurt into the shower, so much and so hard that my vision goes black. But when I come back into my body, I find my hand resting on the shower wall, matching perfectly against hers.

We stare at our hands, then at each other, and the tension is so thick I can taste it in the air. Becca's looking at me with a hunger in her eyes I don't think I've seen before, and it makes me absolutely fucking crazy. I want to take her back to bed and ravage her, just like the tiger in my tattoo.

We stand there silently, the hiss of the shower filling the silence, unable to look away from each other. This could be more. So much more. My resolve breaks, and I reach for her—but then the doorbell rings.

"Shit!" Becca whispers and darts back to her shorts. "Who's that?"

"I have no idea. I'm not expecting anyone. Maybe it's just a delivery or something?" I guess as I turn off the shower and pad out of the bathroom to the bedroom to find the clothes I'd thrown away in my earlier hurry. But the truth is, I'm not expecting a delivery either, so I don't have a clue what's going on.

I slip on my boxers and a pair of jeans I find draped on the back of the armchair in the corner of the room. "Stay here. I'll handle it." Becca nods as the doorbell rings again, so I rush downstairs. "Alright, alright! Cool it. I'm coming," I shout at the impatient, uninvited guest.

Without peeking through the peep hole, I fling the door open, ready to tear the head off whoever's on the other side. But my two worlds collide and grind to a halt when Becca comes creeping up behind me and sees the same thing I see.

"Uh, hi, Mom and Dad."

Chapter 18

Becca

Oh my god. Oh. My. God.

It's Theo's parents. They're here. My body and brain are still buzzing from the aftershocks of the orgasm I just had, and I'm still reeling from the rule that we bent so far it might as well be broken.

But now here I am, smiling stupidly at my new in-laws as they step into Theo's house. Our house. I do everything I can to keep a stunned expression off my face, but I'm not sure I'm selling it very well. Thankfully, Milo comes barreling into the living room from wherever he was hanging out, distracting everyone.

"Mom, Dad, this is Milo, our new dog." Theo grins as Milo eagerly sniffs his dad's hand before moving on to give his mom the same treatment. "And this is Becca, my wife," he continues, gesturing to me.

Now the spotlight is on me, and I feel a kind of nervousness that even the worst stage fright I've experienced can't compare to.

"It's so nice to meet you, Mrs. Camden," I say as steadily as I can, offering a hand for his mom to shake.

"Please, call me Anne." She smiles at me and reaches for my hand, but she spots my ring and seizes on it instead. "But oh my goodness, your ring is beautiful, Becca!" She takes my hand in hers to lift it up so she can examine the ring closer. She beams at Theo. "You have great taste, sweetie."

"In rings or in women?" he asks, and Anne laughs before she fixes me with her smile again.

"Both."

I had truly no idea what to expect when meeting his parents for the first time—I didn't expect to meet them at all today, to be fair—but getting such a warm reception right off the bat is probably the biggest surprise of all.

Anne's smile fades into a frown. "But I still wish I'd found out from you instead of from the news."

Theo sighs. "I know, I know. I'm sorry, Mom. I just didn't know when the right time to tell you was. I mean, how was I supposed to break this kind of news?"

"Simple. By picking up the phone and telling us," his dad answers, and Theo flushes.

"Right." He clears his throat. "Anyway, no offense, but what are you doing here?"

Anne smiles at me again, still holding my hand. "We came to meet your lovely wife, of course."

Theo raises an eyebrow at her. "And you didn't think *that* warranted a phone call first?"

"We love you, Theo, but you don't exactly have the moral high ground here," his father chides, and Theo frowns at me.

"That's classic John Camden for you," he mutters, and his dad chuckles. "I'm sorry. It all just happened so fast, and I got so caught up in it," he says as he ushers his parents into the living room to take a seat on the leather sofa. I join Theo and Milo on the loveseat across from them.

Theo leaves out the reason *why* we had to move so quickly, but I'm not complaining. I can tell his parents really love him, and although their dynamic might be a little messy, seeing that they care enough to show up unannounced to check in on their son warms my heart. My mom would never do something like that for me.

"The heart works in mysterious ways. We understand that," Anne says as she pats her husband's knee. "So how did you two meet? And please don't tell me it was through hockey."

She seems totally unbothered by the fact that I'm still in my pajamas and Theo's not wearing a shirt, so either she's choosing to ignore it, or she really doesn't have a clue what he and I were just doing.

Thank god.

"Well, it was sort of through hockey. We met after one of my games several months ago," Theo answers.

It's a stretch of the truth, but I'm not about to correct him. As far as I'm concerned, the longer his parents think we've been together, the better. Besides, he knows them and what they'll accept much better than I would, so I'm following his lead.

Because it isn't just the government we have to sell this marriage to.

The realization also stirs up a wave of self-consciousness. What if they don't think I'm good enough for their son?

If I can't win them over, this fake marriage might be doomed before it even starts. I don't know exactly how the process works, but I'm sure the feds will want to talk to our families at some point, so what if Anne and John sink our ship?

"So it was a love at first sight kind of thing?" Anne asks.

"Yeah, definitely," Theo answers quickly, smiling at me as he reaches for my hand. Our fingers link, and it seems to be all Anne needed to hear. She joins him in smiling at me, and tears form in the corner of her eyes.

"Oh, Theo. I'm so happy for you, you have no idea," she says, and it tugs at my heart. She just wants her child to be happy, like any mother would.

Well, *almost* any mother.

I can already tell that I like Anne, which makes me feel awful for lying to her about what's really going on between me and Theo. Hopefully, she won't ever have to find out.

"That makes two of us," John says. "We were starting to worry you'd never settle down again."

Theo laughs. "Wow, thanks for the vote of confidence."

John shrugs. "We can be honest here, can't we? I say it with love."

"Yeah, yeah. I know." Theo chuckles fondly, then glances at the clock on the wall. "You know what? I'm starving. What do you say we go out and get something for breakfast? I've got enough time before practice."

"That sounds great. We had a very early flight, so I didn't have time to eat anything before we left," Anne says and gets up like it's settled.

John doesn't protest, but I hesitate because I need to change my clothes but it's not like I can wander down the hall to my room without raising any questions.

Thankfully, Theo seems to pick up on my problem.

"Well, let us get changed and take Milo out for a quick walk, then we can head out," he says and leads me upstairs to his room. "I'm *so* sorry," he whispers as soon as the door closes. "I really had no idea they were coming."

"It's okay, I gathered that. But what am I going to do about my clothes? I don't want them to know we're not sharing a room."

"Then I guess we're just going to have to fake that for a couple of days too. Lucky for us, we already got a head start."

He smirks a little as he says it, and I feel my cheeks flush again when I think about how we slept together last night. And what we just did in this very room.

"What if they want to stay with us?"

Theo shakes his head. "They won't unless I insist on it.

They've always been respectful about my space, and I'm sure they'll be extra respectful now that you're here."

"Well, that's a relief," I say through a sigh. Theo rests his hands on my arms, just below my shoulders, fixing his eyes on mine.

"Are you sure this is okay, princess? I can tell them you're not feeling well if you want to sit out breakfast."

I shake my head. "No, no. I want to go with you all."

His eyes warm. "Okay. You trust me, right?"

I give him a little smile, the rapid pounding of my heart slowing as our gazes meet. "I wouldn't have married you if I didn't."

"Good. I'll go downstairs and smuggle something from your room for you to wear, then I'll take Milo out while you get ready. Sound good?"

I nod, and he gives my shoulders a squeeze. We break apart, and I try not to watch as he quickly gets dressed. Then he strides toward the door, stopping to turn back to me with his hand resting on the handle.

"Be right back," he promises before he disappears.

I pace the room, unable to stay still while I wait. I don't have any reason to think things won't be fine based on how they've gone so far, but I can't help worrying.

I knew I'd have to meet his parents eventually, but I never dreamed it would be like this. I'm sure I would've felt pressured to win them over no matter how we met, but the pressure really feels like it's on now. The way they showed up unannounced like this also makes me wonder if they're already doubtful about our relationship. And really, who would blame them? Theo is rich and semi-famous, so he's a perfect target for gold diggers.

The thought makes me wince like someone punched all the air out of my lungs—because that's exactly what Shawn called me. But he doesn't know anything about what Theo and I have, and neither does anyone else, so that's all that should matter.

Then again, we seem to be having a hell of a time maintaining the line between what's real and fake lately ourselves.

I can't stand getting lost in my spiral like this, so I decide to do something with my hands while I wait for Theo to come back. I step into the en suite bathroom, run the water in the sink, and splash it against my face repeatedly, until my face is so cold it tingles. I'm toweling off when Theo comes back into the bedroom holding a pair of jeans, a sweater, and my coat.

"It was the best I could do in a hurry," he says. "I hope it's okay."

I can't help but smile, because whether he knows it or not, he grabbed my favorite sweater. "Yeah, this is perfect. Thank you."

"You alright?" he asks, studying me carefully.

I give him a shaky smile. "I'm nervous, but I'll be fine."

"I'm sorry again. Take your time getting ready, I'll keep my parents busy."

"Okay," I say and take the clothes from him.

He hesitates for a second, then leans forward to kiss my forehead.

"You're gonna do great with them. They already like you," he assures me, then heads back downstairs to take Milo outside.

I take his advice and use as much time as I can getting dressed and straightening my bed head. I search every drawer in the bathroom for a brush but come up empty-handed, so I guess it's going to be my fingers doing the work.

I check my reflection in the mirror, decide I look presentable enough, and leave the bathroom. Just as my feet touch the stairs, I hear Theo come back inside with Milo, who barks their arrival. I hover at the top of the staircase, listening to Theo talking to his parents about where to go to eat, and can't help feeling like the outsider I am.

"You ready?" Theo calls up when he notices my feet on the stairs.

I jump a little at having been caught eavesdropping, then hurry down the steps. "Yup! Coming!"

We leave the condo and pile into Theo's car, and he rests his hand on my leg as he puts the car in drive. I smile at him and place my hand on his, then catch Anne beaming at us in the rearview mirror.

"There's a great local place nearby called Daybreak Diner," Theo says to the whole car. "I'm pretty sure I've taken you guys there once before."

"It sounds familiar, but I can't remember. My memory isn't what it used to be," John says, and Anne rolls her eyes, chuckling. It must be a running joke between them.

"Well, I've never been, so let's just pretend it's new for all of us then," I say, and Theo's smile widens as he nods in approval.

When we get to the restaurant a few minutes later, I realize it's not some hole-in-the-wall diner like the name suggests. It's an upper-end, hipster kind of place with rustic, barnyard-meets-converted-warehouse aesthetics. And when I'm seated next to Theo in a booth with a menu, I can't help noticing all the call-outs to farm fresh, non-GMO ingredients.

"It's starting to come back to me now," John says as he looks around the restaurant. "I think it was several years ago, but I remember this place."

"Yeah, it's been a minute since we were here, Dad," Theo says. The waitress arrives, and Theo orders a round of coffees for everyone. When she's gone, Anne turns her focus back to me.

"So, tell us a little bit more about yourself, Becca."

Suddenly, I feel like I'm on a job interview. And I guess in some ways, I am. I laugh nervously, unsure where to start. "Well, what would you like to know?"

"Theo told us you're Canadian. What brought you to the States?"

That's a much more loaded question than she realizes, and I don't know how to answer it. Thankfully, Theo steps in.

"Her incredible dancing talent," he says, patting my leg under the table. "Seriously, she's got moves. She makes me look like a two-by-four in comparison."

"Please." I laugh.

"No, really. Tell them about our little dance lesson the other night."

I'm assuming he means for me to leave out the part where we almost tore each other's clothes off again, so I tell his parents about his two left feet and leave it at that.

"He's just like his father in that regard," Anne says with a smile. "A real handy man around the house, but absolutely hopeless on the dance floor."

John laughs and shrugs. "What can I say? We Camdens aren't dancers."

I like keeping the focus off me, so I stay there. "Oh really?" I grin, glancing between Theo and his dad. "What else do I need to know about the Camdens?"

"They can be incredibly hardheaded," Anne answers immediately, and Theo and John laugh. "And their scrappiness seems to run in the family too," she adds.

I laugh softly, nodding. Based on what I've seen of his time on the ice, I'm not surprised to hear that Theo has always been a fighter.

"Damn, Mom, you make us sound like a mafia family or something," Theo says. "I mean, sure, I got into my fair share of fights in school, but it didn't happen *that* often."

Anne lifts an eyebrow at her son. "Theo, you know I love you, but I lost count of the number of times I had to pick you up from the principal's office for getting into a fight with some boy or other who was twice as big as you, just because they were picking on some other kid."

"Oh my god," Theo groans, covering his face. But I think it's cute. Everyone has embarrassing childhood stories with their family that they'd sooner die than share, so I appreciate the Camdens bringing me in like this.

Theo lowers his hands. "To be fair, if you had a bunch of rich little snobs always looking down their noses at you, you'd probably want to break a few of them too."

"You did have a rough time adjusting when we moved," Anne agrees, and I gather that the Camdens weren't exactly rich themselves back then. So, Theo probably had a lot to prove.

"But you found your place, eventually. I was worried for a while you'd make an enemy out of every kid in town, but your good heart won out in the end. That's another Camden thing: a tough exterior hiding a big, mushy heart," Anne says, looking at me.

"I've definitely seen that already." I grin at Theo, and he smiles back, making my heart swell. Not that I have a healthy model to compare it to, but it seems to me like this is how a family is supposed to be: loving, but unafraid to acknowledge each other's shortcomings.

So maybe I'm not as much of an outsider in this family or with Theo as I thought. The thought reminds me that I never had anything like this growing up, but I don't know how to feel about that either because it makes me feel even closer to Theo. Like he's really welcoming me into his family. But this is all supposed to be fake, so where does that leave us?

The waitress returns during the break in conversation, sparing me from my thoughts. We order food and have some more idle talk while we wait, but the topics stay light. Apparently, Anne and John are planning a trip to Canada sometime next year, so I give them some tips on places to see and places to avoid.

After we finish eating, Theo checks his phone for the time. "Shit, sorry to eat and run, but I've gotta get to practice." His expression brightens. "Hey, you know what? Why don't you all come with me to watch?"

Anne turns to John. "What do you think? Are you up for that?"

Her husband's face lights up like a hockey arena. "Oh, absolutely. It's been way too long since I've seen my boy play."

His voice is full of pride, and Theo blushes as he tosses a stack of cash on the table to cover the bill. "Alright, then let's get a move on."

"You really don't have to pay for us," Anne argues, but he waves her away.

"Are you kidding? I want to. I like taking care of you," Theo says, echoing something he's said to me more than once.

We slide out of the booth we're sharing and pile back into the car. Theo stops by the loft to grab his gear quickly, and when we get to the practice arena, he makes sure we're settled in rink side seats before striding off to change.

Anne sits to my left, with John to hers. I'm not sure what to say to either of them, and I've never been particularly good at small talk, so I ask the only thing I can think of. "Is this your first time at the arena?"

Anne shakes her head. "No, we've been several times over the years. We love seeing Theo play. But it's been a little while since we've watched a practice."

The Aces appear on the ice a few minutes later. They start by doing laps around the ice as a warmup, and each time Theo passes us, he finds me and beams. When he does it on the last lap, Anne laughs and leans over.

"I think I understand why you two got married so quickly now," she murmurs.

I blink in surprise at that. "Really? Why?"

"Well, don't take this the wrong way, but John and I were a little worried after hearing that Theo had gotten married so unexpectedly, especially after the way his first marriage fell apart," she says. I don't really know what she means since I haven't gotten the story on that yet, but I let her keep talking. "But now that we've met you, and now that I've seen the way Theo looks at you, it makes so much more sense."

"How does he look at me?"

My voice drops a little as I ask the question. I'm almost afraid to hear the answer. Not because I don't want to hear it, but because of what it might mean, and how it might change things.

Anne's eyes warm as she smiles softly at me. "Like he can see his future when he looks at you. And I can tell he thinks it's bright."

It's a good thing I'm seated because I feel faint. The Aces glide across the ice, and the arena spins around me. And when Theo finds me again, he blows me a kiss that makes my overactive heart double its pounding.

Because Theo sees me in his future.

Chapter 19

Theo

After practice, Mom insists on taking Becca out for "girl time." I wasn't sure Becca was ready for one-on-one time with my mom, who is well meaning but intense sometimes. But Becca promised me she could handle it, and even seemed excited about spending time with my mom, so I didn't really have a choice. I did offer to come and bail her out if she needed it though.

I just hope Mom doesn't share even more of my embarrassing childhood stories with her. God knows there are plenty of them.

"Hey, where'd you go?" Dad asks, stirring me back into the present. We're down in the workout room installing more full-length wall mirrors and lighting I ordered as a surprise for Becca. I realized after watching her dance in here that it wasn't exactly the most inviting space for that, and the girls being out of the house for a while gave us the perfect chance to put everything together.

"Sorry, just got a lot on my mind."

Dad turns from the screw he's tightening to smile at me,

nearly dropping the other screw he holds between his teeth. "Can't say I'm surprised to hear that."

"Meaning?"

"Here, come hold this still for me, please," he says, so I hurry over to hold up the bottom edge of the mirror he's working on. He finishes screwing it in place, then dusts off his hands on his pants. "I don't mean anything by it other than I'm sure you have a lot on your mind. I like Becca. She seems smart and sweet."

"Why do I sense a very big 'but' coming?"

Dad laughs. "You always had a way with words. Like I said, Becca seems very sweet, and I really do like her. I just hope you're being smart with all of this."

"Again, what does that mean?"

Dad sighs. "There's no way to say this that won't piss you off, so I'm just gonna say it. You rushed into your last marriage too."

I can't help wincing. He's right, but that doesn't mean he has to say it. "I *am* being smart, Dad." I stop just short of telling him exactly what "being smart" means in this situation, about how all of this isn't exactly real. The truth will have to come out eventually, but now's not the right time.

Then again, I'm not sure there will ever actually be a "right" time. Things between Becca and I have been so confusing lately. What's real, and what's fake? It's getting harder and harder to tell the difference, and as Dad and I install all of this stuff for her dance practice, the question bubbles up all over again.

"Okay, okay. I trust you," Dad says with his hands in the air. "You're a grown man, you can make your own decisions. I'm just your dad, so it's normal for me to worry. I don't want to see you get hurt."

"I know."

I don't blame my parents for worrying, especially after the way things went with my last marriage. Really, I don't. But

Becca is about as different from my ex as anyone could be, and this situation between us is completely different too. It's just going to take time for them to see it.

Milo barks upstairs, signaling that the girls have come home already, and a few seconds later I hear them walking around. I hear shopping bags crinkling too, which makes me smile. If Mom wants to go shopping with someone, that means they're already on her good list. But I hope Mom didn't give Becca the third degree while they were alone.

The two of them appear at the top of the stairs, Becca first. "We're home!" she calls down to us. Milo charges past her and comes bounding down the stairs, panting and with his tongue lolling. Dad laughs and scratches his head.

"Who's a good boy?" he says in a baby voice, and Milo barks. It doesn't surprise me in the least that Milo's most bonded with Dad already. My dad has always been a dog kind of guy, but Mom would never let him get another one after my childhood dog passed away. She didn't want to go through the pain of losing a pet again.

"So how'd it go?" I ask Becca and give her a hug when she reaches me, but she's already looking at the mirrors Dad and I installed.

"Is this for me?" she asks, looking around the room.

"It is. We aren't quite finished yet—still have some overhead lighting to install—but that's probably a project for another day," Dad answers, and Becca starts to tear up.

"Yes. We've taken up enough of your time today, so we should probably get going and let you two have some time alone," Mom says.

"Wait, going where?" I ask.

"We got a hotel room downtown," Dad answers. "And before you ask, don't worry about us getting there. We'll call a cab." He smiles and gives me a hug.

"Are you sure? I really don't mind driving you over."

"Positive. But thanks for the offer. Maybe we'll finish this up tomorrow? We'll be in town for a few days."

"Yeah, sure. Thank you for the help."

"Of course. Anytime." He hugs me again, then lets Mom do the same.

"Love you guys."

"We love you too, sweetie. Have a good night," Mom says and leads Dad back upstairs. Milo bounds after them, leaving Becca and I alone. When she hears the door at the top of the stairs click closed, she turns to me with tears in her eyes.

"I can't believe you did this for me," she whispers.

"Well, it was kind of a dungeon down here before, and I know it's important for you to be able to see yourself while you're practicing, so it just made sense."

Becca laughs and hugs me. "You're underselling yourself. Thank you. This means a lot."

"Anything for my wife. But look, I made some more room for you too," I say, gesturing at where the bench press used to be. There were already hardwood floors underneath that section of the gym, so Dad and I pulled up the mats that were there to give Becca a larger dancing area. "We're going to install the lighting above that area."

"Thank you. I can't say it enough." She takes a little tour of the practice space we're making for her and does a spin in the mirrors. I don't know how she does it, but she makes something even that basic look elegant and effortless. "Sorry. I'm just imagining the lighting here."

"No need to apologize. Soak it up," I say with a grin. "The spotlight is yours, princess. Even my parents think so."

"Really?"

"Oh, god, yeah. My mom and dad are terrible at keeping their thoughts to themselves. They both love you. My mom wouldn't have taken you out shopping with her if she didn't. That's an Anne Camden rite of passage."

She blushes, despite the beaming smile that appears on her face. "Well, I hope I passed."

"With flying colors."

"I hope so. I really do. I mean, I know all of this is fake, but I still want them to like me."

I know she didn't mean for it to, but that stings. Because she's right. It *is* supposed to be fake, and temporary. As much as I keep trying to avoid it, it seems like I can't stop bumping up against this elephant in the room.

"I still haven't told them," I admit, and Becca watches me carefully.

"I understand. It's not like it would be the easiest conversation in the world."

"No, it wouldn't be. I think they'd understand. Hell, they'd probably even be supportive."

"Then why don't you just tell them?"

I hesitate, looking Becca in the eyes. The truth is simple, but I'm not sure sharing it is the right idea, especially as we keep teetering on the edge between real and fake. I don't want to complicate things any more than they already are, but I owe her the truth.

"Honestly, I don't want my parents to judge you for a choice that I made," I finally say, and Becca seems to tense. "I really don't think they will, but I can't be sure. And I don't want to expose you to that when you already have so much else going on."

Becca shrugs. "I get it. You're rich and famous, so if I were them, I'd be kind of paranoid about that too. I just hope that when we eventually get divorced, they won't hate me like they seem to hate your ex," she says, and my heart sinks both because I'm not looking forward to that day, and because she'd even think to compare herself to my ex.

I take her by the wrist, gently but assertively, and lock eyes with her. She tries to look away, but I squeeze her hand, bringing her gaze back to mine. "Listen to me. You are *nothing* like her. Do you understand?" I feel her pulse quicken in my grip, and she licks her lower lip before she nods.

And I have to remind myself, for at least the tenth time today, that this is all fake.

Because it's starting to feel more and more like it isn't.

Chapter 20

Becca

Over the next few days, I spend more time with Theo's parents than I think I've ever spent with my mom. Not that that's saying much. Anne and I go shopping—mostly to help stock Theo's empty fridge—while Theo and John continue working on the improvements to the home gym. We catch an Aces game while they're in town too.

I'm having a great time getting to know them. But every day when we get together, I have to remind myself that none of this is real. That as much as I like them, and as much as they seem to like me, I can't get used to it. One day, years from now when all of this is over, they'll know the truth and I'll be gone. Because there's an expiration on this little fantasy we're living. We might not have a specific date yet, but it's coming.

So I shouldn't get attached—to Theo or his parents—but it's so much easier to say than do.

Thankfully, they decided not to stay with us just like Theo said they would, so he and I haven't had to keep up the charade that we're sharing a bed. I would probably have exploded by now if we had to do that. And every time I think about what we were doing when his parents showed up unannounced, my face

196

burns. We weren't just flirting with the line of what's acceptable. We sailed right past it.

In some merciful way, having his parents around has forced us to check ourselves. To get back in bounds and reestablish the rules. Which is good because we definitely needed a course correction.

"Everything okay, sweetie?" Anne asks me as she hovers near Theo's front door. It's their final day in town, and they stopped by one last time before heading to the airport to say goodbye.

"Yeah, it's just... bittersweet to see you go," I whisper, and Anne beams at me. She hurries over to throw her arms around me and squeezes me close.

"Oh, honey, I feel the same. It's been so nice getting to know you. Welcome to the family," she says into my ear, and my heart clenches.

She might as well have pressed a knife into my chest, although she doesn't know it. It's both the sweetest and most painful thing anyone has said to me in a long time.

"Thank you." I wipe my eyes with the back of my hand when we part, and John chuckles as he puts an arm around Anne's waist.

"Well, before this turns into a trip to waterworks, let's get going, dear." He holds one arm out to me, beckoning me in, and the two of them pull me in for one last hug. "It really was nice to meet you, kiddo. Enjoy your new practice space. Theo chose well," he says, flashing a wink at Theo, who's standing behind me and petting Milo's head.

"Thanks, Dad. Hope you had a good trip."

"Any time I get to see my son play hockey is a good trip," he says, then gives Theo a hug too. Theo walks them to the door with Milo on his heels.

"Are you sure you don't want me to drive you to the airport? I really don't mind."

John pulls out his phone, waving the screen at us. "The Uber is already around the corner. But thanks for the offer." Milo mistakes the phone for a toy and barks at John, so he pats the dog and laughs. "Goodbye to you too, buddy."

"Alright, well, have a safe flight. Text or call me when you land, okay?"

"Of course. Love you, son."

"Love you too." Theo opens the door for them, and I wave as they leave. When the door's closed, Theo turns to me, and there's something on his face that I can't quite place. But he replaces it with that grin of his. "Thanks for being so willing to spend time with my parents. I'm sure that wasn't easy."

"Are you kidding? I was happy to," I say, and I mean it. A question forms on the tip of my tongue, and I know I probably shouldn't ask it, but I can't help myself. "Was Valerie not into that?"

Theo grimaces at the mention of his ex's name. "She didn't get along well with my parents, to be honest."

"Really? I don't know how. They're great."

"I mean, I know I'm biased, but I agree. But that was the thing with her. She wasn't who any of us thought she was," he says as he flops down on the couch. Milo jumps up and rests his head in Theo's lap, making him laugh. I join them, keeping an eye on Theo.

"We don't have to talk about this if you don't want to, obviously, but what exactly happened with Valerie?"

"Does it really matter?"

I shrug. "I guess not in the grand scheme of things, but I'm your current wife, so I feel like I should know. Especially if your mom is going to keep bringing her up."

Theo sighs. "Leave it to Mom. Yeah, you're right. Valerie and I met just as my hockey career was taking off. I was on top of the world, and I had blinders on. Thick ass ones. She seemed so perfect on paper, and I was riding so high that I overlooked all the red flags."

"Then why did you marry her?"

He chuckles dryly. "I've asked myself that question more times than I can count. Honestly? I don't know why. It just seemed like the thing to do, just like everyone else I knew. I mean, I loved her... or at least I thought I did. But that was before I knew what that word really meant."

"Did she cheat on you or something?"

"No, no. It wasn't anything dramatic like that. We had good chemistry, and I was young and dumb enough that I thought that would be enough to carry a marriage. But after the honey-moon period ended, I realized quickly that we had nothing in common. She loved the *idea* of being married to a professional hockey player a lot more than the realities of it, and we didn't really want the same things. We tried to make it work for a while, but everything went to shit so fast."

"I'm sorry."

Theo laughs again, patting Milo's head. "Don't be. I'm not. If we hadn't split up, I wouldn't be here with you and the puppo right now."

Milo barks like he's agreeing, and I smile.

A while back, Theo told me that he wasn't interested in trying to find love after his divorce. I didn't really get it at the time, but I'm starting to understand now. He rushed things with Valerie before he really knew her, and finding out who she really was the hard way must have made it hard for him to trust anyone enough to let them in again.

I know the feeling.

"Thanks for telling me. I really do like your parents, you know," I say, changing the subject. Theo's smile returns, and he sits up a little straighter on the couch.

"Yeah?"

"Yeah. I'm glad I got to meet them, even if it was a surprise." Theo's smile widens, but I leave out the part about how it reminds me of the mother-daughter bond I know I'll never have with my mom. Or the same bond I'll never have with my own daughter.

"I'm glad it went well too. Not that I was worried. You're amazing and so are my parents, so it was kind of a no-brainer."

"Easy for you to say. You weren't the one in the hot seat all week," I say, and Theo laughs.

"Fair. But speaking of being in the hotseat, we've got the gala tonight, remember? You'd probably better start getting ready."

Shit. With his parents showing up unexpectedly, I'd completely forgotten about him asking me to go tonight. "Please don't hate me, but I totally forgot. And I don't think I have anything to wear tonight."

Theo leans over to pat my hand. "Yes, you do."

"Oh, so you know my wardrobe better than I do?" I tease, and he smirks.

"Why don't you go to your room and see for yourself?"

~

I can barely believe my eyes when I step into my room and find an understated but no less immaculate, expensive sapphire cocktail dress spread out on my bed. A simple, small bow serves as the center piece, offset to the left of the stomach area. Just from looking at it, I can tell it's the perfect size, but I don't know how he figured that out. Did he go looking through my clothes or something?

Then it hits me: Anne. Of course it was her. She helped me pick out and try on all kinds of things while we were shopping, and I was too oblivious to realize that she and Theo were up to something until now. I check the time on my phone and cringe when I notice I only have about an hour to get ready before we have to leave.

There's no time like the present, so I scoop the dress off the bed and hurry to the bathroom to peel off the rest of my clothes and shower quickly. I do my makeup in a rush, trying to match the shades of blue on my eyes to the dress. After, the dress slides up over my clean legs and hips, slipping comfortably onto my body like a second skin. I shimmy my arms into the sleeves, then turn to look at myself in the mirror and almost start crying because I can't remember the last time I looked—or felt—this good. I have no idea where Theo found this dress or how he knew it would be so perfect, but it is.

A soft knock on the door startles me. "Becca? Are you okay?"

"Yeah, I'm fine. But can you help me zip up?" I ask as I open the door. Theo takes one look at me and steps backward, his eyes wide. Something flashes in them, a heat I'm starting to feel way too familiar with, and I feel my face burning.

"You look fucking amazing," he whispers, his gaze raking over me.

My heart skips a beat in my chest, and I turn around so that he can help me with the zipper. I watch his hands reach out in the mirror, and my breath catches as his fingers graze my bare skin before gripping the zipper. I can see his Adam's apple bob in his reflection, and the air in the room seems to thicken so much that it's hard to breathe.

"Thank you," I whisper as he finishes dragging the zipper up.

He nods, a muscle in his jaw working as he steps back. He looks incredible too. Although I've seen him dressed up in suits plenty of times before games, he went all out tonight, wearing a perfectly tailored dark blue suit that I've never seen before.

I don't know what to do with the overwhelming tension

between us, so I pretend I can't feel it, putting on a bright smile as I do a little spin to show him the full effect.

"What do you think? Am I gala worthy?"

"Are you kidding? You could be a gallery of your own." His gaze lingers on my face for a long moment, and then he clears his throat and glances away. "But you forgot something."

He holds up a hand, then disappears down the hall to my room. I have no idea what he's going after until he reappears a few seconds later and holds out his hand. My breath hitches as I see my wedding ring glinting on his palm.

"Oh. Right."

I hold out my hand, which only shakes a little as he slips the ring on my finger for me. Even though he's done this before, it still feels loaded with meaning, and he holds my hand in his for a lingering moment after my ring is on. Then he nods and releases it.

"Now it's perfect," he murmurs, a small smile curving his lips as he looks at the ring on my finger. "Ready to go?"

I nod. "As ready as I'll ever be."

The truth is, I don't have a clue what to expect at this thing. I've been to plenty of fancy events in my time with Shawn, but I was always more of an accessory to him than a feature, so I usually just sat around sipping champagne and smiling for the cameras—because there were always cameras.

I slip the heels and coat on, and we take turns petting Milo goodbye, then head to the car. Theo drives toward downtown and I realize I don't even know where the event is being held until we arrive at a super ritzy hotel. I can't tell if it's as old as it looks or just designed to come across that way, but it's stunning.

Theo pulls up to the valet parking area and puts the car in park but doesn't get out. Instead, he reaches for my hand. "Don't be nervous. You're gonna be great."

"Thanks. I'll follow your lead."

Theo nods and climbs out of the car, so I do too. It's chilly but bearable, and dozens of people in some of the most expensive looking clothes I've ever seen are milling around the grand staircase that serves as the entrance to the hotel. There's even a red carpet! I stand stunned taking it all in until Theo loops his arm through mine. He smiles and leads me confidently up the stairs like he's done this a million times—he probably has—but when we reach the top, cameras blind me as they flash repeatedly in my face.

"Theo! Mr. Camden! Do you have a minute to talk?" a reporter I can't see through the dancing spots in my eyes asks.

I don't know why, but it didn't occur to me that the press would be here tonight, so my body tenses. Putting on an act for rich people is one thing, but realizing I'll be doing it under the microscope of the paparazzi is a whole different game.

But Theo puts his hand on the small of my back, and I take a deep breath.

"We've got this," he whispers in my ear, then ushers me closer to the reporter, who's finally starting to swim into view now that the camera flashes have stopped popping.

The poor guy is young and about as tall as me, and the tuxedo he's wearing is wrinkled and at least a size too big. The deer-in-the-headlights look on his face gives me the impression he's fresh out of college and can't believe Theo is talking to him.

"T-thank you for your time, Mr. Camden. How are you feeling about this season so far?"

Theo straightens his tux jacket confidently and flashes that camera-ready grin of his. "Fantastic, thanks for asking. But listen, boys, there'll be plenty of time to talk shop later. I need to make the rounds, so if you'll excuse us," he says, ready to leave the reporters shouting after us. And they do.

"Congratulations on your marriage, Mr. Camden!" the reporter shouts, and Theo grins at me.

I laugh breathlessly, still having a hard time accepting all of this is real. Not that long ago, I was convinced I was trapped in a dead-end relationship with a deadbeat guy because it was the only way I could keep living in the States. But now here I am literally walking the red carpet with one of the biggest names in the NHL.

And people are noticing. I see their eyes lock on and follow me as we work our way into the hotel's ballroom and hand our coats to an attendant at the door. I'm sure they're talking about us behind our backs, but I couldn't care less. They don't have a clue what's really going on here, and that's exactly how we want it.

"Want a drink?" Theo asks over the soft jazz music playing throughout the room as he spots a waiter carrying a tray of champagne nearby.

"I won't say no."

"Good," he says and waves the waiter down. He grabs two flutes from the tray and hands me one, then clinks the lip of his glass against mine. "Thanks for coming to this. I know it's a lot, but it would've been way worse to do this alone."

"And the questions would've been way more invasive, I'm sure," I say, raising my eyebrows at him as I take a sip of the champagne. It's some of the smoothest I've ever had, but the bubbles still tingle on their way down. I'm glad for the distraction because Theo is right. This place is overstimulating, and it doesn't help that it's absolutely packed with people.

There are little tables placed throughout the crowd for people to rest their things on and talk, but they're all taken, and there's nowhere to sit. We just got here, and my feet are already starting to hurt from my heels, but I've got to power through it.

"There are Margo and Callie," Theo says, pointing at one of the tables on the other side of the room. Margo is wearing a stunning, flowing red dress and Callie looks equally as good in a shade that matches the champagne we're all drinking. "Why don't you go say hi to them? I need to make the rounds with the managers and the other bigwigs. I'll find you when I'm done."

"Okay," I say, then make a beeline for the girls. They light up when they see me approaching, and Margo lets out an audible gasp before she throws her arms around me.

"Oh my god. You look incredible, Becca!"

"So do both of you," I say then give Callie a hug too.

"Seriously, you look right at home here," Callie says and pulls my hair back over the shoulder where I'd been draping it. When I don't answer, Callie laughs. "Okay, it's a little overwhelming, isn't it?"

"More than a little," I admit, and Margo flashes me a sympathetic smile before putting her hand on my shoulder.

"Well, if it makes you feel any better, we're all in this together. These things don't tend to last very long. The guys make their rounds, maybe give a speech or two, and then we're free to go. So, you don't have too much more to suffer through." She picks up a glass of champagne from their table and raises it to me. "Here's to the wives and girlfriends club."

"To the wives and girlfriends club," I agree, and the three of us knock our glasses together before sipping the surely expensive bubbly.

"Thanks for the pep talk."

"Anytime," Margo says, smiling. "So how are things going?"

"Really well, honestly. Theo's parents were just in town, and I had a great time getting to know them both. I was kind of sad to see them go."

"Now there's something you don't hear about the in-laws every day," Callie jokes, making me chuckle. "Good for you though. I'm glad to hear everything is coming together for you and Theo. He definitely seems like he's in a better mood lately."

"Yeah, you must have some kind of magic or something," Margo adds.

"Well, I don't know about all that, but I'm glad to hear it. Especially after what you told me about the rough season he's been having."

"I don't want to count my goals before they're scored or anything, but I have a feeling that's going to change too," Margo says, her blue-gray eyes dancing. "Noah's had a lot of positive things to say about Theo's playing lately. And I'm sure you have something to do with that."

I shrug. "Maybe."

"Maybe? *Maybe?* Girl, look at you!" Callie exclaims, gesturing up and down at me. "Of course you have something to do with it." I blush despite myself and wave her away. "I'm serious. There's not a man on Earth who wouldn't be affected by all of this."

"Okay, okay. I get your point." I'm embarrassed, but it means a lot anyway. A thumping sound echoes throughout the ballroom, making us all look around. But I realize it's someone I don't recognize tapping on the microphone stationed at the front of the room on a raised stage area.

I glance around the room, looking for Theo, and I spot him off to the right of the stage area. He's leaning against a wall next to a tall blonde woman in a shimmering silver dress who throws her head back, laughing at something he must have said to her.

Her hand lands on his wrist, and although it's innocent, jealousy still slides down the back of my throat like an ice cube, chased by the burn of shame for feeling it at all. For all I know, she's the wife of a manager or something, but seeing him act like this with another woman, regardless of who she is, pulls at me.

This isn't real, and Theo isn't yours. Don't forget it.

I swallow the lump in my throat and take a sip of champagne as the person at the front of the room launches into a speech that I'm not absorbing at all. To be fair, no one else in the room seems to be either, but they're all good at pretending.

I finish my champagne by the time the guy wraps it up, then start looking around for another waiter to replace it. The jazz music returns over the speaker system, and people start dancing all around us.

Theo is gone, and so is the woman he was talking to, thankfully. I'd really like to dance with him so I can ask what that was all about, but before I can find him in the crowd, a devilishly handsome man with dark hair and piercing blue eyes appears wearing a smile.

"Looking for a dance partner?" he asks with his hand extended. I hesitate for a second, then smile and put my hand in his.

"You read my mind."

The guy chuckles and leads me out into the gaggle of other dancers by my hand. There's a slower song playing, so I rest my free hand on his shoulder while he places his on my hip, and we gently start to sway to the beat. I'm not sure he'd win any awards for rhythm either, but he can at least keep tempo, which is more than I can say for a lot of guys.

We're just starting to settle into a groove when someone taps on his shoulder from behind. It's Theo, and he doesn't look happy.

"Can I help you?" the guy snaps at Theo, and that seems to piss him off even more.

"Yeah. You can start by taking your hands off my wife."

The guy immediately drops his hold on me and stands with his jaw flapping like he can't find words. "Sorry. I didn't know," he finally says, then with a confused look in my direction, he hurries off into the crowd to put as much distance between himself and Theo as possible.

Theo takes his place, taking my hand in his, and fixes me with a smoldering gaze. "What was that all about?"

I shrug. "Just working the crowd. I was actually looking for you but caught his eye instead." Theo doesn't say anything, just keeps staring at me. "You're pissed, aren't you?"

"I can't say I'm thrilled."

"Really? Because you seemed captivated by the conversation you were having with that woman."

Theo's serious expression breaks instantly, and he raises his eyebrows. "Did seeing me talk to another woman make you jealous?"

Shame roils in my stomach. "It shouldn't have."

Theo laughs. "That's not what I asked. You're jealous, aren't you?"

We take several more steps together before I answer. Theo's eyes bore into mine, and although I'd rather not admit it, he's right. And why should I hide it?

"Yes."

Chapter 21

Theo

Something inside me roars at hearing Becca was jealous—the more possessive side of me. So I pull her closer, taking her by surprise, and stare into her eyes.

"Good. Because I was jealous of seeing you dance with another man."

A hint of a smile appears on her face, but she keeps it under wraps while we continue dancing. I'm still not the greatest at it but being so focused on her helps me stay out of my head and just *feel* things rather than think about them.

She's so close to me that her racing heartbeats pound against my chest, and it drives me wild thinking about what's causing it. The song has a slower pace, and we aren't moving very quickly, so I doubt it's exertion. But if it isn't the physicality, then that means it can only be one other thing: me.

It's unlikely anyone is paying attention, but in the moment, it feels like everyone in the room is watching us. And how couldn't they be? I don't have words to describe what's going on between us, but it's electric. Primitive. Primal. From the way she's looking into my eyes with an intense expression to the way she seems to be testing me with her steps, it's like we've started a game, trying to one-up each other.

She should know by now that I never shy from a challenge. If anything, it makes me feel more confident because this is my element. Competition is something I understand better than anything else. And if she wants me to fight for her, then that's exactly what I'll do.

But the song ends, abruptly breaking the spell between us. Becca and I stand there, staring into each other's eyes, and I can't bring myself to let her go. My entire body screams at me not to, like it's afraid it'll go into withdrawal or something. But being around her really is like a drug sometimes.

Fuck, I'm losing my mind here.

"You're getting better. I'm gonna go freshen up," she says as she disentangles herself from me. But her eyes linger, and she takes a few deep breaths before she tears her gaze away and snakes into the crowd toward the restrooms.

She's not the only one who needs a cool off after that. I've got to get my mind right and off her, so I decide to find some of the other Aces. It doesn't take long for me to spot Sawyer, who's almost as tall as I am and twice as wide. He's lingering along a far wall talking to Grant, and both look like they'd rather be anywhere else.

I make my way over to them and walk into a conversation about a babysitter, which sounds like the perfect distraction. "Dude, I'm telling you, you need to hire a full-time nanny," Grant tells Sawyer, who sighs.

"I don't know. I'm not sure Jake would like that." People would never guess from Sawyer's serious looks and personality, but he's intensely devoted to his son and being a father. The only thing that comes close for him is hockey, but even that is a distant second.

"Well, it doesn't sound like the babysitter you hired for tonight is gonna work out either, so you might as well try," Grant insists. "Besides, wouldn't that be better than having to find someone new every time you want to step out? It's not like you can't afford a nanny."

"Kid troubles?" I ask as I butt in.

Sawyer nods. "Yeah. I'm worried about the sitter I hired for tonight. She's not very experienced."

"Jake's a good kid. I'm sure it'll be fine for one night."

Grant nods. "He is, but it still seems like doing this all the time is getting too hard for you."

Reese and Noah must have seen the three of us talking because they appear out of nowhere. "I think Grant's on to something," Reese says as he claps Sawyer on the shoulder.

"Agreed," Noah says. "This has really been weighing on you lately. And it's probably hard on Jake having different people come and go all the time."

Sawyer sighs again. "Yeah, you're probably right about that. Okay, okay. I'll give the nanny thing a shot."

Satisfied, Reese turns his attention to me. "So how are things going with Becca?" I follow his gaze and find Becca standing and talking with Callie, Margo, and Violet, Reese's sister who's visiting for a few days for the gala. Becca's holding a half-empty glass of champagne. I watch her tip it to her lips and groan.

"I don't really want to talk about it."

Reese grimaces. "That bad, huh?"

I shake my head, maybe a little too hard. "Not. It's not bad at all. And that's the problem."

Reese raises his eyebrows at me. "What do you mean? Are you falling for her?"

"No, it's not that either," I insist, but is it true? I can't help wondering. There's *something* going on between us, but I don't know what to call it. Or if it even matters. Because even if I am feeling something for her, we have an agreement, and I'm not about to break that. People could call me a lot of things, but I'm a man of my word at the end of the day.

"Isn't it about time for your speech?" I ask Noah, desperate to take the focus off me.

He raises a brow. "Are you actually going to listen this time?"

I grin at him. "Probably not."

"Business as usual, then," he says and checks his phone for the time. "But yeah, I should probably start making my way up there."

"Break a leg," I say as Noah leaves, but he ignores the rib. I decide to linger with the rest of the guys through Noah's speech, but the truth is I'm not sure I trust myself to be alone with Becca right now. As much as I keep trying, I can't stop thinking about the charged energy I felt with her while we were dancing. It doesn't help that she keeps stealing glances over at me.

A few minutes later, Noah's amplified voice fills the ball-room, making everyone fall silent. "Thank you for coming tonight, everyone. It really means a lot to me and the other Aces to see the support," he says to a brief round of applause.

Noah starts into a variation of his usual speech for these kind of things, but I tune out pretty quickly. I can't take my eyes off Becca, who's standing with her champagne flute held in both hands and watching Noah idly. She seems as distracted as I feel, and I notice her swaying a little bit.

Is she drunk? I laugh at the thought. Maybe that was her way of coping with her feelings. I'm feeling a little buzzed myself, although I can't figure out if it's from the champagne I had or whatever the hell is going on inside me.

Noah wraps his speech up faster than usual, and the applause from the crowd brings me back into the room. I clap a few times with everyone else, then tell the guys I'm gonna call it a night. We exchange hugs and fist bumps, then I start making my way back to Becca and the other wives and girlfriends.

Margo spots me first and alerts the others, so they tell Becca goodbye before I get to their table and leave together. When I arrive at her side, Becca's wearing a goofy smile. "There you are," she says and laughs.

"Had a bit too much champagne?" I ask gently, nodding at the glass in her hands.

"They forced it on me," she answers, gesturing after the other women.

"We should probably head home then. I'll call us a cab. I don't think either of us should be driving tonight," I say and reach into my pocket for my phone, but Becca puts her hand on my wrist to stop me.

"Can we walk instead?"

I stare at her, confused. "What? Really? You know it's several miles, right?"

"Not all the way. Just a little. I heard it was snowing and I want to see it."

"Sure, if that's what you want," I say and offer her my arm. She grips it like a lifeline, and I walk her slowly through the dissipating crowd toward the door. Since we're going to be walking, I make sure to stop and get her coat from the attendant at the door, then tell the valet that I'll be back for my car tomorrow.

I don't know where she heard it, but Becca was right about the snow. It's coming down slowly in giant flakes that catch in her dark hair and on the fur of her coat. She beams and holds her free hand out to catch a few flakes as we walk down the hotel stairs.

"It's so beautiful," she murmurs as we pause under the golden glow of a streetlight. It lights her up like the goddess she is, and I don't know what comes over me, but I can't stop myself. I look her right in the eyes.

"I agree." But it's not the snow I'm talking about. She glances over, and our eyes lock. All at once, the surge I felt while we were dancing returns and Becca's face flushes. I'm tempted to kiss her, but I loop my arm back through hers instead and continue walking.

She's definitely drunk though, because she's swerving while we walk. I hold on tight to her arm to keep her from tipping over, and I laugh when she steps on my foot accidentally.

"Oh my god, I'm so sorry. Your beautiful shoes!" she whispers, but I can't even be mad. It reminds me of when we shared the bottle of whiskey on the beach, and just how quickly she got drunk from that.

"You're such a lightweight, you know that?"

Her eyes snap to mine. "No, I'm not!"

"Your swaying says otherwise."

"Okay, fine. I'm a little tipsy."

We laugh and keep walking down the street in the general direction of my condo. I have no idea how long she'll be able to keep this up in a dress and heels, but I'll keep walking as long as she can. I'm just enjoying spending time with her.

She looks all around us like a kid seeing snow for the first time, her eyes wide in amazement. Eventually, her gaze lands on one of the taller buildings along the street, and she lets out a long exhale.

"You okay?"

Becca stops abruptly, staring up at the building. "You know what my biggest dream is? Like, biggest dream *ever*?"

I'm tempted to laugh because she really does sound like a little kid, but I want to know what she's about to say. "Tell me."

She turns back to me with a fierce, determined look on her face. "I want to open my own dance school someday," she says, and before I can get a word in, she charges on. "I know, I know, it's a pipe dream. And I have the partnership with Curtain Call that's probably gonna happen, which I'm super excited about, but I really want my own independent school someday."

"It's not a pipe dream. I think you could do anything you set your mind to."

Becca playfully slaps my arm. "You're just saying that because you're my husband. You're obligated."

"Maybe, but I mean it. You're way more talented and capable than you give yourself credit for."

Becca stares at me blankly. "How much have *you* had to drink tonight?"

I laugh and shake my head. "Not enough to be anything other than clear headed."

"Hm." Becca turns away from me again, staring up at the top of the plain office building and blinking away the snow that catches in her beautiful, long eyelashes. "Maybe you're right."

Without another word, she wraps her arm through mine again and we continue walking to the next intersection. But she almost slips stepping off the curb to cross the street, and I have to hold her up.

"You ready to call a cab?" I ask when we're safely on the other side. She's blushing, but she nods.

"Yeah. Probably not a bad idea. Sorry."

"Nothing to be sorry about, princess," I say and gently tap the tip of her nose. The blush on her cheeks doesn't fade, but at least her smile returns. I pull my phone out of my pocket and tap around until I get a hit for a driver, then help Becca lower down onto a nearby public bus bench to wait. Technically, we aren't supposed to get picked up in places like this, but there's hardly anyone around.

Becca's fingers snake between mine on the bench, but it seems to be automatic rather than intentional. I don't know if she's just feeling embarrassed or what, but I don't mind. We sit there quietly enjoying the gently falling snow and each other's company for a few minutes until a black sedan pulls up to the bench and flashes its headlights.

"Time to go," I say and stand first so I can steady her if she needs it. But she manages to get to her feet just fine, so I escort her to the car and open the rear door for her. She climbs inside a bit clumsily but without incident, and I slide in next to her.

"Thanks for the lift," I tell the driver, who's a woman Becca's age. She takes one look at Becca's flushed face in the rearview and raises her eyebrows.

"She gonna be okay for the ride?"

"Yeah, yeah. She'll be fine. Right, Becca?"

"Totally a-okay," Becca says, making the "okay" symbol with her fingers.

The driver raises a skeptical eyebrow. "Alright. Just let me know if you need me to stop. I don't feel like cleaning my whole car tonight."

"I'll pay for it if you do," I assure her, closing the door.

The driver puts the car in gear and sets off slowly, still watching us in the rearview. But Becca really is fine. She stares out the window, watching the snow and buildings blur by, and her fingers creep across the seat to find mine again.

The driver stops outside the condo a few minutes later, and I help Becca out before thanking the driver and telling her good night. I don't know if the champagne is really kicking in now or what, but Becca seems to be getting more and more unsteady, so I'm thankful we have an elevator and don't have to deal with stairs to get into the unit.

As soon as we step inside, Milo comes bounding from somewhere in the living room, nearly knocking us both over. Becca laughs brightly as she sinks to her knees to hold his face in her hands, talking to him in the baby voice that everyone does with their pets.

"Who's a good boy? Did you miss us? Aw, we missed you too, sweet boy!" She plants a series of kisses on his head, and he throws himself down on the floor in front of her, exposing his stomach for tummy rubs. I join her in rubbing his stomach, and she beams at me.

216

"Are you gonna need any help getting undressed or into bed?" I ask.

She flashes me a playful smile. "Are you trying to get me out of my clothes, Mr. Camden?"

My body tenses at the thought, but I keep it together. "No, I didn't mean it like that. I just don't want you getting hurt."

"Relax, I'm teasing you. But I'll be fine. I appreciate you offering though," she says as she continues rubbing Milo's stomach.

"Alright. Then I'm gonna take this guy for a quick walk, then get out of this suit and get some sleep. Good night," I say and kiss the top of her head before I stand.

"Good night." As I grab Milo's leash from the hook by the door, she adds, "And thanks for a good time, Theo. I needed it."

"You're welcome. Thanks for coming."

"I wouldn't have missed it," she says, rising to her feet too. She wavers for a second, probably from the rush of blood, but steadies herself and starts ambling down the hall toward her room. I wait until I hear her bedroom door click closed before I take Milo out for a quick walk.

Once he's gotten his bedtime treat and is settled on his bed in the living room, I go upstairs. I strip off the tuxedo and dress clothes underneath, then hang them up in my closet. They'll need to go to the cleaners, but that can wait. I should probably take a shower after being out dancing and walking around, but I'm honestly too tired, so that will have to wait too. I'm down to my boxers and peeling back the comforter to my bed when a soft knock on the door startles me.

"Did you need something?" I call, almost afraid to open the door, but Becca doesn't answer.

My heart thuds heavily as I stride over and open the door slowly.

Becca is standing there in nothing but a nightrobe that's very loosely tied. She stares at me, her face full of heat, and something sparks immediately inside me—because I already know where this is going. Her eyes fall to my feet, then slowly climb all the way up my mostly naked body until they meet mine again.

We stand there, eyes locked and tension crackling, for what feels like forever. Then she throws herself at me, and her lips crash into mine. All her inhibitions must have gone out the window because her hands tear across my body, taking big handfuls of any patch of skin she can find. They work their way down to the band of my boxers, but when she tries to yank them down, I grip her by the wrists and pull my mouth away from hers.

"Becca," I whisper, resting my forehead against hers because as much as I know we shouldn't do this, I still can't pull myself away from her entirely. I want her so badly, more than I could ever admit, but I can't take advantage of her when she's drunk like this. And that's exactly what's going on.

She looks up at me, distressed. "Don't you want this?"

I wince because holy shit. Of *course* I want it, but not like this. "That's not the issue."

She scrunches her eyebrows at me. "Then what is?"

I sigh. "You're drunk. It wouldn't be right."

"Oh," she says, and drops her hands to her sides. She turns like she's going to do the walk of shame back to her room, which kills me to see, but she hesitates before turning back to me. "Well, we don't have to do that. But can I stay? With you, I mean?"

I should tell her no. I know I should. The refusal tingles on the tip of my tongue, desperate to come out. But I can't do it. It'll break her heart, and that's the last thing I want. So instead, I sigh and nod.

"You can stay."

She smiles and walks back into my room. "Thank you," she says as she climbs under the sheets. I lie down next to her, and she cuddles up against me, her back to my chest. I wrap an arm around her protectively, willing my body not to react to the intensity of having her so close and so willing. It tortures me not to be able to touch her the way I'm dying to, but I'm determined not to take advantage of her. We'd both regret it.

Silence settles between us for several moments, until Becca starts dragging a fingertip up and down my forearm.

"Maybe I shouldn't say this," she whispers. "But I want you so badly."

Again, my body tenses, and I grit my teeth to keep from saying anything that might get me into more trouble than I can handle. But she keeps going.

"I think about you when I touch myself," she breathes, her voice low and husky. "About the way you fucked me that first night."

My pulse thunders in my ears, and I can feel myself start to harden against her. I take several deep breaths to calm myself down before I speak.

"I do too," I whisper hoarsely in her ear. "All the fucking time."

She turns in my arms to face me, giving me a frustrated look. "Then why won't you fuck me?"

I stare into her eyes, my entire body thrumming with simultaneous desire and resistance, then kiss her as chastely as I can manage. "Get some sleep. You need it."

She doesn't seem satisfied with that, but she eventually sighs and turns back over, nestling up against me again. Probably because of the alcohol, it doesn't take more than a few minutes for her to drift off, confirming I made the right choice—as impossible as it feels.

But I know I won't be getting to sleep anytime soon.

Chapter 22

Becca

Theo plants kisses up the side of my neck while he holds me against him, making me shiver. His body is hot and hard behind mine, and he lifts my leg over his, taking me by surprise. But it's nothing compared to the shock and thrill that race through me when his swollen cock head finds my folds from behind.

"Yes," I whisper, more begging than anything. With another kiss on my neck, he pushes into me and forces out a long, stuttering groan with it as he fills me. It's still shocking to me just how big he is, but it feels incredible. The sensation alone starts a burning in me, but when he reaches down between my legs to toy with my clit, I feel like every nerve ending in my body lights up.

This is everything I've been craving for weeks.

Theo bucks his hips into me, pushing out another groan, and I hold on to his arm wrapped around me like my life depends on it. We ease into a rhythm, my hips pushing back to meet his as he thrusts into me, building me higher and higher. With every stroke he takes, I feel myself climbing into a new level of bliss until my mind can't focus on anything other than the intense feeling of his cock inside me.

I'm about to fall apart in his arms. "Oh god, Theo!" I urge as he matches the rhythm of his thrusting to the circles he's drawing around my clit. My eyes snap open as I'm crashing into my orgasm, and his arm is still wrapped around me, but something's different. Wrong. Incomplete.

"Having a nice dream?" Theo whispers in my ear, and dread floods my stomach.

Oh, god. Shit. No, no, no. Please tell me I didn't just say that out loud.

"You aren't fooling anyone. I know you're awake," he continues. "What were you dreaming about me?"

I lie still, hoping he'll stop asking, but he sits up, lifting me along with him. I roll over to face him and feel the fire burning all over my face, but the devious look Theo gives me isn't really helping me to cool off. "Aren't you gonna tell me?"

"Nope."

"Oh. Fine. Then I'll just have to guess until I get it right. But I don't think it'll take many guesses after what I just heard."

I groan and roll away from him, but he laughs and pulls me back. He runs a finger down the length of my arm, jolting my nervous system. "Did it start something like this?"

I was feeling groggy and shitty from all the champagne I had last night, but just this little touch from him clears it. Every nerve in my body responds, and I fill with the aching for him I've been feeling for weeks all over again. No wonder I was dreaming about him. But should I tell him? He was such a gentleman when he refused my foolish, drunken attempt at throwing myself at him.

"I'm so sorry about what happened last night," I say, trying to change the subject. "It was embarrassing, to say the least."

"You shouldn't be embarrassed."

My eyes snap to his. "Why the hell not? That was about as sloppy as it gets."

Theo laughs. "True, but that's why I wouldn't touch you.

You weren't in your right mind. You didn't really understand what you were asking for."

"Oh, I knew *exactly* what I wanted."

"But you didn't get it, so your subconscious spun up a dream about it instead."

"Am I really that transparent?"

Theo stares blankly at me. "Becca. You were basically just screaming my name in your sleep. It doesn't take a Harvard psychologist to decode that one."

"Okay, okay, fine. Yes, I was having a dream about you."

Theo laughs again. "That wasn't just any dream. You were moving in your sleep too, you know."

Fuck, that's even worse. But there's no point in hiding or denying it anymore, especially when it's apparently as obvious as the rising sun. "So what?"

Theo's eyes narrow, and a hungry look flashes behind them as he tugs one lip between his teeth. Electricity courses between us again, and his finger—that never stopped stroking my arm—snakes down to my thigh.

"Here's the thing. If you hadn't been drunk last night, nothing could've stopped me from fucking you," he says, and my breath catches in my throat. I don't know what I was expecting him to say, but it wasn't that. "You have no idea—no fucking clue—how badly I've been wanting you. How even thinking about it has been driving me insane."

Blood rushes in my ears, nearly drowning out his words. Because I've been feeling the exact same way, ever since that first night we shared together. But we had all these rules, all these boundaries we drew up once we got married that even I knew we'd be smart not to screw up. And yet, I kept feeling the temptation, especially as our lives grew more and more intertwined.

But what if we wrote new rules?

Theo's hand slips between my thighs and I can't help shivering against him. His fingertips graze my pussy, and when he realizes I'm not wearing any underwear, he lets out a sound somewhere between a groan and a growl. I purposely left them in my room when I came up here in my drunken determination to seduce him, but I forgot all about it until now.

Theo rolls me onto my back to look up at him. He hovers over me, his fingertips resting against my pussy. I'm still wet from the dream, and I'm sure he notices.

"Tell me to stop," he whispers as he pushes a finger farther into my folds, but that's the last thing that's going to come out of my mouth.

"No," I say confidently, staring him right in the eye, daring him to keep going. He lingers over me for a long moment. His eyes are smoldering as they rake me over, taking in every detail of my naked lower body splayed out before him. With one powerful motion, he moves his hand to grip the sash holding my robe closed and yanks, unwrapping the rest of me like a present.

"Last chance. Tell me to stop," Theo says, and there's a desperation in his voice. If we cross this line again, there's no going back. I'm well aware of that, and I don't care. The only thing I want is for him to fuck me again, to take me the way he did our first night.

I say nothing.

Theo lunges forward, pressing his lips into mine, and I catch fire as I kiss him back. All the unspoken tension, the simmering desire, boils over at once. It comes out in the way he seizes desperate handfuls of my skin as he tears my robe off, and in the way his tongue feverishly collides with mine.

"God, you're fucking beautiful," he moans into my mouth. But I don't just want the focus on me, so I reach for his boxers and pull. He laughs and breaks the kiss so I can tug them the rest of the way off.

"You're a hungry little girl, aren't you?"

"Famished."

Theo's expression changes from playful to predatorial in an instant, so when he presses a finger inside me, I gasp in shock and pleasure. But when I don't resist, he smiles. "Good girl."

I nod at him, silently begging, so he slips a second finger inside me. A whimper leaks out of my mouth and my toes curl. I've been so turned on around him for so long that the feeling alone is enough to start a burning in my core. But he abruptly pulls his fingers from me and lifts them to his mouth. He sucks on them, savoring the wetness and leaving me breathless.

Before I have time to process just how much it does to me, Theo pushes me backward and climbs on top of me. He feasts on my breasts, kissing and sucking on my rigid, charged nipples. The pleasure is so intense that it's overwhelming, but when he gently clamps his teeth around my left nipple, I let out a gasp—both because I can't believe he did it or believe how incredible it feels.

"Tell me what happened in your dream. I won't ask twice," he mutters around my nipple, and the vibration of his voice against it makes my head fall back. I can barely think, let alone form coherent sentences, when so many of my body's nerves are lit up like this. But I stumble into a start.

"We were lying together," I groan as his tongue does laps around my nipple.

"Mm-hm." Again, the vibration against my nipple makes it difficult to think.

"And you were kissing my neck," I say, and as I do, Theo moves up my body to let his mouth hover less than an inch away from my jugular.

His warm breath rippling across my neck and collar bone makes goosebumps spread over my skin, and my hands instinctively shoot to his hair. My fingers wind in his dark locks, desperate for something grounding to keep me from floating away.

"Like this?" he asks and softly presses his lips against the tender skin where my neck joins my collar.

"Oh my god, yes," I whimper, so he kisses me again. I feel him hardening against me, and it takes everything I have not to pull him into me right away. The anticipation and teasing is ripping me to shreds, but as maddening as it is, I'm not ready for it to stop just yet.

"And then what?" Theo asks through the series of kisses he plants on my neck, shocking me with each one.

"You teased my pussy with your cock head."

As if on command, I feel his cock graze my folds just like in the dream, and my body tenses. We're so close to what I want. To what I need.

"How did it feel?" Theo whispers in my ear before he nips at my lobe, sending another current racing across my skin.

"Then or now?" I ask breathlessly.

"Both."

"It felt good. It was... amazing."

"Good. That's how I want you to feel all the time," he says and lifts slightly to grip his cock. He drags it across my pussy in agonizingly slow circles, teasing me. "I've had dreams too."

Those words, almost more than anything he's done or will do to me, light me up. My eyes find his and hold his intense gaze. "What happened in yours?"

"Nothing compared to this," he says, and it pushes me over the edge. I angle my hips a little, bringing his cock head against my entrance. I'm desperate for him, and we're right up to the line. One little thrust is the only thing that separates us.

But I want him to be the one to cross that line. I want him to take me.

"Is this what you want, princess?" he asks as he grips my

legs under the knee. His voice is full of hunger and need, and the blazing look he's giving me proves it.

"Yes."

"Then tell me how badly you want it. Beg for it. Beg me to fuck you."

Chapter 23

Theo

Becca gasps, but her eyes ripple with desire. "Please, Theo," she whispers, and her words travel right to my cock like it's a lightning rod. She has no idea the effect she has on me, the way she drives me insane. I can't put my finger on what exactly it is about her, but she's woken something in me that I haven't felt in years—something I swore I'd lost.

It makes me want her even more. Makes me want to see her fall apart for me.

"I think you can do better than that." When she doesn't answer, I prod her with my cock, pushing another gasp out of her. "I said beg."

Becca pushes herself up onto her elbows to look me in the eye. There's a hunger, a fire there, that I don't think I've seen from her before. "Please, Theo, fuck me." It's a command as much as a pleading. This is another side of her I haven't seen, but it's fucking hot. "I want your cock so badly," she continues and wraps her legs around my waist to prove her point. It's not enough pressure to pull me into her yet, which is good, because I'm not ready. Not so fast.

"Good girl. That's more like it. Keep going."

She chews her lip and smiles devilishly while she thinks. "I want you to fuck me like I'm really yours," she says, and it makes me freeze. I'm hanging on her every word like my life depends on it, and I can't wait to hear what she comes up with next. "I want you to fuck me like I'm your wife."

"*Fuck*," I murmur, and almost fall into her from shock. I wasn't expecting her to go there, but she keeps finding new ways to amaze me. And hearing her call herself my wife like that gets me so turned on I can barely stand it. I'm losing my mind with her, but I'm still in control of myself—for now. "I love hearing how badly you want me. Need me."

She nods eagerly. "I need you more than you know," she says and kisses me hungrily, letting it say everything else her words can't. Her tongue collides with mine, and for a second, I lose myself in it. The primal part of me takes over, and my hands reach behind her to cradle her head in mine. I take a handful of her beautiful hair to hold her in place, matching her passion, and she moans into my mouth.

We part, and she breathes heavily while she stares into my eyes. We're so close that our noses graze each other, and I watch her swallow hard. Arousal flares in her eyes. "I want you to fuck me to pieces," she says with a desperate, haunting look, and that's all it takes to burn away the last shred of control I'm clinging to.

I push her legs up and quickly drop my face between them to bury it in her, but she lets out a noise that sounds more frustrated than aroused. Clearly, this isn't what she was begging for, but I'll make sure she enjoys it anyway.

I smirk up at her from between her legs, her perfect face framed between her equally perfect breasts. "Don't worry. I'm gonna fuck you—especially since you did such a great job begging for it—but first I need to taste you again," I say and steal a quick lick of her wetness. That makes her jolt and gasp, and her head lolls to the side. "That hint of you I got from my fingertips wasn't anywhere near enough. I need more."

Without warning, I spread her open and lap at her, taking deep, hungry passes at her folds and entrance. She's already so turned on that she's absolutely soaked, and I can't wait to feel how amazing it'll be to slide my cock into that welcoming wetness, but that's all the more reason to turn up the intensity. She arches beneath me, pushing herself against my tongue like she can't get enough.

After a few seconds of eating her like this, her head falls back against the mattress, and she starts groaning and muttering words I can't make out. So much for her disappointment, but all I need to know is how much she's enjoying it. How good I'm making her feel. "That's it, that's my good girl," I mutter into her pussy. "Tell me how fucking good it feels to be eaten out by your husband."

Her legs shake a little at my words, and she lifts them up to rest on my back, giving me fuller access to all of her.

"So good," she breathes. "So... oh god, Theo. It feels..."

She slips her hand between her legs to reach for her clit, but I catch her by the wrist and pin her arm against the mattress. The only person making her come tonight is going to be me. That job is mine and mine alone.

But since I feel like I'm fucking starving for more of her, I take her lead and move up to her clit to breathe softly on it. She whimpers as her entire body writhes, and I beam at the way even the slightest touch from me makes her come alive. I bet no one has ever made her feel this good before, has never taken their time and dedicated themselves to her pleasure like I am right now.

It's what she deserves, and it's what she'll get from me for as long as she wants it.

I spit on her clit to get it wetter, and she jumps. When I drag my tongue across it, she shudders and writhes beneath me like an earthquake is raging through her.

Good. I want her dancing on a knife's edge and begging to teeter over it before I let her finish. I want her to feel as turned on as I've been feeling for the last few weeks, and then I want to give her the best release she's ever had. That she'll ever have.

I force my tongue into her and pull it back out, fucking her with it, and her writhing intensifies. Her hands snap to my head, and she digs her nails into my scalp, but that only encourages me. Seeing her squirm is one thing, but I have an insatiable hunger for her sounds of pleasure. So I push my tongue as far as I can inside her, opening her up for me, and she lets out a deep groan that makes my cock swell.

"You feel so fucking good," she says breathlessly, and that's exactly what I want to hear. Her legs are trembling, and her grip on my head tightens when I pull my tongue out of her to lap at her enflamed clit.

"That's the kind of treatment my wife deserves," I mutter back, still flicking my tongue against her clit. Each time my tongue touches it, she moans and tosses her head. "I want you to come on my face. Can you do that for me?"

"Oh, god," she cries out, then bites her fist to keep from screaming, which tells me everything I need to know.

I doubt she could hold back the sensations brewing inside her now even if she wanted to. When I fuck her again with my tongue, she inhales sharply and her body tenses briefly before she trembles and shakes. She comes in waves, coating my tongue and chin in her arousal. I lap it all up, still devouring her and working her through it.

Becca shudders from the aftershocks, struggling to catch her breath. Part of me wants to stay down here and eat her all fucking night long. I want to make her scream until she's so sensitive she's begging me to stop, but I'm so hard and so desperate to be inside her that I can't wait anymore. I need to feel her around me, need to see the look on her face when I fill her up.

I kiss my way up the insides of her thighs, alternating between them. She jumps and whimpers each time my lips graze her soft, tender skin. I keep going all the way up her exposed body, planting feather soft touches along her ribs and breasts until my face reaches hers. I hover over her, staring into her simmering eyes. My hips rest between her legs, my cock against her folds.

When our eyes meet, something passes between us. A current, a spark. Our breathing is heavy but in sync, and I feel Becca's heartbeat pulsing when I rest my forehead against hers. We're right up against the line again, but this time I have no doubt we're going to cross it. And I don't know or care what will happen after we do because I'm so damn ready to do it. I've been ready for weeks, and I can't take the tension anymore.

"Are you sure you want to do this?" I ask, and she nods eagerly.

"Beyond ready."

"Then I need to get a condom. I'll be right back," I say and start to move off her to grab one from the bathroom, but her hands shoot to my shoulders to hold me in place. She locks her beautiful brown eyes on mine.

"We don't need one," she says, catching me off-guard yet again. Not that I'm disappointed to hear it. "We aren't seeing other people, and I'm on the pill. I'm fine with going bare if you'd want that."

I nod, my cock pulsing as my heart races. "Fuck yes, that's what I want."

She smiles, her eyes burning. "Good. Because I want to feel you with nothing else between us."

Her words drive me absolutely fucking wild, and it takes everything I have not to ravage her right here and now. But I need to know this is really what she wants. "Are you sure about this? I don't want you to regret it."

"I've never been more sure of anything in my life. Please fuck me, Theo," she whispers, and her words go right to my cock, making me so hard it borders on painful.

I reach down to grab my shaft and drag the tip across her wetness, coating it, then begin working my way inside her. She lets out a little gasp as my head presses into her, so I pause.

"Jesus, I forgot how big you are," she laughs, sending little shockwaves through my cock and turning me on even more. But as turned on as I am, this is about her as much as it is me. I don't want to hurt her or do anything that would make her feel uncomfortable, so I pause and reach out to stroke her face with my thumb.

"Are you okay?"

She nods. "Yeah, you're just a lot to take."

"You can do it, I promise. You've done it before, you can do it again," I say and her face flames as a look of determination blooms across it. "I won't hurt you, you know that." She nods again, so I push in again ever so slightly, and although she winces, she opens up. She's so wet that I slide in without much resistance, despite the way I'm stretching her, and the grip she has on me feels fucking incredible.

"There you go. Good girl, just like that. Breathe in, nice and deep," I encourage her, and I pause again while she sucks in one rushed gulp of air through her nose. As she exhales, I push farther into her and her eyes flutter. But she keeps breathing, and inch by inch, I disappear into her.

I glance down at my cock as the last of it slides into place, and when my hips finally meet hers, she lets out a shuddering exhale. She takes a series of deep breaths to help her body

232

adjust to my girth, and I keep stroking her face. "There you go. You're so beautiful. My beautiful, amazing wife."

She beams at me as she drinks in my body hovering over hers, and I follow her gaze as it works all the way down. The sight of our bodies fully connected like this, and with nothing at all between them, is so fucking hot that it's almost too much for me to bear. Words race through my mind in a blur, but none of them really make sense or cover what I want to tell her.

"God, do you have any idea how good you look like this?" I ask as I lean over her, pushing myself a bit deeper into her. She moans but glances between her legs to see what I mean, and her eyes widen like she can't quite believe she did it.

Part of me can't believe it either, but knowing that she trusts me enough to let me into her and her life like this makes me feel amazing. It wasn't that long ago that we barely knew each other, but all that has changed. The chemistry was always there, but this is something new. Something deeper.

We might have had sex before, but there's no denying that this time is different. More intense. We're connected now, literally and figuratively, in a way that we've never been, in a way that I haven't been connected to a woman in years. The realization makes something stir in my chest. I don't really know what to call of this thing Becca and I have, but "fake" definitely doesn't feel right anymore.

Because whatever this is, it's real. The confusing feelings I've been having for her are too, so I hope crossing this line, one we can't undo, means I don't have to keep pretending they aren't. We had rules for a reason, but the rules aren't working for me anymore. I'm not sure they ever were.

"Theo," Becca whimpers, and I drop my head to kiss her as I pull out slowly. She whimpers into my mouth from the sensation, and when I drive back into her at the same pace, her head falls back. I move my mouth to her neck, kissing and gently biting as I find my rhythm.

Becca clings to me like a rock in a storm, her nails digging into my back, and it's a good thing I can feel the piercing of it because otherwise I'd drift away too. Being inside her like this, fucking her like this, is enough to make me lose what sanity I have left.

Because nothing has ever felt this good.

Chapter 24

Becca

As overwhelming as the pleasure I feel is, I can't take my eyes off Theo's face while he fucks me. The blazing, intense look he's wearing turns me on and makes my heart race at the same time, and every deep stroke of his cock lifts me higher and higher.

He varies his rhythm, driving his hips forward over and over again as he watches me fall apart beneath him. My eyelids flutter, and I know I'm about to come, but Theo's hand finds the back of my neck, startling them back open.

"Keep your eyes open," he orders, and his authoritative tone does nothing to help me hold back the orgasm building inside me. "And keep them on me. I want to see you, princess. All of you. I want to see my wife's face when I make her come."

Oh fuck.

That's all it takes. I fall into my orgasm, biting my lip and crying out loudly as I struggle to keep eyes open. The edges of my vision start to blur, but I will myself to laser focus on Theo's gorgeous emerald irises. A hungry grin splits his face, and he fucks me harder and faster in response, dragging a series of moans out of me with every little movement.

My climax roils through me in waves, each a little less

intense than the last, until it finally subsides, and I come back into my body. My chest heaves, and Theo stops moving while I try to catch my breath. He's beaming at me.

"How was that?"

"Unreal," I gasp because it's all I can manage, and I mean it. He strokes my cheek.

"I'm proud of you for keeping your eyes on me like that."

"It's impossible to take my eyes off you," I say, and Theo's eyes blaze as he hooks one of my legs and pushes it up toward my chest. Every bit of me is still on fire, so even the casual movement lights up my nerves. And when he pushes himself back into me, my entire body tenses.

"I want to make you come again," Theo says, all his playfulness replaced with serious determination. I don't know how he held himself together through my last orgasm, but I can tell from the intensity of feeling in my core that there is at least another one brewing. And I want to give it to him. To my husband.

"Then take it," I say, and Theo's eyes flame.

"Be careful what you wish for, princess." He thrusts into me, making me gasp and grip the sheets. His strokes take on an edge as he rises to the challenge, and it makes my toes curl. There's something about giving myself to him like this, letting him own my body, that makes me feel like I never have. I've had good sex before, but whatever it is between us brings it to a whole new level.

It only takes a few of these forceful thrusts from Theo to get me building toward another orgasm. His hand is still on the back of my neck, holding me up and in place as he drives into me over and over. I want to keep my eyes open for this one too, but the roiling pleasure percolating in my core is too much to bear. When his free thumb finds my clit, I let out a choking gasp and erupt into my second orgasm.

"Fuck yes, let it out," Theo grunts as his strokes stutter and my pussy involuntarily clenches around him. He slumps into me, his forehead crashing into mine, as he pumps out the last of his orgasm in shuddering, irregular strokes. Then his mouth is on mine, his tongue thrashing against mine like he can't get enough. Like he wants to devour me.

We come back down to Earth together, breathing heavily with our lips touching. But neither of us can find words. My eyes flutter open, meeting his, and he's staring into mine like he can see right through me. Right to my soul.

"You've ruined me, you know that?" he whispers, making me shiver. "My wife is so fucking perfect."

I'm still struggling to catch my breath when his mouth travels to my neck, kissing every inch of skin his lips can find. He gently pulls out of me, then continues kissing his way down my body. He can't seem to take his hands off me, to not be touching me in some way.

He ends up between my legs again, and I whimper when his hot breath grazes my pussy. But I sit up quickly as realization and embarrassment surge through me at the same time. He's about to put his face where the mess of my pussy is—his cum and my own arousal smeared all over my thighs and leaking out of me.

"What are you doing?" No one's ever done this to me before, and I'm not sure I'm okay with it.

Theo grins up at me. "I want another taste. Nothing—and I mean *nothing*—could keep me from wanting to taste you." I'm still trying to work out how I feel about it when his mouth descends on my pussy, his tongue pushing apart my folds. It feels so fucking electric that I instantly forget my objections.

What he's doing is absolutely filthy, but that's exactly what makes it hot. Knowing he's lapping up his own cum too turns me on in a way I didn't even know I liked until now. He's so hungry, so ravenous for me that he meant it when he said nothing could stop him from tasting me again, not even his own fluids. That adds to the thrill and gets me climbing all over again.

He smears his tongue across my pussy, dragging it over my clit and coating it with his cum. He fixes me with an intense gaze as he pierces me with his tongue, groaning into me as he does, and watching him devour me like this gets me right up to the edge all over again. My body starts to tremble, and Theo makes a delighted little noise as he ratchets up the hungry licks he's taking at me.

"Oh fuck," I moan as I tense like a drawstring, then snap under his tongue.

Another orgasm rushes through me, soaking Theo's face, but he doesn't stop eating me until the climax passes, leaving me so sensitive that his touch is almost more painful than pleasurable. Satisfied, he pulls away and climbs on top of me, his face hovering over mine, then kisses me greedily.

I taste both of us on his tongue, and it sends heat racing through me. I kiss him back, matching his intensity, until he abruptly pulls back.

"You're fucking amazing," he pants.

I laugh and shake my head. "You did all the work. But god, you have no idea how long I've been wanting that."

Theo collapses onto the bed beside me and pulls me into his arms, my back against his chest. Our skin glues together, a mixture of sweat and ecstasy, but I'm too exhausted and satiated to care. Theo places a soft kiss on the patch of skin where my neck meets my shoulder.

"That makes two of us," he whispers. "It's been next to fucking impossible to ignore the tension between us lately."

"I'm glad I'm not the only one who noticed it. So I wasn't totally mistaken when I threw myself at you last night?"

Theo laughs. "Drunk? Sure. But mistaken? No way. Like I said, if you'd been sober and done that, I wouldn't have been able to resist."

A thought bubbles in my mind, but I hold it back. I know we just crossed a line, that much is obvious, but I don't really know where we go from here. Or what Theo thinks about what we just did, so I don't want to push my luck.

"Something on your mind?" he asks like he was reading it. I roll over to face him, our skin peeling apart in the process, but I still hesitate. "What is it?"

"Maybe we should just throw out the no-sex rule," I blurt, hoping to just get it out there. "It was just making the tension worse, not better. This could be our little pressure release valve."

Theo smirks and kisses my forehead. "I'm on board with that plan."

I'm not really surprised he agrees, but I am shocked he did it so quickly. He's been so measured and considerate throughout this whole process, so the tension must have really been killing him too. In a weird way, it feels good to know he's been as hungry for me as I have been for him.

"And in that case, I've got something else I want to do," he says, then kisses me again. Almost instantly, heat starts building between us again as his hands wander over my body and his tongue explores my mouth. But before I realize what's happening, he's spinning me over onto my stomach.

He grips me by the hips and yanks me up onto my knees, then gropes my ass before his hands snake up my spine. His hardening cock finds my pussy, and he teases me with the head, making me shiver and moan. "Can you take more?" he asks, and I nod without a second to think about it.

"Definitely. But I'm surprised you're hard again already."

"It's what you do to me," he says intensely, then slides inside in one fluid motion. I'm still so wet that there's no friction at all, and that's good because Theo isn't holding anything back anymore. I grip the sheets and bite the mattress to keep my moaning under control as he drills away at me.

"You look perfect from every fucking angle," Theo says breathlessly as he takes another deep, plunging stroke into me. My eyes squeeze shut from the pleasure. He's so big, and even though my body is used to it now, he's hitting me from a totally different angle that's lighting up parts of me I didn't even know I had.

He must be getting close again because his pace picks up, so I match his rhythm, rocking my hips back as he thrusts forward. Our hips crash and slap together, filling the room with the sound of our union. The feeling is so intense that I give up on muffling my moaning. I couldn't control it even if I tried.

"That's it, take my fucking cock," Theo encourages, and my body thrums. I arch my back, letting him in deeper, and the new sensation sends me crashing into my third orgasm. Theo thrusts into me several more times, gripping and clawing at my waist, until he grunts and pulls out abruptly. I glance over my shoulder and watch him come, erupting in thick ropes that paint my back.

When it's over, I collapse onto my stomach. Every muscle in my body is overworked and on fire. I'm totally worked over, but it hurts in the best possible way. I feel Theo leave the bed and hear him pad to the bathroom. The faucet in the sink runs, and a few seconds later, he returns with a wet, warmed towel. He tenderly cleans me up, starting with my back before moving down to my aching, sated pussy.

"Thank you," I say, half asleep and gazing up at him contently.

"I should be the one thanking you. That was fucking incredible," Theo says as he tosses the towel into the bathroom. He goes to lie down beside me, but Milo comes bounding into the room and plants his wet snout right in my ear.

"Looks like someone's ready for his morning walk," Theo says with a laugh as he pats Milo's head.

"Poor guy is probably starving too. We've been up here for a long time."

The sun is already high in the sky, and I realize I have no idea what time it is. Or how long Theo and I have been at it.

"Come on, boy, let's get you some food," Theo tells the dog.

He helps me to my feet, and I slip back into my robe, which ended up on the floor at some point. Then Milo chases Theo downstairs, barking and whimpering the whole way.

When I join them, Milo has his face in his food bowl, and Theo's already making coffee. I walk over and wrap my arms around him from behind, full of a feeling I can't quite describe, and he pulls me around to place another kiss on my forehead.

"Do you have plans after practice today?" I ask, and he fixes me with a quizzical look.

"Not yet. You have something in mind?"

"Yeah. I'd like to take you somewhere."

His brows rise, but he smiles. "Alright. Then let's do it."

"Good. I'm gonna go get showered up. I'll see you when you get home," I say and leave him guessing.

Because it's my turn to do the surprising.

～

After my shower, I spend some time browsing social media for the perfect place for Theo's surprise while he's at practice. Milo sits with me on the couch, his head resting in my lap, while I scroll around on my phone for somewhere to go ice skating.

It would probably be easiest to just go to the arena, but Theo spends enough time there as it is, and it's not exactly the most picturesque or inspiring place for what I have in mind. I'm looking for something like I used to go to when I was a kid, a random frozen lake or pond that the locals turn into a skating rink. This is Colorado, so there must be something similar.

But I'm having trouble finding anything because I'm not sure what to search for. These kind of things tend to just pop up, they aren't plastered all over social media with

RSVPs and whatnot, so I'm just starting to convince myself that I might be out of luck when I decide to give it one last desperate search. I tap into the search bar and type "ice skating pond Denver CO" and hit enter. The results turn up a bunch of unrelated crap—posts about Denver weather, someone organizing a fishing group—but a post made yesterday by a woman who seems to be my age stands out.

"Can't believe I just learned how to ice skate on a frozen pond. How Denver is that?"

Lucky for me, she tagged a location, so I tap on it and the app opens a map that shows exactly the pond she mentioned. Even luckier, it's in a park that's only a couple of miles from the condo. I was hoping for something a bit more isolated, but beggars can't be choosers, so I screenshot the name and address of the park for later.

"There we go, buddy," I say and pat Milo's head. He sighs at me and rolls over without taking his head out of my lap, so I rub his stomach. If the park were a little closer, I'd take Milo for a walk to scope it out, but after our extended romp this morning, I want to save the energy I have left for skating with Theo later. I'm not sure what he'll think of this little surprise, but I'm hoping he'll appreciate it.

And I'm hoping he'll have an extra pair of skates somewhere around here that will fit me. I could search around myself, but I don't want him to feel like I'm snooping, so I'll just wait to ask until he gets home. But I don't know how long he'll be and I'm feeling antsy, so I turn on the TV and try to find something to kill the time.

I'm zoning out to daytime talk TV about an hour later when Theo walks in, still damp from his post-practice shower. Milo barks and bounds off the couch to greet him, jumping up his front and slobbering everywhere. Theo laughs and pets his head.

"Well, hello to you too, boy! Did you miss me?" Milo barks in response. "I'll take that as a yes."

"How was practice?" I ask from the couch.

"Pretty good. But I was a little distracted because I couldn't stop wondering about what this little surprise would be."

"Sorry. It's nothing major."

Theo tosses his bag down on the floor, then joins me on the couch in a flop. "I'm teasing you. But I am curious. What's up?"

I unlock my phone and bring up the screenshot of the park I found online. "I want you to take me here."

Theo raises an eyebrow at me. "The park? That's the big surprise?"

"There's more to it than that. Is that okay?"

"Yeah, of course. This might sound like a weird question, but what should I wear?"

I examine his sweatpants and shirt and shrug. "I think what you're wearing now should be fine. Might want to bring a coat though."

"Got it. Anything else I should bring?"

"Yeah. Your skates."

Theo laughs and nods as the surprise starts to take shape. "Oh, we're going skating, huh? Cute."

"Yup. So I'm really hoping you have an extra pair of skates that will fit me."

"Whoa, whoa, wait a second. You're telling me a Canadian girl doesn't own a pair of ice skates?"

"Well, I used to, but I donated them when I moved to LA because I knew I wasn't going to need them there, and I wasn't planning on ever going back to Canada."

"Right, that makes sense." Theo considers, then grins. "You know what? I think I might have a pair you could wear. I bought them for my mom on one of their visits, but she's too afraid to get out on the ice these days."

"Oh. Do you think they'll fit?"

He shrugs. "Only one way to find out."

"Okay. Then I guess I'll try them on and see."

"Assuming I can find them. Hold on."

He disappears upstairs, then returns a few moments later with a pair of skates dangling from his finger by their laces.

"Bingo," he declares triumphantly. "And they look like the right size too."

He walks them over to me, so I stick out my foot. He sits on the coffee table and puts my foot in his lap, and although it's innocent, I can't help noticing the current that passes between us when he puts his hands on me again. He grips me by the ankle and lifts my foot to slip the skate over it.

His eyes drift up to mine, and he grins at me, activating my nervous system all over again. The skate is a little big, but less than a full shoe size. Theo squeezes the top of the skate, checking to see where my toes reach, and shrugs. "It's not perfect, but it'll do. You'll just have to lace them a little tighter."

"Then we're in business. Ready to go?"

"I'd go anywhere with you."

He grins, dropping his head to a kiss the patch of skin between my leggings and the top of the skate, making my breath catch. Then he slips the skate off my foot, ties it back up with the other, and gives them to me. He offers a hand to help me off the couch, then we take turns telling Milo goodbye and head for the car.

"Let me guess, you keep a pair of skates in your car too?" I ask.

Theo laughs. "When you're a professional hockey player, you never know when you might need them."

I don't know how true that is, but the image of his Aces buddies calling him up randomly for an impromptu game like a bunch of little boys pops into my head. As goofy as it is, I could see them doing it.

When we hit the road a few minutes later, Theo immediately puts his hand on my leg. "This is really sweet of you."

I shrug. "You've done so much for me, so I figure this is the least I can do to repay you."

He turns his intense emerald gaze on me. "You don't owe me anything, Becca. Like I said, I'm doing this—"

"Because you want to," I finish for him. "I know. But I want to do something nice for you in return, even if I don't owe it to you."

Theo beams at me and pats my leg. "Alright. Thank you."

I hesitate with my hand hovering above his for a second before I give in and wind our fingers together. "You're welcome."

We drive the rest of the way to the park in silence, enjoying each other's company and the beautiful winter scenery of frozen trees and freshly fallen snow covering the hilly landscape. The park itself is busy with families and young people enjoying the rare sunny day in winter, so finding a decent parking spot is difficult, but Theo manages.

"I think the pond is toward the back of the park judging by the map," I say as I zoom in on the screenshot I took earlier on my phone.

"Sure is. I know exactly the place. Come on," Theo says and kills the engine to walk around back and fish our skates out of the trunk. I throw my pair over my shoulder like he does, then he offers his hand again, so I take it and follow him to the back of the park.

The "pond" is so big that it covers three-fourths of the area and might be more accurate to call a lake. But the surface seems to be at least six inches thick with ice, and there are at least two dozen people already zooming around across it, so it feels pretty safe. I sit down on a nearby bench to change into my skates, and Theo sits next to me.

"So," he starts as he kicks off his shoes. "Can I ask why we're here?"

I peel off my left shoe and shove my foot into a skate. "When I was traveling around with my mom, I couldn't always train in a dance studio. But I could always find an empty space to practice in, even if it was something makeshift."

"Like a frozen pond," Theo says with a laugh, and I nod.

"Exactly. It didn't really matter where I danced. Ultimately, all I needed was to *dance*. And I think it might be sort of the same thing for you with hockey."

Theo pauses lacing his skate to look me in the eye. "What do you mean?"

"Well, I know you've been having a hard time this season. There's probably a lot of reasons for that, but I think the biggest one is that the passion's gone, you know? We don't become professionals in something just because. We do it because we love it. But when you don't love it anymore—"

"It just starts to feel like work," he finishes for me, and I nod.

"Right. This might be a frozen pond in a public park, but it's about as far away from the rigidity and stuffiness of a hockey arena as you can get. But we've still got ice and skates, so I'm hoping this can help you reignite that love. No expectations or pressure, just the fun of doing something you love."

"With someone you love spending time with," he adds, and I can't stop myself from blushing, which makes him grin. "I think this is a great idea."

"Yeah?"

"Definitely," he says and finishes lacing up before standing and extending his hand to me. I take it and he helps me to my feet. Walking with skates on is always difficult, but we penguin-waddle our way to the ice and Theo drifts out first. He glides without any effort at all, which isn't a surprise for someone who spends so much time on the ice, but it still impresses me how naturally it comes to him.

Meanwhile, it's been several years since I last went ice skating, so I'm a little less graceful when my skates meet the surface. My right foot shoots ahead of me, nearly taking me down, but I get my footing and after a few desperate flails of my arms, I right myself and drift over to him. He's doing his best to bite back a laugh, but it only makes me want to laugh too.

"Shut up," I say teasingly, and he motions like he's zipping his lips but laughs. "I know I probably look like Bambi right now, but it's been a while. I'll find my footing, just give me a second."

Theo extends a hand, so I reach out for it and hold on for dear life while I steady myself. I really am a better ice skater than I'm probably leading him to believe right now, but I wasn't lying when I told him it'd been a while since the last time I did it —so long that I actually can't remember the last time.

But once I have my feet underneath me again, it all starts to slowly come back. It's not all that different from dancing, just a bit more slippery. Theo skates backward slowly, still holding my hand, and I follow him gingerly out onto the ice. Every time I put one foot in front of the other and manage not to fall on my face, I feel a little more confident.

"See? I told you I wasn't a total disaster at this," I say, but Theo only smiles at me. I appreciate that he isn't rushing me, but I also don't want him to think I need to keep the training wheels on all day, so I let go of his hand and confidently skate around his side. "Would a beginner be able to do something like that?"

Theo shrugs. "I don't know, that was still a pretty beginner move in my book."

"Okay, fine. Then let's push things a little farther," I say and charge away across the ice, zipping past other skaters and leaving Theo standing with his jaw hanging open. After the way I stumbled at the start, he probably can't believe how fast I can move.

He laughs and shakes his head, then comes chasing after me. I try to keep my momentum and the distance, but with his powerful, muscled legs, it only takes a few strides for him to catch me. When he does, he playfully slaps my ass on his way by.

"Tag, you're it," he says and zooms away. The other skaters around us are watching, but I don't care. I peel around a couple in front of me and chase after him, and he must be feeling sorry for me or something because he seems to intentionally slow down enough that I can catch him.

I'm just reaching out to slap his ass in return when he jukes at the last second, sending me sailing right past him. I nearly grab the behind of someone I don't know instead, and when I circle around the edge of the pond, I find him skating behind me with a bright red face from laughing so hard. But we'll see who gets the last laugh.

He skates up next to me and offers me his hand again. "I'm sorry, I shouldn't laugh, but that was hilarious. Would've only been funnier if you'd actually grabbed someone."

"Somehow, I don't think the innocent bystander would agree."

"Probably not. But I've got to give you props, you're a better skater than I would've guessed from how this started."

"I'm not sure if I should take that as a compliment or an insult."

Theo's emerald eyes flash as he squeezes my hand. "It was definitely a compliment. I guess there really is a lot of similarity between dancing and skating."

"You didn't believe me?"

"Not really," he says and laughs. "I know both require a lot of skill and coordination, but I just didn't really see the link until I saw you zipping around the ice like it was nothing. You're a natural."

"Now *that* I'll take as a compliment, especially coming from the professional skater," I say, and Theo pulls on my hand to spin me around and into his arms. I almost tip over, but he holds me tight against his chest as we coast to a stop in the middle of the ice. Thankfully, the other skaters pass us without running us over.

"What are you doing?" I ask with a little laugh, my nerves fraying. The only time I like being the center of attention is when I'm on the dance floor.

"Care to dance?"

My heart thuds in my throat. "What? Seriously? Right now?"

"Yes, seriously, and yes, right now."

"But we're on the ice."

"Yeah, and?"

"Hard to argue with such sound logic," I tease, and Theo laughs.

"Are you up for the challenge?"

It's not really me I'm worried about as much as it is him. I've seen his dancing, and it's not the greatest even without skates and ice underneath him. But we're here to have fun and help him fall in love with skating again, so if that's what he wants, I'll do it.

"Challenge accepted," I say, and he nods with a warm smile before he flings me away with one arm, sending me spinning like a ballerina until our linked arms extend all the way and I jerk to a stop. It's not the most graceful move, but people around us start clapping, so it must have looked purposeful.

I glance over at him, unsure what he's up to, but he just wiggles his brows at me, then pulls me back into him. Our hands link in a classic dance pose, and my free hand rests on his shoulder while his wraps around my lower back.

"Ready?" he asks, and I nod, so he takes one stride to his right, and I match his step. Then he moves to the left and back again, and we float across the frozen surface like we're in a production of Beauty and the Beast on ice. The small crowd watching us claps again, and I realize that it's probably because at least some of the people recognize Theo.

"I don't know how it's possible, but you're much more fluid on the ice than you are on solid ground," I say.

"You aren't the first person to tell me that. My mom used to say that I should've been born on the ice because I was always so much more at home on it."

"When did you first learn to skate?"

"I can't remember," Theo says, shaking his head before staring off into the distance to think. "The first time that comes to mind was when I was around five. My dad took me out to a pond a lot like this one, but way smaller."

"Was John a good skater too?"

Theo smiles at me. "Where do you think I learned it from?"

"I figured it must run in the family. Did he play hockey when he was younger?"

Theo shrugs. "All the guys in my family have played hockey at some point or another. It's kind of a Camden thing. But I'm pretty sure I'm the only one who ever had the skill and the ambition to do something with it other than for fun."

"And when was the last time you just went skating for fun?" I ask, and Theo hesitates before he sighs and laughs.

"Can't remember that either, honestly. But I'm having a pretty damn good time now." His green eyes are warm, and I want to kiss him, but before I can make a move, he unexpectedly dips me backward. My head flies back as I laugh, and he stops me just a few inches away from the ice.

The small audience we've gathered gasps and claps again, and when Theo pulls me back up to him, he cradles the back of my head to give me one of the softest, most romantic kisses I think we've ever shared. My body ignites when our lips touch, and if we weren't in such a public place, it would probably escalate quickly.

But I kiss him back with the full force of the intensity I'm feeling instead until he finally breaks and stands staring into my eyes.

"Thank you for this. I needed it more than I knew," he whispers so that only I can hear him. I want to say something back, but my head and thoughts are spinning from the rush of blood after the drop—and the kiss.

Hunger and something else I can't quite place flashes in his irises, and between that and the racing of my heart, I don't think my head is ever going to stop spinning.

Chapter 25

Theo

Before my next game, I pop down into the workout room to tell Becca I'm leaving. I find her mid-stretch, warming up to practice her dancing. She's got one leg lifted on the balance bar my dad helped me install for her with her foot higher than her waist, and she's leaning into the stretch. The sheer flexibility of it, combined with the skin-tight workout uniform she's wearing, gets my imagination running wild.

"God, how I'd love to fuck you just like this," I whisper as I sneak down the stairs behind her. She startles and looks over her shoulder with her cheeks flushed like we haven't fucked dozens of times by this point. It's been a couple of weeks since we agreed to do away with our "no sex" rule and we've been taking advantage of it. A lot.

Becca smirks at me. "Well, if you play well enough tonight and bring home a victory, maybe I'll let you."

"Maybe? Just a maybe for a win against our arch nemeses, the Prowlers?" I ask as I rest my hands on her hips, letting her feel my already hardening cock through my pants as I press my chest to her back.

Ever since we got rid of the no sex rule, things have been so much easier and more fun between us. All the stress and non-stop tension that was there for weeks before dissipated almost instantly—thank god. I would've gone insane if we'd tried to keep that charade up.

But Becca's grin fades at the mention of the Prowlers, and I grimace as I realize why.

"You don't have to come tonight if you don't want to. I'd understand," I say, and she shakes her head.

"No. I'll be there."

"Even if it means coming face to face with Kaplan?"

"Especially because it means seeing him," she says firmly, and a smile cracks my face. "I want him to see how much happier and better off I am without him. And I want the whole world to see it too."

"I'm so fucking proud of you for not letting that prick hold you back," I say and peck a kiss on her cheek. "You'll wear my jersey tonight, right? Just to really rub it in?"

Becca laughs and nods. "Of course I will. But I'm not doing it just for him. I hope I'll be your good luck charm again tonight."

"I don't know how I could lose with you in the crowd," I say and kiss her again. She holds me in place to kiss me back, and although I'd love to take her right here and now, I pull away because I really need to get going to the arena before I'm late. Noah and the rest of the team would never let me live it down.

"I know, I know, you've gotta go," she sighs when we part. "But remember what I said about winning tonight."

She bites her bottom lip as she grins at me, and I slap her ass lightly.

"I won't forget. And I'll hold you to it too."

"Then get out of here. You've got a game to win. I'll see you later."

I leave before the temptation keeps me in place and it's a good thing there's no one around in the parking garage because

I'm still rock hard when I climb into my car—and I'm sure it's noticeable. I crack the windows to get some cold air flowing to cool myself off, then speed to the arena and make it with just a few minutes to spare.

I head right to the locker room to change and find the rest of the guys already gearing up. Grant looks even grouchier than usual, and judging from the looks on Reese and Sawyer's faces, I'm betting it's because they're giving him some good-natured shit.

"There he is! The man of the hour!" Noah shouts when he spots me across the locker room.

"I didn't know I had such a fan club," I say, smiling at the rest of the guys as I start tearing my clothes off near my locker.

"It's nothing compared to mine, apparently," Grant grumbles, but it has the opposite effect from what he probably wanted because the team refocuses their attention on him.

"Who pissed in your Wheaties today anyway?" Sawyer asks with a punch at Grant's arm.

"I was fine until you two started up."

"Please, you've been acting like Eeyore since you walked in here today," Reese challenges. Grant rolls his eyes and grumbles something under his breath, but I can't hear it over Noah clapping to get everyone's focus.

"Alright, alright, leave the poor guy alone, yeah?" Noah chides. "Besides, we've got bigger things to worry about, like winning a game against the Prowlers."

That gets an eager whoop from the entire team, and in an instant, we're all in game mode. I'm glad, because I want nothing more than to kick the ever-loving shit out of Kaplan and his team tonight. Nothing would make me happier, especially after what happened the last time he and I squared off on the ice when he got that cheap ass check that cost us the game.

That won't happen again. Tonight, or ever.

Noah gives a speech to fire us up, but I'm barely listening

because I'm already chomping at the bit to get out there and pound the Prowlers into the fucking ice. I don't just want to win tonight—I want to destroy them. So, they aren't gonna know what hit them from the second I get out there.

By the time Noah finishes, I'm all geared up along with the rest of the team, so we head out onto the ice together for warm-ups like we always do. We start by doing a few laps to get our muscles working and blood pumping, then take turns running drills shooting against Grant while the seats continue to fill up with fans of both teams. He's not as distracted as he was in the locker room, but I still sink my shot like it's nothing.

When it's time to let the Prowlers take their turn, I find Becca in her usual seat in the front row and skate over to press my gloved hand against the glass. She beams and waves at me, and even though she can't get close enough to press her hand against the glass too, I feel like she's right next to me anyway.

But then her expression falls, so I turn to follow her gaze and see Kaplan standing and scowling at us from center ice. Good. Let his sorry ass see exactly what he missed out on, and how much better off Becca is with me.

I turn back to Becca and pound on the glass to catch her attention. Her eyes drift down to mine, so I kiss my glove and smash it against the glass.

"Fuck him," I mouth, and she laughs and nods. But the buzzer sounds to announce it's time to clear the ice so the resur-facer can run to keep it nice and smooth for us.

"You good?" Noah shouts in my ear as we pile off the ice into our team bench, but I can't take my eyes off Kaplan, who's sitting almost directly across from me on the Prowler's bench. Noah laughs and claps me on the back. "I should've known that's what this was about. Don't worry, we're gonna fucking wreck them tonight."

"You're damn right we are."

Noah flashes me a pleased smile. "There's the old Theo I

remember. You keep that fire burning and they won't stand a chance," he says as the resurfacer passes us, temporarily breaking my stare down with Kaplan. But as soon as it's gone, I find Kaplan's eyes boring into mine again. He smirks at me, which makes me want to punch him more than I usually do, but I blow it off. I know he's just trying to get me worked up so he can knock me off my game.

It's not going to work.

It feels like it takes an hour for the resurfacer to finish its work, but when it's finally done, we head back out onto the ice and form up to get ready for the puck drop. I take my place on the right wing, ready to support Noah and any of the other guys on my side—and hopefully steal a goal as soon as possible. If we can get an early lead, that will just corner the Prowlers.

The referee skates into the center, and the crowd roars as he gets ready to drop the puck. I stay laser focused on it, ready to pounce as soon as the black disc leaves his hand. The ref slots a whistle into his mouth, and I tense like a panther, every muscle in my body screaming to spring.

All the noise in the arena fades into a distant buzz, almost like I've dipped my head underwater, but the screech of the whistle pierces it and I attack the ice with my skates as the puck tumbles out of the ref's hand. My stick connects with it just as it hits the ice and I'm flying toward the Prowler's wide-eyed goalie before everyone else can even get their bearings.

Just like I said, they didn't know what hit them. I sprint down the ice with all the power I can muster, then wind back and slap the puck away. The goalie sails through the air to try and intercept it, but it blazes past his left ear to collide with the net behind him.

The crowd goes insane, making the goal buzzer barely audible over all the noise they're making. All the lights and sound pump me up even more as we all square up for the next face off. But the Prowlers seem to be waking up to the fact that

I'm not fucking around, because Kaplan lines up across me. I hate to say it, but he's their best player, so the fact they want him on me is almost a compliment. Almost.

"Don't get used to scoring, Camden," he shouts over the noise in the arena, but I know he's just trying to bait me, so I pay him no mind and get ready to leap for the puck again. He can talk all the shit he wants, but when we're up two to nothing within the first five minutes of the game, we'll see how cocky he is.

The ref tosses the puck and even though I'm fast, Kaplan is unfortunately faster. He bats it away before I can and cuts through the throng of players, but I'm on him. He makes it three quarters of the way down the ice toward Grant before I intercept him. He tries to juke left, but I'm on to his usual tricks and anticipate it by juking with him.

That catches him off-guard long enough for me to swipe the puck away and pass to Noah before Kaplan even puts two and two together. A roar swells in the crowd again from the reversal, giving me all the encouragement I need. I keep Noah in my peripheral as I bolt down the ice with him, ready to catch a pass if he makes it.

The Prowlers' center is blocking his shot, but he somehow manages to shoot the puck right through the guy's legs to me, which makes the crowd lose it. I'm already winding up to take the shot before the puck reaches me, and when my stick slaps against it, I hear it whiz through the air, hovering just above the ice.

The goalie drops to his knees, trying to block the shot with his super padded legs, but he misjudges the angle, and the puck clips his shoulder before bouncing into the net. The arena erupts into cheers and buzzing, and the entire Aces team flies over to dog pile on me, pounding on my helmet and cheering with the crowd.

But as everyone hurries to their positions, Kaplan skids to a halt in front of me. "Pretty good shot for someone who's content with sloppy seconds."

Rage boils in my veins as quickly as if someone had flipped a switch. "What the fuck did you just say?"

Kaplan shrugs. "I'm just surprised you'd want to marry someone who's damaged goods. I thought you were better than that. I mean, Becca might be fun, but she's not really the type you put a ring on."

He's fucking with me, and I know he is, but what pisses me off even more is that it's working. He's getting under my skin. I suck down gulps of air, trying to keep my cool, and smash my shoulder hard into his as I skate by. Kaplan stumbles backward but doesn't fall. He laughs and shakes his head.

"I guess that means she hasn't told you about her little problem yet, has she?"

"She already gotten rid of the biggest problem in her life— you," I spit back and take my position. He wants a reaction out of me, wants to make me do something stupid. But I'm not going to give him the satisfaction. Besides, I don't even know what the fuck he's talking about, and it's probably bullshit anyway. Just like everything else that comes out of his mouth.

But just like I thought, being down two goals must be getting to him because he's glaring at me as we face off again. Knowing I'm the one pissing him off for once gives me a twisted kind of satisfaction, so I can't wait to see the pissy look on his face when I score on him *again*.

But Reese takes the puck this time, probably because I'm too distracted with Kaplan, so I chase after him. I can't really keep my eye on him though, because Kaplan keeps blocking my view. Clearly, he doesn't want to risk me sinking another shot, so I try to fake him out, but he doesn't fall for it.

We keep dancing down the ice like this until Reese pivots near the goal and tries to pass back to me. I reach out for it, but Kaplan slashes his stick down on mine, nearly taking my fucking hand off. That sends me over the edge, and before I realize what's happening, my gloves are off and I'm slamming him against the boards. I rip his helmet away and land a few punches to his smug face before the refs peel me off him and escort me to the penalty box.

It's not until I sit down in a huff that I blink and realize blood's dripping down into my eye from my brow. I must have cut it somehow in the fight. Noah's going to be furious with me for letting Kaplan goad me into a penalty like this, but he fucking slashed me. What was I supposed to do, just let him get away with it?

The prick is lucky the refs were here. I sit stewing and waiting for the refs to penalize Kaplan too, but when the teams form up again and Kaplan's still on the ice, my blood boils. How the hell did he dodge the box?! He openly slashed me, which is what led to the fight in the first place.

There's an agonizing ten minutes on my penalty clock for fighting, which means I won't be able to get back out on the ice until the end of the game. Maybe it's because everyone else is on edge after my fight with Kaplan, but they all seem to have backed off, gotten more tentative. And that only pisses me off more. Now's not the time to waffle! We're up two points to nothing and we need to keep that going.

But three minutes into my penalty, the Prowlers score on Grant. I pound my fists against the bench, furious. At least it wasn't Kaplan who scored the goal, but still. As if he knows I'm thinking about him, Kaplan skates by and scowls at me on his way to the face off. I raise my fist to flip him off but catch myself. I don't want any more time added to my penalty.

Another five minutes pass without a goal for either side, but that only makes me antsy, especially as the teams keep trading possession of the puck. I jump out of my seat with every attempted pass and interception. Someone's bound to score at this rate, and it better be us. We're approaching the final ten minutes of the game.

With one minute left to go on my penalty, the Prowlers sink another shot—this time by kicking it in. The Prowlers' left wing took the shot, but bounced it off the outside of the goal, and before Grant could recalibrate and figure out where the puck landed, Kaplan was there to kick it in. Because of course he was.

I'm not sure what's worse, that they scored a goal like that, or that it was Kaplan, of all people, who did it. When my penalty time finally ends, I'm already standing with my helmet back on and ready to charge out onto the ice. The game is tied now with a little less than ten minutes to go, so it's up to me to bring the fire.

And that's exactly what I'm going to do.

I dash out of the box and take my place on the right wing during the face off. Kaplan's there, giving me his stupid fucking smug smile, but I'm not about to let him goad me into another trip to time out. All we need to do is score one more goal and keep it locked to win the game, and that's the most important thing to me.

"You gonna behave this time?" Noah calls to me, but he's wearing a smile that tells me he's not exactly upset about the fact I beat Kaplan's face in.

"On my best behavior, scout's honor!" I shout back and cross one arm over my chest. Noah chuckles and turns back to the game, so I crouch, ready to spring again. I've got so much pent-up energy from the last ten minutes spent locked in the box that I feel like I could skate a hundred laps around this giant ass area and still not burn it off.

The ref tosses the puck, and I lunge for it, but the Prowlers' right wing gets there first and starts rocketing down the ice toward Grant. Sawyer heads him off as he inches into the defensive zone and forces him to turn around long enough for me to catch up and intercept. I swipe the puck away from the right wing and in one continuous, fluid motion, spin to send it soaring down the ice in the opposite direction toward Noah.

Noah completes the pass like it's nothing, like he psychically knew I was going to spin it back to him, and shoots on a wide-open Prowlers' goalie. Not even their defenseman was prepared for such a quick turnaround in possession, so when the puck soars past their goalie and crashes into the net, he's just as confused as the rest of his team about how it happened.

But the roaring and stomping in the stands overpowers it as the goal lights flash and the buzzers sound repeatedly. Noah meets me at center ice and pulls me in for a hug, pounding on my helmet with his glove.

"That was your goal, you know that, right?" he bellows over the noise. "When we win this game, and we will, it's because of you."

Maybe when the game's actually over and the victory is ours, I'll be able to bask in what he just said, but in the moment, all I can think about is defending our position for the next few minutes until the timer runs out. If we happen to score again, great, but we don't have to. We just have to beat the clock.

The Prowlers seem to be losing momentum—probably because their morale is sinking. They know the odds aren't in their favor. We have the home advantage with Aces fans filling the stands and cheering us on, we're up three to two, and there's less than three minutes left on the clock. The best they can hope for is a tie at this point.

But I'm not going to let that happen, either.

Over the next two minutes, I skate my ass off, intercepting every single play that I can manage and crossing the ice so many times I lose track. The Prowlers are down but not out, and like cornered animals, the closer we get to the wire, the more desperate they seem to get.

During one of our last face-offs with about a minute left on the clock, their left wing gets a penalty for trying to trip Reese with his stick. The Prowlers are furious about it, but they should've thought about that before they decided to play dirty. Because now they're playing shorthanded and know there's next to no chance they're going to turn things around.

We square up for what will probably be the last face off with thirty seconds left on the clock, and although my entire body is screaming with soreness and exertion, I'm still electrified —and determined to win this game. All that stands between me and humiliating Kaplan and the rest of the Prowlers is thirty seconds.

I catch a glimpse of Becca in the stands while waiting for the ref to drop the puck. She's standing with her fists pressed nervously against her mouth, but when she notices me looking, she throws her hands in the air and shouts something I can't make out, but it's all I need to see to take me to the end.

The ref blows his whistle and tosses the puck, and the next thirty seconds pass in a blur. I barely keep track of the puck as it zooms between players, but neither team manages to get it far enough away from center ice for it to matter. And when the final buzzer sounds, and the crowd goes ballistic as the screens above the ice declare our victory, I breathe a sigh of relief.

The Aces pile together around me, shouting and pumping their sticks in the air for the crowd who are still going nuts, and I finally let myself feel the moment as I look around at all the cheering people. We did it. Two of our three goals were mine, and the third one was because of me too. If anything should make the sports rags stop talking about how I've "lost my game," it's having a win like this.

We utterly humiliated Kaplan and the Prowlers, our biggest rivals, so I should feel on top of the world right now. But I can't stop thinking about what Kaplan said.

What the hell did he mean about Becca's 'little problem'? Was he just baiting me? Talking bullshit to try to get under my skin?

Goddammit, I hate that motherfucker.

I leave the ice with the rest of the Aces, aching and drenched in sweat, to take a hot shower and hopefully clear my head. The press will definitely want to talk to me after that game, but they're the last thing I want to deal with right now, so after I shower and slap a bandage on the cut above my eye, I find Noah.

"Think you can handle the journalists for me?"

Noah lifts an eyebrow. "I would've thought you'd be dying to get in front of the cameras after that game. Everything okay?"

"Yeah, yeah, everything's fine. I'm just exhausted and want to call it a night."

Noah punches me in the arm. "You played great tonight, Camden. I'm really fucking proud of you. Welcome back."

"Thanks, captain."

"Now go on, get out of here," he says with a beaming smile. I throw on a coat and ball cap from my locker before I leave, hoping it'll be enough to throw the reporters if they see me sneaking through the arena to the family room to find Becca. Thankfully, no one notices.

Becca spots me as soon as I enter, but she's chewing her lip. She hurries over to me, looking like she wants to hug me, but she hesitates. "Are you okay? Are you sore?"

I say nothing and pull her into my arms instead. She gives in, wrapping her arms around my neck and resting her head on my shoulder. No matter how sore I am, all I need right now is to hold her, to feel her close.

Chapter 26

Becca

I hug Theo back and notice the tightness in his grip. It's like he's afraid if he lets me go, I'll disappear or something. After that incredible game, he should be on cloud nine, but he seems like something is bothering him. Did something happen out on the ice the rest of us don't know about yet? My eyes flutter shut as I squeeze him back, hoping it will be enough to comfort him.

"Aw, how fucking touching, the prince and his pauper."

Theo's body turns rigid, and my eyes snap open to find Shawn standing in the entrance to the family and friends lounge, staring right at us. After the way he swung at Shawn during the game, I know it won't take much to get Theo going again, so I pull back and look him in the eye.

"Ignore him. He's not worth it," I insist. I'm not about to let Theo risk his career over someone as stupid and irrelevant as Shawn. "Take me home. Make me yours."

Heat and possessiveness spark in Theo's eyes, and he smashes his lips into mine, kissing me passionately for the whole room to see. Shawn makes a disgusted noise, but Theo ignores him, continuing to kiss me for several seconds before he abruptly breaks and takes me by the hand. He glares at Shawn on our way out, then leads me from the family room into the labyrinthine halls of the arena.

I don't know where we're going, but as we storm through the halls, I feel the emotion roiling off Theo in waves. And I can feel the tension in the firm grip of his hand in mine. A few seconds later, we emerge from an unlabeled door into the area of the parking garage set aside for the players and Theo makes a beeline for his car.

Inside, I steal a glance at him, and a jumble of emotions rush through me. I don't know exactly what it is I'm feeling or how to express them, but I do know that I want to ease some of the tension that's threatening to make him snap. And I want him, in a deeper, more primal way than I've ever wanted anyone before.

I don't think either of us can wait until we get back to the condo, so once we're out of the parking garage and on the street, I lean over and reach for Theo's pants. His eyes shoot to mine, his brows stitched together.

"What are you doing?" he asks, his voice raspy.

"If I'm yours, then you're mine too," I tell him, surprised by the possessive note in my voice. "And I want what's mine."

His hands tighten on the wheel as I unzip his pants and slip my hand inside. His cock is already half hard, and it thickens and swells when I run my fingers across its head. Theo makes a low noise, his hips shifting forward a little, and that's all the encouragement I need. I gently work his cock out of his boxers, then lean down and draw it into my mouth.

Theo groans, and I can practically feel some of the tension draining away as my tongue works around him. His hand finds the back of my head, and he pushes my hair out of my face to get a better look at me as he glances down. Hunger is written all over his face.

"You dirty girl," he murmurs. "I fucking love it. But you don't have to do this."

"I know, but I want to," I whisper, echoing his words back at him before I take him back in my mouth.

His nostrils flare, his jaw tensing as he presses his head back against the head rest. "*Fuck*, your mouth feels so good. Jesus, princess, you fucking wreck me."

Feeling bold, I keep going, hollowing my cheeks as I start to suck him. It's a lot to fit, but every little groan and grunt he gives me in response just makes me want to do more. And better. Because as much as he's taken care of me, I want to return the favor. I want to make him feel as amazing as he's made me feel for weeks on end.

He's fully hard now, so I pick up the pace, bobbing up and down in his lap. If we stop at a red light or something, it'll be immediately obvious to anyone who looks what's going on in the car. But I don't give a damn who sees, and from the way he's urging me on with his hand, I'm betting he doesn't care either. He's firm with the way he pushes my head down onto his cock, but not rough with it, and that only turns me on more—especially when he winds his fingers in my hair and grips a handful of it, making my scalp tingle.

"Good girl, take it all the way."

He hisses out a breath, pushing me down slowly until the base of his cock meets my lips. He holds me there for a few seconds until I start to sputter for air, then lets up. But I don't come off his cock. Instead, I wrap my fist around him and slide it up and down to match the movements of my mouth.

I try to go all the way back down on him, and this time when my fist reaches his base, I give it a squeeze while I run my tongue over the underside of his cock. He groans, and the car jerks sideways a little, forcing his cock even deeper down my throat and almost making me gag.

His fingers leave my hair as he puts both hands on the wheel again.

"Shit, you make it hard as hell to focus," he mutters, and I peek out of his lap in time to see him correct our course. "You're a damn hazard, princess."

I know Theo is the type to maintain control of the car even in a moment like this, but still, the recklessness and daring of what we're doing goes right to my head. A gush of wetness floods my panties as I lick my lips.

"Do you want me to stop?" I whisper.

He glances down at me for just a brief second, heat burning in his eyes. "I didn't say that."

The look on his face makes my heart flutter, and I slide my mouth back down on his cock. I don't hold anything back this time, sucking and licking at him like his dick will be my last meal, and he lets out a guttural groan after a moment.

"You're gonna make me come if you keep that up," he grunts as his hand finds my head again.

I know he means it as a warning, a chance for me to back off, but I want it so badly. I want to feel him come down my throat, so instead of stopping, I just pick up the pace, squeezing his base harder.

"Oh my fucking god," he says as he starts rolling his hips in time to meet the movement of my mouth. "Holy fuck, you're so good at that. Your mouth is so... fucking... good."

The last word ends on a groan as his entire body goes rigid, and he lets out a low curse as he comes. His cock swells and pulses in my mouth, coating my tongue with his cum. I do my best to swallow it all, but some of it leaks out and dribbles down his cock.

Refusing to let it go to waste, I drag my tongue up his length, gathering every last drop.

He shudders, blowing out a rough breath. "Holy shit, you're gonna kill me."

I'm still running my tongue over him when he puts the car in park and yanks me off his dick by my hair to pull me up to his mouth. His lips crash against mine like he can't get enough, and I feel my clit throb like a second heartbeat.

When the kiss finally breaks, I realize we're in the garage at his condo. Theo's eyes rake over me, two glowing emerald coals.

"You're such a bad girl. You almost made me lose control," he says evenly, but his words crackle with heat, giving me goosebumps.

"If I've been bad, maybe you should punish me," I whisper.

"*Fuck.*"

An almost tortured expression passes over his face, and he grabs me by the back of the neck and pulls me in for another kiss. His hands move roughly over my body, tugging at my clothes like he's going to fuck me right here in the front seat. Not that I'd stop him if he did. I'm so turned on that he could fuck me anywhere he wanted, and I wouldn't care who was around to see.

But he pulls away just as abruptly a moment later and gets out of the car to stride quickly around to the passenger side.

He flings the door open, unbuckles me, and turns me sideways on the seat so that my legs are dangling out the door. His fingers work quickly as he undoes my pants and tugs them down my legs along with my soaked panties. He drags his fingers across the slick spot I left on the fabric and then sucks on them, dragging a moan out of me.

"So wet for me already," he murmurs. "I love how turned on you are, just from that. Did driving me crazy turn you on, princess? Did knowing how hard I had to work to keep my eyes on the road get you this wet? You like teasing me like that?"

"Yes," I whisper, biting my lip.

He smirks. "You really are a bad girl. So I guess I *should* punish you. I'm gonna make you come for me right here. But you only get to come when I say so."

He's wearing a feral look as he gets rid of my shoes and drags my pants and panties all the way off, tossing them aside.

Then he grips my knees and uses that hold to spread my legs apart. He sinks to his knees between my thighs and licks his lips, making me shiver again because I know what's coming.

All I can do is whimper. My brain has turned to mush, but it's nothing compared to the tangle of sensations that explode in my core when his tongue finds my pussy. My moans fill the garage, and I know that the whole complex can probably hear me, but I'm too lost in the incredible feelings he's giving me to care. I lean back against the center console, my hair dangling over into the driver's seat, and give myself over to him.

"That's it, get loud for me," Theo growls into my pussy, and the vibration makes my toes curl.

I rest my legs on his shoulders, and even the mild discomfort of my position as I sprawl over the center console of the car is overridden by the sheer pleasure his tongue brings as he starts to fuck me with it.

He tortures me just like he promised he would, pushing me right up to the edge and then backing off before my orgasm breaks. I whimper plaintively, but he just chuckles against my pussy.

"You're not in charge this time," he murmurs. "It's my turn. Time for me test your patience just like you tested mine."

"Theo, please..."

He adjusts his grip on my thighs. "You can beg all you like. I fucking love the sound of it. Beg me to let you come, princess."

And I do.

It starts off as small whimpers and whispered pleas, but after he gets me close and then backs away two more times, my noises get louder and louder, my words less restrained. I'm barely aware of what I'm saying anymore. All I can focus on is the overwhelming need to feel the pleasure building inside me like a pressure cooker explode, to feel it flooding my veins with the ecstasy that's just out of reach.

269

"Please, Theo. Please, oh god, fuck. I need to come. I'm so... I'm so..."

My voice trails off, wordless sounds pouring from my lips, and finally, Theo's self-control seems to snap.

"I want you to come on my face," he whispers, his lips hovering over my clit. "Do it now. Come for me. Let go."

His hot breath sends shockwaves through my body, and when he sucks my clit into his mouth, I can't fight the plaintive whimper that spills past my lips. He presses two fingers into me, and my vision turns white. I'm so turned on after getting him off that the feeling of his fingers inside me is all it takes to start the cascading waves of an orgasm.

I try to keep my eyes open through it, to peer between my legs to watch him hungrily lapping at my wetness, but the pleasure is so intense that my eyes water and force themselves closed. My hands claw and grab at anything in the car they can get hold of, and Theo presses his face into me, his stubble like a flint sparking against my sensitive skin.

When it's over, I melt across the seats, my chest heaving. Theo stands and zips up his pants, then takes me by the wrists and hoists me up out of the car into his arms, not even bothering to collect my pants and panties from the floor of his garage. I cling to his shoulders as he carries me into the condo, and even as spent as I feel, I'm nowhere near sated.

As soon as we're inside, he sets me back on my feet to press me against the wall. Milo perks up with interest, but he must realize we're distracted by each other, because he doesn't come to greet us as effusively as he normally does.

Theo's palms splay against the wall on either side of my head, keeping me locked in place as he resumes kissing me. He presses himself against me, and I feel his cock swelling again through his pants.

"Fuck, I need to be inside you," he mutters after a moment, pulling back. He scoops me back up into his arms and carries me to the stairs, kissing me the whole way. He's so absorbed in our kiss that he trips on the steps, and we almost go down, but he breaks the fall and then lowers me onto the stairs, pinning me underneath him.

Our eyes lock, our chests heaving in unison, and I realize we aren't going to make it to his bedroom. But that's fine with me.

Like he's reading my mind, he grips the hem of the jersey I'm wearing—*his* jersey—and pulls it off over my head to throw it on the landing below. He thumbs my nipples, making sparks shoot through me.

Then he rises to his knees to unfasten his belt and wraps it around my wrists, making my breath catch. I don't know where he's going with this, but I love it. He hoists my wrists above my head and uses the belt to tie me to the railing.

"Is this okay?"

"Yes," I say breathlessly. "It's more than okay."

"Good. Because I've got you right where I want you, and I never want to let you go."

His eyes burn into mine as he runs his hands down the sides of my naked body. And he's right. I can't go anywhere, but I don't want to—because this is right where I want to be too.

Theo stands and shucks off his pants. His cock juts out, fully hard again and dripping precum as he peels his shirt off over his head. Then he knees my legs open and crawls back over me, his hand cradling my chin.

"I'm going to fuck you just like this. Spread open and needy for me. Is that what you want, wife?"

My body floods with heat, and my pussy so soaked that I can feel it coating my thighs. I nod without breaking eye contact, and he drags his cock head across my clit, making me moan. I can't stand any more teasing, so I wrap my legs around his waist.

"Don't make me wait," I gasp. "Please, Theo. I'm ready."

He nods, his face set in taut lines that tell me he needs this as much as I do.

"Could never deny you anything," he breathes as he lines himself up.

I feel his head start to stretch my entrance and moan in anticipation, and when he pushes into me with a powerful thrust, I gasp as the air leaves my lungs in a rush. He's so fucking big, and even though we've had sex more times than I can count by now, it's still a shock in the best way. His hips meet mine as he bottoms out, and our groans mingle in the quietness of the condo.

"There we go. That's my good girl," he murmurs, stroking my face with the back of one hand. His thumb traces my lower lip, then he presses it inside. I whimper, wrapping my lips around his thumb as my clit throbs.

His hips draw back and punch forward again. A keening moan escapes me, and even though my arms suspended above my head are burning and my back is aching from the stairs digging into it, I don't care.

I don't need to be comfortable. I just need *him*. With my arms restrained, I have no choice but to give in and let go, so that's exactly what I do.

Theo continues his rhythmic stroking, steadily picking up steam with every thrust. His blazing eyes never leave mine, so I hold his gaze. It's hard to put words to what I see there, but whatever it is, it makes my heart thud harder.

"Want to feel you come again on my cock," Theo breathes. "Can you come for me again?"

I nod, because I can never deny him anything either. And with the way my legs are shaking, I know I couldn't stop myself from coming if I tried.

Theo's hand snakes down between us to find my clit, and he drags his fingers across it. The callouses on his skin feel electric against me, and my back arches sharply. When he takes his next stroke into me, he gets even deeper at this new angle, and I can't fight the moan or the shudder that courses through me.

He grips my hips to steady me as he drives in hard, making me cry out as pleasure shoots through me.

"Say my name," he orders, but I'm so overwhelmed that I can barely think straight. "Say it. Say. Who's. Fucking. You," he demands, each word punctuated by a staccato thrust that sends me into the stratosphere.

"Theo," I mumble almost incoherently, my head tossing.

"Louder."

"Theo!"

"And who am I?"

"My husband."

A savage grin splits his face. "That's right. Your husband. *Yours*. And don't you ever forget it, princess."

My body thrums. As if I could forget it. As if I'd ever want to. He might not know it, but he's changed my life in more ways than I could ever hope to articulate.

But words fall away entirely as we lose ourselves to each other. Theo scoops me up by the back of my neck with both hands, cradling my head while he thrusts in an almost animal-istic frenzy. The burning in my arms and wrists gradually fades away as I drift into a blissful pre-orgasmic haze until his thumb finds my clit again, shocking me back into my body and shoving me toward my climax.

"That's it, let go for me. Fall apart," Theo whispers. "I've got you, baby. I'm right here with you."

A ragged moan pours out of me as I do exactly as I'm told. I come hard, and he follows right after me, his hips bucking irreg-ularly and forcefully as he fills me up with his release.

His forehead rests against mine, his eyes boring into me as he sucks in desperate breaths.

We stay that way for what feels like an hour as we slowly start to come down from it all, until Theo finally laughs and kisses me. Without saying anything, he gently pulls out and reaches up to untie my wrists. My arms burn with a sweet, pulsing ache, just like the rest of my body.

But it's the best feeling in the world.

I don't know how he has the energy for it after what we just shared, but Theo lifts me off the stairs into his arms and carries me to his bedroom. He peels back the covers and lowers me into his bed before climbing in beside me with one arm wrapped around my waist and his face nestled in the space between my neck and shoulder. He's still breathing heavily, but I can't tell if it's from the sex, from carrying me, or both.

I'm sated and spent, so I should just drift right off to sleep. But something is bothering me. I try to brush it off, but every time I close my eyes, I see the moment between Theo and Shawn, just before Theo tore off Shawn's helmet and started throwing punches.

Shawn said something that started the fight, I'm sure of it. And I shouldn't give a shit about a single thing my asshole ex has to say, but I want to know.

The blowjob and the sex gave me something to distract myself from wondering immediately after the game and in the car on the way home.

But now that it's quiet, my mind won't stop racing—because I have a sinking feeling that whatever Shawn said was something about me. What else would cause Theo to lose it and end up in the penalty box?

"Hey. Where did you go?" Theo whispers in my ear as he gently drags a fingertip across my shoulder. I let out a little laugh, still shocked I'm so easy for him to read.

"Nowhere. I'm just drifting in the afterglow."

"You're thinking about something. I know you are. What is it?"

I hesitate, knowing if I don't ask now, I'll lose my chance. But I don't want to dampen this moment, either.

Silence falls between us for a moment, and then he adds, "Whatever it is, you can tell me."

I bite my lip, nerves overtaking the relaxed feeling that filled my body after our intense sex. Finally, I let out a quiet sigh and turn to face him.

"What did Shawn say to you about me?" I whisper.

Theo's expression softens. Reaching up, he gently tugs my lower lip free from my teeth, brushing his thumb over it.

"It doesn't matter," he tells me, his voice serious. "There's nothing anyone could say that would change the way I feel about you. Not a single. Damn. Thing."

I smile, leaning in to kiss him, but my stomach twists a little even as my lips move against his.

Because I don't think that's true.

Chapter 27

Theo

I soar across the ice like there's zero friction between it and my skates. We're running drills for practice, and maybe it's because I'm still riding the high of our last win against the Prowlers, but I'm playing like I'm at the top of my game again.

Even Coach Dunaway notices.

"Good work today, Camden!" he shouts as I breeze past the bench and gear up for another shot at Grant, who even through his grated face mask looks exhausted from trying to defend against me.

When Becca first came to live with me, I was probably at my lowest point. And it was even more of a struggle because of how distracted I felt all the time, even when she wasn't around. The tension just wouldn't stop building between us, and it was spilling over into pretty much every facet of my life—just like Noah warned me not to let happen.

But everything seems to have changed lately. I'm playing better than I have in months lately, and it makes me feel great. Now that my no-sex rule with Becca is firmly out the window, the chemistry between us isn't a distraction at all. If anything, it only makes me play harder and better because I know I'll get the best kind of reward for it.

She's like my fucking muse. I don't know exactly what it is about her, but she inspires me to play harder. I can't lie, I fucking *love* working up a sweat on the ice and then going home to play with her and Milo or working a sweat up all over again by fucking Becca.

And things are going well for her too. Surprising no one, she got the job at that dance academy she interviewed at a couple weeks ago. I'm a little bummed that means I won't get to spend as much time with her, but I'm glad for her sake that she'll have something that will inspire her too. And that will hopefully help her make some friends and start to feel more like she belongs here in Denver with me.

Dunaway blows the whistle, signaling the end of practice, and I realize I haven't been paying a lick of attention since I skated by him a few minutes ago. The rest of the guys pile off the ice, so I follow them back into the locker room to change and get cleaned up. After a shower, I grab my phone out of my locker and find a few texts from Becca.

BECCA: Hey, not that you need it, but good luck with practice today!

BECCA: Btw, I'm going to run some errands after I leave the studio today. So if you get home before me, I already took Milo out for his walk.

BECCA: And don't forget we got him those new treats. You can give him one when you get home! *heart emoji*

I smile, my gaze lingering on the little heart at the end of the last text.

"You're grinning at your phone like an idiot, bro," Reese calls, jarring me away from the screen.

I shrug, rolling my eyes at him across the locker room. "Yeah? So what?"

He smirks. "Just an observation. You seem really happy these days. I'm glad for you."

"Oh. Thanks." I clear my throat, rubbing a hand over the back of my neck. "Honestly, things are going really well. I've got my groove back on the ice, and I've got a great girl and an awesome dog. What more could a guy want?"

Reese laughs and nods, although he's wearing an amused look. "I'm happy for you. Although I've gotta say, I didn't think I'd ever hear those words coming from you."

"Is that a good or a bad thing?"

He shrugs. "Neither. Like I said, just an observation. I feel like we haven't had a guys' night in forever. Who's down to fix that?" He addresses that last part to the whole room, and it seems to get everyone's attention.

"You're damn right," Maxim chimes in as he towels himself off on a nearby bench. "What happened to our regular poker nights anyway?"

"Easy. Some of us got domesticated," Noah answers, and everyone laughs.

Sawyer is right though. It's been forever since we got the team together to just hang out and be guys, and it's been so long since the last time we had a poker game night, I can't remember it.

"Why don't you guys come over to my place for a few games?" I suggest.

"You sure Becca will be okay with that? I mean, your place isn't exactly huge, and we aren't exactly quiet," Reese says.

"She's working and running some errands today anyway, so it'll be fine. Besides, I want you all to meet Milo."

The Aces share everything, and I do mean everything, so I still can't believe I haven't introduced them to my dog, but to be fair, things have been pretty busy for all of us lately. Especially me.

Reese nods. "Alright, then I'm game."

One by one, all the other guys agree.

"Cool. I'll head home now to get the place set up. Meet you there," I say as I gather up my stuff to leave the locker room.

When I get home, Milo greets me at the door, and I see that Becca's shoes are sitting nearby too, which either means she must've gotten home already.

"Becca? You here?" I call while I grab a treat for Milo.

"I'm upstairs," she calls back. "Can you come up here? I have something I want to show you!"

Shit, I didn't realize she would beat me home.

I would've asked her first before inviting them over if I'd known she would be here, but I thought she'd still be out. I want to give her a heads up that they're coming and see whatever it is she wants to show me, so I hurry up the stairs, leaving Milo happily munching his treat in the living room.

Becca is waiting for me in the bedroom, and I grin as I catch sight of her.

"Hey," I say, stepping forward.

Then I pause as I notice a mischievous look on her face. She's wearing a coat that goes down nearly to her knees, and I can't figure out why at first—but then she opens the coat and slips it off her shoulders, letting it fall to the floor.

My jaw drops. She's wearing some of the skimpiest, sexiest lingerie I've ever seen in my damn life. It's bright red and made of delicate lace that leaves nothing to the imagination.

"Holy shit. Is this what you wanted to show me? You look fucking stunning," I rasp, all the blood rushing to my cock.

She flushes a little, her eyes heating as she crooks a finger, beckoning me closer. "Why don't you show me how stunning you think I am?"

"I'd love to, princess." I stride over to her quickly and pull her into my arms, crushing my lips to hers.

She melts against me, but just as my hands start to roam, the doorbell rings. Becca jerks in my arms, surprise flashing across her face as we break apart.

"Shit. *Please* don't tell me your parents are here again." She blinks, shaking her head quickly. "Not that I'd be sad to see them, but..."

I chuckle. "Believe me, baby. I know just what you mean. I love my parents, but I'd lock them out of the house without a second thought right now."

"Then who is it?"

Before I can answer, voices rise up from downstairs. I left the door open for them and texted them to let them know, and her eyes widen as she recognizes the sounds of them talking and laughing among themselves.

"Wait, you invited the team here?" she whispers, quickly grabbing the coat and slipping it back on.

I grimace. "Yeah. I'm so fucking sorry, princess. I didn't think you'd be home. You said you were going out."

"No, it's fine. I was trying to surprise you. I guess this is what I get for trying to be all sneaky."

"Theo! Hey, man, you here?" Noah calls from downstairs.

"Uh, yeah!" I call back. Then I lower my voice and tell Becca, "Hang on one second. I'll get rid of them."

"No, no." She stops me with a hand on my arm as I start to leave. "It's fine. I don't want you to kick out your whole team just for me. We can finish this later."

She flashes me a smile, then pads toward the door, wrapping her coat a little tighter around her. I follow close behind as she heads downstairs to greet everyone, my mind still a little hazy with arousal. The guys have thrown themselves all over the couches in the living room, but they light up when they see her.

"Hey, Becca!" Reese grins. "What's up? I didn't think we'd get to see you."

"Yeah, I..." She clears her throat. "I got home early."

She says hi to everyone else, then slips out of the living room toward her bedroom down the hall, presumably to change. But as I watch her go, a sudden impulse fills me.

Muttering an excuse to the guys, I follow her down the hall. She's just about to close the door to her bedroom when I catch her by the waist.

"Hold on."

"What are you doing?" she whispers, glancing over my shoulder in case any of the guys followed.

Instead of answering with words, I push past her into the bedroom and close the door behind us, then spin to pin her against the heavy wood. I kiss her deeply, pressing my body against her so she can feel how hard I am.

"You wanted me to show you how stunning I think you are," I remind her. "So that's exactly what I'm doing. You're so fucking gorgeous, princess. You take my breath away."

"I wanted to surprise you," she says breathlessly against my lips.

"And you did. I fucking love it, can't you tell?" I ask as I grind my cock against her.

"Theo..." She tilts her head back as my lips trail over her throat. "We don't have to do this right now. I really can wait."

"Well, I can't." I nip at her delicate skin as I shove a hand up under her coat to run my hands over the lacy lingerie and cup one of her breasts. "I need you right fucking now, baby."

Maybe we shouldn't be doing this with the entire team in the next room, but I mean it. I can't wait. I fucking *need* her. She picked out this lingerie just for me, which drives me wild, and she deserves to know it.

Hungry to see her in it again, I fumble with her coat, opening it up again and sliding it off her shoulders. It falls to the floor, and I groan.

"You're a work of art," I rasp. "I've never seen anything more beautiful than this."

She bites her lip, a flush rising in her cheeks. "I'm glad you like it."

"It's not just the lingerie," I tell her, meaning every word. "It's *you*, baby. You take my damn breath away."

"Sweet talker."

I chuckle darkly. "Not always sweet. Now turn around."

There's a rough command in my voice, and she obeys immediately, which only makes my cock harder.

"Good," I praise. "Now put your hands on the door."

She follows that order too, and I groan at the sight of her on display for me like this, so willing and needy.

I didn't get the chance to fully appreciate just how amazing she looks in it earlier, but now that I have the time, I can't get enough. The bright red lace is like fire against her fair skin, and it hugs the curves of her lithe frame perfectly, showing off the best lines and angles.

My hands wander across her body on their own, and seeing the rippling waves of goosebumps my touch brings out her makes me groans.

"Goddamn, you're so beautiful. I'll never get tired of fucking my wife."

She presses her ass against my cock, grinding on it. "Then show me."

Desire rushes through me, and like a man possessed, I drag her panties down her legs in one motion.

"Oh, I will," I promise, my voice low. "But you need to tell me how badly you want it first."

"I need your cock in me, Theo," she whispers. "More than anything."

"Fuck." I unzip my pants and shove them down just enough to free my cock.

Gripping myself with one hand, I tease her entrance with my tip. She shudders and moans, quietly enough that no one outside will hear, but loud enough to drive me fucking crazy. I lean forward so that my lips are grazing her ears.

"Can you be quiet?"

She nods eagerly, but when I press inside her a little, her mouth drops open on a soft noise. I chuckle, pumping shallowly halfway in and out of her.

"We'll see about that. I want to make you scream. I want the whole team to hear how good I can make you feel. So that they'll all know you're mine."

"Oh fuck."

She sounds almost wrecked already, and the desperation in her voice snaps any restraint I had left.

I drive all the way into her, filling her up completely. Then I start to thrust deeply, fucking her hard and fast. There's no time for anything more than that, but judging from the way her eyes are squeezed shut and her lip is trapped between her teeth, she's not going to last long either. When she starts driving her hips back to meet my thrusts, ramming me deeper into her, it's almost enough to push me over the edge.

"You feel so damn good. Look at you taking my cock like this. My perfect wife. My fucking dream girl."

I grip her waist and pull her back into each thrust, getting even deeper and filling the room with the sound of our bodies clapping together. But the guys are talking and laughing in the living room, so I'm sure they can't hear it. And even if they could, I wouldn't care. The only thing that matters to me right now is Becca and the way I'm making her feel.

When my balls start to draw up tight and Becca's legs start to shake, I stop thrusting for a moment, giving us both a break to catch our breaths. But she keeps rocking her hips and squeezing my cock with each movement.

"Fuck," I bite out. "Goddamn, baby. If you keep doing that, I'm gonna fill you up."

"Do it. Give it to me. Please, Theo."

The raw need in her voice makes my heart pound. I'll never get over what the sound of her begging does to me. Nothing else in the world affects me like this.

"Anything for you, princess," I say and drive into her again, dragging a whimper out of her. She manages to muffle it, but there's a good chance the guys might have heard. "Are you sure you can be quiet? Or is the whole house about to hear you screaming from how good I'm making you feel?"

She nods, instead arching her back as she meets my next thrust. I'm not sure which question she's saying yes to, but I don't really care. I wrap my arms around her chest and pull her into me, kissing her neck and shoulder as I drive into her.

"That's it. Take my cock, my dirty girl," I mutter in her ear. "My beautiful fucking princess."

Her whimpers build to a fever pitch as I gradually increase the pace of my strokes, and when her jaw drops like she's going to scream as her orgasm hits, I grip her chin and turn her face toward mine, kissing her to muffle the scream building in her throat.

She trembles in my arms and groans into my mouth as she comes, her pussy spasming around my cock as she drenches me.

It takes everything I have not to release with her until she's finished, but when she finally pulls her mouth from mine, I can't hold it back anymore. My forehead drops to her shoulder as I lose it, my thrusts turning wild as my cock pulses. I come with a low groan, filling her up.

When the last shudder finally works its way through me, I pull out of her and spin her around to kiss her again. Her back thuds softly against the bedroom door, and I notice a break in the conversation down the hall. A beat later I hear Noah clear his throat.

"Everything okay in there? Need help finding anything?" he calls down the hall, and Becca freezes.

She pulls away from me and laughs, a blush reddening her cheeks.

"Everything's fine! Just having a hard time finding the tables for our poker game," I shout back.

"Are there even any tables in here?" Becca whispers. I shake my head, and she laughs. "Of course not."

I shrug. "They're downstairs in storage, actually. But there was something I wanted more in this room."

She grins. "I'm glad you liked your surprise."

"Oh, I did." I cradle the back of her head, leaning in to kiss her again. "I really fucking did."

This kiss is less fevered than the ones before it, and she melts a little as our tongues dance. Then she pushes on my chest a little, breaking the kiss.

"You should probably get back out there," she says, looking flushed and gorgeous as she smiles at me. "For real, this time. I'll get dressed and meet you out there."

"Okay."

I nod, but it takes several more minutes before I can pull myself away from her. Even though my cock is spent, I know it would only take minutes before I'd be ready to go again. But she's right. It'd be an asshole move to make my friends wait for that long, and despite all my dirty talk to Becca earlier, the possessive side of me doesn't want them to hear her fall apart for me again.

"Alright," I murmur, breathing heavily as we separate. "I'm going, I'm going."

She laughs, pulling me in for one last kiss before we move away from the door.

I drag my pants back up and tuck myself away while Becca searches her room for an appropriate set of clothes. I slip out the door and close it as quietly as I can behind me, but Noah is standing at the end of the hall and staring right at me, so I know I'm busted.

285

"Sorry, I thought the tables were in the guest room, but turns out they're probably upstairs," I say, going with the cover story I invented earlier. "I must have moved them when Becca moved in."

But Noah doesn't say anything. He's got his phone clutched in one hand, and when I reach the end of the hall and enter the living room, I find all the rest of the guys sitting and staring at their phones too. They look up at me when I walk in, but quickly avert their eyes.

"What's with the weird looks? Is Gretzky coming out of retirement or something?" I joke, but no one laughs.

Instead, Noah claps his hand on my shoulder and flashes me a sympathetic smile as he raises his phone so I can see the screen. He's got a social media post pulled up, and he gestures for me to read it, but I see the words "Shawn Kaplan" and "Becca Summers" and immediately go tense.

"What the fuck did he do?" I ask, dreading the answer.

Noah's expression turns solemn. "A new episode of his reality show just dropped," he tells me. "And Becca is in it."

Chapter 28

Becca

My stomach drops. I wasn't trying to eavesdrop, but there wasn't any way to avoid overhearing what the guys were talking about while I made my way down the hall. I should've known this was coming—Peyton warned me about it right before I left LA—but nothing could've prepared me for the dread that's twisting in my stomach.

Whatever it is, it won't be good.

"How bad is it?" Theo asks Noah, who shrugs.

"I don't know. We haven't seen it yet. The news just dropped, and Margo texted me about it as soon as she heard," he explains.

It's Margo's job as the Aces' social media manager to be on top of that stuff, which I'm grateful for. As awful as this is, at least we got somewhat of an advance notice about it and didn't have to find out from some sleazy reporter hounding us with questions about it tomorrow.

"Put it on," Theo orders, and Noah raises his eyebrows at him.

"Are you sure about that? We don't have to watch it. I'm sure Margo or someone can summarize—"

"I said put it on," Theo cuts him off and storms over to the coffee table for the remote. He jabs it at the TV to turn it on and starts furiously flipping through channels. "Which channel is this trash on again?"

Noah takes the remote from him and finds the right channel, but the episode is already about halfway over, so he restarts it. I sink down on the couch next to Reese, who looks like he's sitting on pins and needles, and Theo sits on my other side. His hand finds mine as the intro finishes, and I hold on to it as tightly as I can because I'm afraid I might float away without something to keep me anchored.

When the intro finishes, the black screen fades to a shot of Shawn sitting in his living room with tears in his eyes. He isn't full-on crying, but the moisture is there, and I can't help wondering if it's as fake as everything else about this damn show. It wouldn't surprise me if his producers made him squirt some eye drops in before the cameras started rolling.

"I never thought I'd have to film an episode like this," Shawn says after a few moments of silence. "But then again, I never thought my girlfriend would turn into a drug addict, either."

Theo's hand spasms in mine, and all the dread roiling in my stomach comes crawling up my throat. I feel like I'm going to be sick right here, because I already know what's coming next.

Shawn stares directly into the camera, his expression serious. "Becca seemed like the perfect girl for me, at least at first. She was sweet, a super talented dancer, and had a bright future. But she had a dark side too."

The shot fades into black-and-white, grainy footage of another living room that I recognize, but only barely. That whole night is a foggy haze in my memory, and I hate it.

The footage shows me sprawled out on a couch, staring at the ceiling, and my stomach twists at the sight. The camera zooms in on me, past the shoulders of a group of other women who are talking in slightly slurred voices. Even though the footage is slightly unfocused, it's not hard to see just how dilated my eyes are, how high I am.

I can't fight the tears that flood my eyes, and the despair in the pit of my stomach churns into rage.

How could Shawn do this to me?

Then again, I know his true colors well enough by now that I shouldn't be surprised. This is who he is, who he's always been. I just refused to see it.

The show cuts back to Shawn, and the fake tears are gone, replaced by a look of somber disappointment. He leans closer to the camera as it zooms in on his face.

"She led me on, led me to believe she was someone she wasn't," he says seriously. "And she was very good at fooling me, at fooling all of you. Becca was just as much a part of this show as I am, a part that many of you loved just like I did. So I'm sorry to have to tell you all of this, but I had to let her go. I can't have a druggie like that in my life."

Again, the shot fades back into the grainy footage of the house party. I blink away the tears that blur my vision, my chest aching as my lungs refuse to function.

It's Shawn's fault that I ended up on drugs that night. It started because—surprise, surprise—he was being an asshole after losing a game.

He insisted on taking me out to a party with him to drink away his frustration. I would've rather gone home, but he wouldn't take no for an answer, so I followed him and a gaggle of puck bunnies he'd met back to a random house party. That should've been the first red flag, but I gave in, just like I always did with him.

Of course, none of that backstory is included in the episode.

What the footage shows instead is me walking into what looks like the basement of a luxurious house where at least a dozen people are already hanging out. As I stare at it, it strikes me that I don't know how in the world his producers even managed to record this.

Was it all a setup from the start? Did they pay these puck bunnies to approach Shawn after the game, hoping to create some fake drama for the cameras that they planted in the house ahead of time? It sounds crazy, but it's exactly the kind of thing they'd do—and the kind of thing Shawn would be on board with.

I remember the beginning of the night very clearly. I had work the next day, so I only planned to have a drink or two to appease Shawn, then leave.

Except someone slipped something in my drink. I'm sure of it, although when I told Shawn later, he gaslit me, insisting that no one would've done that and that I must've gotten tipsy enough to loosen up and willingly accept whatever drug I was given.

The recording shifts to another shot, still in the basement, and in this clip, I look like I'm barely able to sit upright or keep my eyes focused on anything. My throat goes tight, because I don't remember this part of the night at all. And the worst part is, Shawn is nowhere to be seen. He didn't even realize I'd gotten high until I woke up the next day and freaked out, because he was too busy partying to notice or care.

The show cuts back to Shawn in his living room, staring seriously into the camera.

"This is where it all started to go downhill. When Becca changed," he says, then sighs and looks away from the camera. "I should've stopped her. I wish I had. Maybe then all of this could've been prevented. Maybe if she hadn't gotten hooked, she wouldn't have cheated on me."

What the fuck?

I jump off the couch in shock and storm upstairs, my stomach in turmoil.

I can't stand to see another second of the episode or Shawn's lies, and I'm worried I'm going to get sick in front of the entire team, so I dart into Theo's bathroom and kick the door closed behind me before I collapse in front of the toilet. My skin is prickling and burning like I've caught fire, and I want nothing more than to rake my way out of it, but I'm stuck.

I have to live with this. The Aces, my family, Theo's parents, the *entire world* is now going to think I'm a drug-addicted cheater. And I can't escape it.

My mind jumps to my marriage to Theo and how it's almost certainly going to fall apart now. No government official in their right mind would look at that footage and not scrutinize the person involved who's now seeking citizenship.

I'm fucked. Well and truly fucked. And it's all because of Shawn.

Bile gathers in the back of my throat, and I can't hold it back anymore. I let it out, then move to the sink to wash my face and steal several swigs of Theo's mouthwash. It makes me feel a little better, but my stomach is still at war with itself.

A soft knock on the bathroom door startles me, but I'm sure it's Theo, so I spit out the rinse and wipe my face on the towel hanging by the sink before I let him in. I'm half expecting him to tell me to pack my things and get out right now, but the look of worry on his face catches me off guard.

"I told the guys to go home. Are you okay?" he asks, looking me up and down.

I want to laugh because I couldn't be further from okay, but I appreciate his concern and gentleness right now, so I hold it back.

"I swear, it's not what it looked like on tape. Shawn dragged me to a party and someone slipped something into my drink. It only happened once, not all the time like he tried to portray it. And it wasn't even something I wanted! And I swear to god, as much as he pissed me off sometimes, I would *never* have cheated on—"

Theo steps closer, breaking off my spiral. "It's okay. I believe you."

Tears sting the corners of my eyes. "Y-you do?"

"Are you serious? Of course I believe you, princess. Because I know you, the *real* you. And what was in that footage wasn't that. People are obviously only getting part of the story, and I'm sure it's edited to hell and back to make you look as bad as possible."

I almost break down crying because I'm so relieved that Theo gets it. But of course he does. He's as familiar with Shawn's bullshit as I am because he's been on the receiving end of it too. Knowing he doesn't think the worst of me makes it at least a little easier to breathe, and my stomach's churning finally starts to slow.

Theo pulls me in for a hug, and I melt in his arms, full on ugly crying. He rubs my back but doesn't try to stop me, probably because he knows I need to let this all out or it's going to make me implode.

"We'll get through this. I promise," he whispers in my ear. I don't know how the hell he can be so sure, but having Theo in my corner at least makes me feel like there's a shred of possibility that we will. "The Aces have some of the best PR and legal people in the business, and we all know Kaplan just did this to fuck with both of us. We won't let him win."

"Thank you," I murmur as he draws back a little to wipe away my tears with his thumb.

"You're my wife, remember? I'd do anything for you. Anything."

It's supposed to comfort me, and I know that, but it just makes me cry all over again.

I don't know what I've done to deserve him, but I'm so grateful he's here. There's no way I'd survive something like this without him. I'd go to pieces. I already am.

Theo pulls me in for another hug, and I try my best to relax in his arms. Eventually, my breathing slows and steadies, and my tears finally subside. But my phone vibrates in my pocket, and my anxiety spikes all over again—because whatever the notification is, after what we just watched, it probably isn't good news.

"What is it?" Theo asks as I yank my phone from my pocket but hesitate to look at the screen. "Just tear the bandage off. Get it over with."

I turn the phone over and see a text from Caroline, the studio head at Curtain Call. Instantly, my heart plummets into my stomach before I've even read the message. But I can't stop myself. My eyes dart over the text, and dread piles up in me with every word.

"What's going on?" Theo asks, and my eyes snap to his.

"It's Caroline at Curtain Call. They're terminating my contract with the dance school."

"What? Are you serious?"

"Yeah. One of the kid's parents heard about the video and sent an email to Caroline about being uncomfortable with me as their instructor. She said she doesn't want to, but until this gets sorted out, she has to let me go. Curtain Call can't take the reputational hit."

"That motherfucker," Theo growls as he pulls me into his arms again. I feel the rage bubbling in him, the pure hatred toward Shawn, and I don't blame him. "Screwing with me is one thing, but to go after you? I'll fucking kill him."

"He's not worth it."

Theo pulls back to look me in the eye. "No, he's not. But *you* are. I won't let him or any of his asshole friends hurt you. I swear."

As my mind starts to whirl again, a cacophony of anxiety and fear, I cling to him. He's all I have left, the only thing keeping me anchored to solid ground.

My haven in the storm.

Chapter 29

Becca

The condo feels emptier than normal with Theo gone.

He's away for a game, and he wanted me to come with him, but I really didn't think that was a good idea with everything going on. So I insisted on staying home and laying low instead while I figure out my next steps now that Shawn's completely ruined whatever reputation I might have had.

I'm exhausted. I've spent all afternoon calling nearby leads, hoping to find some other work now that Curtain Call's cut me loose. But unsurprisingly after the video, no one will touch me. It's only been a couple of days since the episode aired, but it seems like everyone already knows about the "trashy dancer who is pole hopping from one NHL player to another."

That was seriously a line I saw in one of the equally trashy tabloids who've picked up the "story" since it broke. Of course, not even one of them have reached out to me for comment or my version of the story, but why would they? They don't practice real journalism.

I sigh and slump back on the couch, my phone dangling from my hand, the screen full of job search results. I should take a break, go for a walk with Milo or something, but I'm terrified that someone will recognize and corner me on the street—and Theo made me promise I wouldn't go out alone. So if some shitbag paparazzi who's hiding in the alley ambushes me, it's all over. That's the last thing I need.

It's almost time for my meeting with the lawyer Theo hired anyway, so I decide to call the job search quits and get ready for that. God, I miss him, even though he's been texting me non-stop since he left. Like he sensed it, I get a text from him again.

THEO: How's the job hunt going?

BECCA: Terribly. Nothing but "no, thank yous."
Whatever. I'm leaving in a bit to meet with the lawyer.

THEO: Good. I wish I could be there with you for it. I'm sorry I can't.

BECCA: It's okay, I understand. But I wish you could too. I'm scared.

THEO: It'll be fine. He's the best of the best. But don't forget to call the car service to confirm your ride. I don't want you out there alone.

I've been so wrapped up in my misery that I completely forgot about needing to make that call. Before he left, Theo arranged for a private driver to pick me up for the lawyer meeting so I wouldn't have to drive and, hopefully, could avoid being spotted in public. It's normal to see a lawyer in these cases, but Theo thought the press might have a field day with it if they found out, so he wants to keep it hush-hush.

I don't blame him.

BECCA: Shit, I did forget. I'll call them now.

THEO: Good luck. Let me know how it goes.

BECCA: You'll be the first person I tell.

I scroll back up in our text thread for the driving service's number and tap to call them. Thankfully, they were expecting my call so me forgetting isn't a problem. They tell me the driver will be in the garage waiting for me within the next twenty minutes, barely giving me time to get ready. The perks of being married to a wealthy, well known hockey player!

I feed Milo and make sure he has fresh water before hurrying to my room to rummage around for something business professional to wear to the meeting. True to their word, a driver is already in the garage waiting for me, and they wordlessly step out of the car to open and close the door for me. I never would've imagined I'd be the kind of girl to get private service like this.

The car itself is immaculate, both in its amenities and presentation. It feels like something a Hollywood diva should be driving around in, not a "trashy dancer" like me. I try not to focus too much on the tabloid headlines on the drive to the lawyer's office, but this story is all I can think about anymore. My eyes are burning from lack of sleep and my lids feel heavy, but I have to keep it together for this meeting.

The lawyer, Eric Botti, is all business when I enter the office. He's older, probably mid-fifties, with salt-streaked black hair. And judging from the deep lines on his face behind his thick glasses, he's seen enough in his day to make anyone blush. That's probably exactly the kind of guy I want working on a case like this, but his appearance only makes me worry more. He strides out to shake my head and welcomes me into his private office.

"Good afternoon, Ms. Summers. I wish we were meeting under better circumstances," he says as I sit down on the opposite side of his desk.

"That makes two of us. Thank you for meeting on such short notice, Mr. Botti."

"Please, call me Eric." He rests his forearms on the desk and joins his hands. "I'll cut right to the chase here. I don't like beating around the bush. I've reviewed everything you and Mr.

Camden provided, as well as the TV episode in question, and there aren't a lot of clear-cut options."

"That's the exact opposite of what I wanted to hear," I say, although I'm not surprised. Shawn's an asshole, but he's smart, and he'll have had his own lawyers comb through every piece of footage before anything airs to make sure it's sound.

Eric nods. "I understand. The thing is, you signed a very restrictive contract with Mr. Kaplan, one that basically gives him free rein to use whatever footage the production captured—including the less-than-flattering bits. There's even a clause that says the producers are allowed to edit the footage however they want."

"So, what? You're telling me I'm screwed?"

Eric chuckles wryly. "Not completely. Depending on what Mr. Kaplan decides to do next, or how far he takes things, there might be some avenues we could explore legally. But as of now, my hands are tied. There isn't anything I can do to get the episode taken down or scrubbed. I'm sorry."

"Well, thanks for the time and attempt," I murmur and stand from the desk, feeling utterly defeated.

Eric walks me out of the office, and I get back in the elevator I took up to him. The doors close, and they feel like a perfect representation of the walls closing in on me. I'm a world away from Shawn, but I'm still under his thumb, just like always.

I don't know how I let this happen. I'm smarter than this. But I was so desperate to make a relationship work, to not repeat the mistakes of my mother, that I stayed in a totally toxic situation and let him walk all over me. I see just how toxic it was now, but it's too late. Clarity won't buy my freedom, and at this point, I'm not sure anything can.

By the time the elevator reaches the ground floor, my head is so far off my shoulders that I feel like I left it in Eric's office. Everything is swimming, and I feel like I'm going to be sick again when I step out of the elevator. I stop and lean against the wall by the exit to steady myself while I fish for my phone in my pocket to tell Theo what happened.

BECCA: Botti said

But as I'm typing, my eyes flutter and the world goes dim.

Somewhere in the distance, I hear my phone clatter against the marble flooring of the foyer as it rushes up to meet me.

~

A man's indistinct, muffled voice mixes with a steady beeping sound, pulling me up from the thick haze I'm under.

Everything is so heavy, dark, and slow, like I'm underwater.

"Where is she? Where is my wife?!"

The words cut through the dense fog.

Theo. It's Theo. But where is he? And where am I?

I try to open my eyes, but my lids won't lift. It's like my body is too tired to even manage that. Images flash in my mind, the last few things I remember seeing. My phone screen, the unfinished text to Theo, and the black-and-white blur of the marble flooring as it raced toward me.

A door bursts open, and the noise startles my eyes open too. Theo is there, racing toward me with a deeply concerned look on his handsome face. He races to my side to stroke my forehead, brushing away my sweaty, tangled hair.

"Becca? Becca, can you hear me?" he asks gently. I nod, but it makes my head hurt, so I grimace. "It's okay, don't move. You don't have to say anything. I'm so sorry I wasn't there. I was on the ice when the hospital called to tell me you'd fallen. I left the arena and got on a plane as soon as I got the message."

"Thank you," I croak. My throat is dry as bone. How long have I been out?

I don't get the chance to ask before a doctor walks in behind Theo, wearing an angry expression. He's probably not happy with Theo for bursting in here like this, but I'm glad he did. He takes my hand as the doctor walks around to the other side of the bed, and just that simple act makes me feel like everything is going to be okay.

"Mr. Camden, I understand your concern, but we've run as many tests as we can and as far as we can tell, there's nothing to worry about. Your wife probably just didn't eat enough and got lightheaded, leading to the fainting."

My stomach twists because I know the doctor's right. I was so stressed out and busy trying to find work that I completely forgot to eat. It's an echo of a problem I used to have, one I thought I'd kicked, but stress has a way of bringing out the worst in me. It's the last thing I want to tell Theo on top of everything else that's gone wrong in the last few days, but if there's anything that damn video has taught me, it's that I have to be honest with him. About everything.

"I'm sorry I wasn't here to take care of you," Theo says as he squeezes my hand. I lift the other to point at a glass of water sitting nearby, and he rushes to bring it to me. He puts the bendy straw in my mouth, and I suck down the water like I'm afraid it'll disappear.

"It's okay," I say after a moment, my throat feeling some-what better. "But there's something I need to tell you." Theo's worried eyes snap to mine, and I wince as I explain, "I... I had an eating disorder when I was a teenager."

"Becca..." He squeezes my hand again.

"I've been working on it for a long time. I'm mostly past it now, but sometimes when I'm really stressed, I forget to eat. That's what happened."

The doctor looks at Theo like he's trying to say *I told you so*, but Theo ignores him, keeping his eyes locked on mine. "I won't let that happen to you again. I promise. From here on out, I'll always be here to take care of you."

My heart flutters at the earnestness in his eyes, and then I drift back off to sleep.

Chapter 30

Theo

Becca is still sleeping a few hours later when the doctor comes back to the room to tell me he wants to keep her overnight, just to be safe.

"She did hit her head pretty hard when she fell, and while the x-rays don't show any signs of a concussion, it's better safe than sorry."

"Shouldn't we wake her up then? I'm pretty sure sleeping is the last thing someone with a concussion is supposed to do. I'm a hockey player. I'm familiar with concussions."

The doctor laughs. "No doubt you are. But like I said, I don't see anything to suggest that's what happened. I just want to keep her out of an abundance of caution in case there are any complications from her neglecting to eat."

"I understand. Thanks, doc."

"Of course. You're welcome to stay with her," the doctor says and leaves it at that.

I glance over at Becca, who's still silently sleeping, and my heart wrenches. I knew leaving her alone in the middle of all of this shit with Kaplan was a bad idea. I wanted to blow off going out of town for the game, but Becca refused to let me. She didn't want me getting in any trouble for her sake.

Like she wouldn't deserve it.

But speaking of trouble, I had to leave the arena in a hurry, and it seems like Becca is fast asleep, so I pull out my phone to make some calls while she's resting. I let Dunaway know first that everything is okay and apologize for leaving the game abruptly.

"You don't have to apologize, Camden. It's your wife. I understand."

"Thanks, Coach," I say and hang up, then immediately dial Noah. He answers after one ring.

"Hey. Everything okay?"

"Everything's fine. She passed out from lack of food and hit her head, but the doctors don't think she did any real damage. They're still gonna keep her overnight."

"Probably not a bad idea. I'm glad she's alright though."

"Thanks. Me too. Although I feel like a fucking idiot for leaving her alone," I mutter as I look at her beautiful, peaceful face.

Thinking about what Kaplan did, and the fact that it led to this, makes my stomach boil with rage all over again. It's a damn good thing we weren't playing against the Prowlers tonight, because I would've beat his fucking face into the ice if we were.

I'll never forget the panic and fear I felt when I got the call from the hospital. And I'm so glad I answered it, even though it was a blocked number. I never would've forgiven myself if I'd denied the call. I almost dropped the phone when the doctor told me why he was calling, and I must have looked like a crazed animal on my warpath out of the arena because the only thought on my mind was getting to my wife's side. I *had* to make sure she was okay.

Being so far away from her in a time of crisis was fucking

torture. And now that this has happened, I don't know how I'm ever going to be able to travel for a game. I can't bear the thought of leaving her alone, of something like this—or worse—happening again. But I can't skip all my games either, so she'll just have to travel with me from now on.

I sigh because I know that's not realistic either. She has her own life and ambitions, and I can't expect her to give all that up. She's already put her dreams on hold for years for Kaplan, so I wouldn't be any better than him if I asked her to delay them for my sake. And I'm sure this crap with Curtain Call will blow over as soon as we prove that Kaplan's full of shit, so Becca will probably be back to dancing and teaching pretty soon.

The worst part is that so much of this is my fault. If I hadn't come up with this crazy fucking idea for her to marry me, if I'd just let her go back home to Canada, she wouldn't be laid up in a hospital bed with a borderline concussion right now. Not that I regret it, but I can't help wondering how things might be different.

I can't remember the last time I felt this helpless. I want to take care of her, to protect her, but there's so little I can actually do. Is this what it feels like to be a parent? To care about someone so much but know that you have to let them live and take risks and get hurt?

The thought brings a realization: Becca's mom! I've never talked to her, and I don't even know if she knows I exist, but I owe it to her to tell her what's going on with her daughter. Becca's phone rests charging on the bedside table, so I reach over to grab it and look for her mom's number.

Of course, she has a passcode lock, and I don't know what it is, but she also has the emergency contacts setting turned on with her mom listed, so I tap to place the call. It takes a few rings, but eventually, her Mom answers.

"Hi, Twinkle Toes," she greets, and I can't help smiling. I

know Becca and her mom aren't very close, but that must be her pet name for Becca.

"Uh, hi, Ms. Summers. This is Theo Camden," I start, and the line goes quiet. "I know this is one hell of a way for you and me to meet, but there's something I need to tell you. Becca's in the hospital."

"Oh my god! Is she okay?"

"She's fine, she's fine. She got a little light-headed and fainted earlier today. She hit her head when she passed out, but the doctors don't think there's anything serious going on."

"She didn't eat, did she?" her mom asks, and I chuckle. Apparently, she knows her daughter better than either of us gave her credit for. Becca's always accusing her of being flighty and self-absorbed—and I'm sure she's not wrong about those things—but this is still her mom. And she still cares.

"How did you know?"

"She used to do the same thing when she was younger, especially if she was stressed out. I've told her I don't know how many times how bad it is for her, but you know how teenage girls can be. They don't want to hear a damn word their mothers have to say."

"Well, speaking from personal experience, teenage boys aren't much better."

"I can imagine. Thank you for calling and letting me know. Is she there? Can I talk to her?"

"She's sleeping right now and has been all day. I'll have her call you as soon as she's able to though."

"Thank you, Theo," she says, then sighs. "Listen, I know Becca and I aren't the closest, but she's told me a lot about you. About your marriage. I can tell you're a good husband to her, much better than I ever was as a mother, and I'm glad she finally has someone in her corner."

That catches me completely off guard, which isn't easy for

most people to do. "She does. And she always will with me, I promise you that."

"That's all I need to hear. It's all any mother wants to hear for their daughter. Thank you again for calling, Theo. I'll try her in the morning."

"You're welcome, but hey, Ms. Summers, before you go," I hurry before she can hang up. "Can I ask you something?"

"Anything."

"What were her favorite foods growing up? I want to make something nice for her."

Her mom laughs again. "Well, it's probably a good thing you asked, because she's *incredibly* picky. Or at least she was when she was little. She loved the usual kid stuff—chicken noodle soup, grilled cheese—but she also really loved these little dinosaur shaped chicken nuggets. I don't know if they even make those anymore."

"Well, if they do, I'll find them. Have a good night, and I'll let you know if I hear anything else."

"You too."

I hang up and put Becca's phone back on the nightstand, then use mine to start browsing all the local grocery stores for everything her mom mentioned, especially those dino nuggets. Because when Becca wakes up, I want to give her the best surprise she'll never see coming.

Lucky for me, they do still make the nuggets, so I order a couple of boxes for delivery along with enough supplies to make a giant pot of chicken noodle soup, then pull my chair closer to her bed so I can take Becca's hand in mine and rest my head on the bed beside her.

There isn't a damn thing, not even sleep, that could take me from her side tonight.

∽

"I'm fine, Theo, really," Becca insists as I try to coax her into my bed back home the next day. "Come on, I've been sleeping for the last like eighteen hours, I don't need more rest."

"I didn't say you had to sleep. But you do need to rest. I don't want you falling again."

Becca grumbles but lies down, pulling the covers over her head. I'm probably overdoing it with her because she does seem like she's back to normal, but I would never forgive myself if she fainted again and got hurt. As long as she stays put in bed for now, that's enough for me.

I close the bedroom door behind me on my way out, and Milo follows me back downstairs to the kitchen. The grocery delivery came this morning before I brought Becca home, so the surprise hasn't been ruined.

I'm a terrible cook and open about it, but I think even I can handle chicken noodle soup, so I pull out all the ingredients, chop up the chicken and vegetables into chunks, and combine them with noodles and broth in a large pot on the stove to let it boil.

It'll be a while before it's ready, assuming I don't burn it, but hopefully Becca will be nice and hungry by then. I'll pop the chicken nuggets in the oven just before the soup is done. I don't know what to do while I wait, so I head to the couch and turn the TV on with the volume muted. I don't want to bother Becca while she's trying to sleep.

I spend more time channel surfing than actually watching anything, but it's enough time for the soup to come to a boil. I leave the TV on a commercial to bring the heat down to a simmer, then pop the chicken nuggets into the oven.

"Something smells good. What are you making?"

I turn around to find Becca standing at the bottom of the stairs, clearly ignoring my doctor's orders to stay in bed. But I can't even be upset about it, because the sight of her wearing my clothes as pajamas almost takes my breath away. They're several

305

sizes too big for her, making her dancer's frame look even more petite and hiding the curves of her body.

Even with her face a bit wan and her hair mussed from sleep, she still looks absolutely beautiful to me.

I never want those clothes back.

Striding over to her, I pull her into my arms for a kiss. Her arms wrap around my shoulder as she kisses me back, arching against me a little. Then she wiggles out of my grasp to peer around me into the kitchen.

"Seriously, what are you up to?" she asks.

I lift one shoulder. "I talked to your mom last night, and she told me about some of your favorite foods from when you were a kid, so I decided to make some of them for you to help you feel better."

Her brows furrow. "But you can't cook."

I bark out a laugh. She really does know me.

"Yeah, I know," I admit with a chuckle. "But I'm trying, okay? I want to get better at it. For you. And I want to make sure there's always stuff in the fridge for you. Things that you like and actually want to eat."

Becca blushes. "I told you, I don't really have a problem with the eating disorder anymore. That was a long time ago, I just got so caught up with the fallout from Shawn's show that I forgot to take care of myself."

"I believe you, princess. I really do." I step closer to her, trailing my knuckles along the curve of her cheek. "But that's why *I* want to take care of you. I hate that this shit with Shawn has you stressed out, and I hate even more that you ended up in the hospital because of it. You scared the hell out of me. I don't ever want that to happen again. So I'm going to make sure you always have something to eat and that you're always taken care of. Okay?"

Becca stares into my eyes for a moment, then nods. "Okay."

"Good."

I tilt her chin up and kiss her. She smiles at me as we break apart, although I can still see doubt lingering in her eyes.

Wanting to banish it entirely, I press another small kiss to her lips before murmuring, "I'm really glad you told me about your past. I know it wasn't easy."

"It wasn't," she admits, her voices low. "And I'm grateful you're being so supportive about it, but this..." She gestures at all the groceries piled on the counter behind me. "It's too much. You're doing way too much for me."

"No, it's not enough," I counter, and she stares at me. "It's not anywhere near enough. I should've been there for you, but I wasn't."

Becca's luminous eyes lock on mine. "But you're here now."

"I am. And I always will be." Tears start to form in the corners of her eyes, but she wipes them away and smiles. I turn back to the stove and lift the lid off the pot, blasting myself with steam. "But I think you're just in time because I'm pretty sure the soup should be ready, or at least getting close. Do you want to taste it?"

She raises an eyebrow at me. "I don't know. Is it safe?"

"You're lucky you just got home from the hospital, otherwise I'd never tolerate this slander."

She laughs but approaches the stove anyway, so I scoop up a wooden spoonful of the soup and bring it to my mouth to blow on it. I think it smells delicious, but I'll let her be the judge of that.

I hold the spoon out to her, and she cups her hand underneath it to stop any dribbling as she gingerly sips at the soup. She doesn't react at first, but her face lights up. "Wow, that's... that's actually really good?"

"What's with the questioning tone?"

"Nothing, I just thought you couldn't cook. Maybe you were playing me all along."

"Oh, no, believe me, I really can't. I just got lucky. In more ways than one," I say, beaming at her, and blush paints her face again.

I pull the chicken nuggets out of the oven, then grab a bowl from the cabinet and fill it with the soup before plating a few nuggets. Then I bring both of dishes over to the kitchen table, gesturing with my chin for Becca to follow me.

"What are you doing?" she asks when I set the dishes down and settle onto the seat in front of them. "Are those for me?"

"Yup, they are. Come, sit," I say, patting my lap, and Becca laughs.

"Are you serious?"

"One hundred percent." I pat my leg again. "Come on, before the soup gets cold."

Becca looks uncertain but settles in my lap. I scoop up a spoonful of the soup and blow on it again before raising it to her lips. She laughs and opens wide, so I gently feed her the spoonful, and she whimpers as she tastes it.

"You really don't have to do this. I'm not so weak and tired that I can't lift a spoon for myself."

"I know I don't have to, but—"

"You're doing it because you want to," she says with a smile. "Yeah, I know. I still think it's too much, but thank you. Really."

I kiss her cheek. "You're welcome," I say, and give her a chicken nugget next. "So have you heard back yet from any of the other dance places you contacted?"

Becca covers her mouth while she finishes chewing and shakes her head before she swallows. "No. Honestly, it's been really stressful. I have this awful reputation now, and I don't know if I'm gonna be able to shake it."

"You will. Take it from someone with the bad boy bachelor reputation."

Becca laughs. "Okay, then there's hope." She falls silent after another mouthful of soup, but she's chewing slowly, almost like she's chewing on her thoughts at the same time.

"What's on your mind?"

Becca shrugs. "Call me crazy, but I've been thinking that maybe I should try to start a school separate from a dance company. It's daunting, but it would be way more freeing if it worked out too. It would be all mine."

"There's nothing crazy about dreams. Dream as big as you want. If someone like me can make it to the NHL, you can do anything you put your mind to."

Becca smiles at me, and I feel the warmth spread through my body. Even when she's recovering, she's a ray of light in my life. I love the way I feel about myself around her, the way she makes me feel like anything is possible. Sometimes, when I encourage her like this, I almost feel like I'm encouraging myself at the same time.

"Really? You think I could do something like that?"

"Of course. It's a great idea, and you have the talent, no one can deny that. It's just a matter of getting it started and seeing it through. But you already have the skills you need for that too. And you know I'd help you however I could."

Becca takes the spoon from me to scoop up more soup for herself. The bowl's half empty at this point, which is good. I'm glad she likes it, and that she's getting some food in her stomach. I don't want her going hungry ever again, on accident or otherwise.

When she finishes chewing, she stares into my eyes. "Thank you, Theo. For everything. I really don't know where I'd be right now without you."

"Well, luckily for you, you never need to worry about that. You'll always have a place here with me, no matter what else happens."

I mean it too. More than anything I've ever said. I wouldn't have predicted this on that first night Becca and I spent together, drinking and talking on the beach, but I'm so fucking glad I decided to follow her outside that night.

Becca leans against me, resting her head on my collar. She nuzzles her cheek on mine, and I wrap my arms around her, holding her close. It's such a sweet, innocent moment, and I don't want it to end.

Because the truth is, I'm falling for her.

Hard.

Chapter 31

Becca

I wake the next morning in Theo's bed with Milo sleeping peacefully at our feet, which makes me smile. I don't realize it at first, but when I roll over, Theo is awake too, watching me.

"Good morning. How are you feeling?" he asks, and I drag my fingertips across his pecs.

"A little groggy, but good. Glad to be home, that's for sure," I say, and although it passes quickly, I notice Theo's face light up. And I know why. I think that's probably the first time I've referred to being here, in his condo with him, as "home." But it's true. This is my home now, and I finally feel it.

"That makes two of us," Theo says before I can add anything else. He kisses the top of my head and idly plays with my hair, making my scalp tingle in the most relaxing, wonderful way. I could lie like this with him all day and never get tired of it, so I don't want to ruin the moment, but I feel like I owe him an explanation. Or at the very least, some reassurance that this won't be a common occurrence.

"Listen, about yesterday," I start, half expecting him to shush me, but he doesn't say anything. He just keeps massaging my scalp, listening. "I already told you I used to have an eating disorder. But I really need you to know that it's something I worked through. It's not a problem for me anymore."

"And I already told you that I believe you," Theo says, smiling down at me. "But I'm here if you want to talk about it."

I hesitate because I feel like we should talk about it, but I'm not really sure what I want to say. "It started when I was a teenager."

"That makes sense. That's a tough time for young women with puberty and image and all that."

"Yeah, but the weird thing is that I didn't really have a problem with any of that. I was in good shape already from all the dancing I did, and I didn't hate what I saw in the mirror or anything."

"Hm. Then where do you think it came from?"

I pause to think because it's not something anyone has ever asked me before. "Honestly? My mom and the way we lived. Things were always so chaotic, so out of control and unpredictable. I never really knew if I was going to get a meal with her, or if she would even be there when I got home from school, so not eating gave me some weird sense of control and constancy in my life. And I kept it going. At least then I knew what to expect, you know?"

"That's heartbreaking," Theo says, and it makes my chest clench because he's right, but I've never really allowed myself to feel that way. "I'm so sorry."

"You don't have to be. It wasn't your fault."

"I know, but still. I hate hearing that you had to live like that," he says and squeezes me against his chest. "I promise that will never be something you'll have to worry about with me."

"Neither is the eating disorder. I'm much better now. I think I just got stressed and fell back into bad old habits."

"It's okay, I understand. It's been an incredibly rough few weeks for you. Anyone would crack at least a little under that kind of pressure. I get it."

"Thank you. That means a lot. I just hope you don't think I'm... defective or something now as a wife."

Theo sits up abruptly, his jaw tightening.

"I don't think that, and I *never* will," he says intensely. "And I don't want you to think it either, princess. Not for a single damn second. I hate the idea of you thinking you're anything less than perfect just the way you are."

We stare at each other, and my heart pounds in my chest until he reaches out to cup my face in his hand. His thumb strokes my cheek tenderly, and I think he's going to pull me up for a kiss, but he just holds me there with his gaze locked on me.

The air between us seems to thicken, making it hard to breathe. I don't know what it is or what to call it, but it's there —*something* building between us.

I want to ask him, to ask if this feels as real to him as it does to me, but I'm terrified to say it out loud. I've already caused enough chaos in the last couple of days, so I don't want to complicate things any more than I already have.

And I couldn't bear to hear it if he didn't agree.

But then he does lean into me, gently pressing his lips against mine, and my body catches fire. I climb closer to him, my hands wandering across his chest as his hands slide up beneath the hem of the shirt—*his* shirt—that I'm still wearing. He strokes my back as the kiss heats up, but when my hand drifts down to his cock, he freezes and pulls away.

"I want you, princess," he says, his voice hoarse. "So fucking much. I always want you. But we can't. Not until you're recovered."

I can't hold back a grimace or hide my sexual frustration, even though I understand. Theo has always been protective of me, so it's no surprise that he's even more protective and worried about me right now. As badly as my body burns for him, I know there's no way he'll give in right now. So it'll have to be enough to know that he wants me too.

"Why don't we get some coffee and breakfast?" he suggests, pressing one last chaste kiss to my lips. "You stay here, I'll bring it up to you."

"You really don't have to do that. I'm fine," I insist, but he just gives me a look, undeterred.

He climbs out of bed, and Milo bounds after him as I slump back against the pillows and sigh. I appreciate him worrying about me and taking care of me like this, but I really do feel mostly back to normal.

Theo comes back upstairs about fifteen minutes later carrying a plate and a steaming coffee mug, so I sit up and take the plate from him so he can sit the mug on the bedside table.

"It's nothing special, but it'll get you started right," he says as I look over the scrambled eggs and toast he made for me. I'm not particularly hungry, but I eat as much of it as I can between sips of the coffee. Theo sits on the end of the bed, watching me.

"Acceptable?" he asks, looking worried.

I laugh and nod. "Yeah, it's pretty good."

Relief spreads across his face. "Good. Maybe I'm not such a train wreck at this whole cooking thing after all."

"I love that you're trying to get better at it."

"Really?"

"Yeah. It's so sweet." I smile softly at him, then go back to eating.

When I'm finished, he clears everything for me, making me feel like the princess he says I am. But I feel guilty for letting him do all of this, especially when I'm not feeling all that ill. He seems to love it though, and he won't take any of my no's for an answer anyway, so I decide to just enjoy it.

Over the next several days, he keeps his attentiveness dialed up to a ten. More food appears in the house than either of us know what to do with, along with recipe books and printed, stained copies of recipes Theo finds online. I try everything he cooks, even the stuff that doesn't look or smell particularly appetizing, because I appreciate what he's doing for me and don't want to discourage him.

Besides, this is a total about-face for him. When I first moved in, he told me he rarely, if ever, cooked. But now he's doing it all the time—and doing it for me. It's a simple gesture, but I find it so touching that he's going out of his way to learn and get better on my behalf.

But I won't lie, I'm also getting incredibly sexually frustrated. It's been almost a week since I came home from the hospital and Theo still hasn't touched me beyond hugging and kissing. I've tried, but he's rebuffed me at every attempt. I don't know what I need to do to convince him that I'm healthy enough for sex again, but I really need him to trust me.

And I need him.

By the end of the week, we still haven't had sex once, and I'm starting to believe the only way I can prove to Theo that I'm back to normal is by getting out of the house and back on my feet. So when he tells me he has a home game tonight and repeatedly says I don't have to go if I'm not feeling up to it, I jump on the chance.

"No, I'll go," I say brightly, sitting on the end of his bed while he gets ready. He pauses and turns to face me.

"You're sure? I don't want you overdoing it."

"I've had a week's worth of rest. I think I can handle sitting in the stands at a hockey game. Besides, I'm sure Margo and Callie will be there, and it'll be good for me to spend some time with them."

That seems to seal the deal because Theo smiles and nods. "Yeah, you know what? You're right. And I'm sure they'd love to see you too. They've been worried about you."

"Yeah, we've been texting a lot since the reality show fiasco. We have a group chat going," I say and grab my phone off the nightstand to show him. "They've been really sweet. They don't believe any of the shit Shawn said either."

315

"No one should," Theo says with a scowl as he yanks his pants up to his waist and fastens them. "But good for you. I'm glad to hear you're making friends out here. I can give you a ride to the arena if you don't mind getting there early. I've gotta leave soon."

"I don't mind," I say and spring off the bed to hurry downstairs and change. Theo already moved most of my necessary stuff into his room, but I have too many clothes to fit in here with his, so I left those downstairs for now. I change into something warm but fashionable to keep myself from freezing in the arena and meet Theo in the kitchen a few minutes later.

"Ready to go?" he asks as he fills Milo's food dish by the door.

"Yup."

Theo grabs his keys from the ring on the wall and leads the way out of the condo. He offers me his hand and we walk to the car together. As usual, he opens the passenger side door for me and waits for me to get settled before he closes the door and steps around to the driver's side.

"I'm glad you're coming," he says as he starts the car and links his hand with mine.

"Yeah?"

"Definitely. I always feel and play better when you're there. And it's been hard to stay focused, even at practice, while you've been recovering. You're all I think about."

That's probably one of the sweetest things anyone has ever said to me, so I squeeze his hand. "Thank you. I'm glad I'm coming too. I missed this so much more than I ever thought I would."

"With you there, we're pretty much guaranteed to win tonight."

"What am I, a lucky charm or something?"

As we pull out onto the street, Theo looks me in the eye and grins. "Something like that."

Theo parks in the area reserved for the players and staff at the arena a few minutes later and walks me inside to the family room. Callie and Margo are already there, and they both light up when they see us walk in.

"Becca! You're back," Callie says and darts over to throw her arms around me. "Glad to see you're up and moving again. You feeling okay?"

"Never better."

"We missed you," Margo says as she catches up and hugs me too.

"Me too. The group chat was a real lifeline, but it's not the same thing."

Theo kisses the top of my head. "I'll let you girls catch up. I need to go get changed."

"Good luck tonight. Not that you'll need it," I tell him as I press my head against his chest.

"I already have it." He kisses me once more and disappears.

Callie beams at me when I turn back around after he leaves.

"It sure sounds like things are going well for you two," she says with a teasing expression.

"They are for sure."

"And it seems like the furor over the episode is dying off already too, at least as far as I can tell," Margo says as she scrolls on her phone, no doubt monitoring the social media chatter. "Not that any of us believed that shit for a second. I don't think the public bought it either, based on how quickly the story is already fading."

"That's a good thing, right?" I ask with my chest clenched. This whole thing blowing over without any real fallout seems like too much to hope for, but if Margo is right, that's exactly what's happening.

"Oh, definitely. I mean, people are still talking about it. But that's kind of the way these social media stories go. People move quickly from one outrage to the next."

"Well, I don't wish the firestorm on anyone else, but I'd be lying if I said I wasn't grateful I'm out of the hot seat. At least for now."

"Don't blame you there," Margo says as she pockets her phone. "Anyway, we'd better get you to your seat before the warmups start. I don't want to fight the crowds, and I've got to work this game.."

I follow her and Callie to our usual best seats in the house and get settled in just before warmups start. The Aces are playing against Minnesota's Monarchs tonight, a lower-ranked team that they haven't played against yet this season. It should be a pretty uneventful night unless the Monarchs have really upped their game since last season.

Neither team seems particularly excited when they take the ice for warmups, but that doesn't necessarily mean anything. Theo finds me in the crowd right away, beaming at me through his visor. He's loose and free on the ice, which is a nice change from how I've seen him the last few games, all tense and agitated.

When warmups are over, both teams form up for the face-off, and I cheer with the rest of the Aces fans when Theo takes the puck. He dances down the ice, gliding between the Monarchs like they aren't even there, and attempts a shot. But the goalie blocks it, which seems to mildly annoy Theo, but he bounces back quickly.

At the next face-off, the Monarchs take the puck, but they don't hold it for long. Their center attempts a pass, and Theo's there to intercept it. The crowd goes wild as he drives down the ice in the opposite direction, and this time he sinks the goal. I jump out of my seat to cheer for him with everyone else, and again he finds me in the crowd, pointing at me with this stick and winking.

My face appears on the giant screens above the ice as the crowd cam locks on me, and I instantly freeze. After the crap with Shawn's show, I'm way less comfortable being this visible right now. The mob online will be looking for anything at all to use to tear me apart again. My arms drop, and I look down at my feet until Callie takes my hand and drags it back up into the air.

"Screw them. Don't let Shawn and his goons steal your happiness. Enjoy this!" she shouts over the noise, making me smile. She's right. I love hockey, and I love watching Theo play, so why shouldn't I soak it up? Anyone who's on Shawn's side in this would tear me down no matter what I did, so I might as well have fun.

And Theo really is playing better than I've seen him play all season, which is saying something because he's been on fire the last few games. His first goal seems to have taken the wind out of the Monarch's sails though because they don't put up much of a fight for the rest of the game, and the Aces end up taking it 3-0 with another goal from Theo and one from Reese.

After the game, I head back to the family room with Callie and Margo to wait for Theo. I don't think the press interviews will take very long after a game like that, and I'm right because Theo appears just about fifteen minutes later. He opens his arms to me, and I throw myself into them for him to kiss me.

"Three to nothing, how about that?" he asks when we break. "I guess you were right, my wife really is my lucky charm."

"I don't know if it was luck so much as it was skill. You played amazingly tonight."

"Because you were there watching."

"Now you're just flattering me."

Theo grins and lifts an eyebrow at me. "Is it working?"

"Doesn't it always?"

He laughs, pulling me into his arms. "Yeah, princess. It always does. You ready to go?"

I nod and say goodbye to Margo and Callie before following him back to the car. We break down the best plays of the night during the drive, and come home to a very excited Milo, who jumps all over both of us.

"I think the poor guy has separation anxiety," Theo says with a laugh as he pets Milo. He isn't the only one, but I keep that part to myself.

"Maybe. I'm going to go shower and get cleaned up before bed."

"Okay. Are you hungry? Can I make you anything?"

"There are enough leftovers in this house to feed a small army. I'll nibble on those later if I get hungry."

"Good idea. I don't want that stuff going bad. Anyway, enjoy."

I give him a quick kiss and head upstairs to use his shower. There's nothing wrong with the one in the bathroom downstairs, I just like his big, open stall shower better. I let the water run for a few seconds to warm up, then strip down and climb inside.

My head is still a bit tender where I hit it in the fall, so the water cascading against my scalp is a little painful. I turn my back to the faucet and let the warm water stream down my back instead while I gingerly splash some onto my face. When I'm satisfied it's sufficiently wet, I step out of the stream and blink away the water running down my face and find Theo standing outside the stall, watching me through the glass with a hungry expression.

"Are you okay?" I ask, and he nods but doesn't say anything. His eyes just travel up and down my naked, exposed body as steam billows around it. Desire pricks to life inside me, and although I know he already showered before we left the arena, I think this might be the chance I've been hoping for, so I push the stall door open. "Come on in, the water's fine."

Theo laughs and pulls his shirt over his head in one fluid motion, then drops his pants. He's already semi-hard, which I take as a good sign, but when he climbs into the stall with me, he reaches for my face to cup it while he examines the bruise on the top of my head.

"Looks like it's healing nicely," he says and kisses the tender spot, then reaches for the bottle of shampoo on the shelf built into the wall. He lathers the creamy liquid in his hands, then starts to wash my hair, being careful not to touch the wound. He massages my scalp with his fingertips, just like they do at the salon, and it feels amazing.

"It *is* healing nicely. I have you to thank for that," I say as I look into his eyes.

A warm smile appears on his face. "Nah, princess. It's me who should be thanking you."

"For what?"

Theo takes the detachable shower head off its hook and rinses the shampoo out of my hair before he answers.

"For helping me find my way again," he says when I'm finished blinking away the water that's dribbling down my face. My heart lurches, both because it means a lot to hear—and because I'm not sure I believe it.

"That wasn't all me."

"Okay, you're right, I had something to do with it too. But if it weren't for you coming into my life, encouraging me to be better just by being here, I don't know that it would've happened. I was so lost before you."

My throat tightens as I try not to cry because it's sweet but also heartbreaking to hear.

"Theo..." I trail off, completely unsure of what else to say.

"I'm serious. The only thing that used to matter to me was proving everyone wrong. I had this fucking chip on my shoulder, and I was pissed off at the world. The way I played hockey showed it. It was more of a fight than a game. But I found a new fuel. A new motivation. You."

My heart expands so much and so quickly that it aches. Theo cups my face in his hands and leans down to kiss me, softly and sweetly, but I have so much pent-up desire for him that I add some intensity in the way I kiss him back.

He pulls away, still holding my face. "Not until you're ready, baby. I don't want to hurt you."

I rest one of my hands on his and push it down to my breast, leaving it there so he can feel the thudding of my heart.

"Please," I whisper without taking my eyes off his. "I'm ready. I've *been* ready, Theo. I need you so much."

Something lights in his eyes, and he kisses me again with the kind of hunger I've been craving but that he's been withholding.

I feel his cock hardening between us, pressing against my thigh, so I reach down and take it in one soapy hand to give it a soft stroke. He moans into my mouth, and I realize that as much as I've been craving this, it must have been driving him crazy not to be able to touch me the way he's gotten used to.

He rests his forehead against mine. "I can never get enough of you."

"Me too," I breathe and kiss him again like my life depends on it.

There's so much more I could and want to say, but I don't have the words for it, so I let my body do the talking. I don't know that there are enough words in the English language to tell him how appreciative I am of him, for all he's done for me. The ways he's changed me and my life.

I've never felt as safe with anyone as I have with Theo. And I don't think I'll ever feel this way about anyone else—but I don't want anyone else. I only want him.

Theo presses my back against the wall of the shower stall. I hiss at the cold glass on my skin and he tries to pull me away, but I stop him.

"No. It's okay. I want you to fuck me like this," I say and kiss him again. He's fully hard now, so I work his cock between my legs and groan when it grazes my clit.

"Then you need to beg for it," Theo says when we break,

resting his palms against the glass and pinning me against it. He moves to my neck, trailing agonizingly teasing kisses down the tender skin there before working his way back up to my earlobe. "I want to hear how badly you want my cock. Your *husband's* cock."

I whimper because he's making me insane, so turned on I can barely see straight.

"You're the only one I want," I say, my chest tight with emotion as our gazes lock. Feeling the sheer weight and force of his muscular body against mine, and the power I know that's thrumming in it, makes me lightheaded. "The only one I need."

"Fuck," he groans, and grips his cock to steady it as he pushes into me. A gasp escapes me because it's been so long since I last had him that I have to get used to it again. But he hoists me up, so I wrap my legs around his waist and my arms around his neck to steady myself as he continues sliding into me.

The pleasure that races through me is deep and intense. With my back against the shower wall and my hips raised like this, he's able to get deeper into me than usual, and each time he thrusts inside, I feel like another little part of me leaves my body. It's been so long since we've been together that I can already feel a climax beginning to tingle, working its way from my curled toes up to my core.

And with each increasingly powerful thrust of his cock, I slide a bit farther up the wall. But I can't focus on anything other than the intensity of the burning inside me. I don't want this to be over so quickly since I've waited more than a week for it at this point, but the way he's stretching and pounding into me feels too good to hold it back.

"That's it. That's my perfect wife. Come for me. Come on your husband's cock," he murmurs gruffly in my ear. I can't deny him anything, least of all of this orgasm, so I let out a little yelp as his words send me crashing over the edge.

Through squinted, watering eyes I watch his face, hoping he'll come with me, but he just stares intently at me, his hips bucking all the way through my spasming. I'm sure I must have flooded him, but he doesn't seem to notice. When I finally come fully back into my body, Theo lets out a sound like a growl and peels me off the shower wall where I've melted.

"What are you doing?"

"You'll see," he says and hauls me out of the shower in his arms, still rock hard inside me. I don't know how he manages it, but he carries me to his bed and falls on top of me. We're getting the covers all wet, but none of that matters. I just want him to feel as incredible as he made me feel.

He braces himself over me, using his powerful, veined arms to hold himself up while he resumes pounding me. There's a hunger, a desperation in his strokes, and his breathing turns ragged as our wet bodies fall in sync, slapping against each other and filling the room with the sound. It's like he can't get deep enough into me, close enough to me, but he keeps trying. And every time he rams into me, I feel myself opening more, beckoning him in.

Because I want him as close as possible too. I don't want anything—not a single thing—between us.

"Come with me," I beg into his ear as my second orgasm begins to build. My hands rake his back to encourage him. I want to feel it, want to be filled by him in the way only he can.

He nods, his jaw tight. "I'm close," he grunts, and I let myself fall to pieces in his arms. We crash like opposing waves into each other, and Theo's thrusts shift from sharp and steady to erratic and spasming. Our bodies press into each other, and Theo grunts repeatedly in my ear, but I can barely hear him over the force of the orgasm tearing through me.

But then my eyes flutter back open, and little spots and specks dance in my vision from squeezing them shut so tight.

And there he is, staring down at me with a smoldering intensity that makes me shiver.

Exhausted but finally satiated, I cling to him, hugging him close against me.

I never want to let him go.

Chapter 32

Theo

"Ugh, do we really have to go to this dumb charity thing?" I ask between kisses while my hands cup Becca's beautiful, perfect breasts. We haven't been able to stop touching each other in the few days since we finally ended our dry spell, and today isn't any different.

"I don't want to go any more than you do, but you said you'd be there, so we have to be there," she says, although she gives me another long, lingering kiss. But just as I'm getting into it, she ducks out from under my arms to grab her coat by the front door.

"You're killing me here."

"It's killing me too," she says as she rubs my cock through my pants, driving me crazy. "But it'll be easy and over quickly. It's just an auction. We can get in and get out." She raises her eyebrows at me to emphasize her point.

I grin at her. "We both know I'm pretty good at that motion."

She laughs and shakes her head at me before she hands me my coat. "Yes, you are, but I'll have to take a rain check on testing that. We've got money to raise. Though it seems like something else is already standing up," she says with a grin as she stares at my hard cock in my pants and chews her lip.

I sigh. "Fine, but at least let me help fix your hair before we leave. You look like you were just running through the woods."

"No thanks to you," she says as I run my fingers through her hair to straighten it out.

"What? I can't help it. Every part of you is beautiful, so shoot me for wanting to touch it all."

"Oh, I'm not complaining," she says and closes her eyes like she's enjoying me touching her. "God, that feels amazing. But we better hit the road before I change my mind," she says and slips away out of the condo before I get the chance to actually change her mind. It took us way longer than it should have to get ready since we were so handsy with each other, but at least we managed to get dressed fully.

Even though it's an auction, this is supposed to be a more upscale event, so I'm wearing a classic black tuxedo. We ran out of time to go shopping for a new dress like I wanted to buy for Becca, but Margo let her borrow a sleek black gown of hers that fits her like a second skin—that's part of the reason it was so difficult to keep my hands off her.

Our reflections are warped in the glass of the car's windows, but even so, I can tell we look good. And we definitely look the part of a rich power couple off for an evening milling around with other rich and powerful people. I've been doing this kind of thing for years now, but it still blows my mind that this is my life. When I was a poor kid growing up, I didn't think I'd ever set foot at a ritzy dinner like this once in my entire lifetime, much less make a regular thing out of it.

I help Becca into the car as usual before getting in the driver's seat, and even though we're officially running late, I still lean over the console for another kiss. Her mouth is all too ready to meet mine, and her hands wind themselves up in my hair.

But she breaks the spell and pulls away, breathing heavily. "We have ten minutes."

"Plenty of time for a quickie, especially with the valet taking the car," I say confidently, and although she beams at me, she reaches around to buckle her seatbelt.

"Let's save it for after the event. It'll be more fun that way. You know, build the anticipation even more."

"You're playing with me, but you know what? I like it." I start the car and peel out of the garage. It's a good thing I know the city because, despite my protests, Becca's right—we don't have a lot of time.

We arrive at a relatively non-descript, multi-story hotel just under ten minutes later, and at first, Becca looks convinced we're at the wrong place. I don't blame her for being skeptical, because it doesn't really look like the kind of place that would host a fancy dinner auction. But as we pull around toward the parking area, she spots people in very nice clothing walking into the front entrance and breathes a sigh of relief.

I drive up to the valet and climb out of the car to walk around and help Becca out like the gentleman I am. The driver takes the car, so I escort Becca up the stairs into the hotel lobby where around two dozen people are milling and nursing their drinks. It's a nicer hotel than it looks like from the outside.

"Is this it?" Becca whispers in my ear, and I chuckle.

"Getting used to the lifestyle of the rich and famous, huh?"

"No, I didn't mean it like that. I just thought... I don't know, I thought this would be ritzier."

"You haven't seen the best part yet. Come on," I say and walk her over to the dual elevator, then press the button to call for it. People are recognizing us as we pass, no doubt because of Kaplan's stupid fucking reality show episode, but they at least have the decency to keep their mouths shut. And that's the right idea.

We pack into the elevator with a few other couples and take

it all the way up to the roof. Becca shoots me a quizzical look, but I just grin at her. A few moments later, we emerge onto a massive, covered rooftop where dozens of tables are setup and at least two hundred people are gathered. String lights dangle among the vine-patterned covering, giving the area a soft, warm glow, and well-dressed attendants zip among the crowd carrying trays of drinks and hors d'oeuvres.

"Is this more like what you had in mind?" I ask, but she's speechless as her eyes wander over all the people. And her eyes shoot wide open when she finally realizes she's rubbing elbows with NHL royalty.

I spot players from more teams than I can count or keep track of, and coaches too. Some are current, some are former, but I recognize almost everyone here. And I'm sure she does too, given her love of hockey.

"This is incredible," she whispers, more to herself than anyone else, and I smile as I loop my arm through hers.

"You're right, it is. Ready to meet some of them?" I'm not sure how it's possible, but her eyes widen even farther.

"Are you serious?" she breathes.

"Of course I am. You're part of the club now since you married me. Might as well take advantage of it, right?" Becca's mouth hangs open as she takes another look around the room. "Or we could just grab a drink and a good seat for the auction. Your choice."

"No, let's mingle."

"That's more like it," I say and make a beeline for Andrew Wheeler, the coach of the New Jersey Titans. We've met a few times before, and he's a really nice, friendly guy, so I figure talking with him first will be a good way to break the ice for Becca.

Andrew, who's bald and wears electric blue glasses, lights up when he sees us approaching. "Ah, Theo! I was wondering if you'd ever introduce me to your new wife."

"Well, you're in luck, because here she is. Becca, this is Andrew. Andrew, Becca."

Andrew shakes her hand gently. "So nice to meet you."

"You too," Becca answers. She looks like she's about to say something else, but then her body tenses suddenly, her jaw snapping shut.

I'm not sure what's wrong until I follow her gaze and find the last person in the world I want to see.

Kaplan.

He's staring right at us, wearing the kind of shit-eating grin I'd love to punch off his face. I instinctively pull Becca closer to me, wrapping my arm around her protectively. It makes sense he'd be here, but that doesn't mean I'm happy about it.

I'm even more unhappy about the fact that he's coming our way.

Andrew notices both of us staring past him, and when he turns to see what we're looking at, he quickly excuses himself. I don't blame him for not wanting anything to do with what's about to happen next. The most recent episode of Kaplan's bullshit "reality" show is clearly the elephant in the room, and I'm sure most of the people here have been talking about it. How couldn't they?

As Kaplan gets closer, I notice he's bulked out more than usual. Maybe he's on some new workout routine for the next time we cross paths on the ice? I don't know, and I don't particularly care. All I know is I don't want him anywhere near me or Becca, but it isn't like I can make a run for it. Besides, I wouldn't want to give him the satisfaction.

I take a deep breath and stand as tall as I can to meet him. My heart pounds in my ears and my jaw clenches. He smiles smugly at us when he stops with his hands in his pockets.

"Nice to see you, Becca." She glares at him without answering, and he scoffs under his breath. "As frosty as ever, I see."

"Fuck you," she snaps, and he narrows his eyes.

"Camden must really be rubbing off on you. In more ways than one."

"Get the fuck out of here, Kaplan," I growl. "Neither of us are in the mood for your shit."

"Fine, play it your way," he says, then locks eyes with Becca. "But we all know you'll come crawling back to me one day when you eventually get bored with Camden."

"That will *never* happen," I say through gritted teeth, pressing Becca against my side.

"You sure about that? Once a cheater, always a cheater, or so they say."

I lunge at him, but Becca gets between us, resting a hand on my chest.

"It's okay, Theo. Don't let him get to you. That's what he wants," she whispers, and it's barely enough to calm the rage roiling in my veins, but it works. She's right. This is a fucking charity auction, not a boxing match. So as much as I'd love to pound Kaplan into dust right here and now, I unclench my fist and step back.

"It's a good thing you have your dog on a leash, Becca."

"Leave. Now," she orders, and he frowns at her.

"Fine. I just wanted you to know I miss you," he says with a smirk and turns to disappear back into the crowd. I glare after him, one arm still wrapped tightly around Becca, fuming. It takes a few minutes for me to slow my breathing and calm down, but having Becca in my arms helps.

"Don't believe a word he says. I'd never cheat on you. I didn't even cheat on him. He's so full of shit."

"Oh, I know," I say, but I let it go. The more I think about him or any of the crap that comes out of his mouth, the more I let him win. "I don't know about you, but I could use a drink."

"That sounds fantastic," Becca says, so I flag down the nearest attendant and pick two glasses of red wine off their tray.

"I'm proud of you for not losing it on him," Becca says as she takes one of the glasses from me.

"So am I."

She chuckles, although I wasn't joking at all.

I take a sip of my drink as an announcement is made that the auction is about to start. There's a small stage at the back of the rooftop, and more rows of chairs than I can count are laid out in front of it. Most of them are taken by the time we get there, but Becca and I manage to get a couple of seats toward the middle before everything fills out.

This is a typical auction, so there are little paddles at every seat with a number on it for us to use to bid on something we're interested in. All the proceeds are going toward youth hockey programs in the city, but I don't actually know what's being auctioned today. It's almost a guarantee that there will be a few lunches with players and that sort of thing, if I had to guess, and probably some game tickets too.

Becca and I take our seats, each of us holding a paddle, while a soft-middled dude I recognize as the head of the youth hockey program walks out onto the stage. "Thank you for coming tonight, everyone," he says into the mounted microphone. "We have a lot of things to get through tonight, so let's get this show on the road."

The charity leader steps back, and another guy in a suit takes his place while an attendant brings out a hockey stick. It's hard to see from here, but it looks like it's been signed by an entire team. "First up we have a hockey stick from last year's Stanley Cup, signed by the entire winning team," the new guy says into the mic. "We'll start the bidding at five hundred dollars. Do we have five hundred?"

Someone in the front row throws their paddle into the air immediately, and the auctioneer launches into a classic rapid-fire stream of words to ask if there's another bid. After several rounds, the stick ends up selling for just shy of five thousand dollars.

"We're off to a good start," Becca whispers as she takes another sip of her wine. I'm not surprised something like that raised so much money, but I am kind of surprised we'd start with something that high value. Usually they start with the least interesting things and work their way up.

The attendant walks off the stage with the hockey stick in their gloved hands, and another replaces them, pushing a photo of a dancer on a large easel. "Next, we have a set of three private dance lessons with Becca Summers, the wife of the Aces' Theo Camden," the auctioneer says, and I almost drop my wine glass.

"You didn't tell me you were auctioning off lessons!" I say, and Becca shrugs.

"I wanted it to be a surprise."

I chuckle, a burst of pride filling my chest. "Well, consider me surprised. Now I know why you were so insistent about getting here on time."

"Are you upset?"

"What? No way. I think it's sweet of you," I say, and I mean it. She's always so selfless, so giving. It's one of the things I love the most about her. And she's helping raise money to fund the next crop of NHL players, so what is there to be upset about?

"We'll start the bidding at one hundred dollars," the auctioneer says, and a paddle a few rows ahead of us shoots into the air. But when the person holding it turns around, wearing an all-too-familiar grin, I almost launch out of my chair.

It's Kaplan.

"Is he fucking serious?" I mutter and thrust my paddle in the air to counter his bid. I don't know what the hell he's up to, but if he thinks I'm going to let him be alone with Becca for even one second, he's in for a rude fucking awakening.

"We're off to the races! I have one thousand dollars. Do I have one thousand five hundred?"

Surprising no one, Kaplan counters my bid. Thankfully, everyone in the room seems to know better than to get involved, so Kaplan and I devolve into a bidding war over Becca. I don't give a damn what the price amounts to. I'll spend every dime I have if it means keeping her away from him, and Kaplan must know it because he's not afraid to keep driving the price up.

"I have five thousand, do I have five thousand five hundred?" the auctioneer asks, and I shoot my paddle into the air. Becca rests her hand on my leg, silently begging me to make this stop, but there's nothing I can do other than keep bidding. As much as I hate it, Kaplan's as entitled to bid on her dance lessons as anyone else is.

"I have six thousand, six thousand!" the auctioneer announces as Kaplan's paddle streaks across the air again. "Do I have six thousand five hundred?"

"Eight thousand," I shout, pumping my paddle in the air and causing a gasp to ripple through the crowd of people. They probably think I've lost my mind, and maybe I have. But I don't care. I don't give a single shit what any of them think or what they have to say. The only thing that matters to me is protecting Becca, at any cost.

"I have eight thousand! This is turning into quite the hot commodity, folks! Do I have eight thousand five hundred?"

"Nine thousand!" Kaplan shouts, and another gasp tears through the crowd. I glance over at Becca and find tears in her eyes, which only makes me want to launch out of my seat and pummel Kaplan to bloody bits with his stupid fucking paddle. At what point will he give it up? He has to know I won't back down, not over this.

"Three hundred thousand!" I shout back, and when yet another gasp spreads through the crowd like a virus, I realize I've jumped to my feet. Even from this far back from the stage, I see the auctioneer's eyes widen, but he doesn't miss a beat.

"Three hundred thousand, I have three hundred thousand

dollars for private dance lessons with Becca Summers! That's quite a bid. Do I have three hundred and one thousand?" he asks, and I tense as I wait for Kaplan to counterbid.

But nothing happens.

"Do I have three hundred and one thousand?" the auctioneer asks again but gets no response. The room is tense and silent. "Three hundred thousand, going once. Three hundred thousand, going twice..."

My fists clench so hard that I swear I can feel the wooden handle of the paddle crack in my grip as I wait, ready to bid again if need be. I'll spend every goddamn dollar I have to make sure Becca doesn't have to spend another second with her asshole of an ex.

"Sold, to Mr. Theo Camden!" the auctioneer finally announces to a polite round of applause.

I sink back down into my seat, possessive satisfaction filling me. When Kaplan spins in his seat, he performatively claps for me, a smug expression on his face. I'm just about to jump over every row of chairs separating us like a crazed track athlete when Becca's hand finds mine.

"It's over," she whispers. "It's over. Let it go."

Chapter 33

Becca

Relief floods me as the tension dissipates, and I wilt against Theo's shoulder to fight back the tears stinging in the corners of my eyes.

He just blew three hundred thousand dollars just to spite Shawn. I'm glad he did—I would sooner move back to Canada than spend another moment with my ex, especially after his TV show stunt—but it's still hard to believe Theo was willing to take things that far.

"You didn't have to do that," I say as the auctioneer moves on to the next item, but Theo lifts my chin up with his thumb to stare into my eyes. His own eyes are blazing.

"Of course I did. And I'd do it again in a heartbeat. Besides, it was a fucking bargain."

As if to prove his point, he cups my face with one hand, tilting my head toward him as he kisses me deeply.

It definitely brings my anxiety down, although I can feel every pair of eyes in the space on us, which makes me flush a little. We've already given everyone plenty to talk about, and I'm sure this will create even more gossip.

"Do you want to get out of here?" he asks when we break

apart, his eyes bouncing between mine. "We can leave right now if you want. Just say the word."

My immediate impulse is to say yes, but I consider for a second and then shake my head. I refuse to let Shawn chase me away, refuse to let him win. I won't give him the satisfaction of seeing me flee.

And besides, I know this event is important to Theo. And if it matters to him, it matters to me.

"No," I say, giving him a soft smile as I cup his cheek. "I want to stay. We still have to have dinner, and I wouldn't want to miss it. But thank you for looking out for me."

"Always, princess." His eyes warm, and he kisses me again.

Theo keeps his fingers linked with mine as the auction continues, his thumb rubbing a soothing path over my knuckles. Shawn is facing the stage again, and I can't stop my gaze from darting his way as my stomach turns over.

I don't understand how someone who claims he once loved me can be so cruel. So spiteful. And the more he shows his true colors, the less I understand what I ever saw in him in the first place. I know I shouldn't beat myself up for dating him—I can't judge myself now for what I didn't know back then—but it's hard not to.

I feel so stupid. So blind and naïve. I gave that man everything I had, so much so that I lost myself in the process. Knowing that he still has this power, this influence, over me makes me feel sick to my stomach. Will I ever be free of him? Will I ever cut the cord bonding us that he seems determined to wrap around my neck for having the audacity to leave him? I can't stop myself from wondering how much of his behavior is targeted at me, at Theo, or at both of us. Maybe it doesn't matter.

I sit on pins and needles through the rest of the auction, which is thankfully uneventful. When it's over, Theo and I make a beeline for the tables on the opposite side of the roof where food is already being served. All the tables are immaculately decorated and sporting some of the finest China I think I've ever seen. It looks so delicate that I'm afraid to touch any of it as I sit down and hang my bag from the back of my chair.

There are at least a dozen other empty seats spread around the circular table, but when I glance up, my heart lodges in my throat—because Shawn has taken the seat directly across from me. I feel rage spilling from Theo like a radiator, and I grip his thigh under the table both to calm him and ground myself.

My body tenses all over again, and a sharp pain at the base of my skull throbs. I hate the way even being around Shawn makes me feel. But more than that, I hate *him*.

He looks me up and down with a smirk that makes my skin crawl. I left his ass behind, so I shouldn't have to think about him anymore, but here he is, haunting me. Why the hell is he still so stuck on me? Especially if he thinks I'm such a miserable, drug-addled cheater like he claimed on his show?

After all, he's the one who broke up with me—on the same stupid show. If anyone has a right to be pissed, it's me. But he seems determined to ruin my life, to get back at me for some reason. I don't know or even care anymore what goes on in his fucked-up head, I just want him to leave me alone. For good.

I open my mouth to say something to Shawn, but Theo speaks before I can.

"Are you hungry, princess?"

"Not particularly," I answer, glaring at Shawn, who just smirks.

"Here, let's trade. I know you don't like broccoli," Theo says as he picks up a fork and starts moving the florets off my plate onto his. He gives me his green beans in return, and even though I feel Shawn watching the entire exchange, it makes me smile. I love how my husband is looking out for me, even in the middle of this shitshow.

"Wow, I didn't know you hated broccoli that much, Becca,"

Shawn comments, and Theo drops his fork on his plate with a clatter.

"Almost as much as she hates you. Which you'd know if you ever bothered to ask her about anything important to her," he growls, and Shawn's grin morphs quickly into a sour expression.

Something that feels a lot like love swells in my chest as Theo smiles at me. I don't know what comes over me, but I lean over and kiss him deeply, and he returns the kiss hungrily. I know Shawn is watching, but for once, I'm not doing this for his sake. I'm doing it because I want to. Because Theo makes me happy, and because I want everyone to see it.

Theo beams at me when we break apart, and thankfully, Andrew Wheeler sits down with a beautiful blonde woman in her mid-forties who must be his wife, giving us something to focus on other than Shawn. "That was quite the auction, Camden!"

"Becca must be one special lady. Or an incredible dancer," his wife adds.

"Both," Theo says, his smile widening, and my heart lurches at the sincerity in his voice.

"I'm Julie Wheeler, by the way," the woman says, confirming my suspicion.

A tuxedoed waiter appears carrying a bottle of wine and begins turning over our wine glasses to fill them one by one, interrupting the conversation for a moment.

"The Denver youth league is probably funded for a long while off of your generous contribution alone," Andrew teases Theo when the waiter leaves.

"It's the least I can do to give back to the community that's given me so much." Theo shrugs casually, resting a hand on my knee under the table where no one else can see. My skin prickles at the warmth of his palm through the fabric of my dress, and then my breath hitches as his fingers find the slit in the fabric and trail upward.

"What are you doing?" I whisper to him as the conversation continues on around us.

He leans a little closer, dropping his voice so low that only I can hear him. "I think you know exactly what I'm doing, princess. The question is, do you want me to stop?"

My pulse picks up, thudding rapidly. I do know what he's doing. The way his fingers have found their way between my legs makes that abundantly clear.

And I also know my answers.

"No. Don't stop."

He grins. "Good answer."

He turns away from me, saying something to Andrew. But I can't pay attention to any of his words as his fingers drag slowly over the crotch of my panties, teasing my clit through the fabric. My legs spread on their own, silently giving him better access.

He increases the pressure, tracing circles around my clit, and I let out a slow breath. It takes everything I have to keep a neutral expression on my face, and to hold back the moan building in the back of my throat.

With the way the tablecloth falls from the table, no one can see what Theo is doing to me, but I still can't believe he's doing it in public like this—and right in front of Shawn, no less. The asshole across the table doesn't seem to have noticed anything happening, but I can tell that there's a possessive edge to the way Theo is touching me, as if he wants to prove how much I'm his by making me come in front of Shawn.

And holy fuck, that's exactly what he's going to do. He's barely moving his fingers, careful to keep his movements discreet, but the tantalizing pressure mixed with the adrenaline rush of knowing we could get caught has my heart pounding already.

As if he can tell, Theo leans closer a moment later, his lips brushing my ear.

"Are you gonna fall apart for me right here?" he breathes. "This time, you really do need to stay quiet. Can you do that?"

I dip my chin once in a tiny nod. There's no way I'll let a sound escape, even though I'm a whimpering, panting mess on the inside.

"Good girl."

He grins, taking a sip of his wine with his free hand as he goes back to speaking to Andrew. His voice is steady and calm, giving away nothing—even as he tugs aside the crotch of my panties and slides two fingers into me.

I gasp softly, then clear my throat to cover it, nodding along to something Andrew just said even though I'm not really listening. Julie joins the conversation with Andrew and Theo, and I focus on staying quiet as sparks of pleasure dance up and down my spine.

Theo's talented fingers keep going, fucking me slow and deep as his thumb finds my clit, taking over there and giving me just enough friction to make my legs tremble slightly.

I'm close. God, I'm so close.

I bite my lip so hard that it aches, and when the pleasure finally crests inside me, I suddenly wonder if I lied to Theo. Can I really keep myself from making a noise?

Fortunately, Theo gives me just the cover I need. He turns toward me again, leaning in close like he's whispering something to me. It gives me the perfect opportunity to hide my face against his shoulder just as my orgasm hits. Pleasure pulses through me in waves, and Theo's fingers never stop fucking me as I let out a tiny whimper.

Thankfully, live music starts playing from somewhere, drowning out the din of conversation happening all around us as well as the sound I couldn't hold back. I cling to Theo's forearm like an anchor while the orgasm washes through me, and when it finally ebbs, I look up to find him gazing down at me with a heated, satisfied expression.

His fingers tease me a little more as they work their way out, making me squirm. I can't believe we just did that—or that we seem to have gotten away with it. It's easily the wildest, most reckless thing I've ever done.

But it's also the hottest.

As I slowly start to come down from the high, I realize the music is coming from a band set up on the stage where the auctioneer was earlier. There's a pianist backed by a cellist and percussionist, and they're playing upbeat music that fits the atmosphere of the event perfectly.

Andrew and Julie finish their dinners before Theo and I do, so they excuse themselves with polite nods before melting into the crowd of people now dancing to the music.

That leaves us alone with Shawn, who glances at us with a sour look on his face.

Theo ignores him, tipping my chin up and kissing me before murmuring, "I think we've stayed long enough. You ready to get out of here?"

I nod, because I really am ready to get away from my shitty ex. But I can't hide my grin as I whisper, "Honestly, I don't even know if I can stand without falling over."

"Good thing you'll have me to catch you." Theo winks at me before standing and helping me up.

Although I can feel Shawn watching our every move, I steadfastly ignore him. But once Theo is sure I'm steady on my feet, he surprises me by reaching across the table to Shawn.

"I'll see you on the ice," he says, deliberately extending his hand.

My heart skips in my chest as I realize it's the same hand he just used to get me off. My arousal is still probably smeared on his fingers as he shakes hands with Shawn, and I bite back a wild grin as my cheeks flush.

I'm positive he did that on purpose, and although Shawn has no idea, *I'm* well aware of the possessiveness of the gesture.

Shawn glares at my husband. "Oh, I'm looking forward to it."

Theo smirks, seeming entirely unruffled by the slightly threatening tone of Shawn's voice, then drops my ex's hand and turns away from him as if he no longer exists. He wraps his arm around my shoulder and leads me away.

But as we approach the elevator, I can sense tension gathering in Theo's body. He presses the call button for the elevator urgently, as if he's in a hurry to get out of here all of a sudden.

"Is everything okay?" I ask as the elevator arrives and we step inside.

The doors close behind us as Theo hits the button to take us down to the lobby, and he turns to face me, his green eyes glinting.

He backs me up against the elevator wall, tilting my chin up as a heart-stopping smile spreads over his face.

"Everything is fine," he says, his voice husky. "I just can't wait to get home and fuck my wife."

Butterflies explode in my stomach as his lips crash down on mine.

Chapter 34

Becca

It's a good thing we're in our home gym where no one is around to see, because even at the rate of three hundred thousand dollars for these private lessons, Theo is still a terrible dancer.

"Come on, come on, show me one more time. I'll get it, I swear," he insists. He's sweating and red faced, but he seems determined, which I appreciate. So for what feels like at least the eighth time, I repeat the move, a simple step and spin maneuver. But when I face him again, he's smirking at me.

"What's so funny?"

Theo shrugs. "Nothing. I'm just appreciating the view."

I slap his chest playfully, but he pulls me into him and spins me into a deep dip, making me yelp.

"What do you think of that move?" he asks as I'm still trying to get my bearings.

"No complaints."

Theo lifts me back up and kisses me, and I can't stop myself from giving into it. But before things get too heated, I pull away.

"You're being a very bad student," I tease, although I'm enjoying it as much as he is.

"Oh, you have no idea how bad I can be," Theo says and smacks my ass. I scoff at him, and his devilish grin widens.

"Okay, in all seriousness, I think you're tripping over your own two feet. You need to start with them more spread out. Shoulder width, like this." I plant my feet just like I'm telling him.

"Trust me, princess, it isn't my feet I'm tripping over."

"Oh, trust *me*, it is."

He tips his head back and laughs at that, then mimics my stance. "How does this look?"

"It's a good enough start," I say and walk around behind him to examine. I tap the back of his knees with my hand. "But you need to loosen up here. It's part of what's making you so wooden."

"I'd prefer it if *you* were making me wooden," Theo jokes, so I tickle him.

He bursts out laughing, ducking out of my reach. I lunge for his ribs again, but he catches my wrists and pulls me into him. He wasn't kidding about getting wood—I can feel his semi-hard cock against my stomach, and it makes my blood rush.

I stare up into his eyes, and heat courses between us. He releases my wrists, and my hand drifts on its own down to his cock to lightly stroke it through his baggy sweats that leave little to the imagination.

"Is this part of the lesson?" he asks, his voice dropping.

I bite my lip, my stomach fluttering. "If it is, that would make me a *very* bad teacher."

"Nah." He shakes his head, something earnest shining in his eyes even though his tone is teasing. "My wife is an amazing teacher. I won't let anyone say anything bad about her."

My heart warms at that, but rather than look too deeply into the emotions his words stir up in my chest, I flash him a playful smile.

"Hmm. And what would you do to me if I said something bad about your wife?" I ask with an eyebrow raised.

He pulls me tighter against his body. "I'd have to give you something better to do with your mouth."

"Such as?" I whisper, giving his cock another stroke as he pulses beneath my fingertips.

"Maybe I'd slide my dick between those gorgeous lips to shut you up," he says, his voice a low rasp.

Heat surges through me, curling low in my belly. "Oh really?"

He smirks, his eyes darkening with desire. "You sound like you'd like that. Is that what you want, princess? Want to take a break from our lessons so I can put you on your knees and use that beautiful mouth of yours? You want me to fuck your face?"

Oh my god.

My legs wobble a little bit as images of what he's describing flash through my mind. I nod, unable to find my voice in this moment, but he shakes his head.

"Uh uh. Not good enough. I need your words."

"Yes." My voice is raspy. "I want you to fuck my face."

"Good girl." His hungry smile is almost enough to make me come on the spot. "Now get on your knees."

There's a dominant edge to his voice, and I quickly sink down in front of him without ever taking my eyes off his. When I'm in position, he nods his approval.

"Go on." He lifts his chin. "Take my pants off."

I reach for the band of his sweats and give them a tug, and when they drop, a smile breaks across my face as my stomach flutters. He's not wearing any boxers, and he's already hard for me.

Fuck, I love that.

I grip him in one hand, although he's so big that my fingers can't wrap all the way around his shaft. I give it a slow stroke, and Theo groans.

"Fuck, your hand feels good. But that's not what I want right now. Open those gorgeous lips," he orders. "I want to see you swallow my cock. Wanna watch that pretty mouth take all of me."

There's something about the commanding tone he uses that melts me. It's going to be a challenge, but I'm not backing down, so I open wide and take him in, inch by inch. I fight the urge to gag as his cock disappears down my throat, but when my lips reach his base, it's too much, so I pull back quickly.

"Fuck, baby. So goddamn good," he says as he strokes my hair. "You're so good for me. Try again. Take your time."

I do as I'm told, but I go slower this time, exploring him with my mouth and tongue and pulling a series of groans out of him. He never takes his eyes off mine, even when I have most of his cock in my mouth. I bob up and down on him slowly, hoping he can feel every little sensation.

Theo's hands slip from the top of my head to the sides of my face. He holds me in place.

"Is this okay?" he rasps.

I nod, unable to say anything, and he thrusts himself into my mouth, filling my mouth and hitting the back of my throat again. It almost triggers my gag reflex, but not quite. Surprising myself, I moan my approval, and he grunts as he feels it, thrusting again.

"If it gets to be too much, pat my leg and I'll stop, okay?" he asks.

I nod again, tears pricking at the edges of my eyes. He takes it slow and gentle for a few more strokes, but once he's sure I can handle it, he picks up his pace gradually until he's fully fucking my face, just like he said he would.

There's no shortage of incredible sex I've had with Theo, but this is definitely making the short list. This is the most turned on I've ever been by giving a blowjob. My hand works itself down my pants to toy with my clit, and Theo chuckles when he sees what I'm doing.

"That's my girl. I want you to enjoy this as much as I am," he murmurs, and my body thrums in response.

There's something really hot about him being concerned about me feeling good while I'm the one going down on him—and he's gliding in and out of my mouth so fast that my lips are starting to tingle.

"That's it, just like that. It feels so fucking good," he grunts as his pace gets even faster. It's difficult to breathe, but I don't even think about tapping his leg.

I want this. I want *him*. And I want to make him come just like this, feel him erupt in my mouth from the pleasure it's giving him.

His cock grows so hard and swollen that I'm sure he must be close to coming, but somehow, he keeps going. His head falls back as he thrusts into my mouth one more time and holds me there for a second until I cough and sputter, then quickly pulls away so I can catch my breath.

"Are you okay?"

"Amazing," I gasp, and he grins at me.

"Good, because you had me so close. But I want to finish inside you. I want to feel that perfect pussy clench around me as I fill you up."

Raw arousal rushes through me, and I lick my lips before standing up. Using one hand, I shove down my stretch pants and panties, kicking them off before I take Theo's hand and pull him over to the weightlifting bench.

"What are you doing?" He gives me a playful, heated look.

"Lie down," I say in answer, pushing lightly against his chest.

He sits first, then lies back, his hard cock jutting up from his body. I kick one leg over him, straddling him, and sink down onto his shaft. Our gazes lock as he fills me, and his hands find my waist, fingers digging into my skin.

"Fuck," he groans. "Do you have any idea how damn beautiful you are? Do you have any clue what you do to me? All the things I want to do to you?"

"Show me," I whisper, barely able to speak past the overwhelming sensation of him stretching me. "Show me how you take care of your wife."

Theo bucks his hips, driving the rest of the way into me and making me whimper. His hands move to mine and our fingers intertwine, giving me something to balance on. With my feet on the floor and my hands in his, I start to ride him, bouncing slowly up and down, and Theo looks absolutely lost.

"Goddamn, you're stunning." The awe in his voice makes my heart race. "I'm not going to last long like this."

That only makes me want him more, so I push up with my calves, giving him a tight squeeze with my pussy.

"*Fuck*," he groans, followed by a grunt when I fall back down on his cock.

He's not the only one who's getting close. My legs are shaking both from the workout and the creeping orgasm building inside me, but I'm doing my best to time it so we come together. We find a rhythm, his hips rising to meet me as I sink back down on his cock. His breathing turns ragged, and his hands squeeze mine so tight they turn white. I'm sure he's about to lose it—until a voice drifts down the stairs and pierces the moment.

"Who the hell is she?" someone demands, and I yelp. Theo's arms fly around me, pulling me into him as he sits up abruptly.

"Valerie," he says breathlessly, and my heart crashes into my stomach.

His ex-wife. What the hell is she doing here?

I turn around slowly and find her standing in the doorway, one delicate hand resting on the railing. She's beautiful, like supermodel level of beauty. Long blonde hair hangs past her shoulders in wave. She's perfectly made up and looks exactly like the kind of woman who would marry a famous hockey player.

She also looks like she isn't at all phased by walking in on Theo having sex with me.

My cheeks flush. I scramble off Theo, grab my pants, and hurry out of the room, brushing past her without a word. Valerie smirks at me as I pass, and I hear Theo hissing at her in a low voice as I dart down the hall, but I can't make out what he's saying.

I make it to the bathroom by my room and am just closing the door when Theo catches up to me. He steps inside the bathroom with me, shutting the door behind him as his gaze finds mine.

"Are you okay?" he asks.

I put on a brave face because I don't want him to know how much his ex being here is getting to me. "I'm fine. Go out and deal with Valerie. She looked pissed."

He frowns, never once looking away from me as he shakes his head. "She can wait. She's not the one I'm worried about. All I care about is how *you* feel."

My breath catches in my throat because somehow, Theo always seems to know exactly what to say to disarm me. To get past my defenses.

As if to prove that point, he steps closer, running his fingertips down the curve of my cheek. "I mean it, princess. Are you okay?"

"You know what?" I blow out a breath, unconsciously leaning into his touch. "No. No, I'm not. I mean, your ex-wife just barged in on us having sex. Why is she here? Do you still have feelings for her? Are you—"

"No. I have *no* interest in her, Becca," he says, dropping his head so that our eyes are on the same level. "None. She's not the one I want. You are."

He kisses me, and there's something hungry and forceful in

it, even more so than there was before. Like he's trying to prove a point. Like he's trying to remind me of something.

His hands fall to my hips, and he walks me backward a few steps until my ass hits the edge of the sink. I never got a chance to put my pants on after I scooped them up, and the countertop is cool against my bare skin as Theo lifts me easily, setting me on the counter by the sink.

"What are you doing?" I ask as he spreads my legs and steps between them.

"Proving it to you. There's nothing and no one in the whole damn world that could keep me from finishing what we started."

He kisses me again as soon as the last word leaves his mouth, and I make a plaintive noise against his lips. Even though I know his ex-wife is somewhere in the house, I'm still so turned on—and so close—that I don't care. If she has the nerve to show up here unannounced, then I want her to hear the way Theo makes me feel. Hear me scream his name.

Because he chose me, not her.

"Eyes one me, princess," he demands, tilting my chin up as his cock notches at my entrance. "Don't look away from me. I want to see my wife's face when I make her come."

There's something in his voice as he says *my wife* that makes me shiver, an electric current of need racing through my veins.

I nod, staring into his gorgeous green eyes as he slides back into me, making me whimper. I'm already good and warmed up for him, so he holds nothing back. My fingers dig into his shoulders, holding on for dear life as he pounds into me.

"I want you to come for me. And I want her to hear it," he murmurs in my ear.

"Fuck, Theo." I nod breathlessly, squeezing around him. "Oh fuck. I'm so close."

He adjusts the angle of his strokes a little so that his cock hits my g-spot, and my mouth drops open as I cry out loudly. A fierce, possessive smile curves his lips, and he grips my hips harder, holding me in place as he drives into me again.

"That's it. Scream for me. Good girl."

"Don't stop," I gasp.

"Can't. *Won't.*" His voice is like gravel. "Fucking hell, princess, I never want to stop. Want to spend the rest of my life just like this. Buried inside you. Where I belong."

He continues fucking me like it's his mission in life, repeatedly hitting my g-spot, and when he reaches down to work my clit, I can't hold back anymore. My head falls back against the mirror as my orgasm tears through me.

"Fuck, Theo!" I scream, and he collapses against me as he comes too.

His body tenses, his hips bucking as he thrusts a few more times, and I feel him fill me up with several pulses of his cock. He kisses my shoulder and up my neck until his lips meet mine.

"You're the *only* one I want," he murmurs between kisses, and the intensity of his voice makes me shiver. When we part, he locks eyes with me. "I mean that."

"I know," I whisper with a nod, and he strokes my cheek.

"Good."

He gently draws back, and I feel a gush of cum spill from me as his cock slides out. I reach for a towel to clean myself up, but he grabs me by the wrist to stop me, something sinful burning in his eyes.

"Don't clean up yet. I want my cum inside you, princess. I want you walking around all day with a reminder of me between your legs. A reminder that you're mine."

I can feel a flush working its way up my neck and spreading over my cheeks. I like this possessive, dominant side of him. I like knowing that he's claimed me, marked his territory in a way. It makes me feel a whole lot less fucked up about the fact that his ex-wife is out there waiting somewhere in the loft.

"Okay," I whisper.

Theo's smile widens. "Goddamn. Just thinking about it makes me want to fuck you again, right here and now."

He kisses me, a deep, lingering kiss that seems to go on forever. When we finally break apart, be helps me climb down off the sink and get my clothes back on. Once I'm put back together, he pulls his own pants up and offers me a hand.

"Better?" he asks, studying my face carefully.

"Yeah."

"You don't have to see her if you don't want. You can hang out in your room until I get rid of her."

"No, it's okay." I give him a little smile, squeezing his hand. "I'll go with you. We're in this together, right?"

Warmth gleams in his eyes, and he cups my cheek with his free hand, pressing his lips to mine again. It's soft and tender this time, but it rocks me just as hard as our last kiss. Because there are so many unspoken words contained inside it.

"Together," he murmurs.

His palm is reassuringly warm against mine as I link my fingers with his and follow him out of the bathroom to face Valerie.

Chapter 35

Becca

Valerie is waiting on the couch in the living room when we enter, and when she spots my hand in Theo's, I don't miss the flash of jealousy that passes on her face as we pass. Theo sits down across from her, never taking his hand out of mine, so I join him.

"What do you want?" he asks her point blank.

"I came to get my motorcycle," she says.

Theo's eyebrows shoot up. "Are you serious? You let yourself into my house for that?"

"I'm one hundred percent serious." She waves a hand airily. "It's been in your garage ever since we split, and now I need it back."

"Well, you can't just come into my fucking house, Valerie. We're not together anymore. And in case you missed the news, I'm with someone."

Her gaze flits to me and then back to him, her lips pressing into a line. "Yeah, I noticed. I'm sorry to interrupt you and whatever puck bunny you brought home today, but—"

"She's not a puck bunny." Theo's voice hardens, taking on an edge that makes Valerie's jaw snap shut. "Becca is my wife.

354

So I'd think very carefully before you say another word about her."

Genuine surprise flashes across Valerie's face, and she looks back at me, her gaze lingering longer this time. When she shifts her focus back to Theo, she seems a bit subdued.

"I'm... I didn't know. I've been travelling overseas for months and haven't kept up with the news. I had no idea you were even seeing anyone, let alone that you'd gotten married."

Theo wraps an arm around my shoulder possessively. "Well, we did. Now, if all you want is your bike, you can get it and leave." He glances down at me, his lips curving into the smile that always makes my heart beat faster. "I've got big plans for my wife today, and we were just getting started when you interrupted us. So we don't have a lot of time to spare."

"Right." Valerie clears her throat, looking like she ate something sour. "Can you get it out of the garage for me?"

"If it gets you out of here faster, of course." He shrugs and stands. Before he leaves, he leans over to murmur in my ear, "Will you be okay alone with her for a second?"

"We'll be fine," I say, trying to infuse my voice with confidence.

He kisses my forehead and leaves the condo for the garage. I vaguely remember seeing a motorcycle in one corner of it, but I had no idea it was his ex-wife's. I did notice that it was set far out of the way, mostly hidden by a stack of boxes. Theo probably made sure it wasn't visible because he didn't want to be reminded of it or her.

"Congrats on the wedding," Valerie says, flashing me a somewhat strained smile once it's just the two of us. "You're lucky. Theo is a great guy."

She's right, but there's something about the way she says it that gets under my skin. I don't know what she's trying to imply, but I don't like it. And I decide I don't particularly like her either.

"Yeah, he is," I say simply.

Milo appears at the top of the loft stairs, and when he spots a new person in the house, he comes bounding down to sniff her. But unlike Theo's parents, our dog seems on the fence about Valerie. I can't say I blame him.

She holds a hand out gingerly for him to sniff, and she smiles.

"I'm glad to see Theo with someone sweet, someone who can make him happy," she says, and I can't tell if it's a genuine compliment or a veiled insult. "It's nice to see him so, well, *domestic*. With a dog and all." She chuckles. "I guess he's got everything he ever wanted now. Or nearly so."

"What do you mean?" I ask, curious in spite of myself.

She grimaces slightly. "Well, Theo has always been a pretty traditional guy. Much more so than me. I could never give him what he wanted most: a family. He wanted the whole deal—kids and a dog and everything—and I didn't, which is ultimately why we broke up. We were compatible in so many ways, but that was a dealbreaker for us. So it's nice to see that he's finally with someone who's the right fit for him."

Her tone is pleasant, but even so, I feel like I've just jumped into a vat of ice. My stomach roils, and I'm afraid I'm going to get sick in front of her, but I nod and pretend everything is fine. Perfectly fine.

Thankfully, the door opens a moment later, and Theo appears.

"Your bike is outside," he tells Valerie flatly. "And there's nothing else you left here, so there won't be any need for you to drop by again."

She smiles at me again, gives Milo's head a pat, and stands.

"Right. Well, it was nice to meet you, Becca. Sorry for stopping by unannounced. I would never have done that if I'd known... well, if I'd known that Theo had found someone."

For a second, I think she's going to hold her hand out to

shake mine, and I tense up a little. But fortunately, she doesn't. She turns to Theo, her expression warming a little.

"I guess this is goodbye," she says.

She takes step forward like she's going to hug him, but Theo steps back.

"It is. For good. Goodbye, Valerie," he says and steps aside to open the door for her.

The warmth in her expression dissolves, and she shoots me one more look, the veneer of polite warmth vanishing from her expression for a moment. She looks put out and a bit pissed off, as if she had hoped that coming here to retrieve her bike would somehow give her and Theo a chance to reconnect. I have no idea if she actually thought they'd rekindle a relationship or if she just wanted one last fuck or something—but either way, I'm glad that Theo made it perfectly clear where he stands.

I don't think even the most delusional person could misread the message he was giving her.

He's done with her. Utterly and completely done.

Theo turns to me, worry passing over his features again as he strides closer and wraps and arm around me. He frowns, brushing my hair back.

"I'm so fucking sorry about that, princess. I haven't talked to Valerie in months. We haven't seen each other in a lot longer than that. But I forgot I hadn't reprogrammed my lock after she left. I'll be doing that today."

"After you finish all the big plans you had for your wife?" I ask, unable to resist.

He smirks, his eyes heating. "Yeah, after that. Fucking you just once wasn't enough, princess. It never is. I'm gonna make you scream my name so many times you'll be hoarse tomorrow."

He pulls me close, letting me feel the way he's already getting hard for me again. Then his expression turns serious, and he lets out a quiet sigh.

"There's nothing between me and my ex anymore. You believe that, don't you?"

"Yeah." I nod, wrapping my arms around his broad back. "I do."

And I mean it. As much as her words unsettled me, I'm not threatened by Valerie, strangely enough.

Thinking about my brief conversation with her makes my stomach clench all over again, and I push those thoughts aside. I'll have to deal with them later, but right now, I don't have it in me to dwell on it anymore.

"That was really the last thing of hers that was left here?" I ask.

"Yeah." He blows out a breath. "It took her a while to move her stuff out after we split, and the last few things were pretty piecemeal. She was moving around a lot by then, in and out of the country. She always went wherever the wind blew her. But she won't be coming around here anymore. There's no room for her in my life."

I nod, and when he drops his head and kisses me like he's starving, I cling to him, trying to lose myself in it. To shove down all of the worries swarming in my stomach and enjoy this moment with him while I still have it.

Before the truth comes out, and the illusion breaks.

Chapter 36

Theo

"Holy shit, your ex-wife walked in on you having sex with your new one?" Reese asks in shock as the team is getting cleaned up and dressed after practice. His jaw hangs open as he stares at me.

"Yeah, that about sums it up," I answer.

His brows furrow. "What did you do?"

I shrug. "I finished what I started, then kicked Valerie out."

Noah bursts out laughing. "Are you serious?"

"One hundred percent. She walked into my house unannounced, so whatever she sees is on her."

"I guess that's fair," Noah says with a chuckle. "I mean, your marriage with Valerie barely counted as real. She had one foot out the door the whole time, so it's not like you owe her anything."

I shake my head. "It's crazy how this woman I'm supposed to be in a fake marriage with is more present in marriage than my 'real' ex-wife ever was." Reese and Noah exchange looks, then laugh. "What the hell are you two laughing about?"

"You aren't in a fake marriage, bro," Reese answers. "Not anymore."

"What do you mean? Yes, I am. Becca's still going to divorce me at some point, whenever she gets her permanent residency."

"You sure about that?" Noah asks with his brows raised. "She seems a lot more invested in you than that. And vice versa."

"Yeah, face it, man. You're head over heels for Becca. The way you've been playing lately proves that," Reese adds, and although I want to push back, I can't. Noah smiles and nods knowingly.

"I see the gears turning. So I'll ask you again: you sure this is fake? Or are you falling for your wife of convenience?"

I don't have an answer. I can't deny that I have feelings for Becca, not least of all because every guy in the room would know I was a damn liar if I tried. But isn't that normal? If you spend enough time with someone and get to know them well enough, of course you'll develop some sort of feelings for them.

But I'd be even more of a liar if I said that the idea of Becca eventually leaving wouldn't tear me apart. And that tells me everything I need to know. I can't imagine life without her anymore, and I'm not sure I want to. So what does that mean for the future? I don't know, but hopefully I won't have to face that for at least another year or two.

"Fuck," Sawyer cusses from the bench where he's sitting, grabbing all our attention. He stares at his phone in his hand for a second before he slams it on the bench.

"What's wrong?" Reese asks.

"Just had yet another babysitter cancel on me at the last second for this weekend. The day after a game."

"Oof, that's rough, bro. I'm sorry," Reese says, although he turns to grin at me. "But maybe Theo and Becca could watch Jake for you?"

If Reese were any closer, I'd punch him. What in the world makes him think I'm qualified to babysit? But Sawyer looks up at me with hope in his eyes, and I know I'm cooked.

"Really? Would you really do that for me?" he asks, and I hear the desperation in his voice. I don't know what he's got going on over the weekend, but it must be something important, otherwise he wouldn't be so pissed about the babysitter canceling. I sigh and pull out my phone.

"I've gotta check my calendar and ask Becca if she's okay with it, but assuming she is, yeah, we've got you," I say, and Sawyer's face lights up.

"Now that's what I call teamwork," Noah says approvingly, nodding at me as I fire off a text to Becca.

ME: Hey, uh… do you have plans this weekend?

BECCA: That depends. The way you're asking makes me nervous.

I laugh because I don't blame her. I'd feel the same way if I got that kind of text.

ME: You aren't gonna believe this, but Sawyer's babysitter bailed on him at the last second so Reese volunteered me and you to watch Jake. I kind of already said yes, but if you don't want to do it, you don't have to.

The bubble indicating Becca's typing appears and vanishes several times as she works on a reply. But finally my phone buzzes with a text.

BECCA: And here I thought you were going to whisk me away to Ibiza or something.

ME: Isn't a weekend with a little boy basically the same thing?

BECCA: Close enough.

ME: So… is that a yes?

BECCA: It is.

ME: Thanks, I appreciate it. And I'll make it up to you.

BECCA: With interest.

I laugh and drop my phone in my pocket. "Alright, we're good for this weekend," I tell Sawyer, who drops his head in relief.

"Thank you. You're a lifesaver, for real."

"We'll see if you still feel that way after this weekend," I say, and the whole locker room laughs.

~

Sawyer greets us at the door to his house Friday night. He's dressed well in a button-up shirt and jeans, and I raise an eyebrow at him.

"Hot date, huh?" I ask.

He chuckles, shaking his head. "Yeah, right. I'm just meeting up with a couple of old college buddies. I haven't gotten out of the house in a while except for games and practices, and Noah's been ragging on me about it. Says I need to have a life outside of fatherhood and hockey."

"Right."

I grimace, regretting my comment about the date. It's pretty much common knowledge among the team that Sawyer has pretty much been off the market since his divorce from his ex-wife Miriam—not because he's still hung up on her or anything, but just because the split sort of destroyed his belief in long-term relationships.

I can relate to that. Or at least, I used to be able to. These days... everything feels different.

"Thank you again for doing this," Sawyer tells us, ushering us inside. "I really appreciate it."

"It's no problem." Becca smiles at him. "Really."

He leads us into the living room, where Jake is sitting on the couch in pajamas watching cartoons. I don't get to see the kid very often, so it always blows my mind how much he looks like his dad, even at the young age of six. He spins around on the couch to look at us, fixing us with the same gray eyes that Sawyer has.

"Hi," he greets us tentatively and waves a little hand. His dark hair is tousled, making it look like he just crawled out of bed, but more likely he just had a bath.

"Hi, Jake, it's nice to meet you." Becca walks over to the couch and offers him a hand to shake as she introduces herself.

"Hi, Becca. You're really pretty," he says, shaking her hand tentatively.

Sawyer laughs. "Watch it, buddy, or you'll have Uncle Theo to compete with."

"And we all know how seriously I take competition," I say and wink at Jake playfully, but he doesn't seem to get that it's a joke. His brows furrow in confusion, and I sigh. It's a good thing Becca is here, because she already seems like a natural with kids. I don't have the first clue how to handle them.

She sits down on the couch beside him. "What are you watching? It looks really cute."

"Bluey," Jake answers. "It's about a dog and her family."

"Oh, I think I've seen this before."

Jake lights up, turning to face her. "Really? Who's your favorite character?"

She pauses to think for a second. "Hm, I'm not sure of her name, but I really like Bluey's little sister."

"You mean Bingo?"

"Bingo," Becca answers as a joke, and Jake giggles. Okay, so at least he gets *her* humor. And at least he seems to like Becca. This would be a very long night if he didn't warm up to either of us.

"Seems like we're off to a good start," Sawyer says quietly to me, then checks his phone for the time. "Shit, I really need to get going before I'm late. Thanks again. There are some leftovers from last night in the fridge you can heat up for dinner, and feel free to help yourselves to them too, but don't let Jake eat any of those microwave meals no matter how much he begs. He loves them, but I'm trying to limit them."

"Got it. Anything else we should know?"

"I'll be back no later than ten. His bedtime is nine, even on a Friday, so don't let him fool you. Because he'll try."

I chuckle. "So typical kid stuff. No problem. Have a good time with your friends tonight. You deserve it."

"I'll try my best." He nods, then steps over to the couch to say goodbye to Jake. "Alright, buddy. I'm leaving for a little bit. You be good for Uncle Theo and Aunt Becca, okay? I won't be home until after you go to sleep, but I'll see you in the morning."

"Okay," Jake says. "Love you, Daddy."

"You too, bud."

Sawyer kisses him on the top of the head and musses his hair before he leaves. When the door closes behind him, I don't know what to do with myself, but Becca swoops into action.

"Have you eaten dinner yet, Jake?" she asks, and he shakes his head. "Are you hungry?"

"He's a growing boy, so he's always hungry. Right, Jake?" I chime in.

This time he laughs at my joke, grinning and nodding.

While Becca's on entertainment duty, I go to the kitchen and open the fridge to look for the leftovers Sawyer mentioned. Several sealed containers sit inside but it's hard to see what's inside them, so I grab a few and spread them out on the counter to investigate. It's just like Sawyer, all serious and dad-like, to leave steamed vegetables and perfectly portioned cuts of meat for his kid. What kind of uncle would I be if I gave the poor kid this?

I open the freezer to check the microwave meals and see a few of them in there that look infinitely more appealing, even if they are carb-conscious versions.

"What Dad doesn't know won't hurt him, right?" I mutter and pull out one of the loaded macaroni and cheese dishes, then unbox it and peel off the plastic film before throwing it in the microwave. Sawyer won't be happy, but if he asks, I'll tell him I ate it.

The microwave dings a few minutes later, and I pull out the steaming dish. Its smell fills the room, and Jake must notice because he calls from the other room.

"Are you making mac and cheese?"

"Uh, kind of!" I call back as I try to avoid burning myself transferring the contents from the plastic dish to a plate.

A series of little footsteps pounds against the floor, and he appears in the kitchen entrance. "That's my favorite! How did you know?"

"Uncle's intuition," I answer and carry the plate to the small wooden table up against the window. There are only two seats, which I guess makes sense because there's only Sawyer and Jake, but the sight makes my heart twinge. Jake yanks out one of the chairs and climbs into it while I search for a fork, and when I come back with one, he's sitting on his knees and practically drooling.

"Daddy never lets me have these."

I hand the fork out to him, but when he tries to take it, I don't let go. "This will be our little secret then, okay? If he asks, tell him I ate it."

Jake giggles and nods. "Okay. Thanks, Uncle Theo."

I let him take the fork, and he digs right in. Becca leans against the doorway to the kitchen and fixes me with a look that's somewhere between amused and disapproving. I grab the cardboard box for the macaroni off the counter and fold it up, then tuck it in my back pocket.

"We'll burn the evidence. Sawyer will never know."

Becca laughs and shakes her head before joining Jake at the dinner table, so I go back to the leftovers to make something for us to eat.

"Are you guys married?" Jake asks with his mouthful of macaroni, and I freeze, but Becca handles it gracefully.

"Yes, we are."

"Why?"

Becca chuckles, and I glance over at her face to see she's flustered. She gathers herself and smiles at him. "Well, because that's what adults do when they love each other."

"How did you know you liked her, Uncle Theo?" he asks, putting me in the hot seat.

I stop scooping veggies on a plate to turn and face him. "I mean, look at her, buddy. What's not to like?"

Jake giggles again. "You're very pretty, Aunt Becca," he says, and she beams at him.

"Thank you, Jake. You're very sweet to say so."

"You're welcome. I hope Daddy finds a girl as pretty as you so he can marry her."

"I'm sure he will someday. Your dad is quite handsome himself. It must be where you get it from," Becca tells Jake, and he blushes before taking another huge bite of macaroni.

"But really, Uncle Theo, how did you know?" Jake asks again when he's finished chewing.

"I'm not really sure, buddy. But Becca was beautiful and sweet and everything I'd been hoping to find, and I felt like I wanted her in my life forever. That's how I knew," I answer truthfully.

Now it's Becca's turn to blush. Her eyes linger on mine, and I'd give anything to know exactly what she's thinking right now.

I don't mind Jake asking these questions—I'm sure he's just curious because he's figured out his dad went out on a date tonight—but I do feel like we're dancing on a knife's edge with the truth here. I can't tell the kid my marriage to Becca is fake, and I wouldn't even if he asked. But I can't help thinking about the shit Reese and Noah were giving me earlier, either.

Because as I stand here babysitting with Becca, our "fake"

marriage feels more real than ever. And I wonder if she feels it too.

"Did you have to wait a long time to find her?" Jake asks, piercing the moment as he looks back and forth between us.

"A few years, yeah. But it was worth the wait."

Jake sighs and drops his fork on the plate. "I hope Daddy won't have to wait that long. I think he's been sad since Mommy left."

Becca reaches across the table to rest her hand on Jake's. She smiles at him. "It's okay to be sad when something like that happens. It's a big change."

Jake scrunches up his face. "Yeah, I guess so. We don't see her very much anymore."

That twists my heart. When Sawyer got divorced, his ex-wife didn't even want custody of Jake, and although I know my teammate tried to shield his son from the truth of how disinterested his mother is in parenting, there's only so much he can do.

Becca shoots a glance my way before squeezing Jake's little hand. She knows a bit about Sawyer's situation from conversations we've had, and sympathy flashes in her eyes as she looks back at Jake.

"Well, one thing I know for sure is that your dad loves you very much," she promises. "You're all he thinks and talks about, even more than hockey. Right, Theo?"

"Oh, one hundred percent. He's your number one fan, kiddo."

That brings a smile back to Jake's face, and he picks up his fork to shovel in another mouthful of macaroni. But before he's finished chewing, he's asking more questions.

"Do you think you and Uncle Theo will ever get a divorce?" he asks Becca, and I watch her face as she works through her answer mentally.

"I honestly don't know. No one really does. But I hope with

all my heart it never happens," she finally says, and I nod my approval.

"Me neither," Jake says as he continues chewing. "I like you two."

"Aw." Becca smiles broadly, her eyes warming. "We like you too."

I finish heating up the veggies and chicken for Becca and me, then bring a plate to her. Jake really must've been hungry, because he finishes his macaroni long before we finish ours.

"Can I go watch TV?" he asks when he's done, even though he's already shoving back from the table.

"That's fine. We'll be there in a minute. Maybe we can find a movie to watch together or something," Becca says.

"Okay! I'll pick something out," Jake says and runs back into the living room. While Becca and I are alone, we stare at each other with unspoken feelings and thoughts coursing between us. There's so much I want to say, but I can't find the words, and now isn't the right time anyway.

Leave it to an innocent little kid's questions to stir all of this up.

I join Becca at the table to finish eating in silence, then clean up the dishes while she joins Jake on the couch. I hear them talking about different movies, and when I come back to the living room, I find Becca with one arm around Jake and his head resting against her. For a second, it almost feels real. Like this is our family, our son.

I shouldn't be thinking like this.

I shake my head and sit down on Becca's other side. "What did we settle on?" I ask since the opening credits are already rolling.

"The Mario movie!" Jake answers enthusiastically. "It's my favorite."

"Does that mean you've already seen it?"

"He told me he has it memorized, so we'll see how much he

remembers," Becca says with a smile as I snuggle up against her. We settle into the movie, which is cute and pretty funny, and it turns out Jake does in fact have the majority of it memorized.

About halfway through the movie though, Becca's phone vibrates in her pocket. It's resting against my leg, so I feel it too. She pulls it out to check it, and a few seconds later, she grimaces.

"What's up?" I whisper, not that Jake would notice as he's reciting the movie line by line. Rather than answer, Becca turns the screen to me, and as soon as I see Kaplan's name on it, my mood sours.

SHAWN: I want to talk to you. I owe you an apology.

I grab the phone from her and immediately start typing out a reply.

BECCA: It's Camden. That's the least of what you owe Becca, but she doesn't need shit from you —not even an apology. She has everything she needs with me.

I send the text and tap into his contact info to block his number, then pass the phone back to Becca. She looks unsettled by the whole interaction, so I put my arm around her shoulder and pull her into me. My body immediately responds to her proximity, but I know that's not the real reason my heart is hammering.

It's just... her.

Noah and Reese were right. Nothing about this is fake.

Chapter 37

Becca

I toss down the pen I've been gripping like my life depends on it and sigh.

How am I ever going to do this?

The more I think about and list out all the little logistical details that would go into opening a dance school of my own, the more my head hurts. It's not something I would've ever pursued before, but after Curtain Call canceled my contract, Theo really put a bug in my ear about it. I want to believe it's possible, but it feels so far out of reach.

How am I going to get funding? And how am I going to find and lease a place big enough? And then what about recruiting students? With my recently tarnished reputation, no thanks to Shawn, it's not like parents are going to be lining up to leave their kids alone with me. That's what got my contract canceled, after all, and people aren't going to just forget about it.

My stomach rumbles, distracting me. Good thing Theo's at practice so he can't hear it. Still, I don't want him worrying about me not eating again and I don't want to take another trip to the emergency room, so I decide to take a break from my planning to make something to eat.

There are plenty of leftovers from all the stuff that Theo's been cooking lately. For every less than stellar dish, there are at least three amazing ones now. He's getting really good at cooking—no doubt thanks to all the cookbooks he's been buying.

One of them is still lying open on the counter by the fridge, and when I peek at it, I see that he's got notes written all over in the margins in his distinct, almost boyish chicken scratch. Some are corrections to ingredient amounts, while others are little reminders to himself of what not to do. For this baked lemon chicken recipe, he scribbled, *Forty minutes at four hundred degrees is way too long. Burnt to a crisp.*

I chuckle and open the fridge. Each of the little plastic containers has a note of some kind attached to the top in the same handwriting. At first, I assume they're labels of what's inside, but when I get closer, I see that they're short notes to me. I reach for the nearest one, a fettucine alfredo that Theo made a few nights ago, and read the note on top.

I know you said you always wanted to go to Italy, so here's my attempt to bring a little bit of Italy to you. I'll take you there someday, and you can find out what REAL Italian food should taste like. I promise.

A laugh softly to myself, a smile breaking out across my face.

I love that he pays attention to little details about me like that—and that he thought to leave a note about it. It amazes me that someone can be this attentive, that he cares about me enough to do something like this. He really does make me feel like the princess he insists I am.

I take the container out and empty the contents on a plate to reheat it in the microwave. We have way more food in the house now than either of us will ever be able to eat, but it's so nice not having to worry about cooking anything. I've always hated cooking, mostly because of the time it takes and the cleanup afterward. But Theo, the budding home chef, takes care of it all—just like he promised me he would.

I'm just pulling the alfredo out of the microwave when Milo appears in the kitchen. I don't know where he's been, but his eyes are still heavy and crusted with sleep, so I bet he's been upstairs in bed. The smell of the food must have woken him up because he's staring up at me and whimpering.

"No, boy, this isn't for doggies," I say as I maneuver around him, but he whimpers again. "Okay, okay, how about a treat?" Milo barks his approval, so I set my plate down on the kitchen island and grab a dog biscuit from a box we keep on the counter by the stove. Milo runs in circles excitedly, but I don't give him the bone right away.

"Alright, boy, can you sit for me?" I ask, hiding the biscuit behind my back. "Sit?" I tap his behind with my free hand to try to encourage him, but he just keeps staring up at me with his adorable puppy dog face tilted to one side. "If you can't sit, you can't have a treat."

Milo's nose leads him to my rear, and I try to spin to keep the biscuit hidden, but he moves with me. Clearly, this isn't going to work, and my food is getting cold, so I eventually give in and drop the biscuit into his waiting jaws. He devours it in a few chews, and I sigh.

"If I can't even teach a dog a new trick, how am I ever going to teach kids?"

My only answer is a knock on the door, which startles me. We never have visitors, and immediately my mind jumps to the worst possible conclusion: it's Valerie again. I'm tempted to ignore it, but whoever's outside must have heard Milo barking and know someone's home because they knock on the door again, harder this time. I step quietly to the door to look through the peephole and my stomach drops.

Because Shawn is waiting on the other side.

Other than Valerie, he's the last person I want to see. I

haven't talked to him since Theo blocked his number on my phone, so I'm sure that's why he's here. But what in the world could be so urgent to make him fly all the way to Denver from Los Angeles? And why did he have to show up when Theo isn't home?

I just want him to go away. I want to pretend he doesn't exist and never did. But he raps on the door again.

"Come on, Becca, I know you're there. I heard you," he says impatiently, and my heart lodges in my chest. I can't avoid him, as much as I'd love to, so I steel myself and unlock the door, but I only crack it.

"What are you doing here, Shawn?"

"I told you, I want to talk. To apologize."

"You could've called, sent a letter, anything. When Theo finds out you showed up here unannounced, he's going to—"

"What, kill me?" Shawn interrupts with a scoff. "Please. Besides, I tried to call, but you blocked my number, remember?"

"I don't know what you want, but whatever you have to say, I don't want to hear it," I say and move to close the door, but he wedges his shoe into the crack. The one eye of his I can see locks onto mine.

"Come on, Becca. I came all this way. At least hear me out. Please?"

He's the last person on Earth who deserves my sympathy or my time, especially after the way he treated me with that disgusting episode of his show, but he's clearly not taking no for an answer. He pushes his shoulder into the crack, forcing the door open farther. Milo growls at him, but I pat his head.

"It's okay, boy." Shawn glances down at Milo but doesn't seem deterred. He pushes the rest of the way into the condo, and he looks disheveled and a little wild-eyed, so I step back. "What do you want?"

Shawn sighs and drops his hands to his sides. "I... I want you back."

373

It takes everything I have not to burst out laughing, but I do let out a snort. Destroying someone's reputation on national television isn't exactly how I'd go about winning them back. But there's an edge to Shawn as he paces back and forth in front of the door that makes me wary.

He stops his pacing abruptly to look me right in the eyes. "I'm serious," he insists. "Seeing you with Theo made me realize how much I miss you."

"That's not true, and you know it isn't. You just want what you can't have, what Theo has. This is just another part of your weird fucking rivalry with him."

Shawn shoots me a mocking look. "Seriously? Why do you think he married you then? Because he *loves* you?" His words cut right through me, even though I know I shouldn't believe any of them. He jabs a finger at me. "See? You already know it. It's because he wanted to fuck with me. He's using you, Becca. Can't you see that?"

"You're delusional, Shawn."

He shakes his head frantically. "No, it's you who isn't seeing things clearly. You know damn well you'll be better off with me. Camden's career is tanking, but I'm going places. Big places."

He locks his already-wide eyes on mine, and they continue to expand. He looks as crazed as he sounds, and my heart starts to pound in my chest. I don't know what he's up to, but I shouldn't have let him in—because I don't know what he's going to do. He steps closer to me, and I match it with a step away as every hair on the back of my neck stands up.

"I'm going to fucking take over the NHL," he insists, nodding as he talks like he's trying to convince himself too. "They won't fucking know what hit them."

His pupils are dilated, and he's so close now that I can feel the wild, electric energy pouring off him in waves. My stomach dips as I piece together what he's talking about. He looks bulkier than he did when we were together, and with the erratic way he's acting...

"Oh my god, Shawn," I whisper. "Are you on steroids?"

He chuckles, his lips curving up in a smirk. "Everyone said I shouldn't fuck with the stuff, but they're idiots. Ever since I started, I've been killing the game. And I look good, right?"

I'm not trying to feed into whatever warped game he's playing, so I don't answer. I just keep trying to back away, but eventually I collide with the kitchen island. I can't get any farther away from him as he takes another step toward me.

"You should get back together with me while you still have the chance," he says, dropping his voice a little as if trying to sound persuasive. "Before my star gets even bigger. Because I'm fucking going places, Becca. To the very top. Don't you want to be there with me?"

"No," I say as firmly. "I don't."

I try to step around the corner of the island, but Shawn lunges and boxes me up against it. The countertop digs into my lower back as he presses me into it with his hulking body and grabs both my wrists, pinning my hands on the counter. Milo growls at him, clearly picking up on the tension in the air.

Shawn moves his face closer to mine, so close that our foreheads are almost touching.

"We both know that's a lie, baby girl. I know how to read you. I know what you really want to say. So just say it."

He moves in to try to kiss me, but I turn my head away and slam my shoulder into his chest, trying to break free of his grip.

Milo erupts in loud barking as Shawn grabs me roughly by the upper arms and shoves me against the island. Fear spikes in my chest, but I try to shove it down. I can't let it win. I can't let him see how scared I am.

"Get your fucking hands off me and get out," I snap.

He stares at me contemptuously. "What are you gonna do, call the cops? I thought you loved me."

"You're sick, Shawn. Get. Out."

He opens his mouth to say something, but he never gets it out. He whirls away from me, and I close my eyes and scream because I think he's going to hit me, but when I re-open them, I find Theo dragging him away by the back of his shirt.

Chapter 38

Theo

All I see is red—bright, burning red—as I haul Kaplan away from Becca and slam his back against the wall. I crash my fist into his face, connecting with his jaw and making his head snap to one side. But Kaplan's not going down without a fight, so when he swings back at me, Becca lets out a little shout of shock, but it barely registers as I jump out of his way.

Kaplan roars and charges at me like some kind of 'roided-out bull, but I sidestep and kick his feet out from underneath him. He might be stronger than me thanks to the juice, but he's a terrible fighter, and I'm fucking pissed.

He spins at the last second but still goes down hard on his back, and I'm on him again, straddling him so he can't get away. He glares up at me with raw fury in his eyes when I lift him by the shirt, but my fist rains down on his face again with a sickening crunch and he goes slack. I've been wanting to beat him into a pulp for years, and I've never had a better excuse to do it than now, so I slam my fist into his jaw again. And again. And again.

All I hear is the crunch of his bones, my grunting with each punch, and Milo's distant, shrill barks in the background until Becca shouts.

"Theo, stop!"

I freeze with my fist drawn back, ready to continue making meatloaf of Kaplan's face, but the look of fear in her eyes snaps me out of my rage. I throw Kaplan down, and he groans with his bloody face in his hands while he writhes in pain. He's lucky Becca was here to stop me, otherwise I probably would've killed him, my career be damned.

Becca's crying with her hands over her mouth, so I stand and approach her and she lets me pull her into my arms. As soon as her chest meets mine, she dissolves into tears, and a fresh kettle of rage boils in my stomach. I knew Kaplan was a shitbag, but I never thought he'd dare put his hands on Becca. So when I spot bruises on both her upper arms, I lose myself and charge back over to him.

I lift him by his torn, bloody shirt so his lolling, unfocused eyes face mine. I slap him once to bring his attention to me.

"Look at her," I command, pointing at Becca. "Look at what you've done. If you ever go near her again, I'll fucking kill you. Do you understand me?"

I give him a chance to nod or gurgle an answer, but he says nothing, so I slap him again. "You will not speak to her. You will not look at her. And you will not go anywhere near her ever again. *Ever.* Do I make myself clear?"

This time, he nods, so I sling him back to the ground and go back to Becca. It takes a few minutes, but eventually Kaplan gathers himself enough to crawl off the floor and stumble out of the condo, leaving a trail of blood on the floor.

As soon as he's gone, I slam the door shut and lock it, then pull Becca close to check her for other injuries. With Kaplan out of the picture, my heart hammers against my ribcage and I feel sick with worry. If anything happened to her, I'll never forgive myself. And I'll never let Kaplan escape my wrath. I'll fucking ruin him.

"Are you okay? Are you hurt?" I ask, but she just shakes her head and presses her face into my chest. I stroke her hair, careful not to get blood on her. "What happened? Tell me everything."

Whining, Milo cautiously approaches us and sniffs Becca's dangling hand before he licks it gently. I'm so glad he was here to protect her in case I hadn't gotten home in time to do it myself, so I pat his head and he whines again.

"I—I was making something to eat and giving Milo a treat when someone knocked on the door," Becca starts. "At first I thought maybe it was Valerie coming back or something, but it was Shawn. He wouldn't go away. I just thought he wanted to talk, to say whatever bullshit he needed to say, and... I'm so sorry, Theo."

Her voice break as she lets out a soft sob, and my chest squeezes.

"It's not your fault, princess. None of this is your fault," I assure her as I squeeze her and rub her back. "How did he get in?"

"He forced his way in. I cracked the door at first, and he just shoved through."

My entire body tenses with anger at her words, but I have to keep myself under control for her sake. The only thing that matters right now is comforting her.

"What the hell did he want?" I ask, although I'm not at all sure I want to know or am ready to hear the answer.

Becca scoffs and looks up at me. "You'll never believe this, but he was seriously trying to get me back."

It takes everything I have not to burst out laughing. "How fucking delusional is this guy? He just put you on blast on national TV, and now he thinks you're going to get back with him?"

"It gets worse. He told me he's juicing, that he's playing better than ever and that he's going to take over the NHL."

This time I do burst out laughing. "So he's not just delusional, he's actually fucking insane."

"Yeah..." Becca trails and looks down. But I tilt her head back up to me.

"What is it? What else did he do?" Becca looks away and tears start welling in her eyes again. "Tell me, Becca. Whatever it is. Just tell me."

She swallows hard but doesn't speak for another few moments. "He said you were using me to fuck with him. That you married me just for that."

"He's pathetic," I snap immediately. "And you know that's bullshit. Just like everything else that comes out of his mouth. You know exactly why I married you, and it has nothing to do with his worthless ass."

"I know." Becca swallows, nodding. "Believe me, I know. But the way he said it, he sounded so sure of himself."

"Of course he did. He's unhinged. Look at the way he put his hands on you," I say as I gently run my fingers over the bruises on her upper arms. "That's not love, that's fucked up."

"He tried to kiss me too. Right before you got home."

The thought of that roach trying to put his lips anywhere near her makes my skin crawl and my rage swell all over again. He has no idea how lucky he is that he didn't.

Becca steps back from me to look me in the eyes. "This is so fucking crazy. What are we going to do?" she asks, and determination builds in my chest because I already know the answer.

"We're going to take Kaplan down. For good," I say and pull out my phone to call the police.

Chapter 39

Becca

Theo invites his lawyer, Eric Botti, over the next day. We sit on the couch together while he tells Eric his version of what happened with Shawn, but Theo can't seem to keep his hands off me. If he's not holding my hand, he's rubbing my leg, or wrapping his arm around me and pulling me into him.

After we finished giving our statements to the police so they could file a report, Theo held me all night, wrapped his body around me like a human shield. Like he refused to let anyone but him get near me ever again. And he promised that he'd never let anything hurt me.

After what happened with Shawn, I didn't think I'd sleep at all, but when Theo told me that, it was like a switch flipped and all the exhaustion I'd been holding back finally overtook me. I slept for ten hours straight, until right before Eric got here. Theo woke me up to tell me that the lawyer was coming, and that I didn't have to talk with him if I didn't want to, but I needed the reassurance that all of this shit with Shawn would finally be over.

"Walk me through what you experienced last night, Ms. Summers. And please be as detailed as possible," Eric says calmly as he looks me in the eyes. He's wearing a serious but concerned expression, and the crow's feet behind his thick glasses crinkle when he offers me a solemn smile. But something about his detached demeanor and crisp navy suit puts me at ease. If Theo trusts him to handle this, so do I.

Theo keeps his fingers linked with mine, like he's trying to encourage me. To give me strength. I sigh. "Well, Shawn has always been pushy and loud, even aggressive, but last night was something else entirely."

"What do you mean? How so?"

"He was erratic. Unhinged. Like he was on drugs or something."

"Theo mentioned that he said something about steroid use. Do you think that's what it was?"

I nod. "Probably."

"Then his unpredictability makes sense if that's true. Though there's no telling if anything else was in his system at the same time," Eric says as he scratches a note on the yellow pad of legal paper resting on his knee. "What did he say he wanted?"

"He wanted to get back with me. We used to date before Theo and I were married. I don't know if you knew that yet," I say, and Eric nods. "He'd sent me a text a few nights ago about how he was sorry for the reality show stunt and wanted to talk."

Eric raises an eyebrow at me. "And did you respond?"

"I did for her," Theo answers.

"What did you say?"

"I told him it was me and that he needed to get lost before we had a problem. Then I blocked his number and I thought that was the last of it."

"Until he showed up at your doorstep while you were away," Eric says, filling in the blanks. "That is definitely erratic behavior. Do you think he knew you were home alone, Ms. Summers?"

I nod. "Yeah, probably. He's in the NHL too, so I bet he figured out Theo would be at practice somehow."

"Did he knock? Or did he force his way into the property?"

"Both," I answer, and Theo squeezes my hand. I hear his breathing get heavy.

"It might be easier if we just showed you," Theo says as he pulls his phone from his pocket. "The whole condo is on camera, mostly for the times when I'm away for games in case of a break-in or something." Even I didn't know that until now, but it makes sense, and I'm grateful to have the footage.

Theo taps around on his phone a few times, then rests it on the coffee table between us and Eric. He pulls it closer to himself and taps the play button on the screen. I don't need or want to watch it again, to relive it, so I look away. Thankfully, Eric keeps the volume low enough that I can't make out what's being said in the recording, although I do hear muffled voices.

I stare at Theo instead, watching his jaw clench and unclench while he keeps his eyes on Eric's face. As upsetting as the footage is for me, it must be just as bad for him. To know that something much worse could've happened if he hadn't come home when he did must be eating at him.

A clattering in the recording grabs my attention, and I see Theo dragging Shawn away from me on the screen as Eric taps to pause it and scribble some more notes. If I had to see any part of the video, I'm glad it was this one because watching Theo charge into the condo like a battering ram makes emotion rise in my chest.

If he hadn't stopped himself, he probably would've beaten Shawn to a bloody pulp. Well, he *still* turned Shawn into a bloody mess, but it would've been much worse. The last thing I want is for Theo to get into any trouble over this, or to face any repercussions with the NHL.

Eric looks up at us with his brows raised. "Well, since it's clear from the footage that Mr. Kaplan forced his way into your home, threatened you, and physically assaulted you, Ms. Summers, that's more than enough evidence to secure a restraining order at the very least. I'll get that drawn up and served to Mr. Kaplan immediately."

Theo nods, his jaw clenched. "Is that it?"

"No. The tape also clearly has Mr. Kaplan admitting to doping. I'm sure the NHL would be very interested to know that about one of its star players. I'll handle that as well, but I'll need you to send me a copy of this recording so I can forward it to the proper parties."

"Of course." Theo takes his phone back to work on it right away.

"What's going to happen to Shawn?" I ask Eric, who shrugs.

"Well, at the very least, he'll probably face a suspension for doping, although it's more likely that a permanent expulsion will come. The NHL has zero tolerance for this kind of thing, and the evidence is coming right from the horse's mouth, so to speak."

"Will he go to jail?"

"Possibly. But I can't say for sure. The courts will have to decide that, assuming you press charges. And I recommend that you do. You did file a police report, I hope?"

"Yes, immediately after," Theo answers for me, and Eric nods.

"Good. That will help you. Make sure to provide the police a copy of this recording too if you haven't already."

"I did."

I glance at Theo, then back to Eric. "And what about Theo? Will he face any punishment for this?"

Eric's expression goes blank. "That I can't answer definitively since it's ultimately up to the NHL to handle the enforcement of their policies. But given that Theo was protecting you from a violent intruder in your home, Theo hasn't committed any crimes, so I would guess the NHL wouldn't have any grounds to discipline him."

I breathe a sigh of relief because that's exactly what I needed to hear, and Eric starts packing up his things, signaling he has all he needs from us. Theo turns to me, smiling encouragingly, and although I still feel a little shaky, I'm better now that the adrenaline has passed and I know that something's going to be done about all of this.

Theo stands with Eric, and they shake hands.

"I'll be in touch with any updates or if I need anything else from you," Eric says.

"Thank you. I appreciate it, man."

Eric nods and sees himself out of the condo, and Theo takes me by the hand to pull me up off the couch.

"What are you doing?" I ask, although I'm too exhausted to refuse.

"You look like you could use some rest and relaxation. Come on, I have an idea," he says and leads me upstairs to his bedroom, where he has me sit down on the foot of the bed where Milo's sleeping. He must be wiped out too because he doesn't stir at all.

"Wait here."

He steps into the bathroom. A few seconds later, I hear the water rushing in the bathtub, and I smile because I know what he's doing. I strip off all my clothes and throw them on the floor by the bed, and when Theo returns, he freezes to stare at me.

He looks like he wants to say something, but he just smiles at me and beckons me to the bathroom, so I pad over and take his hand. He walks me to the lip of the massive tub, and I notice that the jets built into it are going, making the surface of the water roil. He helps me stay steady as I kick one leg over the lip and step into the water.

It's warmer than a normal bath, but it feels incredible. And when I sink up to my shoulders, I can't stop the sigh of relief that leaks out of me. The jets pound against my back, and I close my eyes and lean into them, losing myself. When they flutter back open, I see Theo standing naked by the tub, still smiling. He climbs in with me and sits, then pulls my back against his chest.

"I'm so sorry for all of this," he murmurs into my ear as he massages my shoulders.

"It's not your fault. You had practice. You couldn't have any idea Shawn would show up all strung out and crazy like that."

"I know, but I should've been here. He never should've been able to get his hands on you. And he never will again."

I twist around to look him in the eye. "You came at just the right time. And you handled the fallout. That's all that matters to me. I don't know what I would've done if you hadn't come home."

Theo shakes his head. "I don't want to think about it. I was fucking *furious* when I saw Shawn touching you. Something in me just... snapped." He cradles my face in his hands and stares intensely into my eyes. His are like flaming emeralds. "I can't deny it anymore, Becca. I can't go another second without saying it. I love you."

My heart races, so many emotions flooding my chest that it's hard to breathe.

"I love you too," I whisper.

A smile splits his face, and he presses his mouth to mine like he's trying to seal those words. To taste them lingering on my lips.

"The first night we met, you swore you'd never fall in love again," he reminds me, drawing back just enough to meet my gaze.

"So did you," I breathe, my heart racing.

He trails his fingertips lightly down the side of my face, his eyes crinkling a little at the corners.

"And I meant it," he says, his voice quiet. "I didn't fall in love again. With you, I fell in love for the first time. Because I didn't have a fucking clue what real love was until I met you."

Happy tears burn my eyes, and he brushes them away with his thumbs, his touch more tender than I've ever felt it. Then he tilts my chin up, pressing his lips to mine.

I kiss him, desperate and raw and real, letting it say all the things words are too small to express.

Chapter 40

Theo

I'm still gearing up for the game when Sawyer comes striding up to me, something glinting in his eyes.

"Did you hear the news?" he asks.

I shove my foot into my skate and shake my head. "No? What news?"

"Shawn's been banned from the NHL." He flashes a satisfied smile, holding out his phone so I can read the headline of the article he has pulled up. "The Prowlers dropped him too. And there are rumors that he's gonna lose his reality show because he's not a top NHL player anymore, he's just some low-life asshole with a history of abuse."

I grin savagely because I can't summon even a little bit of sympathy for Shawn. That fucker brought all of this on himself, and he absolutely deserves every piece of shit that's getting slung at him. I make a mental note to send Eric a nice bonus and thank you.

While I'm sitting on the bench, my skates still unlaced, my phone vibrates in my open locker. I reach up for it and find a message from Becca, who's out in the stands. She traveled with me for this away game, and I'm glad she's here to bask in this with me.

BECCA: Good luck tonight! You're going to kill it.

I smile down at my phone because I'm sure I'm going to kill it too. How couldn't I after this amazing news?

ME: Thanks. Having you in the stands is all the luck I need.

I silence my phone and tuck it into my locker, then finish getting geared up and ready to hit the ice with the rest of the guys for warmups before the game starts. It never should have taken Shawn roughing Becca up to get his ass ousted, but I'm over the moon that it's finally happening—and that I'll never have to come face-to-face with his smug fucking smirk on the ice ever again.

A few minutes later, as I file out onto the ice with the guys at the Titans' arena in New Jersey, I spot Andrew in the stands. He waves at me, so I lift a gloved hand in response, but he looks anxious. He admitted to being scared to face the Aces this season during the fundraiser, and with the way we've all been on our game lately, he's right to be.

Our warmup passes quickly, and we form up for the face-off against the Titans. As we all stand crouched and ready to spring into action, anticipation and tension crackles between us. I don't know why, but I have the feeling that this is going to be one hell of a game and it hasn't even started yet.

My eyes find Noah's, and he nods at me like he's reading my mind. Meanwhile, the guys I make eye contact with on the Titans look worried, especially as they start to pick up on the energy that's growing on our team. The crowd falls eerily quiet while they wait to see what happens, but when the ref slings the puck down, they erupt as the players scatter.

I lose track of the puck for a second in the fray but find Noah peeling away from the pack with a small lead on the Titans' center. The others streak after him, and their left winger tries to intercept, but Noah dances around him and sinks a goal like it's nothing. There aren't many Aces fans in the stands—it's a long journey to New Jersey from Colorado—but the few who are there lose it.

I'm already feeling fired up, but Noah's goal and the fans cheering it only makes it stronger. So when we square up for the next puck drop, I'm determined to give them something else to cheer about. I blaze forward as the puck falls and poke it away from the Titans, then swerve through the reach of both their left and right wing to barrel down the ice toward their tense goalie.

Maybe it's because he's already off-kilter from the easy first goal that Noah took, or maybe it's because he knows my reputation, but either way, the poor guy looks like he's shaking in his gear as I close the gap between us and wind up to fire off a shot. I psyche him out by leaning right, then reverse at the last second into a shot on his left side. It soars over his shoulder and catches the net, and again our fans go hysterical.

I find Becca's beaming face in the crowd and point my stick at her. "This one's for you!" I bellow over the noise, and although I know she can't hear me, I'm sure she knows what I mean. Because every shot I score is for her. She's the one who reminded me of my love for this game, who brought me back into it.

Noah plows into me from behind, beating on my helmet with his glove. We aren't even five minutes into the game, but we're already up two to nothing. I steal a glance over at Andrew in the Titans' box and find him with his head in one hand, looking distressed. He has to know they aren't winning this game. There's no way in hell.

After Noah and I score another two goals back-to-back, the Titans might as well throw in the towel. The next time I skate past their box, Andrew looks deflated and defeated. I shrug sympathetically at him on my way past, and he at least manages a smirk.

"You're on fire tonight!" I hear him boom as I skate away. At this point, all we have to do is defend our lead, and that's exactly what we do. The game ends at four to nothing, and I find Becca losing her mind in the crowd with the other Aces fans. This only could've been better if it was the Prowlers we destroyed tonight, but a win is a win.

I shake hands with the Titans and leave the ice in a hurry to get to Becca. I don't care about anything other than being with her right now, so I strip out of my gear and take one of the fastest showers I've ever taken, then rush to the family lounge. Becca must have been waiting on pins and needles for me, because as soon as I walk into the room, she dashes over and throws herself into my arms.

"Oh my god, you were so amazing tonight!" she shouts, barely getting the words out before I pull her in for a kiss.

"This won't even be the most amazing part of the night," I whisper in her ear so no one else can hear. Her face immediately flushes, and I feel her shiver in my arms. The effect I still have on her makes me grin. I can't get enough of the way she responds to every word, every little touch.

"You two coming out with the rest of us?" Noah asks, pulling me away from the trance Becca always puts me in. He's arm-in-arm with Margo, and the rest of the team must have spilled in around me while I was talking to Becca because they're all standing and staring at me expectantly.

"With this kind of peer pressure, who could say no?" I ask, and Noah beams at me.

"That's what I was hoping you'd say."

"Is that okay with you?" I ask Becca quietly, and she nods enthusiastically.

"Of course. We have to celebrate a win like this!"

We pile outside and into Ubers to go to a local bar, Black

Cat, that's legendary. Becca and I end up in a car alone, which is fine with me because I can't keep my hands off her, can't get her close enough to me. Truthfully, I don't even want to go to the bar at all. I'd much rather take her back to our hotel room and show her exactly how amazing I'm planning the night to be, but I have to be a good sport for the rest of the team.

It feels amazing to be back on top of my game like this—and to have the others acknowledge it. I have no idea if the rumors about my contract with the Aces not getting renewed was ever true in the first place, but I can't imagine they're in any hurry to get rid of me now. I might be cocky, but even I'm not arrogant enough to say I'm the Aces star player. But without me, the team wouldn't be half as good as it is, and I think Dunaway and the rest of the management know that without a doubt now.

I turn to Becca in the backseat, my hand massaging her leg. "Thank you for coming with me."

"Are you kidding? I never would've forgiven myself if I'd missed a game like this," she says with a bright smile. "Poor Andrew though."

I laugh and nod. "Yeah, he's gonna have a hard time living that one down. But I mean, he knew what he was in for. He at least knew to be scared."

"I think everyone's going to be afraid of the Aces now, and rightfully so. You all played so well tonight. It was honestly amazing to watch, like you were part of a hive mind or something. You were just perfectly in sync."

"That's how it should be every game, and I think we're going to have a lot more of those going forward," I say, and I mean it. I still don't really know what was hanging over me and knocking me off my game before, but it doesn't matter because I don't plan on ever going back to that version of me.

And with Becca at my side, I'll never have to. I'll never run out of inspiration to play my best.

"Yeah?" Becca asks, still smiling.

"Absolutely," I say and lean over to kiss her cheek. My hand drifts a little farther up her thigh, just to tease her a bit, and she unconsciously spreads her legs. "I don't know about you, but I really don't want to stay very long at this bar."

"You're reading my mind," Becca says, then chews her lip. "A game like that deserves a reward."

"One drink then?"

"That's plenty," Becca says as we pull up to the curb outside the bar. I climb out of the car first and offer a hand to her to help her out, and even in the dim light from the bar's lighting, she looks incredible. I still can't quite believe I get to call her my wife, but there she is, beaming at me with her hand in mine.

We walk in together, hand in hand, and it looks like we're the first ones from the Aces there, but that gives me a chance to scope the place out. As famous as Black Cat is, there aren't many people here, but that's fine by me. If the Titans had turned out a win tonight, the place would probably be crawling with their fans, but given the way we blew them out of the water, there are only a few people in Titans jerseys sitting around.

I lead Becca to the bar, and we take stools next to each other. The bartender recognizes me right away, and although he looks a little downtrodden, he greets us. "Man, I hate to say it, but after a game like that, you and the pretty lady deserve a round. On the house."

"What? Are you sure? I really don't mind paying."

"No way, man. You paid your dues tonight. What'll it be?"

"Two house drafts, please," Becca answers, and I grin at her.

"Coming right up," the bartender says and steps over to fill the mugs for us. He returns a few seconds later with two frosty mugs that Becca and I clink together.

"Cheers to sweet victory," she says with a sweet smile and takes a sip, giving herself a foam mustache. I can't help myself, so I lean over to kiss it away from her. She presses into me, the tension surging between us, and I already want to carry her out of the bar and back to the hotel.

A commotion draws my attention, so I glance over my shoulder to find Noah and the rest of the guys spilling into the entrance of the bar, loud and rowdy as ever. It's probably a good thing there aren't many Titans fans around because I can already tell my guys are going to make a ruckus.

"There he is! The man of the night!" Noah shouts as he leads the rest of the team and their girls toward us. The whole gang is here, so I'm glad Becca will have someone to talk to about something that isn't hockey. Because I'm sure the guys are going to want to recount every play and goal until they're drunk and repeating themselves—not that they don't deserve to.

"I want some celebratory shots! First round is on me," Reese declares as he sidles up to the bar. To his credit, the bartender is a good sport and takes care of it for him by lining up a counter full of shots. Reese lifts one at me. "Camden, you in?"

"No thanks, I've already got my beer."

"Oh, come on! You carried the game for us!" Reese protests, but when I don't say anything, he just shrugs. "Fine, more for me." He knocks back the shot that should've been mine and slides the rest to everyone else.

"Do the honors, Noah," Sawyer says as he claps the captain on the back. Poor Noah's always getting put up to stuff like this, but part of me thinks he likes it in some weird way. He steps into the circle of us and clears his throat, holding his shot in his hand.

"What an amazing season this has been for the Aces," Noah starts, and Reese pounds his fist on the bar top, splashing the shots and our beers with his powerful hands. Becca laughs and takes a sip before he shakes the whole glass empty. I don't know if it's just because of the game we won, Shawn going down, or both, but the whole team is fired up. I'm right there with them.

"Seriously, it's been a real turnaround," Noah continues,

turning to look at me directly. He raises his shot glass to me. "And I have to give you the most credit for improvement, Theo. Not that any of us ever doubted you'd get your groove back."

"Thanks," I say and raise my glass to him.

"We should be thanking you for all the goals this season! I really don't think we'd be in the position we're in now without you. Hell, I know we wouldn't."

I glance over at Becca, who's beaming and nodding at me, and that makes all the difference. Having Noah sing my praises is great, and I know he means it, but none of this would've happened without Becca. I put my hand on her leg, and she rests her hand on top of mine to give it a squeeze.

It's such a simple gesture, something we've done thousands of times by this point, but it means more to me than I think I'll ever be able to tell her. *She* means more to me than I have the words for. And that's exactly why I'll have to prove it to her the only way I know how: with our bodies.

Like she can hear my thoughts, Becca's eyes meet mine and she blushes. I stroke the inside of her thigh with my thumb, and the fire spreading on her cheeks turns into a blaze. Her beer is already halfway gone, although I'm not sure if that's because she drank it or because Reese spilled most of it. Either way, we're that much closer to our one drink agreement.

And that much closer to going back to the hotel.

A younger version of me would've been game to stay out all night, later than all the rest of the guys, to celebrate this win until the sun came up. But tonight, one drink is more than enough. Because there's only one person I want to be with until the sun rises, and she's sitting right next to me.

I suck down most of my beer while Noah finishes his impromptu speech. He compliments everyone, not just me, and when he's finished, I join the whole team and extended team family in applauding. I'm just as proud of myself and the Aces as they are because Noah's right—this really has been an amazing turnaround, both for the team and for me personally.

I finish the last dregs of my beer and set the glass down on the counter, then lean into Becca.

"You ready to get out of here?" I whisper, delighting in the trail of goosebumps that ripple down her neck from my breath.

"Never been more ready in my life," she answers, so I flash a grin at Noah, who's watching us across the bar.

He raises a second shot glass at me, silently giving me his blessing, so I throw down some cash on the bar for the bartender's tip. Then Becca and I slip out of the place while everyone else is distracted.

Chapter 41

Theo

The city is hopping thanks to the game, so getting another Uber back to the hotel doesn't take long. And in the car, I still can't keep my hands off Becca. I wrap my arm around her and pull her into me, her head resting on my shoulder. I feel her heart beating against mine, and her hands find my cock through my jeans, giving it soft, teasing strokes.

I run my fingers down her exposed neck, making her shiver, and all I can think about are the many things I want to do to her when we're alone and undressed. It's a twenty-minute drive back to the hotel, but I'm so turned on that it feels much longer —and I'm so hard that it hurts. I'm literally aching for her.

Before the car even comes to a complete stop at the curb, I fling the door open. The driver flashes me an annoyed look in the rearview, but I'm way too into Becca to care, so I help her out of the car and walk her through the lobby. Her face is still bright with blush, but I can't tell if it's from arousal, the booze, or both.

The elevator ride is almost as agonizing as the Uber, and it doesn't help that it makes several stops on the way to let other people out. When we're finally alone in the enclosed space with only a couple more floors to go, I pin her against the wall and kiss her with the passion that's been mounting for what feels like hours. I taste her hunger on her tongue, and it only makes me crazier for her.

My hands are shoving her shirt up her stomach when the elevator dings our arrival, so she pulls away with a devious smile and drags me out into the hallway. "This feels like déjà vu," she says. "Let's see if you can get the door open without kicking it in this time."

I laugh as I dig in my pocket for the room key because I know exactly what she's talking about. "Hey, it's not my fault. You make me lose my mind." She sidles up next to me as I'm inserting the card in the slot built into the door.

"I want you to make me lose mine," she whispers, and desire floods me.

"Fuck," I groan as the door clicks open, and I pull her inside to kick it shut behind us. Before it closes, I hold her gently by the face to kiss her again, as deeply and intensely as I can. She moans into my mouth as her hands wander across my body and we stumble toward the bed, tearing each other's clothes off until we're in nothing but our underwear.

I softly lower her down onto the foot of the bed and spread her legs apart, then flash a grin at her as I tug her panties off and fling them on the floor. I kiss my way up her bare thighs, racing the goosebumps that follow, and stop just short of her pussy. She's already dribbling wet, so I reach to swipe the trail away with my finger then pop it into my mouth.

"You taste so fucking sweet," I whisper to her as I move my hand back to her pussy. She spreads her legs farther, giving me full access, so I gently ease a finger into her folds. She tosses her head back and groans in delight. "That's my princess. I know you're going crazy for me, so just let it out."

When my finger disappears completely into her, I arch it up toward her g-spot, then slowly drag it back out. She whimpers and shudders, her hips rolling toward me automatically. She's already loosening up, so I slip another finger into her. She lies back with her feet resting on the foot of the bed while I continue finger fucking her, slowly picking up the pace.

"This is a beautiful fucking view," I say over her moaning. "But I want more." I pull my fingers out of her and grab her by the hips to turn her onto her stomach. She doesn't fight me, instead rolling with the motion, and when she's in place, I grab a pillow from the top of the bed.

"Lift up," I order, and she raises her ass in the air a little so I can tuck the pillow under her pelvis. "Perfect. I want to fuck you just like this."

She moans her approval, so I step out of my boxers and kick them away, then climb on top of her legs. I tap my swollen cock against her plump ass cheeks, then shove it down into her wet, welcoming folds.

"Yes," she breathes as I slide into her effortlessly from behind.

The sheets twist in her fists as she grips them, and she rolls her hips backward to pull me deeper into her. The motion spreads her ass cheeks, revealing her perfect little hole. I reach down to lube my fingers in her wetness, then bring them back to her ass.

She jolts when my thumb starts tracing circles around the tight ring of muscles, but I thrust my cock back into her, and she lets out a shuddering breath and relaxes, her muscles slackening a bit.

"That's it," I praise. "Be a good girl and open up for your husband."

Becca looks over her shoulder at me with her brows stitched and her face pleading. She chews her lower lip, and the desperation makes me wild. I reach up with both hands to grip her by the hips and pull her backward to drive into her again, and her back arches as she gasps. She flings her head to the side, her hair sweeping across her back, but my gaze drifts back to her asshole.

I spit on my fingers to toy with it again, then try slipping one inside. The feeling of her squeezing me as I enter her with both my finger and my cock makes me swell with arousal, and Becca's back arches even farther.

"I want to fuck you here," I mutter.

Becca looks over her shoulder, locking her eyes with mine as she nods. "Please. I want that."

My balls tighten as heat flashes through me, but then I groan when I realize I don't have any lube.

"What's wrong?" she asks.

"I don't have any lube, and we're definitely going to need it for that. I want to make it really good for you."

"I have some in my bag," she says, and desire floods me all over again. There's something fucking incredible about the fact she thought about this possibility, even planned for it—and wanted it.

"You really are a dirty girl," I say with a smirk as I push my finger back into her ass. She whimpers and nods, so I slap her ass before I step away to get the lube from her bag.

"It's in the big pocket, down at the bottom," she says over her shoulder, watching me. The moonlight streaming in from the sliding glass balcony door hits her arched ass perfectly, and my cock responds with a surge.

I find a bottle of lube in a plastic bag at the bottom of her bag, just like she said, so I unzip it and drizzle some onto one palm. She watches every movement, but when I climb back onto the bed, her expression shifts, especially when my cock brushes against her ass cheeks.

"Don't be nervous, princess. I promise I'll take such good care of you," I say softly and lean over her to kiss her.

She rises up to meet me, and I give the kiss everything I

have. I need her to know that she's safe with me, that she always will be. I'd never do anything to hurt her.

"If it hurts at all, just tell me and I'll stop, okay?" I say when we part. "We don't have to go any further than you're comfortable with."

She nods and her tense body relaxes underneath me. "Okay."

"You're such a good girl," I praise as I start to smear the lube across her hole with my thumb. Then I start to apply pressure, gently pressing into her until my first knuckle slips inside. She gasps and her eyes widen.

"Are you okay?" I murmur.

"Oh my god, *yes*," she breathes. Her forehead falls onto the bed as I work my thumb in and out of her, opening her up. Tiny shudders wrack her body as she whimpers, "That feels amazing."

"Is it okay if I add another finger?"

She nods again. I pull out my thumb and press into her with my index and middle fingers, aware of the way her breath catches as she adjusts to the intrusion.

"Good girl, you're doing so fucking well. Take a deep breath. I've got you. I'll make sure it feels good."

Her chest rises and falls as she takes a series of breaths, relaxing into it and allowing my fingers to slide into her with ease. She moans softly as I start to fuck her gently with those two fingers.

"There you go. Perfect. Work your clit too, it'll help you open up," I instruct.

She reaches between her legs obediently, biting her lower lip. As soon as her hand finds her clit, she squirms back against me, giving me deeper access. She starts to lose herself in it, and I can feel every response in her body as I get her ready for me.

"Just like that." I nod, my heart pounding. "Fuck, this is so hot. I can't wait to feel you around my cock."

"I want that too," she gasps. "I want you to fuck me like this."

Blood rushes to my cock at her words, and I groan as I draw my fingers out of her slowly.

"I can't fucking wait, baby. It's going to feel so amazing. God, you're beautiful like this."

"Please. Fuck me now. I can't wait either, Theo, oh god..."

Her voice is raspy, and her free hand clenches the sheets as I pull my fingers out entirely and settle on my knees behind her.

"You're ready for me, princess? You want to feel me fuck your ass?"

"Yes," she whispers hungrily.

I reach for the bottle of lube lying on the bed beside us and coat my cock in slickness, then line my head up to her tight back hole.

"Take a deep breath," I murmur.

She does, her eyelashes fluttering as her lips part slightly. As she releases the breath, I shift my hips forward, pressing inside her.

"Oh god," she whimpers.

I drag a hand down the curve of her spine. "So good, baby. You're taking me so well. Such a good fucking girl for me."

"Yes. Yes. Oh fuck. More."

She takes another breath, and I wait for her to release it, then roll my hips forward until another inch or so of my cock is buried inside her. I'm amazed she's able to open like this for me, because I know how big I am, but she's taking it so well.

"That's my good girl. Open up for me," I encourage her as I palm her ass.

"Fuck me, Theo," she begs, and her words hit me right in the chest. "I need it. I need you."

Hanging on to my restraint by a thread, I slowly push the rest of the way in. I want to make this incredible for her, so I'm more focused on her pleasure than on mine—which is probably the only reason I haven't come already, because she feels fucking amazing.

"Keep breathing, nice and slow. There we go," I whisper as inch after inch of me disappears into her. When I finally bottom out, she lets out a hungry, plaintive sound.

"Can you take more?" I ask, my voice hoarse. "You want me to fuck you? Can you take it hard?"

"Yes!" She nods almost desperately, her fingers still working her clit. "I want to come like this. Please, Theo. Make me come."

She's so tight, and I'm already so turned on from all of this that I know I won't last much longer. I lean over her, my mouth hovering just beside her ear.

"Your sweet ass has me so close already," I tell her, and she whimpers. "You feel so amazing, but I want to make you come first."

She reaches for my hand and pulls it between her legs to rest it against her clit. We start toying with it together, rubbing soft circles around the little nub, and Becca groans in pleasure as I draw almost all the way out.

Her entire body trembles as I slide out of her, but I don't let up on her clit, not even when I shove back in, and she lets out a shuddering moan.

"Oh my god," she gasps, so breathy her words are barely audible.

I can tell from the way she's tensing up and stroking her clit hungrily that she's getting close. So I repeat the motion, fucking her harder as our sounds mingle in the air around us.

"So good," I grunt. "So fucking good. Come for me and then I'll fill you up, baby."

"Don't stop. Right there, please... don't stop!"

Our bodies rock on the bed as I slam into her over and over, and I choke out a curse when I feel her clench around me.

She tenses beneath me, holding on to the sheets with her free hand while her other furiously works her clit. I've never felt anything like this, and the sensation is too much for me to hold back. Just as she's reaching the peak of her orgasm, I crash into mine, pulsing inside her ass. It roars through me, one of the most intense climaxes I've ever had, and when I can finally breathe again, I slump forward on top of her as she collapses onto the bed, careful not to crush her.

We lie like that, spent and breathless with my cock still inside her, for several minutes while we try to catch our breath. But eventually I soften enough to slide out, so I roll to her side and pull her against my chest, holding her close to kiss her.

"That was so fucking good," I say through a laugh when we part, and she shoots me a filthy grin.

"Honestly, if I'd known it could be like that, I would've done it a long time ago."

I chuckle, possessiveness roaring through me. "Selfishly, I'm glad you didn't. I like being the only man in the world who's had you like that."

Her smiles softens, turning warm and full of emotion. "Yeah, I like that too. A lot." She leans in to kiss me. "Thank you for making my first time so good."

My heart squeezes. I kiss her again, as deep as I can this time. Even after what we just shared, I still feel like I can't get close enough to her. Can't get enough of her.

After the game and the incredible sex, I'm already feeling drowsy, and it doesn't take long for me to start drifting off. Her chest steadily rising and falling against mine, our breathing in sync, lulls me the rest of the way.

As my eyes flutter, I realize she's the last thing I want to see before I fall asleep, and the first thing I want to see when I wake up.

Forever.

Chapter 42

Becca

My plane touches down in Denver the next afternoon. Despite the snow capping the beautiful mountains on the horizon, the sun is shining brightly. I'm thrilled to be back because the city is starting to feel like home. Like it's where I belong.

My trip to Jersey was sort of a last-minute thing, and I wasn't able to get on the chartered team plane with Theo and the rest of the Aces. They left before me, but that just means Theo is home already and planning to pick me up from the airport.

Which is something Shawn never did.

I still find it hard to believe how hard and fast my ex tumbled from grace—not that he didn't deserve it, the abusive piece of shit, especially after the way he treated me in Theo's home. In *my* home. If there's any justice in the world, and I'm starting to believe there is, I'll never have to see Shawn again. Now that he's been expelled from the NHL, I probably never will.

Eric, our lawyer, called Theo while we were still lying in bed together this morning to tell him that the restraining order we filed against Shawn had been granted. He also told us that Shawn's reality show had officially been canceled, thanks to the scandal of his drug use and the loss of his NHL contract, not to mention the fact that he basically stalked and tried to assault me.

I've never considered myself a vindictive person, but there's something viciously satisfying about knowing that Shawn destroyed his own life. He had everything once, but because of the kind of person he is, he's lost everything now. And now that he doesn't have the prestige of a TV show and a spot in the NHL, he's about to find out how many of his friends were people who really cared about him, rather than just hangers on who never really cared about him beyond his fame.

Eric offered to try to set up a few magazine interviews for me to tell my side of the story, but I turned him down. I'm ready to just move on and focus on what's next. Shawn has already ruined his own career and reputation, so he doesn't need any help from me. And the fallout from his behavior has already cleared my name anyway.

I reach for my purse tucked under the seat in front of me for my phone, then flip it off airplane mode as we taxi toward the gate to send a text to Theo.

BECCA: Just landed, heading toward the gate. Have to get my bag so no rush.

The bubbles indicating he's typing appear immediately.

THEO: Okay, already on my way there. Meet you at the door.

I smile and check the other notifications on my phone while I wait for the plane to get to the gate. There's an email from Eric, forwarded from a reporter at Sports Illustrated, but I archive it without reading it. Shawn and all his bullshit have already taken up enough room in my life and mind, I'm not giving them more.

The plane comes to a stop at the gate a few seconds later, so I unhook my seatbelt, grab my purse, and stand to stretch. I flew first class at Theo's insistence, and there wasn't anyone sitting in the aisle seat next to mine, so I breeze off the plane and past security heading for baggage claim. Amazingly, it only takes a few minutes for my bag to show up, so I grab it off the belt and head outside.

True to his word, Theo's car is already parked right in front of the door. He climbs out when he spots me and hurries to the curb to take my bag for me and plant a kiss on my lips.

"Welcome home, princess. I missed you," he says with a warm smile.

"I missed you too," I murmur.

And it's true, even though it was only a few hours we spent apart. After everything we've been through with Shawn, and what we shared together last night, I feel closer to Theo than I ever have.

He loads my bag in the trunk, then closes it and fixed me with a big smirk and a glint in his eye.

"What's with the look?" I ask, raising an eyebrow at him.

"Are you up for a little ride? I want to show you something."

Curiosity gets the better of me, so I nod, and he beams as he opens the passenger side door for me. He leans in to kiss me again as I buckle my seatbelt.

"Good. You're gonna love it."

He hurries into the driver's seat, and we leave the hustle and bustle of the airport, cruising through the beautiful, mountainous eastern outskirts of Denver. The airport is quite a ways away from the city, but about thirty minutes later we arrive. With his hand on my thigh, Theo drives us the usual path like we're going back to the condo, and we actually pass by it.

"Where are we going?" I ask.

"It's a surprise. We're almost there," he says, so I decide to just enjoy the ride. We end up in a more residential area that's littered with houses, most of which are huge. They're more mini mansions than homes. I'm still unsure what we're doing until Theo parks on the curb in front of one of the houses, which is easily the biggest on the street.

There's still a for-sale post in the massive front yard so I'm a little confused until Theo gets out of the car and walks around to the passenger door to open it for me. He offers me a hand to help me out, so I take it and he beams as he waves at the house behind him.

"What do you think?" he asks.

"I... what do you mean?"

He laughs and squeezes my hand. "I want to buy this house. For you. For *us*. I want it to be our home."

His words hit me so hard that all the breath rushes out of my lungs. Maybe I should've put two and two together faster. I don't know what I was expecting, but it wasn't this.

"But... we already have the condo," I stammer.

Theo laughs again and leads me up the driveway of the massive home to stop at the front door. "I know, but I think we need something we can grow with and grow into."

My heart swells, but I choke on the words that won't seem to come at the same time—because I know what he's implying. What he wants. And that I can't give it to him, no matter how badly I might want to.

The realization crushes me, and I feel like I'm shrinking right in front of him. I want to say yes so badly, to throw myself into his arms. I want to have that future with him, to be married to him for real and know there's no expiration date. But I can't, and it's never been clearer than it is right now. I shake my head slowly, and it breaks my heart as I do. He shoots me a confused look.

"What's wrong? Don't you like it?"

"It's not that. I love it. It's perfect, it's just..." I trail off, my voice trembling and raspy. I can't bring myself to say the rest of it.

Theo's expression falls, and he looks stunned. "Just what? What's wrong?"

I stare into his eyes, and with the way mine are burning I know I'm on the verge of tears. I don't want to say this. God, I don't. It's going to ruin him, ruin everything we've created together, but I have to do it. I've dodged and danced around the truth for months now, but I can't do it forever. I owe it to him to be honest.

Tears stream down my face as I lose control, and Theo looks totally confused as he takes both of my hands in his. "Shit, Becca, talk to me. What's going on? Are you okay? You're scaring me."

"I can't have this future with you, Theo," I finally blurt through the strain in my throat. "It's not possible."

"What are you talking about? Why not?" he asks, and the last of my resolve breaks.

I'm full on crying now, and my face is flaming with shame so I bury it in my hands because I can't bear to look at him. To say the rest of it. Theo tries to pull me into him, to hold me, but I resist because I know if I give in now, I'll never find the courage to tell him.

"I can't have kids," I choke out through my fingers. "I know you want that, and I know it's part of what broke you and Valerie up. She told me."

Theo stares at me in shock, his mouth hanging open, and it only makes me feel worse the longer he stares at me. It feels like my heart breaks a thousand times over in this awful silence between us while he searches for words. Finally, he finds them.

"Why didn't you say anything before?" he asks quietly.

"I'm sorry, I know I should have, and I feel terrible that I didn't, but it didn't seem to matter when we were only ever supposed to be in a fake marriage," I rush. "But then all of a sudden, it started to feel like more, but I still couldn't tell you."

"Why? You could've told me anything, you know that."

I look away because I can't stand the pain playing out on his face. Or the shame of admitting what I'm about to say. "I made that mistake before. I told Shawn, and he never let me live it down. He made me feel like shit about it, over and over again, every fucking chance he got. He made me feel like I wasn't a full woman, that I would never be enough for him or any man because I couldn't give him kids."

Theo just stares at me like he can't find words, which only makes me feel worse.

"I should have told you. I know I should have. But I was falling for you, and I wanted to have this little sliver of happiness, even if I knew it had to end," I whisper to fill the silence and to keep myself from completely falling apart. I can't stop myself. The words just keep pouring out of me.

"I'm sorry for hiding it from you. I never meant for it to be like this. But I can't stay married to you. Maybe it's better if we just end everything now rather than dragging it out for years. It will only hurt more then."

Still, Theo doesn't speak through the look of anguished confusion on his face. I hurt him, and I hate myself for it. And now all my fears are coming true all at once. He wants a family I'll never be able to give him, and he won't want me ever again after all of this.

"Say something, please," I whisper, but Theo just stares at me, his expression unreadable.

My heart splinters into a million jagged pieces, because I know what that look means.

It's over. I ruined this. Ruined *us*.

"I'm going to stay with Reese and Callie for a few days until we can get the divorce finalized," I say, shoving down the sob that's welling in the back of my throat. "You can have Eric draw up the papers."

My chest feels so tight that it's hard to breathe, and I turn away from him before I lose my resolve.

Tears blur my vision as I hurry back to the car to haul my bag out of the trunk, then hurry down the street with my phone in my trembling hand to call for an Uber.

Chapter 43

Theo

I drive back home in a numb, detached haze. One second, I'm standing on the curb outside the house I wanted to buy for Becca and me, and the next thing I know, I'm in the living room of the condo with Milo jumping all over me.

But even that barely registers. I pet his head absently, but I don't feel it. I don't feel anything at all, not even the searing pain that's bubbling beneath the surface. I don't let myself get close enough to that fire because I know it'll consume me if I let it. And I'm afraid.

More than anything, I'm hurt. I can't believe Becca kept something like that from me, no more than I can believe that she just walked away from me. Walked away from everything I thought we had. It all just fell apart in an instant.

I sink down on the couch with my phone in hand. I should call Reese to make sure Becca got there safe and that she's okay, but part of me doesn't want to make the call. Because hearing she's there will make all of this real in a way that I'm not sure I can handle right now.

None of this was supposed to happen. Today should've

been one of the best days of our lives, but instead it's one of the worst.

I tap Reese's name in my contacts to call before I fall to pieces. He answers in the middle of the second ring.

"Hey, she's here. But she won't tell us what happened. What the hell is going on, man?" he asks, skipping the small talk.

"I'm not feeling good enough to talk about it right now. Is she okay?"

"I mean, no. She's a wreck, but she's safe, if that's what you mean."

"Good. Is it okay if she stays there for a couple days?"

"Of course it is," Callie answers in the background, so Reese must have me on speaker.

"Can I talk to Becca?"

"I don't think that's a good idea right now. She doesn't want to talk anyway," Reese answers and my heart clenches painfully.

"Okay. I'll try again tomorrow. Tell her... tell her I'm here whenever she's ready."

"Alright. Are you good?"

"No, but I need some time alone. I'll talk to you later. Thanks for taking Becca in."

"Of course. We're here if you need us. Don't do anything crazy on us, man."

"I won't."

I hang up and drop the phone on the couch beside me, feeling empty. Like completely hollowed out. Milo must pick up on my mental state because he whimpers and climbs up on the couch, then plops down with his head in my lap.

I feel so lost. Adrift. And I don't know how or if we're going to be able to fix this. I wilt over Milo, holding him as close as I can to keep from spinning away into the emptiness swirling inside me, and try not to fall apart.

~

Eric draws up and sends over the divorce papers a few days later, just like Becca wanted. I haven't been returning his calls since I reluctantly asked him to do it, and I haven't left the condo in days, so he had one of his interns slip them under the door. I knew what was inside the nondescript manilla envelope as soon as I saw it, but I couldn't bring myself to open it.

Until now.

But now that I'm staring down at them splayed out across the living room coffee table, I feel sicker than I thought I would. I've had days for it to sink in, to accept that it's over, but I still feel like I'm sleepwalking through a nightmare. This isn't the first time I've been here, not the first time I've had to do this with a woman, but even as much as it hurt with Valerie, it pales in comparison to how this feels.

And I can't bring myself to sign the papers. I've been clutching the pen in my hand so hard for so long that it's cramping and leaving a semi-permanent mark on my palm. Frustrated, I sling it down on the table and reach for my phone on the table. My fingers fly across the screen on autopilot, tapping to call Becca for at least the twentieth time over the last few days.

I already know what's going to happen, but I lift the phone to my ear anyway and listen to the dozen or so rings before the line cuts over to her voicemail. I'm disappointed, but unsurprised. I hang up without leaving a message and drop the phone in my lap.

I promised myself I would sign these today, but I still can't do it. Not until I talk to her, to make sure this is what she really wants, because there's no going back. We can't undo this once we sign and file the papers.

But I need to get to practice anyway, so I leave the documents on the table and head for the arena. At least this will give me something to take my mind off everything. The Aces haven't played a game since we destroyed the Titans, but we've had practice and even with all of this upheaval going on, I'm still playing better than ever.

I know it's because of Becca. She gave me back my love of hockey, so even if I don't have her, I'll always have that part of her with me.

Still, I pass through practice on autopilot, just going through the motions. It does help me stop thinking about Becca for an hour or two, but I'm still not feeling like my usual self. And I'm not sure when or if I'll ever get that feeling back.

During our lineup for practice shots, I score several times on Grant, but I'm barely even paying attention. And before I know it, the buzzer sounds the end of practice, so I leave the ice, dreading going home because I don't want to spend any more time in the empty-feeling condo than I have to. Most of Becca's stuff is still there, but I moved what she had in my room back to the spare just so I wouldn't have to look at it. I don't need the reminders.

I'm kicking off my skates in the locker room and getting ready for a shower when I spot Noah staring at me. When my eyes meet his, he gives me a sympathetic look. "How are you doing?"

I shrug. "I'm surviving. That's about the best I can say."

He frowns. "Well, it could be worse than that, I guess. Do you need anything?"

"Other than my wife back? No, not that I can think of," I say, and when he grimaces, I sigh. "Sorry. Didn't mean to be a dick."

"No need to apologize. I get it. I'd be just as much of a mess if something like this ever happened between me and Margo."

Reese steps around the corner into the locker room and finds us talking. He puts two and two together quickly and tries to go back the way he came, but he's not fast enough.

"Hey, how's Becca? Is she okay?"

Reese freezes with his back to me, but eventually turns around to face me. He gives me a worried look. "She's not doing great, I won't lie. She seems wrecked."

Worry spikes in my gut. "Is she eating? Make sure she's eating! I don't want her passing out again."

"I know. We've got that part under control." He strides over to rest a hand on my shoulder. "Callie and I care about her too. We're doing our best to look out for her."

I let out a shaky breath, feeling sick. "Thank you."

He nods solemnly. "Callie has been a good support for Becca, I think. She has someone to talk to, at least. She'll get through this. So will you."

I think I say something in response, but I'm not even sure. My chest feels like it's caving in at the thought of 'getting through this.' I don't even know what that means. What that would look like. Does getting through it mean getting to a point where I'll be able to imagine my life without Becca? Where I won't feel like I'm drowning without her every single day?

Because I can't picture ever getting through this, if that's the case.

Reese gives me another sympathetic look and then leaves. One by one, the rest of the guys file out of the locker room until I'm all alone with my elbows on my knees, drifting in the wreckage that is my thoughts. But the bench creaks, and I glance over to find Sawyer sitting beside me. I didn't realize he'd stayed.

"Hey. I'd ask how you're holding up, but I have a feeling I already know the answer," he says with a small smile, and I chuckle roughly.

"I appreciate the self-awareness."

"Well, you know I've been in your shoes before, so I have some experience. You want to tell me what really happened? You don't have to."

I shrug, blowing out a breath. "I'm gonna have to tell everyone eventually anyway, so no point in delaying the inevitable."

My teammate listens as I spill everything, from the nitty gritty details of what went down with Shawn all the way to how Becca and I broke up—and why. Sawyer lets out a long exhale when I get to the end and how Becca told me she couldn't have kids.

"Damn, man. That's rough. Really fucking rough."

"Yeah, tell me about it. It's a complete dumpster fire. I want to talk to Becca more than anything, but there's this huge divide between us now. I've tried calling her more times than I can count, but she won't answer."

"So what are you going to do about it? Are you going to go through with the divorce?"

I sigh and grind my fists into my eyes. I'm so tired, so depleted. I haven't been sleeping since Becca left. How could I?

"I don't know. Part of me feels like I should just let her go and move on if that's what she wants."

"But the other part of you feels, what, exactly?" Sawyer asks, and when I glance over at him, he's studying my face as if he's looking for something. He must find it because he smiles. "That's what I thought."

"What are you talking about?"

"From one divorced guy to another, we both let our first marriages end because when shit got hard, it wasn't worth fighting for. So we let it end."

"Yeah, and?"

Sawyer's smile deepens. "That's why you can't go through with the divorce this time. You still think it's worth fighting for, you're just too scared to admit it to yourself." He nudges me with his shoulder, lifting a brow. "So I'll ask you point blank: you think Becca's the one worth fighting for, don't you?"

The one worth fighting for.

Something burns in my chest as those words replay in my mind, and my throat goes tight as a sudden rush of emotions fill me.

I've been a fighter my whole life. I've fought on and off the ice, gaining myself a reputation as a bad boy of the NHL. But I haven't been fighting for the thing that matters most to me.

Becca.

I nod slowly, dragging in a deep breath. "She's the *only* one worth fighting for," I tell Sawyer, my voice raspy.

He chuckles, as if he knew that was exactly what I was going to say. "Then what the hell are you doing here, man? Get your ass out there and fight for her."

Chapter 44

Becca

Time passes in a haze. Has it been a few days or a week? I've lost track, and I don't particularly care. All I know is that I'm trapped in this cycle while I wait for Theo to sign the divorce papers. I can't go back to Canada until then, so I lie around Reese and Callie's place like a house cat, sleepy and disinterested in everything.

But how can I care about anything after this? My entire life has blown up twice in just the last few months. I thought I found forever with Theo. We might have started out by faking it, but until yesterday, neither of us could've denied we had something real. We could've found some way to make it work—if I hadn't screwed everything up.

I can't stop thinking about the broken look on his face when I walked away from him. I know I dashed his dreams for a life together, for a family. I would give anything to go back and tell him I couldn't have kids sooner. It might not have changed the outcome, but it would have spared us both this awful situation.

And it would've meant I wouldn't break his heart the way I did.

A soft knock on the spare bedroom door jars me out of my

downward spiral. "Becca, are you hungry? I brought some lunch."

It's Callie, taking care of me like she has since I got here. Truthfully, I don't have any appetite at all, but I don't want to end up in the hospital again, so I force myself off the bed in the empty, spartan room and open the door.

Callie smiles cautiously at me, although I can see in her eyes that she's worried. I must look like hell. I don't think I've showered in the last two days.

"Glad to see you up and about," she says and extends a plate toward me. A grilled cheese sandwich, cut diagonally, rests on it. The sight is a knife in my side because it instantly reminds me of Theo cooking for me when I got home from the hospital after my fall. "I heard that this is one of your favorites when you aren't feeling well."

She doesn't say his name, but I know she must have talked to Theo. He's called me more times than I can count. And it's just like him to care enough to tell Callie my favorite foods, even after I ruined everything. But the appetite I already didn't have retreats farther at the thought. I didn't deserve his generosity then, and I damn sure don't deserve it now.

I take the plate from her anyway and bite off a piece of the sandwich to choke it down and placate her, then carry the plate back to the bed and sit on the foot of it. Callie follows me inside and stands watching me, like she's afraid I'm on a hunger strike or something and will throw the food out the window if she doesn't watch me eat it.

"Can we talk?" she asks gingerly as I take another half-hearted bite of the sandwich. I'm not hungry, but I know I need to eat.

"What is there to talk about?" I say through a mouthful, and she fixes me with a disapproving look.

"I'm worried about you. Like really, truly worried." She sits down on the bed next to me and puts her hand on my knee. "And I say that as a concerned friend."

"There's nothing to say. My heart is in pieces, and I don't have anyone to blame but myself."

I drop the sandwich on the plate, the small amount of appetite I managed to muster up evaporating as my throat goes tight.

But Callie shakes her head, squeezing my knee affectionately. "No, no, no. We're not playing the blame game today, girl. You're entitled to your heartbreak about what happened, and I'm not here to tell you otherwise, but I'm also not going to let you sit here and beat yourself to a pulp."

"If it's not my fault, then whose is it? I'm the one who lied to Theo."

"I'm not saying it was right to do, but I get it. I really do. I mean, hell, you'd just gotten brutally dumped and abandoned by a guy who repeatedly told you that you weren't worth a damn because you couldn't have kids. Then you fell in love with someone who meant the world to you, and you didn't want to lose him for the same reason."

I lose it at her words because she's one thousand percent right. I set the plate on the bedside table, the only other piece of furniture in the room, then collapse into her arms. Callie hugs me tight and rubs my back while I cry.

"I miss him so much," I breathe. "I hate that I let this happen. That I let myself fall in love with him under such bullshit pretenses."

Callie thrusts me away from her to look me in the eye, staring fiercely at me. "No, don't say that. It wasn't bullshit. You really love him. We all know you do."

"Then why did I keep this from him? Why did I break his heart with it?"

"Because you love him, and you were scared to lose him."

"Then what the hell do I do now?" I whisper and melt into

her again. She resumes rubbing my back as I blink away the tears blurring my vision.

"I don't know. Maybe you should try talking to him," she offers gently.

"He doesn't want to hear from me."

"Really? Then why does he keep blowing up your phone?" I laugh at that because she's right. Theo's been calling several times a day since I got to Reese and Callie's place, but I've ignored them all.

Right on cue, my phone starts vibrating on the nightstand, so I free myself from Callie's arms and reach for it, fully expecting to see Theo's name on the screen. But it's not him—it's my mom. I don't know if I have the heart to talk to her right now, but I haven't heard from her in weeks so decide I should probably take the call anyway.

"It's my mom. Can you give me a minute?" I ask Callie as I wipe my tears with the back of my free hand.

"Yeah, of course. I'll check on you in a bit," she answers and closes the door quietly while I answer the phone.

"Hi, Mom," I say, trying my best to sound like my usual bright, cheery self.

"Hi, Twinkle Toes," she greets me, and a genuine smile comes to my face. "Just wanted to call and check in on how you're doing. Haven't talked in a while."

"Everything's going well here," I lie, but true to her pattern, she doesn't seem to notice.

"Glad to hear. I've been having man troubles myself," she says with a laugh. Apparently, she's more interested in talking about herself than hearing what's going on with me—not that that's a surprise. "This guy, I swear. He's so hot and cold. One minute he can't get enough of me, the next he can't get far enough way."

"How long have you been seeing this one?" I ask, shifting the phone against my ear.

"Just a few weeks now. We met at the bar during karaoke one night, shared way too many drinks, and he ended up driving me home."

How romantic. Somehow, I manage to keep that thought to myself.

"That first night, Becca... it was magic. Like real magic. I haven't felt this way about a guy in a long time," she gushes, as if she hasn't said those exact words a million times before. "But ever since then, he's been flakier than a bowl of Frosted Flakes. But anyway, you don't want to hear more about my Jerry Springer life. How's your husband?"

I almost drop the phone in surprise. Not because she remembered I'm married—for now, at least—but because she bothered to ask.

"Did I ever tell you Theo called me the night you were in the hospital?" she asks when I don't reply because I don't have the faintest clue how to answer that question. "He wanted to know what your favorite foods were, all the stuff I used to make for you when you weren't feeling well."

My heart swells that Theo would do that, then bursts at the thought of how I hurt him, and I can't stop myself from dissolving again. I don't want to cry to my mom, don't want her to know what's really going on, but I can't contain the heartache.

"Oh my god, what's wrong? Did he hurt you?" she asks protectively.

"No. Nothing like that. But things are over between us."

"What?! What happened?"

"I don't even know where to start," I say, my voice shaky.

"Tell me everything. Start at the beginning." So that's exactly what I do. I confess to everything in a gush—the toxic relationship and public break up with Shawn, Theo offering to marry me for a green card—*everything.*

"It started off as just an arrangement, a convenience thing, but it turned real. I fell for him, Mom, and then I broke his heart because I can't give him the thing he wants the most. It could never work."

When I finally finish, Mom sighs. "I'm so sorry, Becca. And I mean that. I never met him, but he seemed like a great guy, and I never would've known things didn't start off real with you two. But speaking of being real..." She trails off, and my heart skips a beat. "Don't be like me. Don't be a runner."

I don't know what to say. She's never been this honest with me, or even showed that she cared enough to try. I sit there speechless, gripping the phone like I'm in some sort of dream and waiting to wake up from it.

"That's what I've done my whole life, but you know that. You were there too. Whenever the going gets tough or the feelings get a little too real, I bolt. But do you want to know why?"

I have a feeling I know where she's going with this, but I indulge her anyway. "Why?"

"Your father," she says, and my heart lurches. "He bailed and disappeared on me, and when that happened, I promised myself I'd never let it happen again. I'd never let a man make me hurt the way he did ever again. So I turned into the person who runs. It's so much easier to be the one doing the abandoning than it is to get left."

This is probably the most honest she's ever been with me, about anything. I still don't know what to say, but she's not finished, so I brace myself.

"But you know what the funny thing is about running? Once you start, it's next to impossible to stop. So don't you run from Theo. Don't you dare. You were always stronger than me, and way more responsible. And you have such a big, tender heart. I know it's hurting right now, baby, but that's because you're trying to do what I taught you and your heart knows better. You were never supposed to end up on the same path as me."

My chest clenches and my entire body aches. My mom has *never* given me this kind of loving, motherly advice before. And even if she'd tried before, I wouldn't have listened because I would've sworn she didn't have a clue what she was talking about, given her abysmal track record with men.

So this hits particularly hard because Mom has a point—a good one. I've always hated the cycle of starting over that my mom subjected me to repeatedly as a kid, so am I really about to do it to myself right now? Am I really going to walk away from the best thing that's ever happened to me, the only man who's truly loved me, just because I can't give him kids?

"Are you still there?" Mom asks gently, and I nod even though she can't see me.

"Yeah. Just taking it all in."

"Good. I'm glad it's getting through. Listen, I love you more than you'll ever know, sweetheart. I know I have a bad way of showing it, but I do love you. And I know that man loves you too. I heard it in his voice the night you were in the hospital. Don't let that go."

"Thanks, Mom. I needed this."

"I know you did. Call me in a couple days to let me know how things are, okay? And make sure you're eating. I know how you get when you're stressed."

I laugh and pick up the cold grilled cheese from the plate next to me and take a bite. "I'm eating right now, actually."

"Good. I love you. Talk soon."

"Love you too, Mom," I tell her, and for the first time in what feels like years, it's because I mean it, not because it's what I'm supposed to say. "Bye."

I end the call and put my phone back on the nightstand with my head whirling with Mom's words. I need someone to process them with, so I take the grilled cheese with me to the door and step outside to look for Callie. Hushed voices echo upstairs from the living room, so I go downstairs and find her sitting on the couch having a whispered conversation with Reese. They both glance up at me when I enter, and I get the distinct feeling they've been talking about me.

"Everything okay?" Callie asks, and I nod.

"Yeah. My mom had a lot to say, but I needed to hear it. What's going on? Is something wrong?" I ask.

But before either of them can answer, someone knocks on the front door. Reese shoots me a worried look as he climbs off the couch to answer it, and his wide frame blocks the view as he opens the door.

"Hey, man," he says to whoever it is, speaking in a low tone. "What are you doing here?"

A familiar voice answers him, sending my pulse racing.

"I'm here for my wife."

Chapter 45

Becca

When Reese steps aside and Theo appears, my heart lurches. I've missed him so badly that his presence now is like gravity, an invisible but no less noticeable pull.

"I came for my wife," Theo repeats and thrusts up the divorce papers in one hand. "I've got them right here."

My heart aches again because I don't want to sign them. I really don't. But if this is what he wants, how can I say no?

Theo steps toward me. "But I want to talk to you first. Can we do that? Please?"

I bite my lip, but after the conversations I had with Callie and my mom, I'd be an idiot to say no. So I nod, and he breathes a sigh of relief.

"Thank you," he says quietly. He glances over my shoulder at Callie and Reese, who are still watching us. "Can we... go somewhere else? Somewhere more private?"

"Okay."

I steal a look back at Callie who smiles and nods encouragingly at me as I follow Theo outside.

He helps me into his car like always, then we head off somewhere. For the first few minutes, the silence and tension between us is almost unbearable. I wish he'd say something, anything at all, or at the very least put his hand on my leg like he always does, but he just grips the wheel and stares straight ahead.

Even though neither of us are saying a word, it's like there's an elephant riding with us in the backseat. There are so many things I want to say, so many things that need to be said, but I don't even know where to start. Somehow, saying "I'm sorry" doesn't feel anywhere near adequate so I just keep it to myself.

But finally, Theo breaks the quiet.

"How have you been? Have you been eating?"

The fact that he cares enough to ask, even after all of this, touches me.

"I have. Callie has made sure of it."

He nods. "Good. I knew you were in good hands with those two."

"What about you? How have you been?"

He grimaces but wipes it off his face quickly. "Not good," he admits, his hand squeezing the steering wheel. He sighs and looks me in the eye. "I miss you so much it's been hard to breathe, much less do anything else."

Tears instantly well in the corners of my eyes because I feel the exact same way, but knowing I hurt him that way makes my heart ache so badly that it feels like it's bruised. But he doesn't say anything more, instead letting silence fall between us again as we keep driving.

Eventually, we end up in downtown Denver, and I start to recognize the area. We're near the hotel where we went for the gala a while back. It looks different now in the daylight and without the snow, but it's still beautiful.

A few minutes later, Theo parks on the curb outside of a nondescript building, and I turn to look at him, confused. If he wanted to talk, why bring me here of all places? I thought we'd go to a park or somewhere a bit quieter and more private.

"What are we doing?" I ask.

"Look closer," Theo says, pointing beyond me at the building to my side. As I'm craning my neck to look up at it, he climbs out of the car and walks around to open my door. He offers me a hand to help me to my feet, and as I'm standing, everything clicks.

I recognize this building. It's the one I noticed in my drunken haze as we walked the streets of Denver in the snow, the one I said would make a perfect building for a dance studio —although I never dared to dream it would actually be possible.

My eyes shoot to his, my heart skipping a beat. "Theo..."

He says nothing, just leads me by the hand through the front doors of the building. I'm not sure at first why the doors are open for us because the building seems to be empty, but it's hard to focus on that when the raw beauty of the space strikes me.

It's open and spacious, with large windows that allow so much light to pour into the area that it makes the room feel almost spiritual, like an altar. Specks of dust twinkle in the light like stars, and the beams bounce off the incredible stained hardwood floors that look like they date back all the way to the original construction. Floor-to-ceiling mirrors line one wall, and a balance bar is built into it as well.

Visions flash through my mind of the room filled with students. When we first saw this building weeks ago, without ever seeing the inside, somehow I knew it would be perfect as a dance studio. But seeing the interior now makes me realize it's so much more perfect than I ever could've imagined.

"It's beautiful," I stammer, because I'm at a loss for any other words.

Theo flashes me a warm smile. "I'm glad you like it— because it's yours."

My heart stutters. "What?"

"It's all yours, princess. The renovations to turn it into a proper studio aren't done yet, but we'll get there," Theo clarifies, but I can't process his words. "I bought this building for you instead of a house. Because you deserve to have your school and not be beholden to your past with Shawn. You shouldn't have to wait for someone else to decide if you're good enough to teach. Because I know you are."

He reaches into his back pocket and pulls out the divorce papers, holding them up.

"I won't sign these—not until the time is up and your residency is permanent. Because you deserve to live your dreams, even if it's not with me. Even if you never want to see me again."

I can't stop the tears streaming down my face, and I wouldn't even if I could. I can't believe he's willing to do all of this for me, even if we split. It's too much. But the thought of actually divorcing him tears at my heart, and just thinking about it makes the tears fall harder.

But when he sinks down to one knee, still clutching my hand, my heart stutters. I can barely breathe.

What is he doing?

"Becca... I know you thought we couldn't be together because I didn't know the truth about you going into it. But now I do. I know you can't have kids, and I don't care. All I want is to be with you," he says.

A lump builds in my throat, the tears blurring my vision before I blink them away.

"I didn't break up with Valerie over the kids issue." Theo shakes his head, his eyes shining intently. "If she made you think that, she's wrong. It was because we weren't right for each other. In so many ways. And I know that better than ever now, because I realize that every beat of my heart wasn't for her—it was for you. So I want to ask you again, for real this time. Will you marry me?"

I stare down at him, speechless. I want to say yes with all my heart, but I'm scared. No, more than scared—I'm terrified I'll disappoint him again, that at some point down the line he'll realize he does want kids and that he made a mistake giving me this second chance. Because there's no "fixing" this thing about me. It's permanent. So I have to make sure he really understands what he's asking.

"Theo, I'll never be able to give you a family. Not now, not ever. Are you sure you can live with that for the rest of your life?"

He rises to his feet, taking both my hands in his, and squeezes them hard as he gazes directly in my eyes.

"I know. But I don't care. Because there is *so* much more to you than that. I won't let you talk about yourself like that's the only value you have."

More tears stream down my face, and not just because of the words themselves—but because I can tell he means them. He's not just saying this. He believes it. And that means more to me than anything he or anyone else could ever say.

"You're an amazing woman, with an equally amazing future ahead of you, and I want to be part of that future," he continues. "So as long as I'm around, I won't let anyone talk or think badly about the woman I love with all my heart. And I'm damn sure not going to let anyone say she's not worthy of that love—not even you. Because you *are* worthy. You don't have to say yes, but I want you to know that I love you with my whole heart, and I always will. Even if it's from a distance, if that's how it has to be. I couldn't stop even if I tried, princess. I honestly don't know how to *not* love you."

My throat is so tight that I can barely breathe, much less speak, and tears are pouring down my face, making it difficult to see anything. I swallow hard because I have to say something. I have to tell him how much this means to me, even if my words could never be enough. Because everything he's just said to me has broken my heart open and rebuilt it all at once, piece by piece.

"All I want is to be with you," I choke. "I love you so much. I love the way you see the best in me, the way you make me feel like the most special person in the world. Like a princess."

Theo chuckles hoarsely, his lips twitching into a small smile. The more I speak, the more I find my voice, so the easier it gets. The words start to flood out of me so quickly I can barely breathe between them.

"I honestly don't think I've ever known what real love is until I met you. How could I? Between my mom's rollercoaster love life and the shit I put up with from Shawn, it's probably one of the most obvious things in the world to everyone other than me. But I couldn't see it until I met you and you started showing me that love is care. It's in the little things, like cooking for me and making sure I eat. And supporting my dreams in every way you can. It's believing in me."

"I really do. You're fucking amazing, Becca," Theo says with a little laugh as he swipes the back of his hand across his face. "And I hope you see what I see."

"I still have some work to do on that, but I'm starting to. And it's all because of you. I don't know who or what brought you into my life, or what I did to deserve you, but I'm done questioning it. Because whether or not I deserve you, I want you. With all of my heart."

Theo stares up at me, his watery emerald eyes wide and hopeful. He squeezes my hand still locked in his. "Is that a yes?"

"It's definitely a yes," I answer, and he surges to his feet, pulling me into his arms and peppering me with kisses as he spins me around in the room's streaming, beautiful light beams like we're the winners on some sort of dancing competition. My heart soars as the room whirls around me, and I give in to the moment, to the pure joy that's flooding me.

It feels like a lifetime ago that my life as I knew it with Shawn fell apart. At the time, I really thought life was over for me, that I'd have to go crawling back to my mom in Canada with my tail between my legs and give up on every dream I had about building a better life for myself, the life I'd always wanted.

But little did I know life was just getting started. That the true dream was unfurling in front of my eyes. All of that had to happen to bring me here, to this beautiful moment with the man I love more than I'll ever have the words to convey.

When we finally stop twirling, he sets me back on my feet and cups my face in his hands. "I want every day to feel like this for the rest of your life," he says and leans forward to kiss me again like he can't get enough.

But I cling to him and kiss him back because I feel the exact same way.

Chapter 46

Theo

I feel Becca's heart thudding in her chest, and it matches the heavy pounding of mine. I can't stop kissing her, can't take my hands off her, because I'm afraid if we break contact, she'll vanish, and I'll wake up from this incredible dream and realize none of it was real. That my mind is playing a cruel trick on me.

But it has to be real. She has to be truly mine. I can't imagine my life any other way. So I cup her face again and pull her in for another kiss. "I love you."

"I love you too," she whispers between lip locks, and her words light me up with desire. It's not enough to tell her how much I love her. I need to show her. I need to make sure she feels it in every nerve of her body.

"You have no idea how much I missed you. Missed this," I say as I steal another kiss. "I still feel you even when you aren't around. It hurt in the weirdest way, like this dull ache that wouldn't go away. Like a phantom limb. You were still there, I could still feel you, even though you were cut off."

"Theo, I'm so sorry," she says breathlessly as a fresh round of tears appear in her eyes. But I swipe them away because I don't want her to feel anything but the love I have for her that's overflowing from me. With her face still cupped in my hands, I look her right in her beautiful brown eyes that are sparkling from her tears and the soft light in the room.

"You don't have to apologize. I understand, I really do. You were scared."

"No, I do need to apologize. I just walked away from you, from everything you've done for me. And I know I hurt you. I can't forgive myself for that."

"You don't have to because I already have."

Becca makes a small noise in her throat and throws her arms around me. Again, I feel her heart hammering in her chest, racing just as hard as mine is.

I can't lie, her walking away hurt like hell, but not in the way she thought it did. It wasn't her leaving that hurt the most, it was that she thought I would abandon her and treat her like Kaplan did just because she couldn't have kids.

But I'm not angry. After something like that, I don't blame her for keeping it from me, and I don't blame her for being scared that the same thing would happen with me when I found out the truth. And that's exactly why we're here. I knew that all the words in the world wouldn't be enough to convince her that none of that mattered to me.

I had to prove it to her.

"You mean the world to me, Becca," I whisper, my voice hoarse. "I would do anything and go anywhere for you. You're everything I need. Everything."

"I can't believe you bought me a dance studio," she breathes, letting out a shaky breath as she leans back to look into my eyes. "I've never had someone do anything like this before. You... you *care*. About me, about my dreams. My future."

"It's all I care about." I swallow, wrapping my arms more tightly around her. "All I want is for you to be happy, to be and do everything you've ever wanted."

"I think I do." She smiles despite the tears still streaming down her cheeks, looking more beautiful than I've ever seen her. "I have you."

"That's a given, baby. Forever." I brush her tears away. "And now you've got this studio too. All you need is students to fill it. I'm sure they'll come now that Kaplan's gotten tossed out of the NHL and pretty much proved everything he said about you was bullshit. I'll do everything I can to help you advertise too. You're going to be the best teacher ever."

Her gorgeous brown eyes are luminous as she gazes up at me. "Thank you," she whispers. "For everything."

"You're my wife. You *are* my everything," I say, hoping she can hear the honesty in my voice.

I never want to lose her again. When she told me about her inability to have kids and left me on the doorstep of what should've been our home, it almost broke me. But I'm so glad that Sawyer talked some sense into me and that I didn't let her go. That I fought for her.

Because I don't ever want to live without her, without this.

I lean forward to kiss her, to show her how I feel in the best way I know how. She reciprocates, her hands resting on my chest, and I lose myself in the glow of the moment. The sun streams through the windows, lighting her and her dark hair up like the perfect angel she is, and gratefulness washes over me.

"I couldn't imagine never kissing you again," she whispers when we part, making my chest ache. "I never would've forgiven myself if I kept running from you. My mom told me not to run, and I'm so glad I listened."

"Me too," I breathe, then lean in to kiss her again like I'm trying to make up for lost time.

It's soft and tender at first, our kisses slow and almost tentative, like we're both afraid that the other person is going to disappear or turn out to be a dream.

But the feeling of her body against mine, her breaths teasing my lips every time we break apart for a second, is solid and real.

I kiss her deeper, sliding my tongue into her mouth and tasting her, inhaling her familiar scent.

My hands start to roam, need building inside me until it's all I can feel.

I almost lost her, and now I have her back.

And I need to fucking make her *mine*.

My hands start to roam, rough and possessive as I nip at her lower lip. Her breath hitches, and she rises up on her tiptoes to kiss me harder, one hand slipping down to palm the growing bulge in my pants.

"Fuck, princess," I groan. "Need you. Right now."

"You too," she gasps.

I kiss her again, hungrier this time, and we stumble backward while we tear at each other's clothes until we meet the far wall of mirrors. Her ass presses into the balance bar built into the wall, and with her pinned there, I scrape my teeth over her collarbone and then drag my mouth upward, kissing her exposed neck and throat.

"I need you," I repeat, my voice rough.

"You have me. I'm yours. Forever," she whimpers back, and my blood rushes as I tug off her pants then reach for mine.

We stop kissing just long enough for her to pull her shirt up over her head and throw it to the ground behind us. She's not wearing a bra, and the sight of her beautiful bare chest just makes me want her that much more. In a matter of seconds, we're both naked, our exposed bodies pressed together.

I cup her perfect breasts, my thumbs stroking her nipples until they're swollen and full. Then I turn her around so she's facing the mirror and run my hands along her incredible silhouette.

"I want you to watch. To see what you do to me, and how perfect we are together."

"God, Theo..." Her voice is full of so many emotions that it makes my heart thud against my ribs.

"I know, baby," I tell her, catching her gaze in the mirror. "I know. I feel it too."

"Show me how perfect we are together," she whispers. "I want to see."

I smile, my heart so full it could burst. "I will. Now be the good girl I know you are and bend over and grip the bar."

She bites her lip and bends over quickly, exposing her perfect pink pussy to me. I tease her folds with the head of my cock and smear the wetness that's already leaking out of her onto myself.

"Look at you," I growl. "So fucking perfect." My eyes find hers in her reflection again as I add, "Keep your eyes on me."

"I will."

I place one hand on her lower back to brace us, then slowly slide into her from behind. I watch as her face goes slack with pleasure and her back arches under my hand. A moan claws its way out of her throat, and I can't help groaning with her as I continue burying myself inside her. When our hips meet, I give her ass a rough squeeze, and she bites her lower lip, driving me crazy.

She still feels so tight and incredible that I can barely hold back, but I don't want to rush this.

I want her to feel in every little movement exactly what she means to me. I want her to feel the love and care in each stroke until she can't stand it anymore and she's begging me to take her over the edge just to make the anticipation stop.

"Look at how well you take me, princess," I murmur as I slowly drag my cock out of her, and although her eyes flutter from the sensation, she never takes her gaze away from mine. The needy look on her face goes right to my cock.

She wants this just as badly as I do.

She needs me just as much as I need her.

"I was made for you," she mutters, and it drives me wild.

I push back into her, a bit faster this time, and the last vowel of her words stays frozen on her face as her mouth drops open in shock and pleasure at me opening her up again.

"That's right, you were. No one has ever been as perfect for me as you. You're it for me, all I'll ever want and need."

I grip her hips, slamming into her again. But it's not deep enough, not close enough, so I lift her upper body by the waist until she's more upright. Her breasts and cheek press against the mirror as I keep fucking her, the new angle making things even more intense.

She gasps against the mirror, fogging it up, and even though she's finally broken eye contact with me, I don't even care. The sight of her lost to the pleasure I'm giving her makes my cock swell, adoration filling my chest.

"That's it," I rasp. "Show me how good your husband makes you feel. How badly you need me."

I thrust into her again as I speak, and she rocks her hips backward to meet me. Her hands splay out against the mirror, and her breathing intensifies, making the fog on the glass spread. I lean over her and crush my mouth against hers, kissing her deeply as I continue moving, going harder and faster with each stroke.

When she abruptly stops breathing and her entire body tenses, I know she's close, so I pick up the pace again, pushing her over the edge. Her orgasm wracks her body as she clenches around my cock, but I need more.

Gritting my teeth to hold back the pleasure, I draw out and spin her around, lifting her up to balance her ass on the bar. Her legs wrap around me automatically as I drive into her again, and the feel of her wet heat surrounding me again is enough to set off my own climax.

"Fuck, Becca. Oh *fuck*."

Her hands wind around my neck and she tries to keep her eyes open as I come, but she loses that battle. They fall shut as she squeezes me tightly, milking my cock as I shudder and groan.

But I never take my eyes off her. Because I want to savor the lost look on her face, the way I know I'm making her feel something no man before or after me ever will.

Because she's mine.

Now and forever.

In the aftermath, my legs start to wobble, and we slide down to the floor together. I turn to lean against the mirror, and she ends up in my lap, facing me. I brush her messy hair out of her face as we smile at each other, basking in the warm glow. I could stay like this for the rest of my life, just gazing into her beautiful eyes and stroking her soft cheek with the back of my hand.

She's perfect, more than she'll ever realize. But that won't stop me from trying to convince her of it. I'll spend every day telling her just how incredible she is.

"I guess we've christened the studio," she murmurs, her eyes gleaming.

I laugh, pulling her closer against me as my cock slowly starts to soften inside her. "Hell yes, we did. Don't worry, it'll be our secret."

She grins, and then her expression turns serious as she runs her fingers through my hair. "I can't believe this is real. I feel like I've been living without oxygen and now I can breathe again. Everything felt empty without you."

"For me too," I tell her softly. "And you were wrong about the fact that you couldn't give me a family."

She blinks. "What do you mean?"

My hand cups her cheek, and I tilt her head up to meet my gaze as I rest the other hand on her chest, just above her heart. "This right here? *This* is my family."

Chapter 47

Becca

The stadium explodes in cheers as Theo scores the Aces' third goal against the Arizona Outlaws in the Stanley Cup playoffs—and I'm right there with them. Theo's mother throws her arms around me and we jump up and down together. Anne and John flew in to watch the playoffs, and I'm glad they're here because I know they're just as proud of him as I am.

"Did you see that?" my mom shouts over the noise as she throws her arms around both of us. She's the most excited I think I've ever seen her, which isn't something I ever thought I'd say. Though she's always been supportive of my love for hockey, she's never shown an interest in it herself.

But when I told her that Theo and I had patched things up and that his team was going to the playoffs, she insisted on coming down to watch the game. And Theo was all too happy to buy her a plane ticket because without her encouragement, we might not be together right now.

Still, with my arms around Anne and my mom's around both of us, the moment feels surreal. Like two worlds colliding. But the fact that it's happening at a hockey game feels perfect because Theo and the sport are what tie us all together. Amazingly, our moms are getting along really well too. It's one of those things I never would've dreamed would happen for me, but then again, so is my relationship with Theo.

"I still can't believe the Aces are in the playoffs!" Callie, who's sitting two seats to my left next to my mom, says as the crowd calms down and retakes their seats. But after the way they've been playing this season, I don't find it hard to believe at all. Especially now that Theo is firmly back in the game.

"God, look at him! Theo Camden is *so* dreamy," I hear a woman sitting behind us say as he skates past our seats. I wave to him, and he flashes me his signature grin and a wink. The woman behind us practically dissolves. "Oh my god, did you see that? He totally just winked at me!" she hisses to the people sitting with her.

Callie chuckles and turns around to face the woman. "I'm pretty sure that look was for his wife. You know, the beautiful woman sitting right in front of you. The one wearing his jersey and his ring."

She smirks, pointing at me.

"Oh, shit!" The woman sounds instantly chagrined as I turn around to look at her too. She blushes, putting her hands over her face. "I'm so sorry! I didn't know he was married."

"It's fine." I shake my head. "But that wink was definitely for me."

"Right." Her blush darkens even more as her friends laugh. She looks like she wants to sink into the seat and disappear, and when Theo does another lap past our seats, she glances at the ice and then back to me. "You're a very lucky woman."

I chuckle. Although hearing her talk about my husband ruffled my feathers a little, igniting a possessive instinct in me that I never had before I met him, the truth is, I have no reason to feel even the tiniest bit threatened.

Because I know exactly how lucky I am.

Theo is mine, just like I'm his, and he makes sure I never

have a moment of doubt about that. Every day, multiple times, he tells me how much he loves me. And more than that, he *shows* me.

Even in the middle of being in the freaking Stanley Cup playoffs, he's dedicated every spare moment he has to helping me get my dance school up and running. The renovations are finally almost done, and with Eric's help, he's taken care of all the legal and admin side of things. We even have a few students who've already expressed interest in signing up once the school opens.

Theo truly is the most supportive husband a woman could ever ask for. So I'm not threatened in the slightest that other women see it because I know without a shadow of a doubt that I'm the only one he has eyes for. There's nothing in the world that could ever make me question that again. He's mine, and I'm his—just like it should be. Neither of us would have it any other way.

The players take position for the next face off. There's only a few minutes left on the clock, and with Theo's latest goal, the Aces are up 3-2 against the Outlaws. All they have to do now is hold their lead. This has been an incredible game, and even though the Aces are playing the tightest I think I've seen them so far this season, their opponents aren't slacking off, either.

As the guys all tense up on the ice and prepare to spring into action, I sit on the edge of my seat, gripping the arm rests so hard that my knuckles are turning white. Mom puts her hand on mine. At the same time, Anne, who's sitting to my right, does the same. Neither of them realize they're trying to comfort me in the same way at the same time, but it makes me smile, regardless.

"Let's go, Aces! We've got this!" I bellow just as the referee slings the puck onto the ice and the players turn into a blur of motion. Keeping track of an individual player is like trying to watch an individual rain drop in a thunderstorm, but eventually,

Theo emerges from the fray, streaking toward the Outlaws' goalie with their center hustling after him.

"Come on, Theo!" I shout so hard it hurts my throat. It's hard to tell from this angle, but I'm pretty sure he's about to score again. He winds up and slaps the puck with his stick, sending it rocketing toward the goalie. I can't see it from this far away, but when the net swishes and the goalie slumps to his knees, I leap into the air, still holding Anne and Mom's hands.

We jump up and down together with the rest of the fans, all of us downright losing our minds, as the buzzers sound and the score updates on the screens. The Aces are now up 4-2 with less than two minutes on the clock, so it's all but guaranteed they'll be moving to the next round of the Stanley Cup.

When I glance over at Anne and John, I see they both have tears in their eyes. They must be unbelievably proud of their son. What parents wouldn't be if their kid was not only a successful professional hockey player, but a potential finalist in the freaking Stanley Cup? Even though I'm standing there holding Anne's hand and watching the whole thing too, I can barely believe it myself.

If he's anything like me, Theo probably doesn't even realize or appreciate how amazing he is. For him, this is probably just something he does. Something he's worked hard and practiced for, sure, but it's second nature for him at this point. Just like dancing is for me. He doesn't have to think about it, he's just *in* it, and it's amazing to watch. Especially now when he seems like he's at the very top of his game.

Based on the way he's dancing around the ice tonight, it's hard to believe that just a few months ago, there were gossip articles being written about Theo getting cut from the Aces due to his poor performance earlier in the season. Anne told me about one she'd read in Sports Illustrated, and I could barely believe her until I found a scan of the article online and read it myself.

I bet that writer is eating a lot of crow now, and rightfully so.

The guys form up for what might be the final face off with this little time on the clock, and my eyes land on Theo, just like they always do. He's magnetic, and I'm sure I'm not the only one watching his every move tonight. I'm still holding Mom and Anne's hands, and I'm squeezing them so tightly that they're probably going numb. Not that there's any real risk here, but I want Theo and the Aces to win so badly!

The ref tosses the puck and the Aces and Outlaws tussle over possession of it several times, intercepting and passing in an exhilarating but nerve-wracking back-and-forth, until finally the Outlaws' right wing skates away with it. But as he soars toward the Aces' goalie, Sawyer appears out of nowhere and steals the puck, then whips it across the ice toward Noah, who's lagging near center ice. He just barely misses the pass, but it doesn't matter. There's now less than a minute on the clock, and everyone seems to know it's over because none of the players seem like they're in a hurry to chase after it.

The end-of-game buzzer sounds, and I launch out of my seat again to cheer for the Aces and Theo. He weaves through the tangle of other players toward us and stops in a spray of ice that showers the glass, then blows me a kiss that I snatch out of the air and hold to my heart. I send one back to him, and he pretends to stumble backward from its force when he catches it, making everyone watching in the audience laugh.

I never would've thought we could be this open about our relationship, let alone play it up in public like this, but I feel nothing but love and support coming from the Aces fans surrounding me.

"You two are way too cute. I can't handle it," Mom says in my ear, and when I glance over at her, I see she's tearing up too. I throw my arms around her because I'm overwhelmed with gratitude. I don't know if she and I will ever have the kind of relationship I wish we could, but her being here now and being

445

so supportive of Theo and me, is definitely a step in the right direction.

"I'm glad you're here," I say as she squeezes me back, so tightly it's hard to breathe.

"I wouldn't have missed it, sweetheart." She plants a kiss on my cheek, and I slip my hand back into hers to walk with her, Callie, and Theo's parents out of the stands and into the family lounge to wait for Theo and the rest of the Aces. Mom slips out of my grip to catch up with Anne and John.

"You must be so proud," she says and puts a hand on each of their shoulders.

"Oh, definitely. But we aren't the only parents with children to be proud of," Anne responds, smiling at me, and it brings a tear to my eye because I finally feel like I've found the family I've always wanted—no, the family I've always *needed*—but never dared to dream I would actually have.

We spill into the family lounge together with Mom talking animatedly with the Camdens, recounting every play like it was the most incredible thing she's ever seen. Callie wraps an arm around me and gives me a little half hug.

"These families coming together is something to see," she whispers, and I chuckle.

"None of it would've happened if you hadn't given me an intervention. I'd probably still be a starving, sobbing puddle in your spare bedroom."

"Well, I had some help from your mom, but you're welcome anyway." She flashes me a teasing smile, but I lean into her again. I really don't think I could've gotten through the near-miss with Theo if it hadn't been for her, and I hope she knows that.

But when Theo appears in the entrance a few minutes later, I rush from Callie's arms and into his. He kisses me while the rest of the family members give him a little congratulatory round of applause, but when I pull back and rest my hands on his chest, he winces, and my heart skips a beat.

"Oh, no. Did you get hurt during the game?"

"No, I'm fine. That area is just a little, uh, tender."

"Well, if you aren't hurt, then why is it tender?"

Theo winks and grins at me. "Don't worry. I'll show and tell you all about it later."

But I'm not taking no for an answer, so I cross my arms over my chest and fix him with the most serious look I can manage. "No, you can tell me now."

Theo's eyebrows shoot up his forehead, and he lets out a little laugh that turns into a devious grin. "I like it when you're bossy like this. But fine, I'll show you, but it's for your eyes only."

He grabs me by the hand and pulls me off toward one of the corners of the room. Thankfully, no one questions it or tries to stop us. They probably know we'd like a private moment after an amazing game like that. I half expect him to kiss me again, just to sell the moment to anyone who might still be watching, but instead he reaches for the hem of his shirt and hikes it up toward his shoulder, exposing his chest.

I don't know what I'm supposed to be looking for at first, but when I spot the bright red, irritated skin that's a telltale sign of a fresh tattoo on his left pec, my heart skips a beat. I lean closer to get a better look, and there, right next to my favorite tattoo of a snarling tiger, is another. It's a simple but elegantly drawn ballerina, caught mid-pirouette, spinning right above his heart.

"Remember how I told you that every tattoo I have is for a significant moment in my life?" he asks quietly, and instantly tears spring to my eyes because I know what he's going to say next. "Well, falling for you was far and away the most significant."

"I love it," I say, choking on my tears. And I really do. My finger gently strokes the ballerina's outline on his tender skin, and although he winces, he doesn't recoil. I'm both touched and turned on by the tattoo, and Theo must be picking up on it because he leans forward to kiss me. It's a hungry, needy kiss, and I can't stop myself from giving into it, despite the fact the room is full of his family and friends.

Anne clears her throat, and Theo freezes, although he doesn't break our kiss.

"Yeah, save it for the bedroom, lovebirds," my mom adds, and Theo groans before finally peeling himself away from my lips. I shouldn't be embarrassed—I love my husband, so what?—but my cheeks flame anyway.

"Don't worry, we'll finish this later," I whisper in his ear, and his eyes flash devilishly when he looks down at me.

"I'll hold you to that, wife," he whispers back.

With a shiver of anticipation dancing down my spine, I walk back to the center of the room with him to rejoin our family—the family we've built together.

Epilogue

Theo

I'm still fighting with my tie for the grand opening of Becca's dance studio by the time she strolls into the room. Her reflection appears in the floor mirror as she enters the frame, and the gorgeous, seafoam green dress she's wearing trails after her. My heart always stutters at the sight of her, but the way the dress fits her and makes her gold-flecked eyes pop makes my heart race.

"You look gorgeous," I say in awe as she comes up from behind me to help me with my tie.

"Sweet talker."

She smiles at me in the mirror, her warm brown eyes flashing, but the expression she wears underneath them is a little jittery, so I turn to face her.

"Is something wrong?"

She sighs, biting her bottom lip. "I'm just worrying about nothing, as usual."

"Don't downplay your feelings. What are you worried about?"

"I'm nervous, that's all. Like... what if the school flops? What if no students show up? What if none of it works out?"

she asks as she finishes tying my tie for me, and when her hands stop moving, I take them in mine, resting them on my chest.

"What if it *does* work out?" I ask, then lift her hands to my mouth to kiss both of her palms. "Have you allowed yourself to think about it like that? Because I have, and you know what I think? It's going to be incredible, just like you are."

Her eyes fill with tears, but they don't fall.

"I mean it. I'm not just saying that to make you feel better. You're the most amazing woman I've ever known, and the fact that you want to help kids by giving them an outlet in dance the way that you had when you were younger? That's amazing. You're going to make the world an even brighter place than you already do just by being in it."

Becca chuckles through her tears and dabs her eyes with the back of her hands, careful not to smudge her makeup. "How do you always know exactly what to say?"

"Because I know you. And I love you more than anything."

"I love you too," she says, and leans in to kiss me, so I meet her. It's gentle and sweet at first, but when she swipes her tongue across my lower lip, desire catches fire inside me. My hands find her waist and work their way upward, my fingertips dancing lightly across her delicate ribs like piano keys.

I take her cheeks in my hands and intensify the kiss, parting her lips with my tongue. She whimpers into my mouth as she surrenders herself, wilting into me, and I spin us both to the nearby wall. She's pinned with her back to the wall now, but she doesn't resist. Her hands find my belt buckle, and she starts fumbling with it, trying to unfasten it. I fondle her breast, giving it a lustful squeeze, and she yelps and pulls back from me.

"What's wrong? Are you okay? I didn't mean to hurt you," I rush. That was a different kind of gasp than she normally makes —and I've made her do it enough to know the difference.

"I'm fine," she says, but the look on her face still makes her seem a little uncomfortable. I flash her a worried look, and after a second, she bites her lower lip shyly. Deviousness dances in her eyes.

"What is it?"

"Well, I was going to surprise you with it later, but I guess I might as well show you now," she says and reaches for the left strap of her dress. She tugs it downward, exposing her shoulder and breast, and there on the soft, tender outer edge sits a fresh, red-and-inflamed tattoo. It's a small, elegant illustration of an ice skate and a ballet shoe with their laces tied together.

My heart swells at the sight, and I can't stop myself from reaching out for it. Very gently, I run my fingertip alongside it, careful not to touch the tattoo itself. "When did you get this?" I ask hoarsely.

"Earlier today. Callie took me," she says, her eyes slowly moving from the tattoo back to mine. "It hurt like hell so I'm probably not going to get one for every major event in my life, but I wanted to get one for the best thing that ever happened to me: marrying you."

My love for her overwhelms me, and I kiss her again, letting it pour out of me through my lips. She responds in kind, again tugging at my belt buckle, and it takes everything I have not to tear her dress off and take her right here and now. But there are people outside waiting for us, for her, and the last thing I want is to distract her from her big moment.

I pull back, keeping her upper lip between mine. "We should save this for later," I whisper, and she moans like a kid being told they can't have candy.

"I know you're right, but I hate it."

"There'll be plenty of time for this later. Think of it as your reward."

Her eyes flame as she stares into mine. "Like I said, you always know exactly what to say." She gives my crotch a lusty grope, and I swipe my thumb across her lower lip to fix the lipstick I smeared, then tap her affectionately on the nose.

"Let's go, Mrs. Camden."

She beams and loops her arm through mine, and we walk out of the backstage dressing room together into the main studio space. The renovations are even better than I thought they'd be when the contractors showed me their proposal drafts.

There were already plenty of windows in the building, but they installed more. Now, floor-to-ceiling windows line the front of the building, offering anyone who walks by a view into whatever the class of the day is working on—its own bit of genius self-advertising—and plenty of light for the dancers inside. Becca insisted on keeping the original hardwood flooring, which I was happy about because it's beautiful, so I had the reno crew re-stain and finish it, making it look brand new.

We also installed a series of sliding dividers built into the floor and ceiling so, if necessary, Becca or whoever is instructing the class that day can create separate practice spaces. And of course, no dance studio would be complete without a killer sound system, so I made sure Becca got the best of the best with that too. A full wireless speaker array is built into the ceiling so that anyone can connect to the system and play whatever music they want.

I pull my phone out of my pocket, which is already connected to the sound system, and cue up some easy listening jazz. Soft, twinkling piano fills the room with rich sound, and Becca looks around lovingly at all the preparations.

I hired a catering company for her grand opening event, and they've done an amazing job decorating. Two long tables line the far wall, each basically buckling under the weight of the food, drinks, and deserts they've prepared, and gold-and-silver balloon displays are tastefully littered throughout.

"Are you ready?" I ask as we walk through the space toward the front door to unlock it. There are already at least two dozen people outside, all dressed up and waiting for the main event. With Margo's incredible PR skills and social media know-how, we put together an online marketing campaign for Becca's launch, so while I'm sure at least some of them are here because of my ties to the NHL, I'm not the real star.

She is, and rightfully so.

We open the doors together, and people start streaming inside. Surprising no one, the entire team of Aces and their families are here, and they file in and give us both hugs one-by-one. By the time Becca's finished hugging them all, she's in tears.

"Thank you all so much for coming," she says. Callie pulls a tissue from her bag and passes it to Becca so she can dab at her eyes without ruining her perfect makeup.

"Hey, you're Theo's family, so you're our family now too," Noah says, and I beam at him because he has no idea how much it means to me to hear him say that. I never blamed him for being skeptical about my relationship with Becca at the start, even though I didn't like it. But the fact that he's come around, that he's seen just how real our initially fake marriage has become, is worth more than any win or trophy.

I clap him on the back and pull him in for a hug. "Thank you for saying that."

"Of course. But don't let us keep you, Becca. You can talk to us any time. You've got parents to charm and students to recruit," Noah says, gesturing at the parents and kids already helping themselves to food and drinks.

Becca takes a deep breath to steel herself and nods. "Wish me luck."

"You don't need it," I say and kiss the top of her head as she drifts past me to greet her potential new clients. She's just as warm and friendly with people she's meeting for the first time as she is with anyone else, and watching her talk with them this effortlessly makes me even surer that she's going to crush this business.

She makes the rounds, making sure to stop and talk to every single person in the studio, but I hang back with the rest of the

Aces to let her shine. This is her moment, and I'm more than content to watch her work her magic.

"She really is something else," Noah says, following my gaze as I track Becca. "But you'd better watch out, bro. At this rate, she's gonna be making more money than you."

"I hope she does, for her sake."

Noah smiles and nods. "And that's how I know you love her. You want to see her win, want to see her dreams come true."

"That's all I've ever wanted for her, from the very beginning."

"I never would've guessed you were so altruistic," Noah says, and I shrug.

"What can I say? She brings out the best in me."

"And we're all grateful for it. For real. Congratulations, Theo. You deserve all of this."

"Thank you," I say and clap his shoulder again before I excuse myself to go grab some food for Becca while she's between greetings. I know her well enough to know that she's enjoying this so much that she's not going to stop anywhere near long enough to eat, so I take a plate of veggies and dip and a cup of water and bring it to her while she has a second.

"Seems like it's going well," I say as I hand out the plate to her. She takes it and kisses me on the cheek.

"Always thinking of me," she says and swipes a baby carrot in the dip before popping it into her mouth. "And yes, it's going incredibly well, just like you said it would. I've already had half a dozen parents tell me they're going to sign their kids up."

"See! They love you. Not anywhere near as much as I do, obviously."

"Not that it's a competition or anything, right?"

"Exactly."

She laughs and continues eating, but her eyes drift over to two little girls in matching pink dresses playing some sort of game together. They can't be any older than ten, and they look so similar that they must be sisters. They're singing and clapping their hands against each other's, but one girl misses the other's hand and almost hits her in the face, and they burst out laughing.

Becca turns back to me with a warm smile and something in her eyes that I can't place. She bites her lower lip and idly pushes around the veggies on her plate with her finger.

"What's on your mind?" I prompt, and she hesitates before she eventually drops the broccoli floret she's been twisting between two fingers.

"I've been thinking..." She trails off, her gaze floating back to the two little girls.

"About what?"

"About adoption," she says, and before I can say anything, she rushes forward. "I mean, it's okay if you don't want that. It's just something I've been thinking about and—"

Her words break off as I pull her into my arms. I kiss her forehead gently, then tilt her chin up, gazing into her luminous eyes.

"I want it, princess. With you, I want everything."

She beams up at me, and when I press my lips to hers, I know that I'm holding my future in my arms.

Epilogue Two

Sawyer

I don't know if it's the excitement of being around other kids, getting to do something outside the house with me, or both, but Jake is positively buzzing. I've watched him tear across Becca's new dance studio with a group of other kids his age more times than I can count, but none of the kids seem to be losing any energy at all.

Becca and Theo are still arm-in-arm, talking privately on the far side of the studio. I'm so happy for Theo. All the Aces are like brothers to me, but Theo and I have more in common than the rest, and one big thing in particular: divorce. After seeing everything Theo went through with Valerie and how in love he is now with Becca, I want to believe there's hope for the other divorced guy on the team.

They share a hug, then Becca parts with him and heads toward the center of the space where there's a microphone on a stand waiting for her. She taps it a few times to check that it's on, and the muffled noise grabs everyone's attention.

"Hello, everyone," her warm voice fills the studio as she smiles at the gathered crowd. "Thank you all so much for coming today. I don't even have the words to tell you all how much it means to me. Starting a dance school like this is a dream come true, something I've wanted to do ever since I was the same age as some of my future students here today, so it's hard to believe it's happening. But it is!"

I join the rest of the audience in giving her a round of applause before she carries on with her speech.

"But I got to thinking... I know we're all a little too dressed up for this event, but what kind of dance school grand opening would this be without any dancing?" she asks and glances around the room with a playful smile. The kids in the room erupt in cheers, and Jake is jumping up and down excitedly with the rest of them, but instantly, my body tenses.

Oh fuck, please don't tell me she's going to make us all embarrass ourselves by dancing.

"Okay, glad I'm not the only one who was thinking it!" Becca says with a laugh. "So I've put together a few little steps for us all to learn. Everyone's welcome to join to the best of their ability. Just go ahead and line up here in front of me, okay?"

Jake and the rest of the kids bolt to form a line, but I hang back. I'm hoping she only means the kids, but when some of the other parents start joining, I realize I'm doomed. Jake spins around looking for me, and when his little gray eyes find mine, my hesitance melts. I feel silly, and this is something I would normally never do, but I'm not about to squash Jake's enthusiasm just because I'm uncomfortable.

I'd do anything for this kid—even if it means making a total fool of myself in public.

So I walk over to him and take his outstretched hand. He beams at me and bounces in place, and I can't help laughing at his enthusiasm. He's such a happy kid, which is surprising after all the crap he's been through with my separation and custody battle with his mom. I hope he holds onto that happiness, and I'm going to do everything I can to make sure that he does.

"Alright, looking good, everyone! Now who's ready to shake

their groove thing with me?" Becca asks as she swishes her butt from side to side. The kids erupt in laughter and start trying to replicate her movement, which even I have to laugh at. "Okay, okay. I see you're all experts already!"

Becca has a natural talent with kids, and they seem to love her. I could see her hosting her own children's show or something someday, and I'm sure it would be a hit.

"So like I said, we're gonna keep it simple so we don't ruin our amazing outfits," Becca continues as she walks to the center of the line in front of her. "But first I think we need to shake off the jitters because you seem a little scared. So come on, shake them off with me!" she says and starts shaking her arms erratically like they're covered in ants she's trying to throw off. The kids devolve into laughter again but join her, their little hands flailing everywhere.

"Okay, I think we're loosey goosey now. What do you think?" Becca asks.

"Yes!" the kids scream in unison, making her laugh.

"Good, good. Now what I want us to do is a simple little number that starts a little something like this," she says and juts one leg out to the side with her toes pointed down. The kids mimic her. "Good! Now put your hands like this," she continues and places both hands on her hips. The kids follow and although some of them laugh at how silly they look, most don't seem to care. Becca's eyes find mine and she points a finger at me. "Hey, that goes for the adults too!"

"Yeah, come on, Dad!" Jake says, tugging at my hand to get me to put it on my hips like the rest of them. My face is burning, and I know I'm probably blushing, but I push it down for Jake and smile at him as I make a show of sticking out my leg and putting my hands on my hips. Jake thinks it's the funniest thing ever, and hearing his little laugh makes my heart swell.

"There we go!" Becca says. "Okay, now I want us to shake our hips from side to side, just like this." She demonstrates the move, which the kids also find hilarious as they try to copy her. When Jake's seemingly got the hang of it, he looks over to see how I'm doing and just laughs even harder.

"Alright, I think we've got the first move down pat. Great work! But now comes the hard part. Are you ready?"

"Yeah!" the kids bellow.

"Good, I think you are too. What we want to do next is to roll our fists together, like we're punching a punching bag. Like this," she says and drops the mic so she can demonstrate the move. It's simple so the kids catch on quick. "Perfect! Then we're gonna turn to the other side and do the same thing." She demonstrates again. "Alright. The last part of this is a little jump, like this," she says and jumps into the air, throwing both her hands up above her head. The kids don't wait to copy her, they all just spring up like jumping bugs.

"I think you've got it, so now it's time to put it all together to some music. Hit it, DJ!" she says over her shoulder to Theo, who laughs and taps the screen of his phone. The song "I Like to Move It" by Reel 2 Real starts playing over the speaker system, and when the main refrain of the song kicks in, Becca starts the dance routine.

She puts her hands on her hips, one leg stuck out, and bounces for four counts, then changes to the punching move for another four counts, and finally jumps into the air just as the song shouts, "Move it!"

The kids catch on like it's nothing, and even though I feel silly as all get out doing it with them, I have to admit I'm having fun. But a big part of it for me is just watching Jake being happy and goofy. I repeat the moves a few times with the kids before I eventually see myself out, retreating to the corner where Noah and Reese have been watching—and no doubt cracking jokes.

"Damn, man, I didn't know you had such killer moves," Reese teases before he takes a sip of his drink, and Noah snorts.

But I roll my eyes at them because I don't care. I'd do anything for Jake, and they know that.

"Yeah, yeah, yuck it up. I can only imagine the pair of left feet on you two."

"There's a reason I'm not out there 'shaking my groove thing,'" Noah says, using air quotes.

"Probably for the best. We wouldn't want to scar these poor children for life," Reese says, and even I can't help laughing at that. "But in all seriousness, man, I'm glad to see you and Jake out and about. It's good for you both."

"Thanks. And yeah, I agree."

"I take it that means your babysitter situation still hasn't gotten sorted out?" Noah asks, and I sigh.

"No, it's been pretty rough. Lately, it feels like Jake changes sitters more often than his underwear, the poor kid." Noah snickers. "But it's not for lack of trying. Seems like there are too many kids and not enough qualified sitters. I just wish I could find one solid person I could depend on, you know? I hate having this rotating door of people with Jake. With the divorce and the custody fight with his mom, he really needs someone he can get to know. Someone consistent."

Reese raises his eyebrows at me as he sips his drink again. "Which is exactly why you should reconsider the whole nanny thing, bro," he says when he's finished.

"I have been, actually."

Reese's eyebrows climb farther up his forehead. "No shit?"

"Yeah, I just haven't pulled the trigger on it yet." I sigh again. "I dunno, man. It's been two years since my split with Miriam, but I still feel like I'm floundering half the time. Like I'm doing this single father thing all wrong."

Noah smiles and claps me on the shoulder. "I don't know, Jake sure looked like he was having a blast out there dancing with his dad. That kid loves you way more than you think." His words make my throat clench. He's right, and I know he is. I just want to do right by Jake, more than anything, especially after what he's been through with my divorce."

"I think he wants to see you happy too," Noah adds. "Have you thought about getting back out there? Maybe getting remarried someday?"

I snort because I can't help myself. "After Miriam, I'm not sure I ever want to get back on the horse again. I've got Jake to focus on, and that's all I need. I'm staying single, thanks."

Noah and Reese exchange looks, not even trying to hide it, but I ignore them. The conversation dies, and I can't help noticing their gazes drifting toward Margo and Callie. They look at their fiancées with such adoration, such love, that it makes me jealous—and feeling that way makes me feel like shit. These are my best friends, I should be happy for them, not jealous.

"I understand you feeling that way now, and it's totally valid," Reese says, breaking the uncomfortable silence. "But I still think one day some woman is going to crash into your life and turn it upside down."

I open my mouth to argue, but a little hand clamps around mine, cutting me off. I glance down to find Jake staring up at me. "Daddy, can I have some cake?"

I laugh and nod. "I think you've burned enough calories to justify it. Come on," I say and wave to the guys before walking Jake over to the table stacked with plates of pre-cut cake to make sure he doesn't take a gigantic piece he doesn't need. I pick up plates for both of us and hand him one with a fork, and he tears right into it. His face lights up at the first bite.

"It's *so* good!"

"Well, I can't just take your word for it, can I?" I ask and cut off a bite of the cake with my fork to taste it. It looks like a simple vanilla cake with chocolate frosting, and that's exactly what it is, but Jake's not wrong. It tastes amazing. "Wow, you weren't kidding! That's really good."

But Jake's already halfway through the piece I picked out for him, too consumed with sugar to pay much attention to what I have to say. Just a kid being a kid. While I pick at my cake, my eyes drift back to Reese and Noah on the opposite side of the room, and what Reese says plays on repeat in my head.

Some woman is going to crash into your life and turn it upside down.

He's probably full of it and just saying that because I'm one of the few guys left on the Aces who doesn't have a woman. Maybe he feels sorry for me or something, I don't know. But I meant it when I told him I wasn't interested. The other guys don't get it, what I've been through, and the way it's changed me. Not even Theo, who went through a pretty messy divorce himself.

At the thought of him, my gaze shifts to the center of the studio where he's currently slow dancing with Becca. I can tell from the way they look at each other that they're head-over-heels for one another, and I'm happy for him. I really am.

But I don't need a relationship or love. And I'm not even sure I want it, honestly.

Or at least that's what I keep telling myself anyway. I have Jake, who I love more than anything, and who makes me happier than I've been in a long time.

So then why does it still feel like something is missing from my life?

Books by Nikki Lawson

Books by Nikki Lawson